RUDGER RUMP AND THE MAGE OF AGES

DR. SCOTT SIMERLEIN

To Caitlin,
A magical tome
for every gnome!
Enjoy,
Dr. Scott Simerlein

Hydra
Publications

Cover art and illustrations by Dr. Scott Simerlein

ISBN: 978-1-948374-78-1

Hydra Publications

Goshen, Kentucky 40026

www.hydrapublications.com

For my mother, Mary Lucia Simerlein,
whose tireless support and encouragement helped make this work of fiction a reality.
Nothing is impossible.

AUTHOR'S NOTE

Rudger Rump's tale is brimming with fantastical words, some known to the human world and others entirely new. When you encounter a "weird wyrd" in his story, take a moment to turn to his Logofile at the back of this book. He may have jotted its definition there. If he didn't, take up his quest by seeking out the nearest unabridged dictionary. Add your own entry to the Logofile to become Rudger's assistant lexicologist!

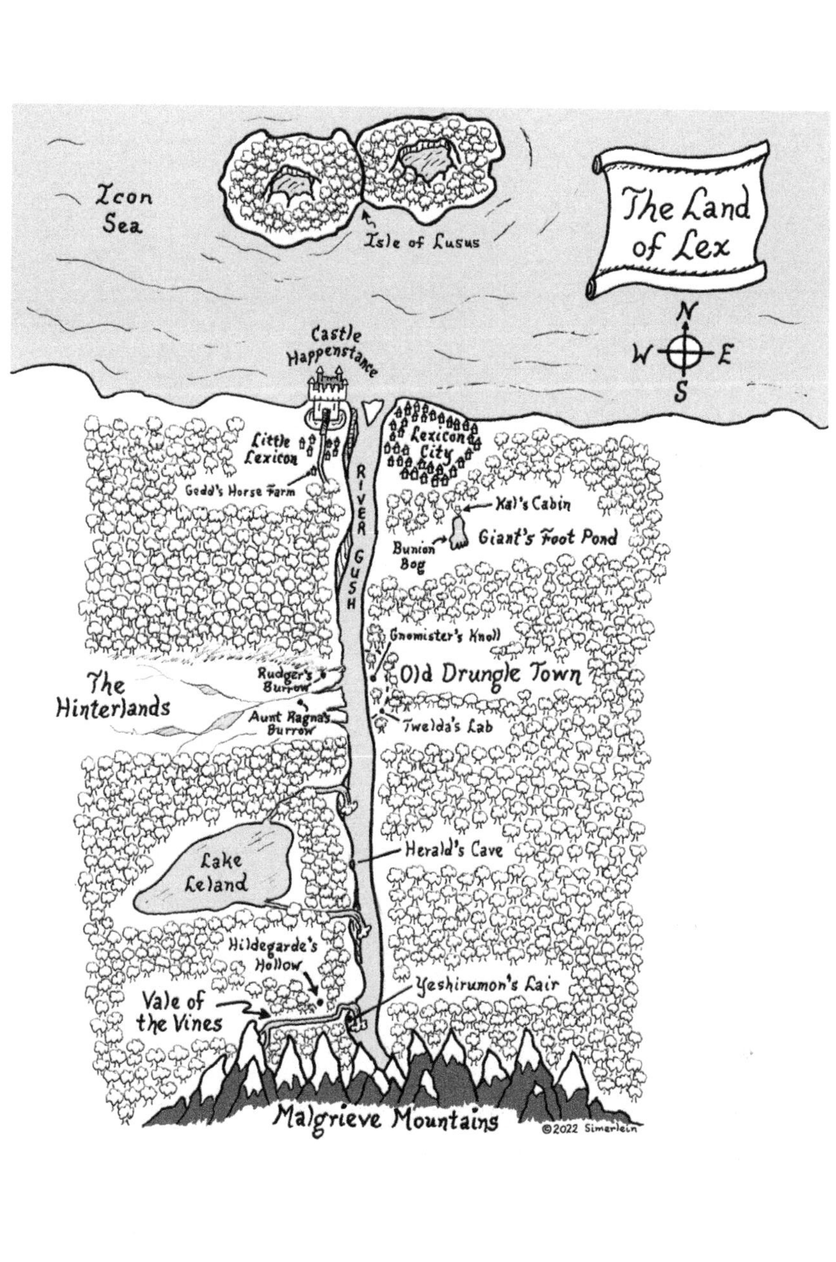
The Land of Lex
Icon Sea
Isle of Lusus
N
W
E
S
Castle Happenstance
Little Lexicon
Lexicon City
RIVER GUSH
Gedd's Horse Farm
Kal's Cabin
Giant's Foot Pond
Bunion Bog
Gnomister's Knoll
Old Drungle Town
The Hinterlands
Rudger's Burrow
Aunt Ragna's Burrow
Twelda's Lab
Lake Leland
Herald's Cave
Hildegarde's Hollow
Yeshirumon's Lair
Vale of the Vines
Malgrieve Mountains
©2022 Simerlein

CHAPTER ONE

"Why do we have to stay with Aunt Ragna, Mum?" Rudger Rump complained as his triplet siblings raced and chased each other down the sun-dappled path before him. "I'm old enough to watch the Terror Trio for a couple of nights."

"Don't call them that," his mother scolded as she watched the threesome rip puxa pods from the bushes and bean each other with them. The pods ruptured as they hit their targets, leaving yellow-white tag marks that oozed like pus over the triplet's freshly laundered brown jumpers. She sighed. "And you're *no*where near old enough to handle those three."

"I'm fifteen," he said defensively.

She scoffed. "You're practically still a gnomeling, and a good decade away from your beard. We'll talk when your whiskers start coming in."

Rudger scowled under his pointed tan cap. "But Aunt Ragna's weird," he grumbled. Then, switching to his most dramatic whisper, he added, "Everybody says she's got *daft disease*."

"Your aunt isn't weird, Rudger. She's...*Put that poor thing down, young lady!* You know the rules! No lobbing of living creatures, even if they do have a shell!"

Rani, the self-appointed leader of the three-gnomeling wrecking crew, pushed her lower lip out in a pout. Then she shrugged and tossed the terrified tortoise over her shoulder.

Her mother turned back to her eldest son. "As I was saying, your aunt isn't weird. Or daft. She's just...eccentric. Yes, eccentric. That's a much nicer word to describe her. And eccentricity isn't catching, so you and the triplets are stuck staying with her until I get back from helping your father in Old Drungle Town."

Rudger blew out his cheeks in frustrated resignation. His mother was not to be swayed on the point, but at least he had acquired a new word for his trouble. He stopped under the shade of a large thatch of reeds and extracted a sheaf of yellowed parchment from his traveling bag. Pulling his ever-present quill from its perch atop his right ear, he made a new entry in his loose-leaf Logofile.

Ecsentrick = weird like Aunt Ragna

"Will you *please* keep up?" his harried mother called, pacing back up the path toward him. "It's hard enough to manage your brother and sisters without having to stop every ten minutes for you to scribble in that silly book of yours."

She glanced at his entry. "And you've misspelled it. Two *C*'s, no *K*."

He made the correction:

Ecentric ~~Ecsentrick~~ = weird like Aunt Ragna

"No, no. I said *two C*'s, not one."

"It has two *C*'s, Mum." He pointed to the beginning and the end of the word.

"Argh! Three *C*'s, then! By the Five Elements, Rudger Rump, sometimes you're every bit as exasperating as *they* are."

She stopped short and began to fuss with his hair. "Tuck those red locks of yours in. Can't have your aunt thinking you're a leprechaun, all mischief and magic. The scandal of it all! We Rumps are *respectable* Humdrungle gnomes in dress, as well as speech. So none of those crazy words you're so fond of spouting. Just good, sensible, no-nonsense language while you're here, you hear?"

Far down the path in a well-lit clearing, Roni could be seen announcing her arrival at Aunt Ragna's burrow. But instead of calling out "Gnome a-home?" as was expected by any gnome of good breeding, she instead performed a tap dance on its wooden flaphatch. She was presently hip-checked off her tiny stage by Rani, who insisted on calling herself by an unapproved nickname, thereby violating their clan's long-standing tradition of adopting names beginning with the letter *R*.

"Maca beats Roni!" Rani cried as she gleefully took up the tap dance. "Maca! Roni! Maca! Roni!"

Rudger suppressed a giggle as he watched his mother's left eye twitch with annoyance. He had never admitted it was he who had planted the nickname in his suggestible sister's head.

Upon the twelfth repetition of Rani's thunderous Maca-Roni step, it was clear that Roon, their brother, was preparing to add his own talents to the show. The third act was preempted, however, when the flaphatch flew open, catapulting Rani with a gleeful shriek into the air. Her hang time seemed to Rudger a shade longer than gravity should permit, and she landed with a certain sluggishness in a nearby patch of grizzlegrass. The conundrum of Rani's flight took a back seat in Rudger's mind as a mass of frizzy brown hair rose from the flaphatch aperture.

Aunt Ragna was a fierce-looking gnomette, well into her fifties, but still sharp and spry as she approached the midpoint of her life. Her emerald-green eyes sparkled with an intelligence and spirit that lent an elfin quality to her faintly creased visage. As the lithe gnomette climbed lightly out of her burrow, apparel mostly adherent to the customary mode of dress of the Humdrungle gnomes came into view. Though her pointed cap was missing, she wore a tan jerkin with simple, woven leather accents and brown breeches that were only a shade greener than the approved norm. Her boots were fashioned of dillyhog hide with leather laces to match the inlay of her vest. But it was her blouse that defiantly announced to the whole of Humdrungle society that she would not be bound by its rules. The chemise was an eye-scorching shade of scarlet, puffed at the shoulders and shimmering in a most undignified manner. In a way, it was this outrageous nonconformist touch that put Rudger at ease.

The patch of grizzlegrass bobbed and shook with Rani's laughter as she righted herself.

Rudger quirked an eyebrow at his mother and tilted his head toward his aunt. "You think *she'll* be a better babysitter than me?" he whispered. "I'm insulted."

Shushing her son, the beleaguered mother-gnomette greeted her older sister. "Ragna! May the Elements grant you serenity."

Ragna's intense eyes locked on her sister. "Bilge," she said. "The elements care nothing for me or you. Learned that a long time ago. Still, I will bid you hello, Redna."

"I'm *Ridna*, Ragna."

"Ridna, Redna, you twins always did look alike," Ragna said dismissively. "Frankly, all I want is to be Ridna the lot of you. Took me twenty years to earn my solitude, what with eight of you whippergnomers to raise. And now you bring me four more!"

"Just for a couple of days, three at the most," Ridna assured her. "Their father needs me in Drungle Town. It's an emergency."

"He's a tailor, right?" Ragna said. "What's the emergency? A shortage of burlap sacks threatening the height of Humdrungle fashion?"

Ridna gave her sister a withering look. "There's no need to be snarky. I didn't want to discuss this in front of the 'lings, but it seems that their grandparents aren't faring so well.

They're confused and having trouble speaking. Rondo's worried they may have had strokes."

"Both of them?" Aunt Ragna questioned. "At the same time? I'm no healer-gnome, but even I know that would be quite a coincidence."

"Regardless, I need to go and tend to them. All our brothers and sisters have households of gnomelings, so I figure you're the one to leave mine with. Oh! Did you know that Redna just had her eleventh child? Anyway, this fine fellow, here, is Rudger; he'll be no trouble to you. The triplets, however…" She paused to look around. "The triplets…Where have they gotten to?"

The three fell silent, listening for a clue as to the gnomelings' whereabouts. The only sound Rudger could make out, aside from the singing of the dayna birds, was a faint squelching noise.

"Ah!" cried Aunt Ragna with a disturbing grin. "Bet the little tykes have made the acquaintance of the arachna shrubs."

"Arachna shrubs?" repeated Rudger as he pulled out his Logofile.

Ragna marched off, leaving Ridna and Rudger to stare at each other in bewilderment. A moment later, they were chasing after their peculiar relative.

"What are arachna shrubs?" Rudger asked as he struggled to keep hold of the loose pages fluttering in the breeze.

"Arachna shrubs are a handy little botanical specimen to protect your garden from pests," Aunt Ragna explained. "Picked them up on one of my trips to Flaxenrod years ago. Haven't lost a single buffa beet to the blunderelk since I planted them. Yep! Just as I suspected."

Ridna let out a strangled cry as a hideous hedge came into view. Thrice the height of a gnome, it bristled with short, black, hair-like blades set on long tendrils that thrashed about in the gathering twilight. The wriggling mass called to mind a tangle of gyrating serpents, but no serpents ever made the horrible sucking noise they now plainly heard. Near the base of the hedge were three distinct bulges wrapped in runners. The gnomeling-shaped lumps undulated sickeningly with each repetition of the wet, gulping sound.

"*En garde*, arachna fiends!" Aunt Ragna bellowed with relish. "You've enjoyed many a fine repast in your sentinel duty, but these are not meant for you."

She drew a dagger from inside her jerkin and set upon the shrubbery with a wail. A dozen slashes, and a very frightened Roni appeared. She was shaken and had a few welts on her face and arms but seemed otherwise unharmed. She ran to her mother, who inspected Roni for injury and then clutched her daughter close.

In short order, the other two triplets emerged, equally upset, but none the worse for wear. Aunt Ragna continued to battle the marauding tendrils as they sought to ensnare her in retaliation.

"Learn your place, wily weeds!" she cried as she hacked the foliage into submission. "My nieces and nephews shall never be the object of your carnivorous cravings!"

"Carnivorous?" Rudger asked, quill at the ready.

"Means meat-eating, lad," Aunt Ragna commented over her shoulder as she continued to slash at encroaching branches. "These shrubs have a taste for it. *Ruffians!* But that I had our family sword Vicarius in my possession. Vic would carve you into a mewling topiary!"

With a grunt, Ragna separated from the beaten bushes. Straightening her jerkin with an emphatic tug of triumph, she looked at Ridna and her cowering triplets.

"*Never* wage battle with an unknown enemy," she declared, as if to sum up a lesson.

"Oh, Aunt Ragna," Rudger said sadly. "Your beautiful blouse. It's ruined."

The garment's sleeves were in shimmering tatters, exposing far more musculature than any middle-aged gnomette ought to boast. Ragna's biceps flexed as she placed her hands on her hips.

"Your father can sew me a new one as a reward for liberating his precious children," she said with a wink. "Electric blue, this time, I think. All right, whippergnomers. Dinner awaits. Hup, hup!"

And with this, Ragna turned on her heel and marched back toward her flaphatch.

The Rump family stood aghast at the events that nearly provided a carnivorous hedge with a three-course meal. Rudger was the first to recover. A grin spread over his face as he turned to his stunned mother.

"Still think Aunt Ragna'll be a better babysitter than me?" he asked.

CHAPTER TWO

"Bedtime, the lot of you," Rudger Rump decreed in the most authoritative voice he could muster. "Into the sack, and no lipflap."

"But Aunt Ragna said we could stay up to see the moon and the stars dance," Rani and Roni whined in unison.

"That won't be for hours," Rudger countered. Then he raised his bushy red eyebrows and added, "Do I need to remind you what Mummers says about gnomelings up after dark?"

They looked up at their older brother with shining eyes. "Yes! Yes!"

"No, no," Rudger teased. "I'm sure you haven't forgotten."

"We forgot! We forgot!"

"Well," he sighed theatrically, "I guess I have no choice but to remind you. But only if you're in bed by the count of fifty. One, two, ten…"

The girls shrieked their objection to Rudger's creative

counting and raced down a tunnel to their sleeping quarters. Their brother, however, made no move to disentangle himself from the roots that protruded from the hearth room's earthen ceiling.

"Roon," Rudger chided gently. "Hurry up, or you'll miss the story."

Roon's inverted face descended into Rudger's line of sight.

"You can bribe the sisturds with that silly old poem, but not me," he said with gusto as his unruly blond hair swung in lank strands below him. "*I'm* going to see the moon rise."

Rudger reached up and snared his little brother by his dangling locks. "Don't call them that," he growled over Roon's cry of surprise. "And you're going to see my *dander* rise if you don't stop acting like a boughbrat."

Rudger had just managed to extract Roon from the snarl of roots when his ears picked up on shenanigans in the bed quarters. "Thirty-five!" he called as he propelled his brother toward the tunnel. "Forty-one!"

A pair of off-stage squeals shattered into giggles. Roon turned to stick his tongue out at Rudger before trotting off to join his sisters.

Rudger gave another sigh—bona fide, this time—and then cupped his hand toward the kitchen. "All clear, Aunt Ragna," he reported.

The gnomette stumped unsteadily into the room. Her frazzled hair was dotted with bits of burbled wurblebird egg—the result of a cooking lesson gone horribly awry.

"I raised eight humdrungling brothers and sisters in this burrow," she stated in dumbfounded contemplation, "but *never* have I endured the likes of those three willow-the-winks. Now

I understand why your poor mother stopped with just the four of you."

Rudger shrugged apologetically. "Crazy stuff like that happens all the time in our burrow."

"Thank the good Elements they didn't come out identical," Aunt Ragna continued. "Your mother and her sister, Redna, were bad enough with that twin thing between them, but identical *triplets*?" She shook her head in dismay, dislodging a glob of egg which bounced off her short nose. "That caliber of birther magic doesn't bear thinking about."

Rudger found himself lost in the emptiness he always felt when somegnome brought up his siblings' relationship. The triplets were extraordinarily close, and even though he was their brother, Rudger couldn't help feeling like an outsider in their presence. The sadness was replaced with curiosity, however, as his brain processed his aunt's last remark.

"Magic?" he asked her, almost ashamed. "But Humdrungle gnomes aren't magical. That'd be improper."

Aunt Ragna laughed. "My sister's got you good and buttoned down, doesn't she? Well, I've got news for you, Rudger Rump. 'Respectable' gnomes like your mum may denounce magic in their hallowed circles, but it's there, nonetheless. And multiple-birth magic is a wild variety that can't be repressed. You think those wurble-eggs exploded of their own accord? I think not."

Rudger stared at his aunt, realization dawning. Rani's gravity-defying flight that afternoon played through his mind. It wasn't the first time he'd seen her bend the laws of physics. Of course, he'd never mentioned this or any of the peculiar happenings surrounding the triplets to his parents. But, for some reason, the idea that the triplets could harbor such a flaw made him feel a little bit less alone.

"Why, even I've had the odd encounter with magic," Aunt Ragna admitted. "Did your mother ever tell you the tale of Vicarius the sword?"

"Sure. But I thought it was just a bedtime—"

"Oh, *Rud*-ger!" came a two-part singsong call. "We want our *stor*-y!"

Rudger gave his aunt a look.

"Go," she bade him. "We'll talk later. Can't have anything else exploding, can we?"

Snagging Ragna's cloak from its peg in the entrance hall, Rudger tossed it over his shoulders and pulled up its hood. Then he paced into the bed chamber in full character. The girls twittered with glee. Roon pretended not to care. Rudger drew a dramatic, wheezy breath and began to recite:

"Comes the human, looming closer,
Cloak of darkness, stalking closer,
Hushful footfalls, ever closer,
Gnomelings, fear ye well.

"Comes the human, creeping closer,
Gnarly fingers, reaching closer,
Snatch the gnomelings, dreamy dozers,
None can hear them yell.

"Runs the human, over, under,
Steals away its precious plunder,
Kidnapped gnomelings *ripped* asunder!
Sound their ghastly knell!

"Make thee not this fateful blunder;
Tucked in bed, thy covers, under,
Gnomelings spared this wicked wonder,
Till the morn, sleep well."

Rudger's enthusiasm had escalated through the performance, and with the final words, a curious wooziness came over him. He stumbled and grabbed at the bedpost for support. As his balance returned, he heard no applause or laughter. He was confused by the image of his sisters clutching one another, their little faces drained of blood. Roon had vanished entirely. Further investigation revealed his two widened eyes peering at Rudger from around the foot of his bed.

"Now, *that,*" Aunt Ragna commented from the doorway, "was gruesome, even by my standards. Does your mother know you tell these three such horrific tales?"

Rudger blinked. "Uh, actually, it's her story, Aunt Ragna," he said distractedly. "She tells it to them all the time."

"Not like that," Rani broke in, her voice quaking. "I…I don't think I like that story anymore."

Rudger frowned. "What's the matter with you three?" he asked. "I've told you that story before."

"Not like that," Rani repeated quietly, a tear rolling down her cheek.

Rudger shook his head in befuddlement. "Sure, I have. This cloak is new, but it's basically the same story Mummers tells you."

Roon poked his head over the bed. He looked like a terrified flufferbunny.

"You changed the ending," he whispered. "I couldn't understand it."

"And you got big," Rani added.

"Big and scary," Roni sobbed.

"This is ridiculous, you three," Rudger said, throwing the cloak off his shoulders. "It's just me. Right? And it was the same ending as always. 'Till the morn, sleep well.'"

"And that is good advice for us all," Aunt Ragna broke in. "We're all safe, all together. There are no nasty humans prowling about tonight. Everygnome can just settle down for a nice sleep, okay?"

She went to the bed Roon was hiding behind and coaxed him back onto it. Then she tucked in the girls, stroking each one gently on the cheek. Leaning over to blow out the lantern's candle, she fixed Rudger with an appraising look.

"You'll sleep in the room at the end of the tunnel," she told him.

"But I always stay with them," he protested. "They can't fall asleep without me here."

"They will tonight."

With a puff of air, the room was plunged into semi-darkness. Aunt Ragna trundled her bewildered nephew back to the hearth room.

"I don't understand it," he said. "I really scared them with that story—one they've heard a hundred times before."

"But not here, in an unfamiliar place," Aunt Ragna pointed out. "And you *were* a bit intense, dear, considering they're so young."

"They *love* that story! And it ends happily enough. I just don't get it."

"Happily?" the gnomette asked, her eyebrow quirked. "You call that a happy ending?"

"Well, yes," Rudger replied. "Compared to the rest of it, at least."

"Just what were those last lines again?"

He recited them to her.

"That's not what you said in there," she told him. "Nothing about being spared, that's for sure. Far darker and words the likes of which I've never heard before."

"What words?"

"I'm not sure." She thought for a moment. "Something like, 'Gnomelings fear their endless slumber, *corporsapiensi* spell.' Your voice got all husky and thick when you said it."

Aunt Ragna smiled indulgently at her nephew's slack-jawed expression. "Now, now. You look every bit as frightened as those three did. It's nothing to worry about. Just sit yourself down, and I'll bring you some somna root tea. Settle you down for a good night's rest, it will."

As his aunt bustled off to the kitchen, Rudger absently approached the desk where he'd placed his Logofile for safekeeping. He extracted a sheet of parchment from the bundle, one with another nonsense word inscribed upon it. Below it, he added:

corporsapiensi = big and scary?

Aunt Ragna's rattles and clinks from the kitchen were a

small comfort as his eyes dragged back and forth over the weird words. He longed to crumple the parchment and toss it into the fire. If only his fears could be reduced to cinders so easily.

Nothing to worry about, Aunt Ragna had said. Everygnome's safe. No dangerous humans out there.

But what if the real danger was him?

CHAPTER THREE

The mid-night hours trudged heavy and humid through Aunt Ragna's earthen burrow. Rudger Rump's harried mind flirted with sleep, landing in that curious limbo that yields willful dreams. Scooping up a well-worn memory, Rudger's subconscious concocted the scene.

She was screaming. Her cry of distress was a melody to Rudger's inner ear. True, her voice had not been so lovely, her hair not quite so flouncy and radiant, but Rudger's brain wasn't concerned with historical accuracy at the moment. A grin crept onto his semi-sleeping face as he settled in for the unreal show.

His view panned outward, revealing the fullness of the human girl's peril. She struggled daintily in the villainous clutches of a huge dragon.

Wait, his semi-conscious mind interceded. *Not big enough. Enhancing, enhancing...* The girl seemed to shrink in the monster's expanding claws. *There! That's a proper dragon. Resume.*

She struggled daintily in the villainous clutches of a *gargantuan* dragon, long of teeth and evil of intent. She screamed again, her dulcet pleas plucking at his heartstrings. He charged into the vibrant green meadow.

"A dwarf?" the damsel asked crassly.

Despite his ego's attempts at rescripting the dream, the girl's original sarcastic words came through. He wrested control from the true memory before answering.

"Nay, a noble gnome," he said broadly with a gallant sweep of his cape. "I have journeyed from afar to free—"

"My knight in shining armor is a beardless little *dwarf*?" she grated again. "High skies! I should think I'd rate a human hero, at least."

The grin on slumbering Rudger's face slipped. Again, his subconscious mind tried to redirect the plot.

"Foul beast!" he proclaimed grandly. "Unhand this ray of loveliness, lest you taste my—"

"And that red hair," she interrupted with a scoff. "Not ginger or auburn, but garish *red*? No dignified savior could boast such a ghastly mane."

Dream-Rudger rounded on the disparaging damsel, his infatuation brimming despite his annoyance.

"Pray, do you prefer liberation or ingestion, fair lady? For if it is the latter, this sinister serpent is certain to oblige."

"'Twould be a pox on my reputation to be saved by one such as you," she answered primly.

"Better a pox than an agonizing death in a dragon's belly," he pointed out.

"I choose the belly, halfling hero. Consider yourself dismissed."

Slumbering-Rudger's snort of outrage startled him to full wakefulness. The glamour of the dream fell away, revealing the actual memory. The lady grew less lovely; the dragon contracted to a less prodigious size; the brilliance of the colors leached from the scene.

The dragon lifted the maiden, her attention now locked on her reptilian captor. Gone was Rudger's wondrous cape and gilded tongue. His knees knocked with fear as the formidable foe advanced.

And then his memory failed.

It returned to reveal that the dreaded dragon had vanished. One moment, it was bearing down on Rudger, its great orbs alight with murderous intent, and the next, he was alone with a heap of a girl, splayed out upon the trampled grizzlegrass.

Real-Rudger opened his eyes to the dank darkness of his underground bed chamber. Swinging his legs over the side of the unfamiliar guest bed, he rose and fumbled to light a lantern on the rough-cut bedside table. His loose-leaf Logofile lay in a careless stack upon it. Rudger lifted the top page and looked again at the nonsense word he'd supposedly uttered back then, supplied by the human girl.

dwindiminish

That was the non-word he'd supposedly cried just before the dragon disappeared, if the human girl was to be believed. And yet, he had never so much as thought of such a non-word before. And never another since.

Until tonight.

He'd managed to pack away the terrifying memory of the dragon and the maiden, concealed in a shroud of stalwart denial. But after the events of this evening, fear and self-doubt were pressing upon him anew. They were turned back, however, by the faintest of sounds audible to a young gnome's sensitive ears.

A sprinkle of soil cascaded down the dirt wall before him. He straightened and found himself eye-to-eye with a subterranean hackerpede.

"I say!" it exclaimed as Rudger took a hasty step back. "I *do* beg your pardon. I was under the impression that this earth was uninhabited. Misled by the First Element, it seems."

Rudger wondered if he was still dreaming.

The tiny creature protruded its head from the wall, looking first left and then right. By some means unfathomable to Rudger, it straightened a tiny red bowtie fastened about its neck.

"Well, since I've intruded, I might just as well inquire," the hackerpede went on. "You wouldn't happen to know the way to the one-hundred-sixteenth Bibliorinctum, by chance?"

Rudger continued to stare in abject disbelief.

"Not too bright, eh?" the dapper little 'pede surmised. "Or perhaps you're mute? Hmmm. I don't suppose you can read? I'm quite adept at twisting myself into letter-shapes, though it *is* rather exhausting. *W*'s are a particular challenge, as you might imagine."

"I-I can speak," Rudger said at last, eyes closed as he frowned and shook his head. "I'm just surprised to hear a hackerpede do it."

"It's an unusual talent, I'll admit," the creature conceded. "Either that, or most worms don't have much to say. Anyhoo, since it turns out that you're a sapient sort of fellow, I suppose I should introduce myself. I am called Vermis von Higglesbreath. The Fourth. Oh, and for the record, I'm a vermitome, not a hackerpede. Nasty blighters, those."

"Vermitome?"

"A bookworm, in the common vernacular." The worm produced a tiny pair of spectacles. Again, by some unknown means, it manipulated them onto its face. Overcome by the peculiarity of it all, Rudger dropped the parchment page he was holding back onto the Logofile and sat heavily on the bed.

"Hmm," Vermis mused. "Capable of speech, but lacking in etiquette."

"Beg pardon?"

"Your name, son. When someone introduces himself, it's customary to return the gesture."

"Oh. I'm Rudger Rump. The first."

"I'm sorry."

"Why?"

"It's a most unfortunate surname."

Gnome and vermitome considered each other for a moment. When it became clear that Rudger was at a loss for anything to continue the conversation, Vermis cleared his tiny throat.

Gnome
Sweet
Gnome
©2022 Simerlein

"So do you know?"

Rudger frowned again. "Do I know what?"

"The way to the one-hundred-sixteenth Bibliorinctum."

"Oh. That. I don't even know what a Biblio-whatever-you-said is."

"Don't get out much, huh? It's a convention for vermitomes. Only happens every five years, and I'm late."

"What exactly do vermitomes do at a convention?"

"We consume knowledge, of course."

"Consume knowledge?" Rudger repeated dubiously. "What does that mean?"

"Best if I demonstrate," the bookworm said. Running his body out of the hole in the wall, he drifted elegantly down to the tabletop. The vermitome was nearly three inches long with multiple legs like a hackerpede, except that each one ended is a shiny, miniscule shoe. His body was pale green in color and consisted of eight rounded segments, each of which sported a small vermilion spot on either side.

Vermis scuttled across the bedside table and up onto the Logofile. There, he aligned himself with Rudger's latest nonsense entry, *corporsapiensi.* Lowering his head, he advanced across the page. When his segmented body cleared the sheet, the word was gone.

"Hey!" Rudger objected. "You erased my note."

"Not erased. *Consumed.* And it was delicious, too. Savory, with an exotic spicy zest."

Rudger jerked the page out from under the bookworm. Pulling the quill from his ear, he rewrote the entry and then glared at Vermis. "I need those words, so you can stop eating them right now."

"*Consuming*," the vermitome corrected. "It has nothing to do with nourishment. I'm not even hungry."

"Whatever," Rudger grumped. He grabbed the rest of his precious Logofile and jostled the bookworm off. But Vermis caught sight of the title as he slipped past.

"Logofile, eh? I'm afraid you misspelled it."

Rudger scoffed. "No, I didn't."

"Yes, you did. It should be a *ph*, not an *f*." The surprisingly supple centipede contorted his body into each letter as he said it.

"It's a file of words," Rudger argued. "*Logo-* means 'word,' and *file* is spelled with an *f*."

"Ah. I thought you meant a 'lover of words.' That's spelled *L-O-G-O-P-H-I-L-E*. Ouch. I forgot *H*'s are hard, too. I think I sprained something."

"Serves you right for showing off," Rudger muttered as he jotted down the new spelling and its definition. Then he looked up at the cheeky vermitome suspiciously.

"Are you sure that's a real word?"

"Of course, it is!" Vermis snapped. "I'm a real, live book-worm, aren't I? I suppose I should know a thing or two about vocabulary."

"If you say so."

"Okay…*So*," the vermitome quipped, forming the two letters with flair. "Look, I've been consuming knowledge for so long, I know just about everything."

"Everything?"

"Yep. Everything. Trouble is, I can't remember it."

Rudger knitted his eyebrows. "That's…"

"Unfair? Frustrating? Inconvenient?" Vermis supplied.

Rudger shook his head. "I was going to say, 'hard to believe.'"

The tiny worm's body stiffened, its vermilion spots expanding in size. "Doubt?" he cried indignantly. "You dare to doubt the word of Vermis von Higglesbreath the Fourth?"

"Keep your voice down!" Rudger warned. "You don't want my aunt finding you in here."

"Ah. Would that be your Aunt Ragna Riggle, once-owner of the enchanted Switching Blade, Vicarius?"

Rudger's jaw dropped. "How do you know about Vic?" he asked.

"I told you. I know everything. And here's something else I know. Your grandparents in Old Drungle Town didn't have simultaneous strokes. Their speech was stolen from them."

"How do you know about my…" Rudger began. Then he interrupted himself. "Hold on. What do you mean, 'stolen?'"

The little worm shrugged, in as much as a creature without proper shoulders was able. "I *told* you, I'm something of an expert when it comes to words, written or spoken. And that one of yours I just consumed? It's still wriggling about inside me. My gut is literally telling me that you might be the only person in the kingdom who can save your grandparents and stop the Logoleech."

"Logoleech?" squeaked Rudger. "What in high skies is that?"

For the first time since Rudger had met him, Vermis seemed sincerely serious.

"A poacher of words. A thief of knowledge."

Rudger eyed his sheaf of parchment. "Kind of sounds like what you do."

"Hardly. If I nibble, the Logoleech devours. And it's here, in the Land of Lex. Your grandparents are just its appetizers."

The loquacious worm took a deep breath and sighed extravagantly. "So, it seems our little palaver, pleasant though it has been, has come to its terminus. Are you going to act on the information I've imparted?"

"Well," Rudger considered, "I *am* worried about Grampers and Grammers. And if what you've told me is true, maybe I should go to them, though I don't know what help I can be."

"More than you can imagine, if I'm not off my mark," the vermitome said.

"Well, okay. But I have to tell Aunt Ragna, Rani, Roni, and Roon that I'm leaving for Old Drungle Town before I go."

"Agreed. Now, lend me an ear."

Rudger stopped short. "What do you think I've been doing for the last ten minutes?" he asked.

The worm rolled his eyes behind their tiny spectacles. "I mean, lend me an ear, literally. I need a place to ride with you. Cozy little holes in the earth are my preferred habitat, but your auditory canal will do in a pinch. Lean over."

"Great gobs!" Rudger cried with a shiver of revulsion. "That's disgusting! There's no way I'm having you talking my ear off from the inside."

"Hmph! Probably plugged up with earwax, anyway. Fine. Your left nostril, then. I'd suggest your mouth, but I've never fancied them. Unless you have impeccable oral hygiene. Do you floss?"

"*Blech!* I'm not carrying you in my nose or mouth, either!"

"Well, there *is* a fourth option, but I can't say it would be particularly pleasant for either of us."

"Holy toadstools!" Rudger exclaimed. "You're not taking up residence in *any* of my orifices, okay? Look, don't you have a Biblio-something-or-other to get to? You said you're already late."

"Oh, pish-posh. There'll be another one in half a decade. But what we have brewing here…"

Vermis flashed the discombobulated gnome a winning smile.

"…*this* has the makings of a quest!"

CHAPTER FOUR

"So which way now?" Rudger Rump asked as he approached a fork in the rising forest road. To the left, early morning dew glistened on vines entwined about stout bricklebark tree trunks. To the right, wispy trailers of fog curled like beckoning fingers as they rolled off the dirt path and down a steep embankment. A bit beyond, the terrain widened to support a gauzy blanket of condensation that undulated lazily around jagged, protruding rocks.

"Left, I say," a tiny voice answered at his temple. After a bout of intense negotiation, Rudger had reluctantly agreed to provide Vermis a riding perch—around his ear rather than inside it.

"But," the vermitome continued after a pause, "right *does* have its attraction, don't you think? Such a quandary, left or right? The impact of such a decision could be—"

"Whoa, whoa, whoa," Rudger interrupted, coming to a stop. "Are you waffling?"

"Certainly not!" Vermis said in a petulant tone. "A self-respecting von Higglesbreath settling for *those* pathetic puckered pancakes? I should say not. Blintzes. Now, *there's* a proper breakfast edible. Or better yet, crepes. Mmmmm. Crepes with blunderbutter and just a dollop of coagulated quagmire cream. Scrumptious!"

"What are you babbling about?" Rudger said irritably. "I wasn't asking for your breakfast order."

"Pity. I'm an excellent tipper."

"What I meant was, don't you *know* which path leads to Old Drungle Town?"

"No. Should I?"

"You're the navigator of this operation!" Rudger exclaimed. "Knowing which way to go is part of the job description." He hesitated. "You *have* been to Old Drungle Town before, haven't you?"

"Indubitably."

"Then which way do we go?"

"Search me. I'm all turned around up here. Earth tunneler, remember?"

"Are you telling me I've been faithfully following directions from a directionally challenged worm *ever since we left Aunt Ragna's burrow this morning?*"

"Yep. And look how far it's gotten us."

"*Argh!*" the gnome growled. Shaking his head vigorously in frustration, he stomped off down the righthand path.

Sixteen tiny shoe soles flailed for purchase about Rudger's left ear as a piercing cry of protest assailed it.

"*Mas*ter Rump!" the bookworm enunciated in outrage. "Do maintain a proper carriage of the cranium if you expect me to ride in so precarious a position. Elsewise, I shall be forced to seek stabler accommodations. Your tragus, for example."

"My *what?*"

"Your tragus. It's that teensy flap of cartilage in front of your earhole. I do believe I could wedge myself ever-so-snugly into your auditory fossa and use that ledge as a lovely chinrest."

"Not on your life, worm. Make one move in that direction, and I'll stuff you under my cap."

The tension between the unlikely traveling companions grew nearly as palpable as the fog that had since engulfed them. Bricklebark boughs bent broodingly above, blocking all but the most exuberant rays of sunlight. Rudger's reckless stride faltered as his vision grew increasingly useless.

"Shall we return from whence we came," queried the vermitome, "and follow the path I so wisely selected?"

"*Randomly* selected," Rudger grumped. "And no," he continued, though his instincts begged to differ. "This fog is sure to lift soon. Besides, I hear flowing water. Aunt Ragna said Drungle Town's on the river."

"How did she take the news of your imminent departure?" Vermis asked after forty more sightless paces. It was like wandering about in a grounded cloud at dusk.

Rudger answered in hushed tones. "Uh, not so well. She didn't mind my leaving so much except that it meant she'd be left on her own with the Terror Trio. Can't say I blame her. Those three are a real hand—"

Rudger's commentary ended in a yelp. The fog had abruptly thinned, and Rudger was a single step away from walking off a cliff and plunging into turbulent river water thirty feet below.

Vermis recovered first. "Great gobs!" he cried. "That might have constituted a tragic end to our noble quest. Hmm. Do you suppose the words *tragedy* and *tragus* have the same origin?"

Heart thudding in his chest, Rudger could only manage a dismayed groan.

"Because I know *tragus* means 'goat's beard,'" Vermis went on. "It's called that on account of the ear hair that grows there. That's something the males of your species and humans have in common. When you get old, vibrissae grow *everywhere.* Out of your *noses*, out of your *ears*. You get such a crop on the tragus, it resembles a goat's beard. And if you ever saw one up close, you'd agree that it—"

"Vermis! Pinch 'em," Rudger ordered.

"Pinch what? What's that supposed to…? Oh. You mean pinch my lips, right? Is that how you gnomes say, 'shut up'? I guess I am a bit of a nervous talker, but that's no reason to be rude. Besides, vermitomes don't *have* lips, but if we did, we wouldn't pinch them for the likes of you. We don't have ear hair or nose hair, either. Any hair at all, really. So that's another way we're superior to—"

"Vermis, *please!* Stop talking."

"Why should I?"

"Because I thought I heard something. And because all that chatter is *ear*-itating."

"Irritating?" the little worm began in outrage. Then he stopped short. "Oh, wait. I see what you did there. I say, that's clever. Quite so. Excellent word play, Master Ru—"

The vermitome's compliment erupted into an ear-splitting shriek, accompanied by a sharp blow to the back of Rudger's head. The gnome stumbled forward, teetering anew at the precipice. Windmilling both arms, Rudger fought for his balance as the projectile reversed direction and came at him again.

This time, Rudger ducked, and the bird-sized bullet grazed his left shoulder. Snatching his brown cap from the air with one hand and his dislodged rider with the other, he saved both from plummeting into the river below. In an impressive maneuver, Rudger stashed Vermis in the hat, pivoted, and advanced on his assailant.

Faster than the eye could track, the orange blur closed in on him, this time targeting the pointed cap in his hand. Rudger moved to protect the hat's occupant, drawing it in to his torso. The missile altered its course and collided with the young gnome's breastbone. The impact loosened Rudger's grip on the cap, which landed on the rocky precipice just as Rudger tipped backwards into a freefall.

The chilled, churning water of the River Gush swallowed Rudger Rump, driving the air from the gnome's small chest. Rudger's reeling mind reacted without his volition, setting his short limbs into frenzied motion. They propelled him to the surface, where he coughed and sputtered vehemently as he fought to reload his lungs with precious air.

The river coursed over a modest ledge, dunking the drowning gnome once again. Awareness crept back to Rudger, but slowly, like a beaten dog to its master. He knew he must act or succumb to the water. There was only one means to prevent the latter.

Thrashing again to the surface, Rudger found his chance. Drawing spray-laden air from between gouts of river water, and inspiration from some unknown wellspring, he croaked a Weird Wyrd.

Hydroscleros!

Water tightened about the gnome's limp body, encasing him in a translucent prism. Its geometry was poorly defined, borders growing and eroding as liquid washed against it, but the makeshift buoy held. The raging current buffeted the mass about, eventually discarding it in the shallows on the far side of the river. There, the magical buoy disintegrated, leaving its exhausted passenger unconscious on the pebbly bank.

"That's quite enough lounging about for you," a voice grated, piercing the layers of slumber that cocooned Rudger's mind. "Fair warning: I am prepared to interpret your lack of response as tacit approval to occupy whichever of your cavities is most convenient."

The threat roused Rudger's sluggish mind, prompting him to cover varied entry points. He cracked an eye to find Vermis peering right back through his tiny spectacles. Rudger had, heretofore, been unaware that vermitomes could produce a toothy smile.

"That's more like it," Vermis said. "Now, up, up, up. You have a new trekster to meet."

"Trekster?" groaned Rudger.

"Yes. I thought I'd try my hand at coining fanciful words after witnessing what that one did for you back there." The bookworm's face fell as he sighed. "Sad to say, it seems I lack the talent for Logomancy."

"Logomancy?" echoed Rudger.

"Yes, yes. Word magic, if it must be defined," Vermis said testily. "Have you no training in etymology at all, boy? With the masterful Wyrdcraft you worked in the water, I should think you'd had years of instruction. What was it you said? 'Hydro-scleros' or some such?"

Rudger rubbed his face and shifted his body in an effort to ease the pain caused by the rocks beneath him. "I haven't studied, et-…etta-…whatever it was you said. I haven't formally studied much of anything, really."

"Great gobs of ignorance, why not?" Vermis asked.

Rudger shifted a little more. "Because there aren't any Humdrungle schools in the Land of Lex, I suppose. And certainly not for magic." His groggy mind made a connection. "Say, how did you hear what I said from way up on that cliff?" Another connection, and he added, "Come to think of it, how did you get down here?"

Vermis grinned and gestured with several of his legs to a spot over Rudger's shoulder. The unseen trekster spoke.

"If you have not gone to school, how do you come to know so much about language?"

Rudger rolled over with difficulty to set eyes on the source of the question. They widened at the sight of a small, orange, four-legged creature sunning itself on a nearby rock.

"Uh, I'm gnome-schooled, I guess," Rudger answered. "Words fascinate me, so I write every new one I hear in my Logofile, Mister…"

The creature blinked at him balefully. "I have found no need of a moniker, such as I am."

"Oh." Rudger paused uncertainly. "I'm sorry. I have to ask," he apologized. "Are you a lizard?"

"Lizard, chameleon, salamander, newt," it said carelessly. "Call me what you like. It's irrelevant. But your talent—*that's* what matters."

Rudger looked askance at the little orange quadruped. "You were the one dive-bombing us up on the cliff, right?"

"I prefer to characterize it as a skilled aerial assault," it replied.

"But if you were airborne, where are your—"

It lifted a pair of thin wings, making the completion of Rudger's query moot.

"So you flew Vermis down here. But why were you attacking us?"

It cocked its scaly head. "I was in need of breakfast," it answered, "and the grub, here, seemed a likely meal."

"Grub, indeed!" Vermis huffed. "*I* am a vermitome."

The lizard creature peered over Rudger's chest at the bookworm. "You must admit, hanging over this poor fellow's ear like that, you did look rather like a parasite."

"*Parasite?* Master Rump, I have changed my mind. This uncultured, winged newt is not worthy of joining our quest."

"Winged newt," Rudger mused. "Hmm. That's as good a name as any."

"Beg pardon?" Vermis said.

"'Wingnut.' We have to call him something."

"Wait," protested Vermis. "We're taking her with us?"

Rudger frowned. "Her? Isn't Wingnut a boy?"

They turned in unison to gaze questioningly at the newt.

"I have found no need for a gender, either," Wingnut reported.

"Well, I guess that makes you an 'it', for the time being," Vermis surmised. Then he turned to Rudger. "Unless Master Rump is harboring covert knowledge of the anatomy of newts."

Rudger caught the vermitome's eye. "Oh, no. I'm no expert in…a*newt*omy."

As gnome and vermitome guffawed at the quip, Wingnut rolled its reptilian eyes.

"I thought there was something punny about you two," it lamented.

CHAPTER FIVE

An ear-stabbing whistle pierced Rudger Rump's merriment like a spear thrust into a grummermelon. Its shrillness robbed the young gnome's heart of its rhythm then drove it into a panicked patter. He looked anxiously at Vermis, who offered a single whispered word of warning.

"*Human.*"

Wingnut responded by vaulting its body into the air. The brush of its wing as it whizzed past Rudger's head broke the whistle's paralytic power. Blood rushing into his cold, wet limbs, Rudger snatched up the vermitome and bolted upland from the riverbank.

Old Drungle Town wasn't an obscene human city with brazen buildings and denuded roads to blight the mother land. Like its humble Humdrungle denizens, Drungle Town concealed itself beneath the folds of the forest along the River Gush. Truly, an unaware sojourner might traverse its full breadth and never suspect that underfoot lay the largest gnomish settlement in all of the Land of Lex.

But even in his anxious state, Rudger Rump easily spotted the hallmarks of Humdrungle habitation. Driven by the looming threat, his keen eyes seized on the very first flaphatch that marked the outskirts of Drungle Town. Without hesitation, Rudger grasped the flaphatch's handle and jerked upward with all his might.

His teeth rattled in their sockets as he discovered the hatch was locked.

This was highly irregular. Rudger could not recall a single instance of a fellow Humdrungle gnome's hatch being barred to him. But Rudger was a country gnome, and the customs of city-dwellers might be different. A sound like a heavy footfall tweaked his ears. Reining in his racing mind, he forced it into the well-practiced patterns of civil conduct instilled by his mother.

"Gnome a-home?" he inquired, desperately endeavoring to strike a balance between speaking loudly enough for the burrow's occupant to hear and quietly enough not to attract the attention of his potential human pursuer. His heart hammered in his throat as he waited for a response.

"Gnome a-home."

Relieved, Rudger advanced his request in the prescribed manner.

"Home to loan?"

"Go and roam."

Rudger could scarcely believe the response.

"How rude," Vermis griped from his perch on Rudger's ear. "Here you are, a fellow gnome in dire straits, and this imbecile tells you to go roam. Frankly, I don't think he deserves the honor of our presence."

"Vermis, pinch 'em!" Rudger hissed as he hurried to the next hatch. It, too, was barred.

"Gnome a-home?"

"Gnome a-home."

"Home to loan?"

"Go and roam."

"Really!" raged Vermis. "These so-called brethren of yours are positively inhospitable! Wait. Why are we leaving? You should impress upon that domar the urgency of your need."

"That's not how the Entry Entreaty works," Rudger explained between gasps for air. "Once you're refused, there's no recourse. You're duty-bound to move on. I really don't understand this, Vermis. I've never known a gnome to turn down the Entreaty. They must be afraid of the human, too."

The pursuing footfalls were growing louder, and Rudger was forced to skip the next six burrows to buy some distance. Over and over, the Entreaty failed to produce the response he so desperately required, "Welcome, gnome." Without that, he would surely be overtaken by his long-legged pursuer.

To his right, Rudger spied a group of four flaphatches prettily arranged at the base of a flowering jawjackle bush. It was as close to actual landscaping as Humdrungle burrows ever boasted. Perhaps it meant important gnomes resided there. Looking to his left, he saw a lone hatch, practically obscured by an unkempt patch of grizzlegrass. Bucking the odds, Rudger veered left.

He skidded to a stop in front of the solitary flaphatch and

hopelessly tugged on its rusted ring-handle. To his surprise, the hatch yielded, exposing an aperture beneath. An enormous shadow rose up behind him, but Rudger didn't turn to look. He dove into the tiny hole and jerked the hatch shut behind him.

He crouched there, panting in the darkness, weary muscles tensed as he waited for his foe to pry the flap open. Thunderous footfalls loosed bits of soil from the roof of the gloomy space, but soon all went quiet. Had the human not seen him duck into the burrow? Rudger strained to suppress his ragged breathing as he imagined the giant above puzzling out his hiding place. At last, the footsteps resumed. Rudger exhaled as they faded into the distance.

"Vermis?" he called tentatively, once he was confident the human threat had passed. "Vermis, are you all right?"

"Yes, no thanks to you," the bookworm answered peevishly. "It's a wonder I haven't suffered cardiac arrest! First, you get us lost in the fog and decide to take a long walk off a short cliff. Then you try to feed me to a winged newt while you're taking a refreshing dip in the river. Now we're hiding from a human who wants to stomp us flat. I ask you, what kind of quest are you running here?"

"What?" Rudger said, mystified by the worm's interpretation of recent events. "Vermis, this hasn't been a picnic for me, either!"

"I believe it shall have to be a picnic for one from now on," the vermitome declared. "All of this has taught me it is far more dangerous to make your own adventure than to consume one from a nice, safe book."

Rudger felt the little vermitome's weight lift from his ear.

"Vermis?" he asked, reaching up to confirm that his traveling companion had gone. "Vermis, you're not going to leave me here alone, are you?"

"I regret that I am returning to my original itinerary. With luck, I will find my way to the Bibliorinctum without further incident."

"But what if that monster comes back?"

"I suggest you do the sensible thing and stay underground where it can't find you," Vermis replied. "I guarantee you that's where I'll be. In the earth, where it's safe."

"Vermis, please stay. I haven't found my grandparents' burrow yet."

"I'm sorry, but I shan't be dissuaded. I bid you adieu."

The dank, silent darkness of the unfamiliar burrow seeped into Rudger's spirit. A wisp of hope lifted it slightly when the vermitome's voice returned.

"May our tunnels cross again, Master Rump. *If* you live long enough."

CHAPTER SIX

Rudger Rump stared apprehensively down the twilit tunnel he now faced alone. Drawing a shaky breath, he invoked the Entry Entreaty for the tenth time in as many minutes.

"Gnome a-home?"

The packed, earthen walls absorbed his quavering voice. Scoffing at his own timidity, Rudger cleared his throat and called out with more conviction. The air itself seemed to close in and extinguish the words. The gnome listened until his last whit of hope conceded there would be no response. Twiddling a button on his jerkin, Rudger budged his legs into motion. It seemed ill-advised to antagonize the silence with another vocal outburst.

The tunnel extended before him, growing blacker with each step he took. While accustomed to the requisite economies of underground living, Rudger found the passage uncommonly tight and long. Indeed, the flaphatch of his parents' burrow opened directly into their hearth-room, and Aunt Ragna's led to a staircase contained in a compact entrance hall. The young gnome had never encountered such a protracted, snaking entry to a Humdrungle abode.

Even with their exceptional adaptive ability, Rudger's eyes strained to form an image of the space around him. He wished he'd thought to pocket some of Aunt Ragna's phosphofungus before he'd left that morning. It wasn't an oversight—burrows were practically never devoid of the luminescent plant. But as it was, Rudger was forced to hobble along, his sense of touch guiding him along the tract as it sloped ever deeper underground.

Negotiating a narrow *S*-turn rewarded Rudger with a bit of illumination, and as he approached the tunnel's outlet, the oppressive silence joined the darkness in its retreat. At first, the sound was little more than an unintelligible garble with the barest hint at order and meaning. Intrigued, Rudger edged forward and poked his head through a doorway cut into the tunnel's wall.

The chamber within was awash with a reddish-orange light that spilled from a squat fireplace carved into the wall opposite. The area before it was dominated by a long wooden table loaded with implements and apparatuses Rudger imagined might be found in a wizard's hovel. Glass beakers, flasks, and covered jars sparkled in the firelight wherever they weren't obscured by disorderly sheaves of parchment and open-face books. Here and there from this clutter protruded iron tongs and forceps and calipers so large that it seemed to Rudger it would take two gnomes to manipulate them. The meager floor space was littered with pots and pans with their lids askew plus vast, rotund receptacles that could only be called cauldrons.

In the chamber's most distant corner, Rudger could just make out a straw pallet and rumpled bedclothes. Beside it stood a prodigious trunk, which appeared to be in the process of disgorging the whole of its contents.

It was these commonplace, quotidian objects that reminded Rudger he was intruding upon the home of a Humdrungle gnome. The occupant was not visible, but the garbled sounds Rudger had heard were now identifiable as gnomish speech. Rudger had to concentrate to discern the hurried words.

"…come-to-me-only-when-all-else-has-failed-and-expect-a-miraculous-solution-for-which-I-won't-get-due-credit-but-what-else-is-new-for-I-have-never-gotten-a-fair-shake-in-this-moldy-old-town-with-its-stodgy-council-and-insufferable-gnomister-who-can't-see-past-the-nose-on-his-face-his-way's-not-the-only-way-or-even-the-best-way-and-just-because-I-don't-see-things-the-way-he-does-is-no-reason-to-bar-me-from-the-healer's-guild-and-worse-make-me-a-laughingstock-but-they'll-all-see-this-extract-will-work-and-when-it-does-they'll-be-falling-all-over-themselves-to-place-the-healing-hood-upon-my-shoulders-which-will-be-shaking-with-laughter-of-vindication-which-can-only-be-truly-savored-when…"

Rudger gasped as he hauled his mind out of the dizzying torrent of words. Even as he shook his head to dislodge some of the verbal vomit, the bewildering logorrhea rolled on. When his brain could manage a thought of its own, Rudger found himself questioning the mental status of the maniacal monologuer who never seemed to pause long enough to draw air.

Rudger strongly considered going back the way he had come. Then the young gnome remembered with a chill his narrow escape from the human. He had heard that city burrows tended to be interconnected so it was possible to travel around town without going topside. If this was true, it would keep him safe from his pursuer and allow him to locate his grandparents' domicile quickly.

"Uh, excuse me? Sir? Madam?"

The gabbling went on unabated. Apparently, the gnome couldn't hear Rudger over his or her own yammerings.

Feeling a mounting trepidation, Rudger Rump stepped away from the relative safety of the doorway and into the burrow proper. He gingerly picked his way through the multitude of pots and pans strewn about the floor and carefully avoided the glassware and iron utensils that stuck out from the tabletop. At the far end of the room, a sickly-sweet odor like flowers gone sour filled his nostrils. He peered around an overburdened wardrobe to spot at last the garrulous resident in an alcove, still prattling away. The gnome was hunched over a basin with its back to Rudger, who cleared his throat. Still, the commentary continued, and it occurred to Rudger that waiting for a polite moment to interrupt this gabster's roll might result in his remaining in this cluttered hole until his whiskers sprouted.

"Beg pardon, honored one, but…"

The figure's shout of surprise was upstaged by a thunderous crash as it dislodged a double rack of skillets from the wall in front of it.

The startled gnome jerked back, forgetting the stool upon which it stood. Teetering precariously, the gnome cried out and grabbed wildly at shelves on either side, inadvertently adding their contents to the clamorous cascade. Rudger jumped back as the collection of clattering crockery covered its owner, capping off the catastrophe with a cacophonous conclusion.

Rudger hopped over rolling rolling pins and tumbled tumblers in his haste to aid his accidental victim. "Are you all right, sir? Madam?" he cried as he dug through the debris. Tossing aside a dented tea kettle, he found an arm. Gently, he used it to extract the rest of a very disheveled gnomette not half a decade older than he. Remarkably, she was still talking at breakneck speed.

"…contemptible-trespasser-who-dares-to-invade-my-happy-hollow-and-clobber-me-with-cantankerous-kitchen-ware-which-constitutes-assault-and-battery-in-addition-to-breaking-and-entering-and-just-those-crimes-will-get-the-gnomister-to-shackle-and-yoke-him-let-alone-the-even-worse-offense-of…"

"Wait! Let me explain!" Rudger tried to break in. "I was being chased, and you didn't answer the Entreaty. I'm really sorry I startled you, but—"

"…say-you're-sorry-now-but-you-won't-know-the-meaning-of-sorry-until-I-let-you-have-it-with-this-frying-pan-but-it's-too-heavy-to-wield-so-maybe-I-should-work-my-way-over-to-the-lab-bench-where-all-of-the-pointy-implements-are-that-I-can-jab-into-your…"

"Whoa!" Rudger tried again. "There's no need to get violent. I'm just a harmless gnomelescent who's—"

"…gnomelescent-my-foot-you-can't-be-more-than-fifteen-and-the-harm-has-already-been-done-my-poor-kitchen-is-in-a-shambles-and-a-week's-worth-of-jawjackle-blooms-wasted-which-endangers-every-gnome-in-this-city-because-now-I-have-to-start-the-delicate-distillation-process-all-over-and-that's-days-of-work-assuming-there's-even-enough-blossoms-left-to-collect-enough-nectar-because-the-leaves-aren't-half-as-good-and-take-weeks-to-process-and-the-roots-are-even-worse-because-of-the-impurities-that-I-have-to…"

Rudger's head was spinning. "Please, please! Just slow down a little. Don't you ever stop talking?"

"…can't-stop-this-jawjackle-jabber-with-the-concentrated-fumes-I've-been-inhaling-all-morning-but-it-will-all-be-worth-it-when-I-show-those-healing-harpies-up-but-come-to-think-of-it-you-shouldn't-be-here-or-you'll-start-jabbering-too-which-would-actually-serve-you-right-for-destroying-my-burrow-and…"

"That's exactly what I want," Rudger interjected. "To get out of here and find my grandparent's burrow. They live in Drungle Town, and I need to find them right away. Can you help me?"

"…be-ridiculous-why-should-I-do-anything-to-help-you-when-you—"

"Look, I'll make you a deal, okay? Let's get you out of these fumes and into some fresh air. Then you can give me directions to my grandparents' burrow. After I see them, I'll come back and help you clean up the mess I caused. I'll even help you collect those jawjackle blossoms you need. Okay?"

"…seem-to-be-telling-the-truth-so-I-guess-I-can-trust-that-you'll-do-as-you-say-and-I-really-could-use-the-help-with-the-blossom-collection-all-right-we'll-get-you-to-your-grand-parents-and-then-you're-my-assistant-for-the-rest-of-the-day-but-before-we-can-go-I-have-to-bottle-whatever-jawjackle-juice-I-can-save-to-test-on-one-of-the-patients-and…"

"Fine," Rudger said in exasperation. "Just please hurry. Oh, and can I ask you a favor?"

"…seems-kind-of-nervy-to-ask-for-a-favor-after-all-the-trouble-you've-caused-but-I-am-a-magnanimous-gnomette-who-tries-to-see-things-fairly-so-I-suppose-I-will-hear-your-request-although-that-doesn't-mean-that-I'll…"

"I just want to know if you have any earplugs," Rudger blurted. "And if you know a vermitome named Vermis von Higglesbreath. You two would have *so* much to talk about. Eesh!"

Twenty minutes later, Rudger was patrolling the vicinity surrounding the jabbering gnomette's flaphatch. He was on alert, watching for the human he had evaded. He hoped the stories he'd heard about the limitations of a human's attention span were true. With luck, the wretched thing was off somewhere terrorizing a colony of fairies or chasing some leprechauns a league away.

Suddenly, Rudger realized the barrage of words coming from the gnomette was breaking up. There were still spits and sputters of the jabber-jaw, but now they were interspersed with moments of silence between.

Rudger pulled his fingers out of his ears. He hadn't had the patience to wait for the gnomette to provide something soft to stop up his overtaxed ear canals. "Feeling better?" he inquired.

The gnomette had seated herself on a rock just a few yards

away from her flaphatch. She gave Rudger a tentative thumbs-up. Apparently, she feared speaking might set off another bout of logorrhea.

Rudger waited a few more minutes before asking, "Think you're ready for a simple question? Like, 'What's your name?'" He raised his hands in a gesture of restraint. "Just that. Don't try to elaborate."

The gnomette steeled herself with a deep breath and opened her mouth. "The-name-and-moniker-by-which-I-am-rightly-known…" She clamped both hands over her renegade mouth and then rolled her sea green eyes in frustration. She suffered three more false starts before she managed a succinct answer, "Twelda Greeze."

"Okay. That's progress, I think. My name is Rudger Rump." He stuck his elbow out toward her. "Pleased to make your acquaintance, Miss Greeze."

Twelda moved to reciprocate the greeting but swung her elbow away at the last second.

Most Humdrungle gnomes would take offense at such a slight, but Rudger understood. Stifling another word-surge had forced the gnomette's breach of protocol. After several spectacular paroxysms, Twelda managed to squeak out, "Rump?"

"Well, okay. I guess the human's gone. It's probably safe to bump a rump," he commented, thinking she was inviting him to sit down. Once beside her, his eyes drifted to the jawjackle bush a stone's throw away. "So that's the source of your vocal vexation, eh?"

Twelda uncovered her mouth and, with a prodigious effort, converted a word-surge into a strangled stutter. "Y-y-y-y-yes." She took a breath and went on. "Gnomes 'round these parts know that jawjackle tea loosens the lips and helps-get-a-conversation-going-so-I-thought-about-it-and-hypothesized-that-if-I-concentrate-the-nectar-from-the-flowers-to-make-a-tonic-I-might-be-in-a-position-to—*Arrgh!*" She used all eight of her digits to pinch her loquacious lips together. Once she'd regained control, she blew out a stream of air that lifted her blonde bangs. "Guess it's more powerful than I thought."

"It was kind of hard to catch everything you were spewing down there," Rudger said, "but I gather the extract is meant to be some kind of cure?"

"Right. I deduced that if a small infusion of jawjackle juice gets healthy folks talking, a stronger dose might serve as a remedy for those who can't."

Rudger looked at the fetching gnomette appraisingly. "Hypothesize? Deduce? You don't sound like any wizard I've ever read about."

"That's-because-I'm-not-a-wizard-or-magician-or-sorceress-or-conjurer-or-enchant—"

She slapped her cheek to stop the jabbering. A raised finger signaled Rudger to wait until the spell had passed.

"It's because I'm a different kind of wonder-worker," she finally told him.

"Oh? And what is that?"

"Well, humans would call me a scientist."

Rudger frowned. "Sigh-and-kissed? What's that supposed to mean?"

The gnomette suddenly grunted and pursed her lips.

"Hackerpedes!" Rudger cried as he leaned back. "Are you…?"

Several awkward seconds ticked by before she could

manage an answer. "No, Rudger, I'm not trying to kiss you. I was just suppressing another jabber. And I said 'scien*tist*.' It's a kind of wizard who doesn't use magic."

The concept boggled Rudger's mind. "A wizard who doesn't use magic? That doesn't make any sense."

Twelda Greeze stood up and smoothed her long-bodied tan smock. "Haven't you read any human writings?" she asked. "I don't claim to fully understand science, but it seems to be a kind of anti-magic. It relies on deductions and logic and reasoning to form hypotheses, which are guesses about how the world works. Then scientists test these hypotheses by—"

"You're jabbering again," Rudger accused.

"No, I'm not," Twelda reported. "Scientists test hypotheses to see if their observations support them. It has nothing at all to do with magic."

"Or reality."

"All right, Mr. Doubter. We'll do some science right now. Go on. Observe something."

Rudger was beginning to think the daffy gnomette had taken one too many frying pans to the noggin down in her burrow, but he decided to humor her. She seemed his only hope of locating his family in this unfriendly town.

He rose to his feet and cast his eyes about the forest around them. Nothing stood out until his gaze fell upon the soft ground in front of Twelda's flaphatch.

"Okay," he announced. "There's an enormous footprint in front of your hatch. What does your science make of that?"

"Easy," Twelda replied with a shrug. "Humans have no toes."

Rudger's brain imploded. "*What?*"

She went over to the print and squatted beside it. The impression was almost as long as she was tall. "Notice the contours of the forefoot," she said, tracing them with her finger. "There are no demarcations for digits. It's a perfectly smooth arc. Ergo, human feet are toeless."

Rudger advanced. "But humans wear *shoes*, like we do. That's why you don't see toeprints."

Twelda pointed to Rudger's own footwear. "Shoes indent between the digits."

"Well, gnomish shoes do," he admitted, wiggling the four toes on his left foot, each wrapped by an extension of the shoe's boughbrat hide. "But that doesn't mean human shoes have to."

Twelda rose and placed her hands on her hips.

"Have you ever observed a human barefoot?" she asked.

"I try my best not to observe humans at all."

"Then you have no evidence to support your argument," she declared. "I've observed dozens of human tracks, and they all looked like this. Therefore, science says humans have no toes. Or, possibly, that they only have one big one per foot. But that pretty much amounts to the same thing."

Rudger had had enough of this incredibly peculiar female. He backed away from her, saying, "Fine. I'll concede the point. And I think it'll be best if you go back to your sciencing. In your burrow. Right now."

"But what about our deal?"

"Null and void," he said, spreading his hands. "You're off the hook."

"Wait a minute. You're the one on the hook, buddy. *You* trashed *my* burrow, remember? And, besides, you need me."

Rudger had reached the quartet of flaphatches surrounding the jawjackle bush. "Oh, don't feel the least bit obligated," he said soothingly. "I'm sure one of these nice gnomes can help me." He leaned toward the nearest flaphatch. "Gnome a-home?" he inquired urgently.

"You're not getting off that easy," Twelda said as she closed the gap between them. "If you don't want to help me clean up that mess, then you can even the score by being the control subject in my jawjackle juice experiment." She pulled a vial of blue liquid out of her pocket and shook it in front of his face.

"Me? Take that?" Rudger squeaked. He sidestepped to the next hatch. "Uh, I'd be honored, but I can't. I've got sick grandparents to tend to."

"*Sick* grandparents, you say? Both of them?"

"Uh-huh," he replied distractedly. Cupping his hand over his mouth, he directed his next words at flaphatch number two. "Gnome a-home? Little help here?"

Twelda closed the gap again. "What's wrong with them?" she pressed.

"Um, they had strokes."

"Strokes?"

"Yep," Rudger told her nervously as he retreated to the third hatch. "You know, can't talk, that sort of thing. Gnome a-home? Anybody?"

"Nobody's answering the Entreaty," Twelda said, crossing her arms. "We're on lockdown due to the Mute-ation."

"Mutation? My, my. That sounds unpleasant."

"Do you know what the Mute-ation is, Rudger?"

"Uh, something about gnomelings being born without toes?"

"No. It's an illness that's robbing gnomes of the power of speech."

"Really? That's too bad."

"Ugh! Don't you get it?" she asked in exasperation. "Your grandparents can't speak. The jawjackle juice I've been distilling is for them! You're a Rump!"

"Hey, now. No need to call names."

"No, I mean *your* name is Rump. So's theirs. I talked to your father about letting me try the jawjackle juice on them. Experimentation, you see. It's a science thing."

"How nice for you," he said indulgently. Now at the fourth and final flaphatch, he stomped on it frantically. "Gnome a-home! Gnome a-home! Aw, come on, guys. Let me in!"

The overzealous gnomette reached out and caught Rudger's face with both hands. She fixed him with a piercing stare. "No one's going to answer you, Rudger."

He swallowed nervously. "Why not?"

"Two reasons. The first I've already told you. We're on lockdown due to the Mute-ation."

"What's the second reason?"

"Those aren't burrows you're stomping on."

"Oh…what are they?"

Twelda grinned sardonically. "You country gnomes would call them latrines."

"Oh, poop."

"Precisely. Now, stop acting like a turd and come with me. We've got some grandparents to save."

CHAPTER SEVEN

Rudger stuck close to Twelda Greeze as they traversed the forest overlying Old Drungle Town. Rudger's heart was racing, so convinced was he that his human hunter would leap out from behind a moss-covered tree trunk. And although she was mostly recovered from the jabber-jaw, Twelda's residual vocal outbursts only added to Rudger's discomfort.

"Are you *sure* we can't find some kind-hearted gnome to let us into their tunnels?" he asked. "Look—there's another flaphatch. Why don't we try it?"

"Because that 'burrow' is a composting station," Twelda deadpanned. "Look, haven't the last twelve Entreaty refusals gotten it through your head? Nognome is going to let us in. The Mute-ation's causing mass xenophobia."

Rudger's curiosity trumped his nerves. "Xe-no-phobia," he enunciated appraisingly. "That's a cool word. What does it mean?"

"The fear of strangers," Twelda told him.

Rudger eagerly reached into his pack. "Awesome! How do you spell xen-…oh, smut."

"Hey! Watch your language. You happen to be in the presence of a lady."

"What? Oh. Sorry." All the vim had drained out of the young gnome.

The gnomette turned around. "What's wrong?"

Rudger slowly pulled a handful of wet pulp out of his traveling bag. Regarding it miserably, he said, "I love words. I've loved them ever since I was a 'ling. Used to write every new one I heard down in my Logofile here. But now it's ruined." He turned his hand palm down and let the sodden mass plop on the ground.

"That's a shame," Twelda said with empathy. "How'd it get so wet?"

"A flying newt knocked me into the river."

"Flying newt, you say? I've never seen one of those in these parts."

"Afterward, it told me I should develop this 'talent' for words I have. That's what it called it. A 'talent' for Logomancy."

"The newt *spoke* to you?" Twelda asked. When Rudger confirmed it, she added, "Well, I can't say I'd take advice from a talking lizard, but I feel your pain. I've had plenty of accidents back in the burrow that destroyed data that were precious to me.

"But," she continued in a brighter tone, "it's important to look at such a setback as an opportunity for a fresh start." She pulled a small book out of an inside pocket of her long, tan lab smock.

"Here," she said, clapping him heartily on the shoulder. "Take my notebook. You can start a new Logofile. Oh, and I'm sure I have a spare quill somewhere on me."

"Gee, thanks," Rudger said as she rummaged through her other pockets. The little leather ledger was bound smartly with fine twine stitches. It was far more impressive than the loose-leaf sheaf of parchment scraps he'd lost.

"There," the science-gnomette said as she handed him the quill.

Stowing it behind his ear reminded Rudger of Vermis. He wondered what had become of the little bookworm.

"Now, you can resume your research," Twelda declared.

"Research?" he asked as he opened the book and began to jot down 'xenophobia' and its definition.

"Certainly," the gnomette replied. "A scientist's work must not be long interrupted."

Rudger looked up, his brow crinkling. "I'm not a scientist," he said.

"You're not a wizard yet, either," she observed with a grin.

Ten minutes after receiving his new and improved Logofile, Twelda led Rudger down through an unbarred flaphatch into a public tunnel. It was wider than the one the young gnome had negotiated to reach Twelda's burrow, and there was plenty of phosphofungus to light the way. Rudger was just becoming accustomed to this safe, deserted passage when a burrow-door, the first they'd found open, caught his eye. A dillyquill broom was flicking its bristles through the doorway in a regular rhythm. When the gnomette manipulating the broom stepped into the tunnel, Rudger's pulse quickened.

"Grammers! You're all…right?"

The joyful exclamation lost its punch as Rudger tried to process what he was seeing. There she was, his supposedly stricken grandmother, sweeping dirt out of her burrow as she might do any day of the week. It was a chore he had never understood. After all, the floor itself was *made* of dirt.

The broom continued its work. Thinking she hadn't heard him, Rudger started up their old bit.

"Keep that up, Grammers, and we'll be living in a pit."

The old gnomette missed her cue, failing to play-scold him for his cheek. She continued to sweep mechanically, even after it was clear there was no loose dirt left to clear.

"Is she deaf?" whispered Twelda.

Rudger, consumed with his own quandary, barely registered the science-gnomette's question, but both he and his grandmother recoiled violently when an ear-shattering shriek ripped through the tunnel.

"Ow, Twelda!" Rudger complained as he uncovered his ears. "What'd you do that for?"

"Just testing my hypothesis," she replied. She jerked a thumb at the old gnomette. "Not deaf."

Grammers was crouching in the doorway, clutching at the wall as if releasing it might send her world spinning out of control. Rudger moved to comfort his distressed grandmother, but his mother descended on her first.

Ridna cradled the confused old gnomette in her arms,

oblivious to everything else. "Mother Rump!" she cried. "Why did you scream? Are you hurt?"

The elder Mrs. Rump maintained her anguished silence.

Ridna stroked her mother-in-law's gray hair, which was pulled back in a chignon at the nape of her frail neck. "Please, Mother Rump," Ridna begged. "Just tell me what's wrong. You can do it, dear."

A croak came, not from the old gnomette, but from Rudger, who was still standing in the hall. Ridna's head turned toward the noise, but she saw Twelda first.

"Who are *you?*"

Twelda gasped as if stabbed by the sharpness of the query. Before she could find her tongue, Ridna's eyes tracked farther up the tunnel and seized on her son.

"Rudger! Wh-...what are you doing here?"

Tears abruptly filled his mother's eyes. Two hasty dabs with her sleeve restored the composed parent he had always depended upon.

"I asked you a question, son," she said sternly. "And what have you done with your cap?"

"I-I lost it in the river," Rudger stammered. "Oh, Mummers, I'm so glad to see you!"

The self-professed gnomelescent rushed to his mother like a scared little gnomeling. The two hugged each other.

Twelda cleared her throat. "Mrs. Rump, I am Twelda Greeze. I accompanied your son here from my burrow at the southern edge of Drungle Town. Seems he's had quite a time finding you. Dive-bombing lizard, fall in the river, marauding human—that sort of thing."

"Why, by the High Gnome's whiskers, did you leave your

Aunt Ragna's burrow?" Ridna asked the quivering mass in her arms.

"It was Vermis," Rudger answered, his voice muffled by his mother's embrace. "He told me to come."

She drew him out to arm's length. "Vermis? Who's he?"

"He's a vermitome…a-a-a bookworm. He just popped out of the wall and told me I'm the only one who can save Grammers. Grampers, too. He said the Logoleech is coming, but I don't *want* to learn magic to fight it."

"Well, you're safe now," Ridna comforted. "Nobody's fighting anybody here. And nobody's learning magic, either. But let's get everygnome into the burrow, shall we?"

Ridna wrapped a protective arm around her son's shoulders and ushered him into a smallish kitchen where a cheerful fire blazed in a stone-lined hearth. After settling him into a canfawood chair, she turned and beckoned Twelda to take a seat across from him. Ridna then collected her befuddled mother-in-law from the doorway and led her through the kitchen into an adjoining room. When Ridna returned, she was carrying a pair of afghans which she settled around the two young gnomes.

"Mite bit cold in here," she commented. "The tunnels that got you here are even worse. You two must be chilled to the bone." She pulled the lid off a pot that was suspended over the fire and stirred its contents—by the smell of it, swampkunk stew. Rudger's belly let him know its opinion about being neglected for the past twenty-odd hours.

"Supper'll be ready soon," Ridna announced. As she replaced the lid, a couple of droplets from its inside face fell into the fire, producing a hissing sound. "In the meantime, why don't you tell me what this is all about? From the beginning."

And so they did.

By the time they'd finished their tale, Ridna was tutting like an agitated boughbrat.

"Part of the reason I left you and the triplets at your Aunt Ragna's was to spare you the dangers of the travel here," she told Rudger. "It can be a risky journey. Mine was fairly uneventful this time, but you never know what the wilderness is going to throw at you."

"What's the rest of the reason?" Rudger asked.

"I didn't want you to see what's become of your grandparents."

"So Grampers is the same way?"

"I'm afraid so," she confirmed as she pulled a wooden drawer out of a rectangular hole dug into the earthen wall. From this box, she produced tableware for her surprise visitors. "They're both napping now, but they're hardly any more responsive when they're awake."

"But Grammers was sweeping," Rudger pointed out.

Ridna smiled slightly. "That doesn't mean much, dear. They perform repetitive tasks without really understanding what they're doing. Neither one of them has uttered a word since I arrived, and they don't seem to understand anything said to them."

"Have you tried writing back and forth?" Twelda asked.

Ridna shook her head. "They never learned to read or write. When I heard that awful scream, I was more hopeful than alarmed. I thought it might mean some sort of breakthrough."

"I'm sorry I frightened everygnome," Twelda said. "I was just testing a hypothesis. No harm intended to you."

"None suffered," Ridna replied, adhering to the polite, stereotyped response. Then her eyes narrowed. "Twelda Greeze, you said? Seems to me I've heard that name before. What was it in association with? Ah, yes. Some wild speculation concerning this Mute-ation sickness going around?"

"Yes, except I don't think it's fair to call it wild speculation," Twelda told her. "It's the result of disciplined scientific thought."

"Now I remember," Ridna interjected as she checked the stew anew. "You're that radical wizard-gnomette who rales against traditional living while espousing some cockeyed form of magic nognome understands."

"It's not magic, ma'am. It's *science*."

"Whatever you call it, any decent Humdrungle gnome will have none of it."

"And yet it is this indecent practice that has brought a probable cure for your parents to your doorstep," Twelda said stiffly.

"They're my *husband's* parents, not mine," Ridna snipped. "And it's their doorstep, not mine. See what your 'disciplined thought' has brought you? Two misconceptions in the very same sentence."

"Mrs. Rump," Twelda said through gritted teeth. "The Council of Gaffers has authorized me to investigate a possible remedy for the Mute-ation." She pulled the vial of blue jawjackle extract from a pocket in her long-bodied smock. "Here it is."

"Well, that's nice for you, dear, but we'll be having no

magic potions in this burrow. And certainly not from an outcast like you, if you'll pardon my bluntness. We are simple, proper, non-magical Humdrungles."

"Mrs. Rump—"

"I believe this discussion is at its end. Thank you for escorting my son, but—"

"Perhaps if I spoke to *Mr.* Rump?"

"Rondo is not here, Miss Greeze. He is at the Gnomatorium on important matters of state."

"When will he return?"

"I don't know. Certainly not tonight."

"Well, then, perhaps I can go to the Gnomatorium and—"

"Impossible. He can't be disturbed."

"Why, by the tenets of science, not? They're *his* parents. I should think—"

"No. Actually, you shouldn't," Ridna interrupted nastily. "Thinking should be reserved for gnomes with common sense. My husband cannot see you because he is instrumental in the preparations for the Leprechaun Legion's arrival tomorrow noon. Surely even you, with your outlier status, have heard about this."

Both gnomettes were now on their feet, hurling words at each other across the burled gnarlicwood table. Rudger could tell Twelda was winding up for a return lob, but a hiccup in her thinking preempted it.

"Leprechauns?" she mused. "You're married to the leprechaun ambassador?"

Ridna nearly erupted. "Marry a leprechaun? What a repugnant idea! Nognome in this family would stoop to such impropriety! Whatever would make you conceive of such an offensive thing?"

Twelda looked perplexed. "Sorry. I didn't mean to offend. It just seemed logical that Mr. Rump might be a leprechaun because…" Her voice trailed off as she pointed uncertainly at Rudger's head.

Rudger caught her meaning first. "Great gobs! Just because I have red hair doesn't mean I'm a leprechaun!"

Twelda sounded contrite. "Well, of course, I didn't think you're a full-blooded—"

"I'm not a demi-leprechaun, either! Look, this isn't about me; it's about Grammers and Grampers. They need help, and I found it." Rudger turned to his mother. "Twelda may be unconventional, but I've seen what her jawjackle juice can do."

"Yes," Twelda put in. "I was only exposed to its fumes earlier, and it turned me into a jabbering idiot."

"How could you tell the difference?" deadpanned Ridna.

"Mummers, you've got to give Twelda a chance. If her extract makes normal people jabber, doesn't it make sense giving it to Muted gnomes might get them talking again?"

"This isn't about what makes sense, Rudger. It's about what's proper and decent."

"And it's proper and decent to leave Grammers and Grampers like they are?" Rudger yelled.

The household fell silent as the question hung in the air around them. The furious bubbling of the forgotten stew popped the lid from its pot, producing more hissing as its contents doused the flames. Ridna moved to the hearth to swing the pot away from the fire.

"I will tell you what isn't proper and decent," she said softly as she ladled stew into each of three bowls. "Having a son who has just disobeyed his mother's wishes hollering at her like she's a common imp."

"Mummers," Rudger said quietly, "I'm sorry. I didn't—"

"No, no," she interrupted. "As we have so rightly established, Mother and Father Rump are not my parents. My opinion doesn't matter in this matter. But I cannot allow an untested potion to be given to those dear, old gnomes without their son's consent. That I will *not* stand for."

"Oh, absolutely, Mrs. Rump. I fully—"

Ridna held up a hand to silence Twelda. "So I bid you go to Mr. Rump. You know where he is. If you can obtain his permission to experiment on his parents, which I doubt, I shall stand aside."

"That's more than fair, Mrs. Rump. We'll do that."

"Eat your stew while it's hot, Miss Greeze. Having served it to you, it would be a breach of etiquette to eject you from this burrow before you've completed your meal. And to demonstrate that I bear you no ill will, you are invited to stay the night, and Rudger will accompany you to the Gnomatorium in the morning."

She pushed an errant lock of her mudpud brown hair back in place before continuing.

"Now, if you'll excuse me, I must attend to your guinea pigs in the other room." She filled two more bowls with stew and put them on a wooden tray. When she moved to deliver them, Rudger placed a hand on her forearm.

"Let me, please. I'd like to see them."

"You may come with me. It's likely they'll need to be spoon-fed at first."

Mother and son entered the bedroom to find their patients resting comfortably upon a wurblebird down mattress with an enormous tan afghan covering them both. Ridna awoke the couple, and the vacant expressions in their milk-white eyes tore at Rudger's heart. They were little more than shells of his grandparents, and as Rudger pressed the first spoonful of stew to his Grammers' lips, he resolved to do everything in his power to bring his grandparents back. Even if that meant risking the jawjackle extract.

Or learning Logomancy.

Grammers lifted her wrinkled arm and fumbled at the spoon Rudger held. He relinquished it, allowing her to take over the feeding, but the gnarled fingers slipped, and the spoon dropped to the floor with a thump.

"That's all right, Grammers," Rudger said bracingly, though it was clear she didn't understand. He bent to retrieve the utensil and bumped the nightstand on Grammer's side of the bed. A wad of phosphofungus joined the spoon. Rudger grumbled at his own clumsiness and bent to retrieve the objects.

"Uh, Mummers? Why are there holes under the bed?"

Ridna set her bowl and spoon down on the other bedside table and proceeded to wipe her father-in-law's dribbles with a napkin. "What holes?" she asked distractedly.

Rudger waved his mother to his side and pushed the wad of phosphofungus into the dark space under the bed. Its pale green light revealed eight holes in the dirt floor. Each was big enough in diameter to hold two fingers.

"Hackerpedes," Ridna said disdainfully. "Those pests have been especially obnoxious recently. Gnomes all over town have been complaining."

"I thought hackerpedes tunneled alone," Rudger said.

"Usually, they do. Who knows? Maybe one went crazy and made a bunch of tunnels instead of just one. Doesn't matter. I'll have to call the Soil Squad tomorrow whether it's one hole or eight to fill in."

"Do you have some bricklebark root?"

"Well, I suppose so. Why? You're not going to waste it on those holes, are you? Hackerpedes don't reuse their old tunnels, Rudger. They always dig new ones. There's nothing to worry about."

Rudger's mother's voice faded as his sensitive ears perceived the faint clackety-clacking of armored hackerpede legs emanating from the holes. It was probably just his imagination.

But what if it wasn't?

CHAPTER EIGHT

The Gnomatorium of Old Drungle Town violated every convention of gnomish architecture. Constructed of roughhewn bricklewood and imported elven glass, the above-ground meeting hall rose a dizzying six feet atop its modest knoll. The structure boasted a wood plank floor, thatched roof, and more than a dozen windows—all features that typical Humdrungle burrows lacked. Although the site was well-hidden from outsiders by a ring of interwoven amnesioak trees, the hall was not a usual hotspot of Humdrungle activity. The risks of remaining topside for long periods of time unnerved all but the bravest of gnomes. It was a rare spectacle, indeed, when Rudger and Twelda emerged from the public tunnel and found a crowd abuzz on the Gnomatorium's cropped grizzlegrass lawn.

"High skies," Rudger breathed at the sight. "I've never seen this many gnomes in one place before."

"Well, it's not every day you get to see leprechauns," Twelda commented from behind him.

The young gnome raised his line of sight. "Wow. So that's the Gnomatorium."

"In all its superterranean splendor."

"I've never seen a real building before. Humans live in burrows like that, right?"

"Yep," the gnomette replied. "Except they call them 'houses.'"

Twelda was making little noises of exertion behind Rudger, but he was too entranced by the throng before him to check what she was up to. "So many gnomes," he marveled. "And all topside. You'd think they'd be nervous up here."

"They probably are. I know I am."

"Then why doesn't the Council of Gaffers meet down below?"

"Two reasons," Twelda explained. "One, there isn't a chamber big enough for everygnome. And, two, leprechauns are top-dwellers. They wouldn't take kindly to an underground conference."

"So? They're the ones visiting us."

"You know us gnomes," Twelda said with a sarcastic lilt in her voice. "Can't risk a diplomatic impropriety. Everything has to be done according to perfect protocol." Then her voice became more serious. "Speaking of protocol, aren't you forgetting something?"

"Huh?" Rudger asked distractedly, still ogling the crowd. "What did you—"

"Breach!" somegnome barked in Rudger's ear.

Rudger jumped and turned to find a middle-aged gnome in

a greenish-brown uniform glaring at him. As Rudger stared back in dumbfounded fashion, the black-bearded official cried out again.

"Breach of protocol, boy! Have you no respect for the Gnomister?"

"I'm sorry?"

The glowering gnome pointed at Rudger's feet. "Fix them, or you'll have to go."

Befuddled, Rudger looked down at his footwear. The boughbrat hide lace-ups seemed fine to him. A little dirty, perhaps, but what did the guard expect? He'd just come out of the tunnels.

"Switch 'em!" a whispered voice urged.

Rudger turned around to find Twelda pointing at her own shoes. *So that's what she was doing*, he thought. The gnomette's slippers were now on backwards.

"Well?" growled the security-gnome.

"S-sorry. My mistake," Rudger sputtered as he yanked off his shoes and replaced them on the wrong feet. "No offense intended, sir."

"None suffered," came the gruff reply. He skewered Rudger with another narrow-eyed stare before resuming his patrol.

Twelda smacked the back of Rudger's head.

"Ow!"

"How could you *do* that?" she scolded. "Step onto Gnomister's Knoll without observing the Shoelute? You're lucky that guard didn't toss you in swale!"

"I didn't know, okay?" he said in his own defense. "I'm

from the Hinterlands, across the river. We don't have a gnomister there."

"I'm surprised he didn't cite you for that cap, too," she went on. "You'd better pull it down again."

"Ugh! Why did I have to lose mine in the river?" he complained as he tugged the undersized hat down over his ears. "If this thing isn't squeezing my head, it's creeping up. Grampers' head is *tiny*."

"Or yours is ginormous," Twelda said, appraising his cranium. "I'm guessing the latter."

"Ha-ha. What are you, now? A haberdasher?"

"Oh, it's just one of the many hats I wear," she quipped. "Now, pinch 'em. Here come the Gaffers."

The double doors of the Gnomatorium were opening, and the crowd hummed with excitement. The Gnomister himself emerged first, easily distinguished by his extraordinarily tall, tan pointed cap which brushed the lintel as he passed through the doorway. The pattern of his elaborate tan-and-ochre ceremonial robe was echoed, to a lesser extent, by the garments of the Gaffers behind him. Out they processed, step by pretentious step, the Gnomister alone in the lead with the ten Gaffers following in pairs.

Twelda leaned toward Rudger. "Which one's your father?" she whispered.

"None of them. He's not a Gaffer."

"What is he, then? A Protocaller?"

"Not exactly. Just watch."

After the Council members came two more rows of gnomes, three abreast. Their caps and robes were darker than those of the Gnomister and Gaffers, the approved shade of burnt umber. These rows of Protocallers compacted to fit through the doorway, and one of them brushed its edge with his shoulder.

Instantly, a pair of hands appeared, smoothing the folds in the Protocaller's robe. The nimble hands were connected to a lone gnome dressed in a simple mudpud vest and matching pantaloons. He squeezed past the Protocallers and scurried to adjust a cap here, a hem there, ensuring that each official's raiments were impeccable. He moved with a slightly awkward gait owing to his slippers being on the wrong feet.

"Surely, that gimpy fellow's your father," Twelda speculated. "The one fussing over the robes of the others? What's his title again? The Sartorio?"

Rudger didn't answer; his eyes remained glued to the gnomish procession. Now, a curiously short figure appeared in the doorway. This final member of the retinue was remarkable only in the color of his beard, auburn with ginger highlights at the sides. He wore a modest tan cap, tan shirt, and mudpud brown pants that lacked adornment of any kind.

With a shot of dismay, Rudger suddenly discerned the reason for the gnome's diminutive stature—he was processing on his knees. Rondo Rump struggled along behind all the others, carefully bowing his head in keeping with his subservient station. Only when the Sartorio's own pantaloons became indented during the course of his work did Rondo rise from his knees. He hurriedly restored the breeches' contours and then scrambled back to the rear of the procession to resume his knee-walk down the Gnomatorium's wooden porch stairs.

"Oh, Rudger," Twelda said with sympathy, apparently

realizing this pathetic soul was his father. "How degrading."

"No, no," Rudger responded with false brightness. "It's an honor to be in the procession. A real honor." But witnessing his father's plight for the first time was a blow to Rudger's heart.

With painstaking pomp, the processional party took their prescribed positions; the Gnomister front-and-center, the ten Gaffers in an arc behind, and a troika of Protocallers flanking either side. The Sartorio moved freely, if awkwardly, intervening wherever the breeze dared to stir a lapel or cuff. Rondo Rump remained unobtrusively stage left, only rising from his knees to attend to the Sartorio's own vesture.

The Gnomister had no need to call for the attention of the assemblage; the pageantry of the procession had done this work for him. With a flourish, he lifted both hands, palms down. Grandly, he interdigitated his fingers and then turned his joined hands palms up to open the address.

"Honored gnomes of Old Drungle Town, dedicated denizens of the Fourth City, loyal protectors of Humdrungle propriety, steadfast champions of our Righteous Rituals, unswaying observers of…"

Twelda scoffed. "He does go on, doesn't he?"

Rudger shushed her.

"…we gather here this appointed day to welcome our noble brothers in minikinity, the exalted Leprechauns of Limptenshire. But in light of the fact that fair Helios has not yet reached his zenith…"

"He means it's not noon yet," Twelda interjected. "Why can't he just speak plainly?"

"Quiet, Twelda. I'm trying to listen."

"…ample time to dispense with the business of a most egregious nonconformity perpetrated by an alleged enemy of the Code of Valid Vesture."

The Gnomister paused for effect.

The pause grew pregnant, then awkward, as the crowd waited in silence.

"Proto-call!" one of the stolid Protocallers bellowed.

The outburst stunned the crowd, necessitating a second reminder, voiced in perfect unison by all six of the officials in burnt umber robes.

"Proto-*call*!"

The townsgnomes didn't wait for a third prompt. In belated response to the Gnomister's characterization of the defendant, they offered a chorus of condemnation.

"*Nyuht, nyuht, nyuht, nyuht…*"

Thinking it wise to join in, Rudger vocalized in kind. He noticed, however, that many of the gnomes around him seemed less than enthusiastic about their required response.

"Bring forth the offender," commanded the Gnomister.

Through the hall's open doorway emerged a pair of guards like the one who had berated Rudger. They escorted a short, plump fellow with white whiskers. The elderly gentlegnome fairly jabbered with fear, leading Rudger to wonder if perhaps he'd been hitting the jawjackle tea a bit too hard.

The gabbling gnome was ushered to a spot directly before the Gnomister. Even from clear across the lawn, Rudger could see the poor fellow quaking.

The Gnomister raised both arms.

"Whereas you, Gilder Gaggle, have been accused of the substandard and subversive production of textiles in hues other than those expressly approved by the Council of Gaffers, and whereas, your dye works were inspected and found, in fact, to contain such dyes and textiles of questionable hues, and whereas, you did knowingly utilize these unsanctioned textiles to sew and construct garments of a most ghastly color and nature, intentioned for purchase by the Council of Gaffers itself, be it known to all at these proceedings that it is the required duty of the Sergeant Sartorio to examine said garments and to render true a ruling of their propriety or lack thereof before the open Council."

"B-b-but, sirs," quavered Gilder Gaggle, "I've explained that this was all an innocent mistake! It was a single dye batch, and the umber did not burn adequately. In my efforts to supply the uniforms in the short time frame you offered—"

"Proto-call!" cried the sextet.

"*Please!* I was up all night sewing feverishly by phospho-fungus and lantern. I couldn't detect the rawness of the umber color until—"

"Proto-*call*!"

The gentlegnome tailor bit his quivering lip. He dared not provoke the Protocallers further.

The Gnomister continued, "Sergeant Sartorio, step forward and recite the Inventory of the True Hues."

The Sartorio came forth, puffing out his chest while hooking his thumbs in the armholes of his vest.

"The True Hues are but four, O Whiskered One: Tempered Tan, Mudpud Brown, Drear Ochre, and Burnt Umber. These hues, and these only, are approved by the Council in the dress of the Humdrungle gnomes. The standard of each is safe-guarded by the Sartorio himself."

"As the expert in the subtleties of each Hue, examine the confiscated garment and render your esteemed opinion."

A derisive snort distracted Rudger from the drama unfolding before him.

"What a farce!" Twelda whispered into Rudger's ear. "They've already convicted that poor fellow."

The Sartorio approached the garment and produced a golden loupe from his pantaloon pocket. After a period of visual inspection, his head snapped up to address the Gnomister.

"This heinous hue is closest to the True Hue of Burnt Umber but fails the standard by several shades of green."

"I t-told you it was a mistake in the burn—" began the distraught gentlegnome.

"Proto-call!"

The Gnomister hesitated only a moment before passing sentence.

"To produce such a textile is negligent," he proclaimed. "To fashion it into clothing of any kind is criminal. But to present that clothing to dignitaries of this Council is downright egregious. Shall this knave be permitted to flout the Code of Valid Vesture ever again?"

The Gnomister paused for effect. This time, the crowd was quicker on the uptake.

"*Nyuht, nyuht, nyuht, nyuht…*"

He raised his hands for silence. "Gilder Gaggle, you are hereby sentenced to bear the Amnesioak Yoke for a period of…eight hours."

As Gilder Gaggle wailed his regrets, Twelda whispered, "Great skies, that's *worse* than going to swale! Just an hour in the Yoke leaches away a decade of memories. But eight? They'll be hardly anything left."

Rudger felt the injustice of it boil up inside him. "All this over the color of some clothes? Why *can't* he make green clothes? Why can't we wear anything but four ugly shades of brown?"

Twelda looked around nervously. "Rudger! Keep it down, okay? It's an age-old Humdrungle custom. You don't mess with those."

"Well, my Aunt Ragna does," he challenged. "She has a crimson blouse."

"Shhh!" Twelda hissed. She met the eyes of curious gnomes around her. "He's kidding," she cajoled them. "A crimson blouse? Puh. Who ever heard of such a thing?"

Rudger crossed his arms stubbornly. "I'm not kidding," he insisted. "She *wears* it, too. Well, at least she did until she ruined it fighting her arachna shrubs. She wants Dadders to make her an electric blue one next."

"Ho, ho! What a kidder!" the gnomette grandstanded as she set upon Rudger and forced him into a head lock. Under the guise of giving him a noogie, she whispered in his ear. "Pinch 'em, you domar! Unless you want your father to be next in the Yoke."

A fortuitous arrival drew the attention of the onlookers away from the tussling gnomes. The mischievous, green-clad leprechauns made no production of parading into the clearing, rank and file. Instead, they materialized, higgledy-piggledy, onto the Gnomatorium grounds, eliciting cries of alarm as they caught nearby gnomes unawares.

"How's she cuttin', boyo?" said one as it popped into existence in front of Rudger's trapped head.

Rudger blinked at the sprig of shamrocks that had sprouted about its feet as it continued, "What's this? Why are you and the missus acting the maggot?"

Rudger wrenched his neck upward and found a ladychaun appraising him. "Missus?" he half-said, half-choked. "Great gobs! We're not married!"

The leprechaun cocked her little head, rust-red ringlets dancing on either side of it. "Sure as Saint Christopher, you two'll be hitched someday. I can smell it all over yuh. Then she'll be doin' something about those gammy shoes of yours. Cobbler made a bags of 'em, he did. Don't even fit right."

Rudger pried Twelda's arm from his throat so he could rebuff the uppity minikin.

"Not that it's any of your business, but I'm observing the Shoelute, here."

"Shoelute? That's an odd-un."

"It's a sign of respect to our Gnomister," he explained, suddenly aware that each of his big toes was mashed into the narrowest toe-sleeve of the shoe designed for the opposite foot.

"Oh, would yuh listen to 'im!" the leprechaun laughed. "Sign of respect, he says."

"Which you'd know nothing about," Rudger growled as he continued to struggle against the headlock. "Now, get lost, will you?"

The ladychaun crossed her slender arms. "No need to be a Holy Joe about it. And if you don't mind me sayin', I'd be scarlet in your place, subdued by your future ball-and-chain."

Twelda giggled and eased her hold, allowing Rudger to pull free.

Rising to his full sixteen inches, he glared down at the irksome leprechaun.

"Oh, stop yer gawkin'," she rebuked him. Then she curtseyed to Twelda. "Fair play, missus. Gotta keep those overblown males in their place, I always say."

"Too true," Twelda replied with a smug look at Rudger. "Welcome to Gnomister's Knoll in Old Drungle Town. I'm Twelda Greeze."

The ladychaun doffed her little green hat. "I thank you, Twelda of Old Drungle Town. My name is Triksha Loofe. But you can call me Trixie."

Twelda removed her cap. "Pleasure to meet you. Oh, and this one's Rudger," she added, jerking a thumb in the outraged gnome's direction. "Rudger Rump."

"You don't say," Trixie said with a tinkling of laughter. "Explains a lot, don't it?"

A shrill whistle interrupted the introductions. "Hup! That'd be my cue," Trixie said. "You'll excuse me, won't you?"

The little leprechaun pulled a tiny fife from her coat pocket and added its voice to the obnoxiously upbeat tune that was taking over the enclosure. Rudger shifted his gaze back to the Gnomister's platform party only to discover a small green figure with an extravagantly curly red beard dancing a jig before them. The Protocallers bellowed for decorum, but somehow their cries were woven into the sprightly music from the lutes, panpipes, jugs, and fiddles scattered throughout the crowd. Not until the song and dance had come to its raucous conclusion could the appalled Gnomister get in a word.

"Welcome though you are, Lordling Liverwurg," the Gnomister announced as he glowered at the spectacularly bewhiskered leprechaun taking bows before him, "the good gnomes of Old Drungle Town beg you to observe a modicum of restraint."

The green-clad minikin turned to address the Humdrungle bigwig.

"Don't be getting' yer nose out of joint," he said with a wink. "Everyone knows you're in charge on account of that fierce cap you've got. Tell me, is your head shaped like that, or have you just got serious notions, now?"

The leprechauns tittered at the jibe.

"The cap," declared the Gnomister, "is ceremonial in function. And you would do well to exhibit some decorum."

"Ah, he *is* puttin' on airs, the cheeky bloke," the leprechaun replied. "And here it was him who called us here. Welcome, my eye."

The Protocallers were gearing up for another round of bellows, but the Gnomister silenced them with a gesture.

"We summoned you here—"

"'Summoned,' says he," interrupted Lordling Liverwurg. "What d'ya take us for? Some sort of genies?" Then he slapped his forehead. "Ah, but I mucked that one up, I did," he said ruefully.

"How's that?" shouted a leprechaun from the crowd.

Lordling Liverwurg's eyes twinkled as he took in the whole of the assemblage.

"Isn't it obvious?" said he. "Blarney serve me, I should have said 'greenies' just then."

The leprechauns roared with laughter as the Gnomister

cleared his throat sharply.

"'Summoned' was a careless choice of word. 'Invited' would be more apt."

"Go on, then."

"Very well. We *invited* you here to discuss a crisis of growing proportions. It has become apparent to us that a foul magic is afoot—a magical illness that renders its victims mute. By our count, twenty-one gnomes in our fair town have already fallen prey to this enigmatic Mute-ation."

As the crowd gasped at this news, Twelda bent down toward Trixie Loofe. "Gotta cut Rudger a break here," she told the ladychaun. "His grandmother and grandfather number in that twenty-one."

Trixie peered up at Rudger. "Coo," she sympathized. "Family's got a bad dose of it, eh?"

Rudger acknowledged the question with a nod as the Gnomister continued.

"And so, it was our desire to inquire if the leprechaun population has suffered similarly."

Lordling Liverwurg stopped his playful fidgeting and addressed the Gnomister directly. "Aye. We have."

The gnome bowed his head with dignity. "The Humdrungles express our empathy and admit that we have no natural remedy for this mysterious affliction. Being staunch abstainers when it comes to the practice of magic, we are loath to ask it, but the public welfare demands a solution. Have your leprechaun magic-workers divined a cure?"

Lordling Liverwurg again answered soberly. "Alas, I cannot say we have. However, we have heard a rumor that a creature called the Logoleech may be to blame."

The assembled minikins gasped anew, but Rudger did not join in. Instead, he flashed back to his conversation with Vermis in Aunt Ragna's burrow.

A poacher of words, a thief of knowledge, the Logoleech devours. Your grandparents are just its appetizers.

The Gnomister straightened his black beard and addressed the throng. "With our brother leprechauns as flummoxed as we, the threat becomes even more dire. I call on all within the reach of my voice to remain calm but be vigilant. We shall contact the other members of the Minikinity to seek an answer. Somegnome, or someone, must surely have an insight into this dreaded plague."

Rudger turned to see Twelda clutching her vial of jawjackle juice through her tan laboratory smock.

"Go on," he urged her. "Tell them."

The aggrieved look on her face spoke of a conflict within. "I can't, Rudger."

"Why not?"

She sighed. "Two reasons. One, it would be breaking protocol if I speak here. I'm an outcast, remember?"

"Forget the protocol! Your cure is way more important than a bunch of stupid rules."

"Maybe, but then there's reason number two." She pulled out the vial and peered uncertainly at the blue fluid it contained. "It's just a hypothesis. It hasn't been tested yet."

"It's a far sight more than what those duffers have," Rudger pointed out.

"But what if it doesn't work?"

"It *will* work. It's science, remember?"

His words seemed to embolden her. She closed her eyes

and took a deep breath. As she opened them, she gripped the vial with conviction.

Thunderous footfalls and the screams of a hundred gnomes stole the moment. Rudger's eyes seized on the western edge of the small enclosure where the braided amnesioak branches were shaking ominously.

Another peal of screams assaulted his ears as an arm of enormous proportions broke through the foliage high above his head. The accompanying five-fingered hand tore at the boughs below it, producing a gap that admitted a foot and lower leg as big as any of the minikins present. The enormous foot plummeted to the earth, sending shock waves up Rudger's spine. Behind that massive limb came into view the torso and head of the most dreaded monster known to minikind.

A human.

The giant's purple robes snagged on broken branches as it breached the amnesioak barrier. Humdrungle gnomes ran for the four public flaphatches that represented their only viable route of escape. Meanwhile, the visiting leprechauns offered no magical assistance to their fellow minikins. Taking care not to meet the marauding human's eye, they evaporated from the lawn. To her credit, Trixie Loofe was the last ladychaun standing, but Twelda's pleas for a cloaking charm fell on deaf ears.

"Sorry, Twel. Gotta leg it. Leprechaun's luck to yuh."

Her magical disappearance produced a sprig of heather to complement the shamrocks.

The human loomed overhead, matching the lofty Gnomatorium in height. Rudger watched in amazement as gnomish shoes sailed every which way, their newly discalced owners putting on speed as flat, bare feet slapped against the grizzlegrass lawn. Rudger tried to catch sight of the Gnomatorium platform party, but the Gnomister and his entourage had fled nearly as efficiently as the leprechauns. Into the building they had dashed, probably down some privileged hatch no common Humdrungle would ever conceive of entering.

"Rudger, come *on*!" exclaimed Twelda as scores of panicked gnomes stampeded around them. "What in Terreste are you waiting for?"

"My father," Rudger yelled back. "I have to know if he… Oh, no! Look!"

Twelda followed the line of Rudger's pointing finger. The human was stomping its way toward them, now less than a dozen of its gigantic strides away. Barely visible through its flapping robe and grizzled salt-and-pepper beard, a gnome's capped head and flailing arms could be seen protruding from the giant's right armpit. Its tan sleeves and auburn hair were disturbingly familiar to Rudger. As the monster approached and the mass exodus ebbed, the plaintive cries of the captive were unmistakable.

Kicking off his own shoes, Rudger charged straight at his human foe. The monster seemed to grow in size with every step he took. At over four times his own height, Rudger's attack options were limited. He threw himself at the human's shin, but the billowing robe caused him to misjudge its location. Instead of latching on, Rudger ricocheted off the enormous leg, bouncing between the giant's feet and out through the robe on the other side.

The giant barely took notice of the bungled assault. Transferring Rudger's father to its left armpit, it pivoted to lumber back to the hole it had made in the wall of amnesioak trees.

Rudger righted himself and sprinted after the colossus. Suddenly, Twelda was there, clawing at his arm and shoulder.

"Rudger, stop!" she hollered. "You can't help him! Can't you hear what he's saying?"

Now that his adrenaline rush was subsiding, Rudger found he could make out his father's words.

"Turn back! Don't let the human get us both! Tell your mother I love her!"

Rudger's resolve faltered. Then he imagined telling his mother he'd let the monster abduct her husband. He imagined the tears in his siblings' eyes as he told them their father was never coming home.

The young gnome plowed forward, dredging his brain for a Weird Wyrd that might stop the titanic gnome-napper, but the wellspring refused to open. Twelda kept pace, seeking to lace an arm around Rudger's neck, but Rudger was wise to the move now. He performed a somersault to evade capture.

The giant was at the trees, threading its gargantuan limbs through the ragged gap. Rudger closed in, his grandfather's tight cap working itself free from his head. Red hair exploding into view, Rudger pounced on the human's heel and wrapped his arms around the outsized ankle. His father's entreaties for him to abandon the pursuit ended mid-sentence. Rudger hung on as the ankle dragged him forward into the amnesioak foliage.

Suddenly, the young gnome's thoughts began to crumble; his motivation dribbled away. He struggled to remember why he was being pulled through these jabbing branches, why the urgency he still felt mattered at all.

©2022 Simerlein

A yank on Rudger's own ankles peeled his arms apart. He found himself tumbling onto a grizzlegrass lawn, tangled up with a blonde gnomette wearing a peculiar long-bodied coat.

"Ha!" she crowed as they sorted out whose limb was whose. "That'll teach you to duck my headlock. You're not getting gnome-napped on my watch!"

Rudger stared at the boisterous gnomette. As seconds passed, her triumphant smile began to fade.

"Hello," he eventually said. "My name is Rudger. Do I know you?"

CHAPTER NINE

"Uh-uh-uh! No, you don't," Twelda Greeze chided as Rudger's eyelids began to droop. "That'll be the oak-haze, right on cue. Some gnomes go down for *days* after blundering into a copse of amnesioaks, but you'll have to fight it. That human might come back, and I am *not* slipping a disc dragging you to safety."

Twelda cast her eyes about the enclosure. All four public flaphatches were choked with gnomes trying to reach the safety of the underground tunnels. The sensible thing to do would be to choose a hatch and wait for their turn to exit from Gnomister's Knoll.

Twelda, however, was not feeling particularly sensible at the moment. Heaving Rudger to his feet, she marched the groggy gnomelescent straight up the hill to the Gnomatorium itself.

Trespassing in the Gnomister's private tunnels was an infraction of such enormity that Gilder Gaggle's tailoring faux pas paled in comparison. The science-gnomette knew she ought to abandon the notion of setting foot there, but she drove her wilting companion onward. *This is an emergency,* she told herself. *Rudger can't resist the haze much longer.* She turned a blind eye to the fact that this course of action offered an attractive bonus: the opportunity to flout the rules of a government which had seen fit to shun her.

"So sleepy," Rudger mumbled as Twelda's pokes and prods propelled him up the veranda steps.

"Just stay with me," Twelda encouraged him. "Soon as we're safe, I'll let you sleep it off, okay?"

She urged Rudger forward, through the Gnomatorium's handsome double doors. Inside was a rustic meeting hall girded with roughhewn bricklebark beams and columns. Row after row of varnished benches led to a dais at the far end of the room. On the left side of that raised stage stood a stockade fashioned from limbs taken from the trees that encircled Gnomister's Knoll. Twelda gave the dreaded Amnesioak Yoke a wide berth as she directed Rudger to the other side of the dais. There, behind a podium which bore the Gnomister's seal, a narrow door hung open. The stem of a key protruded from its ornate iron lock.

Beyond the door lay a staircase that began in polished gnarlicwood but changed to packed earth halfway along its span. Using the private stairway to reach the safety of the underground tunnels did little to settle Twelda's jangling nerves. The thrill of defying Council law had abandoned her, and in its place rose the heart-gripping fear of being discovered in this forbidden place.

When Rudger began to moan another complaint, Twelda

clamped a hand over his mouth and hissed in his ear to be quiet. They might be safe from the human marauder now, but the Gnomister and his Gaffers could be equally dangerous. Soon, it became clear her semi-conscious companion was hindering their search for the public tunnels. Rudger would have to be stashed somewhere while Twelda scouted the way alone.

The nervous gnomette half-guided, half-dragged Rudger down a good-sized passage, barely noticing the canfa-wood paneling lining its walls. It wasn't until the earthen floor transitioned to stone that the peculiarity of this particular passage registered with her.

Twelda was seriously considering turning back when at last she spotted a door at the end of the tunnel. Subterranean tunnels in Old Drungle Town rarely dead-ended like this, and the grand manner in which this one terminated disturbed the gnomette. The closed door was pretentious, with an elaborately carved frame and an inset plaque containing four blank wooden panels, each stained a different shade. Supporting Rudger with one hand, she reached out and tried the handle. The door was locked.

"Gnome a'home?" she ventured.

No answer. Some agoraphobic gnome might be napping inside, but her gut told her the room beyond was unoccupied. Perfect for her current needs, if not for that bothersome lock.

Science-gnomes were a resourceful lot, and they knew a lot more than how to extract the juice from pretty jawjackle blossoms. During her nineteen years on the planet, Twelda had made a study of all things mechanical from her collection of taboo human books. Allowing Rudger to slump against the paneled wall, she pulled a small leather case from an inside pocket of her lab smock. The metal instrument she drew from it produced a gratifying click as it tripped the lock's tumblers. Twelda pushed the heavy door inward, grunting softly as bright light forced her to squeeze her eyes shut.

White phosphofungus encrusted the small room's ceiling, bathing its contents in a stronger illumination than typically encountered underground. Mounted on each side of the well-lit, white-tiled chamber were two pairs of metal brackets. Each bracket assembly held a large roll of cloth.

Twelda frowned. It seemed to her a ridiculously elaborate set-up just to store some tailor's wares. Further scrutiny of the room revealed no other trappings of the sartorial profession. No scissors, no thread, no pins or needles. The room was bare but for the four hanging bolts of cloth.

Twelda gave up puzzling over the idiosyncrasies of the Gnomister and his Gaffers. All that mattered was this would be the perfect place to let Rudger sleep off his oak-haze while she found the way back to his grandparents' burrow.

A terrific noise startled the gnomette. She darted out of the white room to find Rudger still propped up against the coridor's wall, face-first, snoring with sufficient vigor and volume to spook the most stalwart blunderelk.

"Rudger! Wake up! We're here," she told him. When her voice failed to rouse him, she resorted to shaking the slumbering gnome.

"Hmm? Huh? Whuh?"

"We're here," Twelda repeated. "Up on your feet. Just a few steps, and then you can nod off again."

"Too bright," Rudger complained as they entered. He threw an arm over his eyes.

"You're in luck," Twelda said. "There's all sorts of cloth in here. I'll make you a pillow from this roll, and you can pull a bit over your eyes to block out the light."

"Cold toes," the young gnome remarked as he plodded over the chamber's pristine white floor. "Chilly in here."

Twelda looked down and discovered Rudger had lost his shoes. "We can fix that, too," she said. She yanked another bolt of cloth off its roller and wrapped the material around his feet. "There. How's that?"

His slurred response seemed to imply contentment, so Twelda pulled down the other two bolts and fashioned Rudger a makeshift quilt. Then she said, "I'm going now. When I find the way back to your grandparents' burrow, I'll come back for you. All right?"

A muffled grunt of agreement emanated from the mound of cloth.

Metal implements in hand, Twelda headed toward the elaborate doorway. She strained to pull the heavy door back into its frame but stopped a head's-width short in order to take a last look at her sleeping friend.

"Sweet dreams," she said. "Hope you remember me when you wake up."

A thunderous snore set Twelda back on her heels. She quickly shut the door and manipulated the lock's tumblers until they clicked.

CHAPTER TEN

Too soon, a tap-tap-tapping sound stirred the tatters of Rudger Rump's mind. Reluctantly, he cracked open his eyes.

There was little to see; a swath of something was draped over his face, allowing only the merest trace of light to penetrate. His hazy brain gradually cobbled together the assumption that he was at home in the Hinterlands, enjoying the drowsy security of his own bed. But the illusion was soon shattered by a ragged recollection of his Aunt Ragna's awful arachna shrubs. Might he be their victim?

The young gnome sat bolt upright, splitting open the cocoon around him. Blinding white light roused him to full wakefulness. His eyes adapted slowly, gradually revealing that he was in an unfamiliar chamber lined with small white tiles. Four slender cylinders were mounted to the walls, two on the wall nearest him and two on the one opposite. Clearly, he was not at home. And unless this stark space was the product of his aunt's eccentricity, he wasn't in her burrow, either.

Rudger scrambled to his feet, kicking loops of cloth every which way. Rushing to the only exit from the white-tiled cell, he jerked on the ornate door's handle. Its carved foliage motif hinted at the freedom of the open woods, but to Rudger's dismay, the portal was locked tight.

The panicked gnome racked his brains, trying to recall how he'd gotten here. He remembered arriving at Aunt Ragna's burrow and his aunt saving Rani, Roni, and Roon from the arachna shrubs. He also remembered he'd somehow managed to terrify the triplets with a bedtime story. But after that, nothing.

His mind was a blank from that point forward. He drew an unsteady breath. How much time was he missing? Where was he now?

And what was making that annoying tapping noise?

Rudger ignored the auditory irritation in favor of taking stock of the room's meager contents. The mounted rods offered no clue to his whereabouts, so he sat down to scrutinize the folds of fabric strewn about the floor.

A tailor's son, Rudger immediately recognized the quality of the material he was examining. It boasted the lustrous sheen of satin combined with the luxurious softness of velvet. Each of the four lengths of cloth was dyed a shade of brown so even and perfect it surpassed any Rudger had ever lain eyes upon. Peering closer, he became mesmerized by a weave that was beyond masterful. Its warp and weft were so incredibly fine it was surely the product of a magically enhanced loom.

"Such a **deft weft**," Rudger murmured appreciatively as the fabric slid over his fingers.

A pulse of energy concussed the metal rods, rattling them in their brackets. Rudger's heart raced in the ensuing silence. The tapping sound—which had ceased—began again, louder and more insistent than before.

Rudger collected himself and set aside the magnificent stretch of cloth to run his ear along the chamber's wall. As he zeroed in on the source of the noise, a puff of powdery grout assaulted his nasal passages. He backed away and sneezed. The offending tile fell, clattering against the floor until it came to rest on his bare foot. A tiny, pale green head popped through the resulting hole in the wall.

"Great gobs of indolence!" its owner cried. "I've been chipping away at that obstruction for ages! Never occurred to you to aid your own rescuer, I suppose."

Rudger was agog. "I beg your pardon?"

"Now, isn't *that* a fine how-do-you-do," the creature said sarcastically. "And for an old friend to boot! Apparently, your etiquette hasn't improved."

Rudger's eyes were stretched so wide in disbelief they hurt. "I-I'm sorry. Do we know one another?"

"Master Rump, you wound me to the core. I admit we didn't part with mutual consent. Some might even characterize my departure as tucking my tail between my legs and running. But considering the fact vermitomes don't technically *have* tails, I hope you will choose to overlook my misstep."

"Vermitomes?" Rudger asked, still trying to process the notion of a talking worm. "I'm really sorry, but I'm not following you."

"That's good because I have no designs on leading you through this madcap quest of yours. Worries enough just trying to be part of it."

Rudger's gob-smacked expression drew a look of consternation from the bookworm. Threading the rest of its body through the hole it had created, the vermitome drifted gracefully to the floor. With a glance up at the confused gnome, it slipped a pair of spectacles and a tiny red bowtie into their appropriate places.

"Recognize me now?" it asked.

"Nope. Sorry."

"Well, if this isn't a fine nest of hackerpedes," the vermitome muttered. Then its head whipped up again. "Speaking of which, I'd be very much obliged if you'd put that tile back in place. Caution is the forebear of defense, I always say."

Rudger did as he was bid. "Who *are* you?" he asked.

"It aggrieves me to require a reintroduction, but apparently it is necessary." The loquacious worm cleared its throat and straightened its bowtie. "I am Vermis von Higglesbreath. The Fourth." It flicked its eyebrows expectantly. "Eh?"

Rudger stared at the worm blankly. "Doesn't ring a bell."

"High skies and sliggen slop!" it exclaimed. "We met only two nights past. In your room in your aunt's burrow. Ragna, I think you said her name is. Surely, you remember that. We had a quest."

Rudger tried hard to recall. "I remember being at Aunt Ragna's. I just don't remember you," he admitted.

"This is unacceptable to the fullest degree." It paused to eye the loose tile. "Well, I suppose there's time. I shall simply have to refresh your appallingly inadequate memory."

And so the vermitome did. At the end of the recountal, Rudger found himself thinking of the little worm as a friend. He was also shaking his head incredulously.

"You think *I* cast a magic spell over the river?" he asked.

"Indubitably, my good fellow. You are a Logomancer of the highest caliber, pending proper training, of course. I've decided to return to your side to guarantee you receive said schooling."

Rudger laughed.

"You dare doubt my earnestness?" the worm demanded, his crimson spots expanding alarmingly.

"No, no," Rudger assured him. "It's just that you've got yourself the wrong gnome."

"Oh?"

"I don't have a magical bone in my body. And even if I did, I *wouldn't* do magic. It's against the law."

"From the knowledge I've consumed," Vermis commented, "I've gathered that your species' peculiar aversion to magic-working is more of a custom than a law."

"Whatever. It's just semantics."

"But that's the crux, here, isn't it? Words have meaning; words have power. And if you're such a good little Humdrungle gnome, what was that magical pulse you put out just minutes ago?"

"That?" Rudger said, glancing at the now-stationary cylinders. "That wasn't me."

"I beg to differ," the bookworm countered. "I never mistake a Glynt."

"A what?"

"Glynt. G-L-Y-N-T," the vermitome spelled, forming each letter with his lithe, segmented body. "It's your magical signature, broadcasted every time you do magic. I recognized your Glynt straight off, though I knew you were in here even before the pulse."

"How?"

"That cataclysmic snore of yours," Vermis answered. "Believe me, after surviving a night of that acoustic horror, I'd recognize it anywhere."

A clacking at the door startled gnome and vermitome alike.

The latter recovered his tongue first. "This might be an opportune moment to wield a Weird Wyrd," he advised as the lock's tumblers turned.

Rudger swallowed nervously. "What's a weird word?" he whispered.

Vermis scoffed. "Only the conduit of your magic!"

Rudger was beginning to wish he had his Logofile at hand. "What's a conduit?"

"A tool of focus," the worm clarified, eyes glued to the door. "Like an amulet or wand for lesser wizards. You, however, need only to speak the right Wyrd."

"Balderdash."

Vermis looked at Rudger and cocked his head appraisingly. "Hmm. Not the word I might have chosen at this particular juncture, but you're the wizard."

"What? No! That's not what I…"

Rudger abandoned his reply as the door swung open. A hunched, knobbled figure filled the door frame. Despite its semblance of minikin form, the bulky brown body, which was balanced upon two spindly legs, seemed to lack a critical characteristic—a face. The lumpy mass that appeared to pass for its head had no discernible eyes, nose, or mouth. Instead, its cranium bore a bizarre, open-ended horn that resembled a crinkled cornucopia.

The monstrosity hobbled into the chamber and closed the door behind it. Straightening up, it plopped half of its bulk on the floor. Through his horror, Rudger realized the deposit was actually an irregularly shaped pack. Then the creature's head pivoted to reveal the comely visage of a young gnomette. Her face—a welcome sight, indeed—was framed by a peculiar apparatus which Rudger could now see included a matching pair of the huge, protruding funnels.

"I'm back," the gnomette announced as she dusted off the front of her long-bodied smock. "I'd ask if you missed me, but I'll settle for just being remembered."

Before Rudger could offer a response, the gnomette let out a shriek. "Hackerpede!" she cried. She stomped across the room with deadly intent.

"Wait! Don't!" Rudger protested as Vermis retreated into a corner. Rudger caught the advancing female by the arm.

She goggled at him. "Why shouldn't I squash it? It's a filthy little 'pede."

"Madam," Vermis said indignantly, "you are gravely mistaken! I am not a filthy hackerpede. I am an immaculate vermitome, and one of great renown. Honestly, I do wish you gnomes would bone up on your taxonomy."

"It…speaks?" asked the gnomette.

"Yes, it does," Vermis snipped, "and a fair sight more

eloquently than you." He used three front legs to point at her raised foot. "Now, kindly put that lethal weapon down and tell us who you are and what that hideous contraption atop your cranium is."

"Oh, this?" she said, removing it and placing it on the pack as she returned to a biped stance. "It's a scientific invention of mine."

Vermis risked a few steps closer to the device. Then he scuttled to the side to gain another perspective. "I give up," he eventually proclaimed. "Tell me, how do malformed funnels strapped to one's head cause children to quarrel?"

The gnomette went slightly cross-eyed. "What?"

"I said, 'How do malformed funnels strapped to one's head cause children to quarrel?'"

The female looked at Rudger. "What in the Elements is it talking about?"

Rudger shrugged. "Maybe it's a riddle."

"It is not a riddle," Vermis snapped. "It is a question, and a perfectly good one at that! You said this thing is 'scion-tiff-ic.' A 'scion' is a child, and a 'tiff' is an argument. But what I don't understand is why youngsters would brawl in the face of that horrific headpiece. Bawl, I could see. But brawl? Not so much."

The blonde gnomette looked at Rudger.

"Are you *sure* you don't want me to squash it?" she asked.

"Better not," he advised. "Vermis, here, apparently knows me, and he seems willing to help. I think. It's hard to be sure. He uses an awful lot of words but doesn't seem to say that much."

"I *beg* your—"

"Anyway, I'm Rudger Rump," the gnome went on, ignoring Vermis' outburst. "You still haven't told us who you are."

The gnomette sighed. "I was hoping I wouldn't have to. My name is Twelda Greeze. You'd know that if those amnesioak branches hadn't stolen your memory."

"So *that's* why he forgot who I am," Vermis interjected. "It all makes sense now. Being a charismatic clan, we von Higglesbreaths are generally remembered."

Twelda rolled her eyes. "You stumbled into my burrow yesterday afternoon," she informed Rudger, "and I escorted you to your grandparents' place. We set out from there this morning to find your father topside, but a human broke into Gnomister's Knoll and took him."

"Took him?" Rudger sputtered. "My father? Are you saying he's been gnome-napped?"

"Hmm. A human abducting gnomes," Vermis commented. "This is most interesting. Tell me, what was it wearing?"

"A long purple robe, not that it matters," Twelda said to the worm. She turned back to Rudger and added, "What *does* matter is that you went after the human and—"

"Details, Miss Greeze, if you please," Vermis interrupted. "Male or female? Young or old? These things are of the utmost importance."

"Arrgh!" She turned on the worm. "It had a gray-streaked beard, so that makes it an old man, okay? And if you interrupt me one more time, I'll feed you to the first wurblebird I see."

"Wurblebirds, Miss Greeze, are rare to be found underground," Vermis pointed out.

"But humans are topsiders, so that's where we're heading, you obnoxious little centipede."

"Ah-ah-ah," the vermitome countered in a singsong tone. "Not enough legs for that, I'm afraid. Sixteen, not a hundred. You'd do better to count before you call names."

Twelda growled and raised her foot. Rudger nullified the threat by pulling the gnomette off-balance.

"Stop it, you two," he ordered. "I'm trying to piece things together, and all you can do is bicker! Let's have some peace while I'm piecing, *capisce*?"

Vermis regarded Twelda. "Ah, me. Such a relief the amnesioaks didn't wipe away his facility with language. It really is a thing to behold."

Rudger frowned at the bookworm. "I don't know if you're being sincere or sarcastic, but either way, this chatter's giving me a noggin-ache. So let's just…" He abruptly noticed the vermitome's footwear. "I'm sorry. Do you normally wear shoes on only half your feet?"

"That's what I've been trying to communicate," Vermis said, waving eight legs simultaneously. "I lost eight shoes fleeing from the hackerpedes. Eight! I evaded capture back at a clump of amnesioak roots, but they're sure to remember who they were chasing presently."

"Then let's get out of here and back to my grandparents' burrow," Rudger suggested.

"We can't," Twelda said. "I left you here after the human attack to find a way out of these restricted passages and to fetch your mother."

"My mother? Oh, wait. I remember. She's supposed to be taking care of Grammers and Grampers. They had strokes."

"But that's just it," Twelda continued. "They *didn't* have strokes. Your grandparents have the Mute-ation, and every-gnome's afraid it will spread, so the Gnomister put a quarantine on them."

"Quarantine? What's that?" Rudger asked.

"It means they have to stay in their burrow because they're sick," the gnomette explained. "No one can go in or out."

Rudger's face fell. "Including Mummers?"

Twelda nodded. "She's quarantined, too, so I couldn't bring her here with me. All I could do was write her a note and slip it under the door."

"Does she know about Dadders being gnome-napped?"

"No. I thought it'd be cruel to burden her with that since she's burrow-bound. I told her you'd be staying at my place until the quarantine is lifted." She narrowed her eyes at the young gnome. "That reminds me. You still owe me a clean-up, and getting amnesia's not going to get you out of it.

"Anyway, I hurried back to my lab and picked up a few things to help us rescue your father." Twelda nodded toward the lumpy pack and the horned contraption on top of it. "And to answer your question, Vermis, I call that headpiece an 'auriculator.' It enhances the hearing of any minikin who wears it. Thought it'd help me avoid getting caught on the way back."

"You thought *wrong*," a voice boomed.

CHAPTER ELEVEN

Twelda Greeze twisted around to find a sour-faced gnome obstructing the doorway. He was large for a Humdrungle male, about twenty inches tall and not quite half that across the shoulders. Under his mudpud brown cap blazed a pair of hazel eyes alight with fury. His knob of a nose sat atop a chestnut mustache and beard which tapered to a point an inch above ostentacious pantaloons that precisely matched his cap in shade. His vest was an equally perfect match while the long-sleeved tunic beneath, in a tempered tan, was the lone dissenter to the otherwise magnificently monotone ensemble. Twelda was taking in the gnome's well-oiled dillyhide shoes when she abruptly remembered where she had seen him before.

"What in the Gnomister's name are you two 'lings doing in this restricted vault?" the Sergeant Sartorio demanded. Then his eyes fell on the tangled mess of cloth on the floor, and he suffered a paroxysm of shock. "*The Standards*," he moaned. "What have you done to the Standards?"

Vermis von Higglesbreath squared such shoulders as he had and marched to the fore. "Astute you are not, you puffy-panted pinhead," he declared. "You are faced, not with two trespassers, but three. Ha, ha!"

Twelda nudged the bellicose bookworm with her right foot. "Uh, Vermis? We're in a situation here. It might be best to keep that kind of information to yourself."

"Perhaps," the vermitome proclaimed shamelessly. "But how else would I offer sorely needed commentary on those tasteless trousers?"

"The Standards. My responsibility," the Sartorio lamented. "Defiled. Utterly and completely defiled!"

"Look at the bright side," Vermis told him. "Now you can chuck the lot and start fresh. I'm partial to periwinkle myself."

The Sartorio glared savagely at the flippant bookworm. "Blasphemer!" he bellowed. "Knave! Heretic!"

"Oh, come, now," Vermis tutted. "Make up your mind."

"You'll all be thrown in swale for this! And if there's anything left of you after, it'll be the Yoke for sure!"

"Please, sir," Twelda implored. "This was all an innocent mistake. My friend over there is Rudger Rump."

The Sartorio's baleful expression betrayed no trace of recognition.

"Surely, you know the name," Twelda prodded. "Rump? As in Rondo Rump, his father?"

The official's visage might have been chiseled from stone.

"You *must* know who I'm talking about," Twelda went on

desperately. "Auburn whiskers with highlights? Works on his knees?"

At last, the hardened face shifted. "You're saying this is the Supplico's lad?"

"Yes! Yes! Rondo was gnome-napped by the human in the purple robe, and Rudger ran afoul of the amnesioaks trying to rescue him. I brought him here to recover, not knowing how important all this cloth was. Silly me! And Rudger—he was in no condition to tell me not to cover him with it. He can't even remember me bringing him here. Oh, and the worm wasn't here at the time, so you see? It was all just a comedy of errors." Twelda giggled weakly.

"You wrapped the lad in the Cloths of Color," the Sartorio said.

"Well, yes. It's kind of cold in here, and poor Rudger lost his shoes."

"You wrapped his *feet* in our Standards?" the gnome asked, his voice rising. "He defiled them with his dirty, bare *feet*? By the High Gnome's giblets, it's the Yoke first, swale second, for you two! You shan't have any of the horrors of swale erased from your minds! And as for that impertinent hackerpede there? I'm going to defile him…with *my* feet!" The official advanced.

"Now, now, Mr. Sartorio," Vermis simpered. "Think this through. You don't really want me smeared all over those snappy shoes of yours, do you? Have you ever tried to get worm guts out of dillyhide? Impossible!"

Twelda hooked the Sartorio's arm, breaking his stride.

"It'd be wrong to kill Vermis," she tried reasoning with him. "He's as intelligent as we are."

"Ooo," Vermis said with a wince. "Insult! I'm an intellectual *giant* compared to all you simple—"

"Vermis, you're not helping!" Twelda barked as she resisted the Sartorio's efforts to shake her loose.

The cornered worm tilted an ear toward the all-but-forgotten loosened tile. "Before I meet my untimely end," he called out, "I feel compelled to set the record straight yet again. I am *not* a hackerpede."

"Oh, yeah?" challenged the Sartorio as he continued to bandy Twelda about. "Prove it."

Vermis grinned.

The unsecured tile shot across the chamber, shattering spectacularly as it struck the wall opposite. Like streaks of blackened oil, the hackerpedes emerged, one after the other, until seven of the six-inch-long horrors marred the pristine whiteness of the wall. Together, the chitin-armored chilopods raised the foreparts of their bodies and trained their glittering black eyes upon the Sartorio and his hanger-on. Barbed mandibles bearing hairy, writhing mouthparts worked furiously; the moist clicking noise they made set Twelda's skin a-crawl.

The gnomette spied Rudger along the infested wall, eyes half-closed and seemingly unresponsive. She broke her grip on the Sartorio's arm and rushed to her friend's defense. The pantalooned sergeant made for the door.

"I leave you now," he announced with a grin, "and I'm locking you in behind me. If the 'pedes don't finish you off, I'll be back to charge you for this heinous vandalism in the morning. It's a blessing Supplico Rondo won't be around when his criminal son is sentenced to lose the *rest* of his memories."

The threats were irrelevant to Rudger Rump. Time, for him, had gone lazy, drawing the Sartorio's words out into a muddled warble. The young gnome's attention had turned inward, onto a sea of billowing thoughts within his own head.

Dark trailers of mist dominated the space. Rudger's attempts at probing only agitated the swirls and whorls; there seemed to be no end to the storm clouds churning around him. Then two of the misty tendrils parted. They revealed a glowing speck in the otherwise dusky mindscape.

Rudger tested the spot. A tiny rent opened in the fabric of his mind, a peephole onto a radiant fount of power. Its light spilled into Rudger's mind, aligning the drifting billows to construct a Weird Wyrd:

Fabrikinesia!

The instant Rudger's tongue released the Wyrd, the limp snarl of Standards beside him stiffened and convulsed. The Sartorio gasped as four bolts of cloth—one tempered tan, one drear ochre, one mudpud brown, and one burnt umber—arced across the chamber to converge upon him. By the time Rudger emerged from his trance, the mummified official's muffled protests could barely be heard.

"Rudger?"

Twelda Greeze's cautious inquiry was laced with wonder…and something else.

Was it fear?

The hackerpedes forced him to break eye contact before he could be sure. One had reached Rudger and embedded itself in his hair. He extracted the beastie, unperturbed by its multitudinous slashing claw-tipped legs and snapping jaw. Only when the 'pede drew blood did Rudger stop scrutinizing it and toss it aside.

Five of the other 'pedes had closed rank around Twelda, who was kneeling as she pried a sixth hackerpede's mandibles off several of Vermis' legs. The bookworm lost the last of his tiny shoes in the struggle, and his blonde savior acquired two unwelcome piggy-backers, each nearly as long as her spine. Rising with Vermis safely coiled about one hand, she employed the other in a wild swatting motion designed to dislodge her hideous riders.

Rudger snapped into the moment and jumped up to de-pede the damsel in distress. Using both hands, he ripped two hundred barbed legs from her lab smock, leaving the garment in a ragged condition.

"Come on," he urged the exhausted gnomette as he led her to the door. Shouldering her bulky pack, he clambered over the swaddled Sartorio. Twelda followed suit, eliciting a second round of "oofs" and "ouches" from the angry mound.

Barreling into the hall, they turned as one and closed the door behind them. Twelda, still breathing hard, rummaged through her pockets to retrieve the appropriate instrument.

"Do you have to lock him inside?" Rudger asked.

"Only if you want to escape," she said as she maneuvered the tumblers. "If he gets out and alerts the Gnomister, we can kiss our memories goodbye."

"But what about the hackerpedes?" Rudger pressed.

"What about them?" Twelda asked with a scoff. "He was willing to leave *us* with them. Besides, the cloth he's wrapped in should protect him if they attack."

"If?"

"Didn't you notice? The hackerpedes were mostly after poor Vermis here."

She looked down at her hand and stroked the dazed bookworm's side. His spots dilated as he moaned softly.

The gnomette looked back up at Rudger. "I think those brutes are more likely to pursue the three of us than to bother with Mr. Fancy-Pants."

"Then let's give them a good chase," Rudger suggested. He hesitated. "Uh, where should we go? We can't go back to my grandparents' burrow. You said it's quarantined."

Twelda gestured toward the pack Rudger had salvaged. "And I already got everything we'll need from my lab."

"Then we go topside," groaned the vermitome. "That purple robe…you said…" His voice trailed off. With a shuddering breath, the little worm went still in Twelda's hand.

"Vermis?"

The gnomette glanced anxiously at Rudger and then back down to the vermitome.

"Vermis? Vermis!" she cried, gently prodding the bookworm's limp body.

"Ah," the bookworm wheezed with a pained grin. "You do care."

"Don't play around like that!" she scolded, though she was visibly relieved. "Ugh. Just when I was beginning to tolerate you. What were you going to say about the purple robe the human was wearing?"

"It's a wizard robe," Vermis answered with a sigh. "In service to the human King. That's where we'll find Rudger's father."

CHAPTER TWELVE

Rudger Rump awoke the next morning in an unfamiliar glade capped by a steel gray sky. He took a certain comfort in being able to remember the two-league-long trek through the woods which had brought him there the night before. He could also recall scurrying through the tunnels of Old Drungle Town with a gnomette named Twelda Greeze and a vermitome called Vermis. But try as he might, he still lacked any memory of either of his companions prior to the Standards Chamber. The appetizing scent of fried wurble eggs pointed out another memory he lacked—that of a recent meal.

"Good morrow, Rudger," Twelda said cheerfully as she poked a stick into the fire beneath a small pan. "How do you like your eggs?"

"Burbled, please," he replied as he got up. He quirked his left eyebrow as he took in Twelda's unconventional mode of dress. "Um, if you don't mind my asking, is there a reason your smock is on backwards?"

"Oh, this?" she asked, plucking at the garment. The gnomette grinned as she beat the egg whites and lavender yolks into an airy froth. "I'm observing the Coatlute, to thank Mother Terreste for providing us breakfast."

Rudger regarded her blankly.

"Never heard of that one either?" she continued lightly. "Oh, there are *dozens* of salutes we townsgnomes observe, Rudger. You did the Shoelute yesterday, of course, but then there's the Crosslute where we walk crosslegged all day to ward off bad luck, and the Caplute where we turn our hats inside-out to honor the one we love. And we mustn't forget the Pantlute. We wear our britches on our heads for that one. Want to guess why?"

Rudger shook his head in bewilderment.

"To tip off naïve country gnomes that they've been had."

A smirk on the gnomette's face stretched into a mischievous smile.

Rudger groaned. "You're yanking my beard, aren't you?"

Twelda laughed. "You don't have a beard to yank," she observed. "But you're right. I'm teasing you. My smock's on backwards to serve as an apron."

"So are all those salutes made-up, or did I really do a Shoelute yesterday? And is that why you gave me these last night?" He pointed to his feet.

Twelda's mirth dissipated. "Oh. I forgot you forgot. Yes, you switched your shoes around for the Shoelute, but you must have lost them when you tackled that human. Those are an extra pair I brought from my lab. Still don't remember any of this?"

Rudger's shoulders fell. "Nope. And I can't remember meeting you before the chamber last night. But for some reason it surprises me you got a fire going. You don't seem like the outdoorsy type."

"Ah," Twelda replied, holding up a forefinger. She turned to rummage through her unshapely pack and pulled out what appeared to be a pair of tongs with sparkly fangs.

"Another invention of mine," she announced. She clacked the device, and a shower of blue sparks burst from it.

Rudger yelped and jumped back.

"Fire-flinger," she told him. "Guaranteed to ignite kindling on the first strike or your money back." She cupped her mouth with her hand and whispered, "The secret is the quickquartz tines. Far more incendiary than plain old flint."

Rudger drew a shaky breath. "But is it safe?" he asked.

"Safe?" the gnomette repeated with a frown. She set off two more sparkbursts, inspiring Rudger to backpedal even farther.

"It's effective," the science-gnomette concluded as her eyebrows smoldered alarmingly. "What more could you want?"

"Wow," Rudger said, looking for a way to change the subject. "Uh, maybe you should put the fire-thinger away and check on our eggs now. I think they're burning."

"Can't be," the gnomette contradicted, but to Rudger's relief, she stowed the flinger back in her pack. "Nope, they're fine. All they need is my special ingredient."

She reached behind her and grabbed a moist toadstool. Crumbling it in her hands, she added it to the eggs.

Rudger swallowed apprehensively. "Uh, you didn't just pick that 'shroom, did you?"

"Fresh this morning," Twelda confirmed. "Why?"

"Well, we can't eat it."

"Why not?"

"Because it came from the wild. It could be poisonous, or worse."

Twelda gave her nervous companion a withering look. "Rudger, you're acting like this is my first time in the field—which is what we scientists call 'roughing it,' by the way."

Rudger acknowledged the statement with a weak grin.

Twelda barreled on. "And *as* a scientist, I know exactly what I'm doing. Honestly, I thought I'd earned your trust last night."

"In rescue operations, yes. But in identifying potentially lethal fungi? Not so much."

Twelda pursed her lips disapprovingly. "Well, I *have* identified this particular species. It's a mishamash mushroom. Perfectly safe to ingest."

"No negative properties?" Rudger asked, peering into the pan suspiciously.

"Puh. Nothing dangerous. Just a harmless little side effect. It's rather amusing, actually."

"What side effect?"

"Bioluminescence."

"Bio-what?"

"Luminescence. That's one for your Logofile, kiddo. Oh, don't bother looking for all those loose pages you had. They were ruined in the river. I gave you a replacement. It's in your inside pocket. You may thank me again."

Rudger didn't recognize the leather-bound notebook he found in his vest, but he did recognize his handwriting inside. "Uh, thanks. So what's bioluminescence?"

"It means mishamash mushrooms glow in the dark."

As he jotted down the definition, he asked, "And why is that so amusing?"

Twelda put a finger to her cheek and rolled her eyes impishly. "Well, let's put it this way. As long as somegnome's been eating these babies, you don't need a lantern to find the latrines at night."

"Blech! That's nasty!" Rudger exclaimed.

"No," said Twelda. "It's biology."

"I propose you two make that the final word concerning the bowel habits of gnomes."

"Vermis!" Twelda cried in delight. "You're awake!"

"A state of consciousness I am rapidly coming to regret," the bookworm replied. "Verily, upon rejoining the land of the living, I had hoped to be greeted in a slightly more erudite—"

"How are your legs?" interjected Rudger.

The vermitome was put off by the interruption, but he shrugged and turned to one side. His three injured legs were tucked up against his spotted body.

"They're tolerable," he reported. "Fortunately, I had the good sense to grow five more on that side. I must confess that I am far more distressed by the loss of my footwear. It's *so* difficult to find my size."

"Would a hearty breakfast make you feel better?" asked

Twelda. She tipped a tiny morsel of omelet into a bricklenut cap.

"It 'shoe' would," quipped the vermitome.

The two chuckled, and Twelda turned expectantly to Rudger. "Well?" she asked, passing the skillet under his nose.

"Uh, none for me," he said. "The idea of my guts glowing kind of turns my stomach."

"Well, I've used all the eggs I gathered," she said as she served herself. "But I'll burble you some plain ones if you go find more. Or will that overtax your delicate constitution?"

Again, the gnomette and vermitome giggled as they tucked into their breakfast. Unsettled as it was, Rudger knew his belly would start growling soon, and there was no telling when food would be available next. Rudger wanted to believe it was this thread of logic that spurred his decision, but deep down, he resented being called delicate.

"Where'd you find those?" he asked, more gruffly than intended.

Twelda pointed to the east. "Over that rise is Giant's Foot Pond. The wurblebirds like to build their nests in the crags there."

"Great," Rudger said as he turned to march up the wooded hill. "Keep the fire going. I'll be right back."

"Watch out for loose rocks," Twelda called after him. "If you lose your footing, you'll drop right into the swamp water."

"They don't call this side Bunion Bog for nothing," added Vermis.

The pond turned out to be large—nearly the size of a lake. Otherwise, it was aptly named; it truly looked as if an enormous foot had punched its way through a vast shelf of limestone, leaving behind a crater that had since filled with water.

To Rudger's right, the shoreline meandered in and out like so many toes. He was on a crest overlooking the biggest one, on a protrusion in the foot's contour that resembled a lumpy bunion. Wurblebirds glided through the air, slashes of white against the overcast sky, their calls melodic and soothing. It might have been idyllic if not for the stench. Down the irregular slope below him, Rudger could see water choked with algae and decaying plant matter. His traveling companions were right; it would be most unpleasant to fall in.

The wurblebird nests were nestled among rocky outcroppings all along the toes of the foot-shaped pond. A natural ledge about two feet wide rested several yards below him. It ran all the way to the big toe's tip, ending below a promising nest there. The trouble was getting down to the ledge safely. One faulty foot placement could send him sliding into the fen.

Rudger knew he ought to return to camp and ask Twelda how she negotiated the treacherous slope. Perhaps she had a rope in that pack of hers which would make the descent safer. But the gnomette's barb still stung, and Rudger liked to think he had some self-respect.

Planning his route carefully, Rudger stuck out a foot and tested the first rock experimentally. When it proved stable, he lowered his other foot to the next. Shuttling back and forth along the irregular rock face, he soon found himself nearly to the ledge.

The sound of claws raking across rock forced him to turn. His heart leapt into his throat as a fanged face closed in on him. He remembered too late that wurble eggs were a favorite of this furry, yellow-eyed beast.

Far more sure-footed than he, the wereweasel scrabbled over the rock face, eager to add gnome flesh to its breakfast menu. In an instant, it was upon Rudger, and the terrified gnome had to make a split-second decision. Hoping his friends could hear him, he let loose a scream as he flung himself at the ledge below. His aim was true, but the brittle rock crumbled beneath his feet, threatening to launch him toward his secondary target, the bog water. Windmilling hard, he lurched backward and landed on his posterior with both feet hanging out over the putrid water ten feet below. With his heart hammering in his chest, he cried out for help once more.

The vocal outbursts weren't only meant to alert his companions. The night before—or was it two or three?—Aunt Ragna had recounted a tale of her youth in which she had fought off a pack of wereweasels like the one he now faced. She'd stressed how sensitive their hearing was and how she'd used that against them. Of course, *she* had been armed with a pair of daggers to generate the noise. Rudger fervently hoped his vocal cords would be a passable substitute.

His shouts seemed to have the desired effect. The beast had not joined Rudger on the ledge. Every time he hollered, it flattened its triangular ears against its skull and hissed in agitation, but the wereweasel was growing bolder as Rudger grew hoarser. It was only a matter of time before the weasel's hunger would drive it to attack again.

Rudger hurried along the ledge, desperate for a route of escape that did not involve a plunge into the fetid fen below. The wereweasel kept pace, lunging down the slope to snap at his head and face. "Helios, shine and save me!" he cried. Aunt Ragna had also impressed upon her audience that direct sunlight drained the aggression from a wereweasel, rendering it a far more docile creature.

Helios remained unmoved behind his wall of clouds. Rudger had retreated to the tip of the lake's big toe, near the very nest he had spied from above. As the beast spit and slathered, the young gnome reached into the nest. His hand closed around a pair of wurble eggs. "Take that, you fiend!" he yelled as he pelted the weasel's pelt with eggy grenades.

Unfortunately, this did nothing but add mucoid drippings to the animal's salivary secretions.

Rudger ripped the nest itself from its rocky base, sending a shower of pebbles into the swamp water below. It was a mistake to watch them fall; when he turned back to his foe, he was horrified to find it on his level, blocking any lateral moves he might make along the ledge. In a last-ditch effort to fend off the monster, Rudger bashed it silly with the nest. Bits of twig and dirt stuck to the wurble egg remnants, but it was clear the blows would not stop the creature's assault. Rudger prepared to jump.

The grayness of the day receded as an unidentified source of illumination intensified. Rudger dropped the crumbling remains of the nest and watched in amazement as the wereweasel's eyes constricted, its fierce yellow irises swamping its pupils. The wereweasel looked up over Rudger's head, its snarls and hisses silenced. Rising on its hind legs, it towered over the gnome, but it failed to press its advantage. It stepped back. Stepped back again. Then it held its position, wobbling precariously on its two back legs.

Suddenly, Rudger knew what he must do. Charging forward, he shoved the hypnotized beast off the ledge. The strange light faded the moment the monster splashed into the bog below. As it thrashed about in the viscous green water, screeching its fury, Rudger found he could breathe again. Who had saved him? He remembered the fire-flinger.

"Oh, Twelda," he said gratefully as he turned to pinpoint the source of his luminous salvation. His breath caught in his throat anew.

There, at the crater's lip, stood the towering figure of a human boy.

CHAPTER THIRTEEN

Rudger Rump had never seen a human being up close before. At least, not that he could remember. Twelda claimed he'd gotten close enough to tackle one the day before, but the amnesioaks had erased his memory of the encounter.

Regardless, Rudger could tell the human looming above him was young. The boy's skin was smooth and his chin beardless, just like Rudger's. And although he was outlandishly tall by gnomish standards, Rudger knew adult humans tended to be even larger—often four times Rudger's height or more.

The lad's wavy hair was darker than mudpud brown, and even though he was making strong eye contact, Rudger couldn't quite discern the color of his eyes.

They stood, regarding one another for a long moment. Neither seemed quite sure how to initiate a conversation. For Rudger's part, he'd just been saved by a Fyreball, bright as the sun, apparently conjured betwixt the hands of a human boy who was probably even younger than he. A combination of awe and wariness stayed his tongue as effectively as the Mute-ation ever could.

At last, the humanling spoke.

"What?" Rudger called out in response. Between the cater-wauling of the vanquished wereweasel below and the breeze coming off the pond, Rudger hadn't heard a thing.

The human tried again. Rudger's sharp ears strained to make out the words. "You're -ine, now."

Rudger, being a well-mannered Humdrungle, had been expecting a polite introduction of some kind. The boy's state-ment seemed an odd way to greet a stranger, but Rudger chose not to judge. This *was* a human he was dealing with, after all.

"Yes, I'm fine now," he yelled up to the boy. "Are you fine, too?"

Rudger could just make out the crinkling of the boy's brow.

"Uh, yes?" he shouted back down in an uncertain, rising tone. "Thanks for asking?"

"My pleasure," Rudger replied, feeling the rawness of his overworked throat. He looked about once more for a path off the rocky wall that might allow him to avoid further contact with the human. There was none. When he looked back up, the boy was still staring right at him. "Let me climb up," Rudger proposed.

The young gnome carefully picked his way along the bluff overlooking Giant's Foot Pond. His strategy was to choose a path that took him as far from where the human was standing as possible. Unfortunately, the boy paced him, for as Rudger neared the top, an oversized, five-fingered hand appeared in front of his nose.

Rudger's innards tightened with apprehension as he accepted the boy's proffered hand. The human pulled him up onto the crest as if he weighed nothing. When Rudger looked up, a wave of dizziness washed over him. The boy was even taller than he'd thought.

"Are…are you going to come with me now?" the giant asked, his hazel eyes staring down at Rudger from their obscenely lofty height.

Rudger's mind had jammed, making it difficult to process the boy's words.

"Come? With you?" he eventually managed to sputter. "Why would I do that?"

The boy bit his lower lip. "Because I trapped you. That means you're mine now, right?"

"Hold on," Rudger said with a frown. "Is that what you said before? 'You're mine now?' I thought you were inquiring as to my well-being."

The human hesitated, as if the idea had never occurred to him. "Gosh. Of course, I'm glad you're okay. But are you going to obey me or not? I did trap you, fair and square."

"You didn't trap me," Rudger argued. "The wereweasel cornered me out on the—"

"*I* sent that weasel," the boy interrupted earnestly. Then he seemed to consider the implication of his words and added, "But I wasn't going to let it eat you."

"Well, thanks for that," Rudger replied sarcastically. "But even if you did send the weasel, I don't see why that means I have to obey you. And why do you keep staring at me like that? If you don't blink soon, your eyes are going to shrivel up."

The boy seemed vexed. "You…you're not supposed to talk to your master like that. I know—I've read all the lorebooks on the little people. You're under my power now, and as long as I keep my eyes on you, you can't run away."

"Master?" Rudger said indignantly. "Why would you ever think—" Then he paused. "Oh, wait. I think I get it."

"Get what?"

Rudger raised his eyebrows. "You don't happen to think I'm a leprechaun, do you?"

The boy cocked his head. "Well, sure. Little man, red hair. Of course, I expected you to have a beard and green clothes instead of brown, but—"

"Sorry, kid. I'm not a leprechaun. I'm a gnome. You've got your minikins crossed."

The boy's eyes widened. "A gnome? Gnomes don't have red hair."

"This one does."

The towering human thought a moment. Then his eyes narrowed, and he stepped closer. "You're not trying to trick me, are you?" he accused.

Rudger's neck prickled with fear. "Uh,…no?" he squeaked. He cleared his throat. "I mean, *no*. I am a Humdrungle gnome. Not an especially tall one, I'll admit, but I'm way too big to be a leprechaun. And I have no musical talent whatsoever."

The boy's menancing demeanor drained away. He dropped dejectedly into a cross-legged funk. "Well, flufferduffs," he grumbled.

Although Rudger still had to incline his head to meet the boy's eye, the reduction in the latter's height was a relief. He soon found himself feeling sorry for the young human.

"Disappointed, huh?"

The boy shrugged. When at last he looked at Rudger, his eyes had lost their intensity. "I thought I was finally going to please my guardian. Now it's ruined."

"Your guardian? You mean like your mother or father?"

"Nah. Don't have either of those. Come to think of it, I hardly have a guardian, either. I've never even met him. But he leaves me instructions, chores. One of them is to capture a leprechaun."

"Why?"

"Dunno. He never explains anything to me."

The boy lapsed into a miserable silence. Rudger tried to imagine being under the thumb of an adult he'd never lain eyes upon. His pity for the humanling increased.

"Cheer up," he said bracingly. "You *did* catch a red-headed gnome, and that's no small thing. We're a rascally lot, you know. I reckon you'll have no trouble snaring that leprechaun when you find him."

The human's eyes were still sad, but the corners of his mouth turned up a bit.

Rudger grinned and stuck out his elbow. "My name is Rudger Rump. How do you do?"

Now the boy giggled. "No, it's not."

Rudger put his hands on his hips. "Yes, it is. I come from a long line of Rumps."

"That's just silly."

"What is? My name? Hmmph! I can think of a very

famous minikin who shares it. Partially, at least. Why, I'll even bet you've heard of him."

"Who?"

"Rumpelstiltskin, of course."

The boy's laughter was gratifying to Rudger. Clearly, this human was no monster. In many ways, he reminded Rudger of his little brother, Roon.

"Now, unless you're like Rumpelstiltskin and can't risk letting people know your name, I would be very pleased to learn it." Rudger waggled his still-extended elbow, invitingly.

The boy leaned forward and bowbumped the gnome. "I'm Kal," he said with a smile. "And I'm very glad to meet you."

"Likewise. Now, if your invitation still stands, I'd like to accompany you wherever you'd like to go."

"Really?"

"Really. But as a guest, not a prisoner. Is it a deal?"

Kal's smile grew even broader. "Deal," he said as he extended a hand.

Rudger looked at it dubiously.

"Humans don't bump elbows to greet each other or seal a deal," the boy explained. "We clasp hands and shake on it."

Rudger tentatively placed his four-fingered hand into Kal's. After pumping it up and down half a dozen times, the boy released it.

"Humans are peculiar," remarked Rudger, still looking at his hand.

"That goes double for red-headed gnomes," Kal replied.

When Rudger looked up, he saw a pair of long legs walking north.

"Come on," the boy said over his shoulder. "My cottage is this way. At the pond's heel."

"Not so quick, gillywick," Rudger called after him. He pointed west and added, "I have a couple of friends waiting at the base of this hill. Stay here, and I'll go prepare them for…" Rudger stopped short, an impish notion tickling his brain.

"On second thought," he announced, "why don't you just tag along with me? Might be more fun."

The boy shrugged and took five of his gigantic strides to close the gap between them. Again, Rudger felt the awkwardness of staring at this enormous being's kneecaps. He squared his shoulders and started down the incline.

"Slow down, Kal," Rudger instructed after a short distance. "I can't keep up. How about letting me get in front? If they see you first, they might run away."

"Who are these friends of yours?" Kal asked as Rudger scurried past him.

"A gnomette named Twelda and a bookworm who calls himself Vermis von Higglesbreath, the Fourth."

When this elicited no reaction, Rudger turned around and craned his neck to look up at the boy. The human's expression had gone sullen again.

"What's the matter?" the gnome asked as he walked backwards down the hill.

"Hmm?" grunted the boy. "Oh, nothing. I was just hoping you'd say one of them was a leprechaun."

"Why? Because you'd try to trap it?"

"Well, maybe. As long as it wasn't a *really* good friend of yours. Oh. Watch out for that root behin—"

Still facing backwards, Rudger felt the tree root twist

under the ball of his foot. For an awful, slow-motion second, he was teetering on the brink as Kal's long arms extended toward him.

And then he was tumbling down the hill. The young gnome tucked his chin as his legs rocketed over his head again and again. By the time Rudger reached the bottom, he no longer knew up from down.

"An impressive entrance," Vermis remarked when Rudger had come to a stop, limbs splayed in every direction. "But reckless, too. Any wurble eggs he collected were surely pulverized during those acrobatic shenanigans."

"Vermis, he didn't do that on purpose," Twelda Greeze chided as she rushed to Rudger's aid. "He fell. He might be —*jumping jawjackles!*"

Twelda froze as a colossal form emerged from the trees. It wasn't as big as the human from Gnomister's Knoll, nor was it as finely dressed. Instead of purple wizard's robes, this smaller monster wore a ragged, cream-colored tunic and old suede breeches that were several inches too long. Gathers of the excess pant material formed a bulky ring around battered shoes that allowed pink toe-tips to show through their fronts. The tatterdemalion giant bore down on Rudger, but instead of attacking, it crouched at the motionless gnome's side.

The giant turned its huge face toward her, concern etching furrows into its mighty forehead.

"Twelda?" it asked expectantly. "You're Twelda, right? Rudger's friend?"

The science-gnomette, who had been preparing to rescue Rudger from a second marauding human, struggled to switch gears. This human didn't seem anything like the first. The panicked look in its eyes suggested a significant difference in its temperament.

"He's not…dead, is he?" the human went on. "He tripped over that root so fast! I couldn't catch him in time."

Twelda approached and checked for a pulse. "He's alive," she reported.

"Thank Helios," the human breathed. Now that her surprise had worn off, Twelda could see it was a young male, a child. She stood up and cleared her throat to get its attention.

"How did you know Rudger's name?" she asked. "And mine, for that matter? As far as I'm aware, Rudger doesn't know any humans."

The boy sat back on his haunches and looked down at the suspicious gnomette. "Rudger and I don't know each other. Not very well, at least. We just met up at the pond. I…I think we were becoming friends. At least, I hope we were. I saved him from an attacking wereweasel."

"Which you sicced on me," Rudger added weakly.

"Oh! You're all right," cried the boy. "Thank the Elements!"

"'Sicced on me?'" repeated Twelda. She looked at the boy. "What does he mean?"

"Well, I might've, kind of…*encouraged* the wereweasel to attack," he admitted. At Twelda's outraged expression, he put up his huge hands. "But I never intended to let it eat him. Honest. I just wanted to catch Rudger because I thought he was a leprechaun. Red hair, you know. But he's not a leprechaun, so I let him go."

Rudger sat up with a groan.

"Kal, you never *had* me to begin with, so how you could you let me go?"

Twelda cupped Rudger's chin and turned his head toward her. "Rudger? Do you remember me?"

To her concerned expression, he replied, "The gnomette with the glow-in-the-dark intestines? Oh, yes, Twelda. I remember you."

"Thank the sister stars! What with your amnesioak amnesia, another blow to the head might—"

"Amnesioak?" interrupted the human named Kal. "Did Rudger get his memories erased by that awful stuff?"

"Yes," Twelda answered. "He forgot meeting me and Vermis both. Can't even remember the human attack back on Gnomister's Knoll. That's where the amnesioaks were."

"Human attack? How long ago was this?"

"Yesterday."

"Hmm. How much time did he forget?"

"A day and a half, give or take."

Kal snapped his fingers. "I might be able to undo that amnesia. That'd make up for siccing the wereweasel on him, right?" The boy turned his attention to Rudger. "Think you can walk?"

"I-I'm not sure."

"Then I'll carry you." He moved to pick the gnome up.

"Hold on, now!" protested Twelda. "We don't know you, human. We're not going anywhere with you."

"But all of my supplies are in my cabin," Kal explained.

"Everything you need to grind our bones, you mean. I know how you humans operate."

"Twelda," Rudger said weakly, "I think it's *giants* that grind their victim's bones."

"What do you think *he* is?" Twelda countered, sweeping a hand from Kal's head to his toes.

"Everything's going to be fine. Kal is a friend," Rudger assured her as he allowed himself to be lifted.

"How can you possibly know that? The evidence is inconclusive at best! Vermis? Vermis! Where are you? I need you to talk some sense into Rudger."

"I am right here, Miss Greeze," the vermitone intoned.

As Twelda cast wildly about to locate the bookworm, a soft rain began to patter against the leaves around them. Frustrated, Twelda eventually looked up at Rudger, now cradled in the human boy's arms. Vermis peered down at her from his perch on the gnome's ear.

"I vote we take this fine young man up on his offer of aid and shelter," Vermis announced. Then he turned his attention to Kal. "And crumbcakes? I would *so* enjoy a crumb or two at this juncture."

The boy looked at the worm uncertainly.

"I have some unleavened biscuits on hand. Oh, and I could drizzle some honey over them to sweeten them up."

"Sold!" cried the vermitome.

"Vermis!" scolded Twelda. "Are you really going to let yourself be bribed with a biscuit?"

"So it would seem," he answered unabashedly. "Besides, this young fellow has a most intriguing Glynt." The bookworm motored up Kal's arm. "Tell me, have you studied with anyone?"

"Vermis!"

The boy turned on his heel, carrying gnome and vermitome into the forest with him. Vermis' tiny head appeared over the human's shoulder.

"Face it, Twelda. The worm has turned. And the human, too." He eyed their fire and its surrounds. "Ugh. Do be a dear and decamp for us, will you? I'd offer to help, but I haven't the foggiest notion how to rein in a human. Yee-haw!"

CHAPTER FOURTEEN

The boy-wizard's cottage was a quaint little affair—canfa-log walls, thatched roof, stout bricklewood door. It might have passed for the dwelling place of a common human farmer, except for one tiny detail.

It was upside-down, balanced on a crooked fieldstone chimney that belched swirling curls of smoke along the ground beneath it.

"Above-ground habitation has always struck me as peculiar," Vermis announced as the topsy-turvy structure came into view. "But *this* is ridiculous."

Kal giggled self-consciously. "My master's pretty peeved about the upside-down thing. He could fix it in a flash, but he won't. He's stubborn that way. Wrote me a letter telling me it's my responsibility to set it right. Trouble is, I have no idea what spell I'm going to use to do this. So how am I supposed to figure out how to flip it back?"

Rudger Rump stirred in the human's thin arms. "What spell you're *going* to use?" he asked.

Kal hesitated. "Uh, right. I have no idea what spell I'm going to use to fix this."

Rudger shook his throbbing head. "That's not what you said. You said you don't know what spell you're going to use to turn it upside-down."

"No, I didn't."

"Yes, you did."

"No, I didn't."

"Vermis, you heard what he said, right?"

"Beg pardon?"

"I said…ugh! You haven't even been listening, have you?"

"Nope. I've been too busy appreciating those inverted rain-barrels up there. See how the water stays in them? First-class sorcery, that. I told you this boy has an exceptional Glynt."

"Grab hold, guys," Kal advised as he broke into a sprint up the cobbled path. "I've found it works best if I do a handspring through the door."

"A *what?*" cried Rudger as he gripped the boy's neck. Suddenly, Rudger found himself tumbling through the air for the second time that afternoon. The jolting flip set Kal's large feet squarely up on the cabin's wooden plank floor. When Rudger's brain stopped sloshing about in his skull, he cracked his eyes open. Bare wooden rafters stretched out overhead.

"Very neat," commented Vermis as he gazed out a window on the west wall.

Rudger followed the bookworm's example but then shut his eyes tight. Trees seemed to extend downward from an unlikely earthen ceiling while raindrops rose to meet them from a pearl gray sky below.

"It takes some getting used to," Kal said as he set Rudger down on a straw-filled mattress. "I can close the shutters, if that makes it easier."

Vermis tutted. "I, for one, welcome a change in perspective."

But Rudger moaned. "Close them, please. We Humdrungles get nervous enough just being above ground, but this? My whole world's been turned upside down…literally!"

Kal moved to shutter the windows but hesitated at the door. "I should probably leave this open for your friend, Twelda, when she gets here," he said apologetically. "How about I make a compress for your head? That should make you feel better."

Rudger waited, trying not to think about the earth hanging somewhere above him. The compress proved soothing to his overwrought equilibrium, its aroma of collybloom and munxmoss quickly lulling him toward sleep. A ticklish sensation about his left ear threatened to rouse him. His hand moved automatically to scratch at it.

"Master Rump!" came an indignant cry. "Whether you recall it or not, this is my agreed-upon perch. Henceforth, I shall thank you not to forget it."

"Huh? Oh, sorry," Rudger replied groggily. "Your feet tickle awfully."

"I assure you I do not relish high-stepping through all of this ear hair without my accustomed footwear."

"Ear hair?" Rudger sat up, fingers investigating his other ear. "My ears aren't hairy."

"I have news for you. It's a wilderness back here. Tome and quill, it wouldn't hurt you to pluck once in a while."

Rudger considered this. "Actually, that *would* hurt."

"Be that as it may, I have returned to your auricle to apprise you…"

"Of the future?"

"…of a grave and timely threat which—wait. What?" Vermis said, derailing his own train of thought. "What did you say?"

"I asked if you're going to predict the future."

"Why in Lunira's name would you ask that?"

"Because you said you returned as my oracle. They predict the future, don't they?"

"Great gobs of homophony!" the bookworm cried as he launched himself into the air and floated down into Rudger's lap. "Here I am, striving to impart critical information, and the lad wants for a grammar lesson!"

He huffed pretentiously and twiddled his bowtie. "What I said, Rudger, is that I returned *to* your auricle. A-U-R-I-C-L-E," he spelled, forming each letter for emphasis. "Not 'as' your O-R-A-C-L-E. Although if I *were* a soothsayer, I'd say your immediate future is imperiled, forsooth."

Rudger frowned as he sifted through the vermitome's verbosity. "Ugh," he groaned, cradling his aching head. "Why can't you ever say anything simply?"

"Prolixity is my passion," the bookworm espoused. "But in the interest of expediency, I shall endeavor to truncate my—"

Rudger cleared his throat pointedly.

The vermitome's mouth drooped.

"Succinctness. Yes," the bookworm said as if to coach himself. He took a deep breath, paused melodramatically, and then spat out, "An 'auricle' is an ear. Kal's Glynt concerns me, and have you noticed *that*?"

Rudger looked where Vermis was pointing. Hanging on a peg between the door and a worn wooden cupboard was a rather magnificent purple robe fashioned of shimmering silk. Handsome indigo cording lined the seams that affixed billowing sleeves to its velvet-trimmed body. Rudger returned his gaze to the vermitome and shrugged.

"You won't remember this," Vermis explained, "but Twelda filled me in while you were frolicking at the pond. Apparently, the human that kidnapped your father at Gnomister's Knoll was wearing a wizard's robe just like that one. Clearly, it's too large to be Kal's, but his master…" Vermis let his voice trail off ominously.

"Where *is* that gnomette, anyway?" the bookworm resumed abruptly. "She should be here by now. And, furthermore, where has that Kal boy slipped off to? His exodus was most fortuitous in light of our need to confer, but—"

A shriek penetrated the cabin through its glassless windows.

Despite Vermis' advice to the contrary, Rudger swung his legs over the side of the human-huge bed and tottered to a window beside the now-closed front door. He pushed the shutter open, and a wave of nausea turned his stomach as he was faced again with the inverted world outside.

At the edge of the clearing stood a figure, glued by the feet to the overhanging earth. It was Twelda Greeze, flailing her arms at the open sky below her. Some airborne creature was harrying her; a deft maneuver on its part managed to knock Twelda's pointed cap off her head. Rudger's brain told him the hat should fall downward into the sky, but instead it leapt upward to nestle against the looming land mass above. Rudger fought to quell his queasiness as the irritated gnomette barked at her assailant.

"Kal *wants* me here, you overgrown dragonfly!" she shouted. "I'm with Rudger and Vermis! Now stop coming at me, or I'll let you have it with this!"

Rudger could barely discern the tiny glass vial she was brandishing before her.

"Extract of bugnought root," she warned. "Best insecticide known to science!"

"I, madam, am no insect," came a faint reply. "Nor am I shirker of my duty to protect. Begone, foul gnome!"

"Hieronymus?"

Kal came rushing into view, calling the peculiar name. He, too, was upside-down, his feet pounding up on the grassy ceiling.

"Hieronymus, stop that! Twelda is our friend. I cast the passmark on her. Didn't I do it right?"

"You did it correctly, Kal. I just don't happen to agree with it."

"Don't be mean," the boy said. "I met Twelda and the others up on the ridge across the pond. I thought the red-headed one was a leprechaun. Sicced a wereweasel on him. That *was* mean, so I'm trying to make it up to them, see?"

"Oh, I see, all right. You're bringing strangers into the cabin when you know it's against the rules."

"Look," interjected Twelda, "if we're a problem, we can just leave."

"No!" protested the boy. "I want you to stay. Master's practically never here, and Hieronymus is going to be nice. Aren't you, Hieronymus?"

The creature zipped around Twelda's head and then hung in the air close enough to count her eyelashes.

"While I am not bound by the boy's wishes, I am prepared to tolerate your presence for the time being."

"Great!" said Kal as he ushered the others toward the cabin. "Now we're all friends. How about we go inside? I can make suzzleleaf tea." He looked at Twelda. "Want me to help you over the threshold? Takes a bit of gymnastics. I could carry you."

Twelda eyed him with disdain. "I'll manage. Thanks."

"Suit yourself," he called over his shoulder as he charged up the path.

Rudger found he appreciated Kal's tumbling maneuver far more as a spectator than a passenger.

"Oh, you're up," the boy observed as he dropped gracefully through the door. "That's perfect! You can join us for tea."

Rudger ducked as the creature called Hieronymus performed a barrel-roll through the window he'd been looking through.

"Apologies," it said politely, as it whizzed overhead. Rudger thought the orange blur was going to land on the mantel across the room, but it came back to hover in front of him instead.

"Rudger?" it asked dubiously, cocking its tiny reptilian head one way and then the other. "It *is* you, isn't it?"

The young gnome was taken aback. "Um…yes," he stammered. "Have we met?"

"Most assuredly. Down by the river, outside Old Drungle Town. Don't you remember?"

"Rudger's memory has been compromised by an unfortunate brush with amnesioaks," Vermis reported from the bed. "But I offer you unreserved salutations, Wingnut—so long as you don't attempt to ingest me again."

A series of thumps accompanied the graceless entrance of Twelda Greeze. She'd failed to perform the required flip and ended up landing on the plank floor headfirst.

Rudger stumbled as he hurried to her side. "Are you okay?" he asked anxiously. Then he noticed the metal bowl she had strapped to her head.

She grinned and pointed to it. "Noggin-guard," she explained. "Another invention of mine. *And* it doubles as a mixing bowl."

Teatime was a blessed stopover in the most frenetic couple of days Rudger had ever known, even if he couldn't remember it all. As it turned out, Wingnut—or Hieronymus, as Kal called it—was a sort of babysitter for the boy while his master was away. Kal clearly did not relish the arrangement. He seemed to think he was of sufficient age to look after himself.

"And just how old are you, if I may inquire?" asked Vermis from his place on the tabletop.

There was an awkward pause as the boy and the winged newt regarded each other.

"Nine?" ventured Kal.

"Ten," Wingnut answered over him.

Vermis furrowed his hairless brow. "There seems to be some disagreement," he observed.

"Well, it's a little hard to be sure," Wingnut explained as it flitted nervously back and forth over the table. "You see, no one's quite sure when Kal was born. He's an orphan."

"Oh," Twelda said with compassion. "We're sorry."

"Thanks, but I'm all right," Kal replied. "My parents died a long time ago before I was cur—"

"*Weaned*," interrupted the newt, zipping into position directly in front of Kal's wide-eyed face.

"Cur-weaned?" Vermis asked. "How curious. Was Kal raised by mongrel dogs?"

"What? Oh, of course not," Wingnut assured them with a fidgety loop-the-loop. "But what about Rudger, here? You said he has amnesioakia?"

"So I've been told," Rudger replied with a sigh. He sipped his fragrant suzzleleaf tea before continuing. "Apparently, I fell afoul of some amnesioaks while trying to stop my father's gnome-napping."

"Gnome *napping*?" inquired Wingnut. "Why would you be...Oh, I understand. Your father must be narcoleptic, and you were trying to keep him awake, right? I had a great-uncle so afflicted."

Rudger looked at Wingnut blankly. "Uh..."

"Allow me," Vermis told his bewildered friend. The bookworm turned to the newt, who had at last alighted upon the empty biscuit plate. "What Rudger means is he was trying to stop his father's *abduction*," Vermis clarified. He twiddled his bowtie. "Really, you must forgive these

Humdrungles. They have a strange way of expressing themselves." Then he turned back to Rudger and added in an undertone, "We'll make an entry for 'narcolepsy' in your Logofile later."

"Logophile? You mean you're a word lover?" interjected the boy-wizard. He regarded the young gnome earnestly. "Are you a lexicologist like me?"

Again, Rudger was at a loss.

"Lexicologist, my eye," huffed Vermis. "Rudger doesn't just *study* words, my good fellow. He invents them. Rudger is a Logomancer."

"Truly?" breathed the boy. His face beamed with admiration. "You can do word-magic?"

Rudger squirmed in his seat. "Well, I wouldn't say—"

"Oh, he's being modest," Vermis cut in. "Needs a spot of training, that's all. I've seen him cast Weird Wyrds twice myself. Remarkable stuff. And you, Hieronymus. You've witnessed it, as well."

"*I'm* studying to be a Logomancer, too," gushed Kal. "It's super hard. At least, that's what my master keeps telling me. Study lexicology, vocabology, etymology, fourteen other ologies. Gotta know all about words and how they're put together, forwards, backwards, and inside-out. But even *that* doesn't guarantee you'll ever be able to do it properly. Oh, you can learn other kinds of magic without much talent. I've been able to control animals and make Fyre forev—well, for a long time, anyway. But Logomancy! *That* requires knowledge *and* talent, you know? I think I'm getting the hang of it, but it's tricky."

"While I'm sure our guests are interested in your studies,

Kal, I seem to remember that I was inquiring about Rudger's ailment," Wingnut reminded him.

Kal was suddenly abashed. "Oh," he mumbled. "Sorry."

"No, it's fine," Rudger assured the boy. "I'm a novice at Logomancy, too. If I were better at it, I might have been able to save Dadders. And then I would remember meeting all of you, the first time around." His eyes flitted from Wingnut to Vermis and then to Twelda. The gnomette's visage bore a shrewd expression.

"The man who took Rudger's father was wearing a robe like that one," she said boldly, pointing at the purple garment in the corner. "It's our only clue to the gnome-napper's identity. What can you tell us about it?"

Kal opened his mouth to answer, but Wingnut vaulted himself back into the air with a volley of rapid-fire speech.

"Oh, that? Not much to tell, really. Belongs to Kal's master. You'd have to ask him about it, but he's rarely here. Spends most of his time at court with the other Wizards of Lex."

"Wizards of Lex?"

"Yep. A whole guild of them. King Emmett is partial to magic-workers."

"He's especially keen on Logomancers," stated Kal, once again regarding Rudger avidly. "That's why I want to be one. And I'm getting there, I think. In fact, I think I can help you with your memory problem. I ran across the Wyrd cure for memory loss just the other day."

The boy jumped up from his seat and crossed to a bookshelf filled with dusty, old tomes. He selected a relatively clean one and began to thumb through it.

Wingnut circled the boy tightly. "Kal, that's very advanced magic. You aren't even supposed to be reading about it yet. I strongly recommend that you—"

"Oh, pish posh," the boy said, apparently resolved to his course of action regardless of the newt's advice. "It'll be my way of making up for the wereweasel thing. Ha! Here it is. It's a logomantic formula, all right. 'Course they can't print the actual Wyrd in the book. It'd spoil the magic if just anyone could utter it. But I've got it worked out. Shall we have a go?"

Kal's strength of conviction curbed Rudger's natural inclination to decline. The boy seemed sure of himself, and Rudger really did want to remember the time he'd lost. He turned to Vermis and Twelda.

"Why not?" the gnomette said with a shrug. "What's the worst that could happen? It won't work, right?"

Vermis thought a bit longer but then concurred. "You really have nothing to lose."

"Kal, no," Wingnut insisted. "I *vehemently* protest this reckless—"

"Hieronymus, I'm doing this," Kal said firmly as he set the spellbook on the bricklewood table. He cupped his mouth with a hand and whispered to Rudger, "He's such a killjoy."

"'*He*,' you say," mused Vermis. "Rudger and I had a debate about Wing—I mean, Hieronymus' gender."

"He's a boy," Kal proclaimed over Wingnut's grumblings. "Now, let's see if we can jog Rudger's memory. I'll need complete silence for this."

Rudger watched anxiously as Kal closed his eyes. A sort of serenity seeped into the young human's face. Rudger wondered if it was anything like the trance he barely recalled feeling in front of the triplets back in Aunt Ragna's burrow. The thought brought a pang of longing. He missed the Terror Trio. Their antics, their laughter, even their silly bickering—

Projectimentum!

Instantly, Rudger sensed something was wrong. Instead of a flood of memories rushing into his head, his face began to prickle horribly. He reached up to discover needle-sharp stubble emerging from his jaw. He yelped in surprise.

"Great gobs," commented Vermis as Twelda's eyes grew round with horror. "Any lexicologist worth his salt knows *mentum* denotes the chin."

Kal was aghast. "I'm sorry!" he cried. "I thought it meant the mind. You know, as in 'mental.'"

"That's *mens-*, you nanny-yammer!" Vermis chided. "Or in some cases, *ment-*. But never *mentum*."

"I warned you this was ill-advised," Wingnut added ruefully.

Rudger jumped down from the human-huge chair and rushed to a window. A hefty bound landed him on its wide sill. He found his reflection in the mirror-like surface of the rain-barrel water. Bright red whiskers were pouring out of his face, lengthening at a shocking pace.

"What have you done?" he moaned as the facial hair spilled over his throat. "I'm not supposed to have a beard. I'm only fifteen! I'm not ready for this!"

"Who ever is?" intoned Vermis. "Why, when I was but a

pupa, my father warned me that puberty brings abrupt change—"

"Not *this* abrupt!"

At last, the whiskers ceased growing, their questing ends coming to rest at Rudger's breastbone. The bewildered gnomelescent tugged disbelievingly at his insta-beard. It was the color of a sun-ripened tomato and had a lustrous sheen.

"Gnomes' homes, this is a disaster!"

"Now, really, Rudger," Vermis said. "It's a few whiskers. I 'mustache' you to get a little perspective."

Twelda and Kal stifled giggles as Rudger clambered down from the sill. He frowned at the unsympathetic bookworm, who smirked down at Rudger from his tabletop perch.

"What did you say?" demanded the gnome.

"I said you're overreacting. Things could've been so much worse, you know."

"How?"

"If Kal's inflection had been even half a tone lower, it could've been your *jawbone* that grew out," the vermitome answered. "Imagine that! You were a *hair's*-breadth away from unspeakable disfigurement."

An undignified guffaw escaped from Kal, which set Twelda into a fit of giggles and inspired a chuckle from the otherwise solemn Wingnut. When Twelda recovered, she eyed the bewhiskered gnome impishly.

"Yeah, Rudger," she said, "I guess you could call that a close shave."

Kal snorted as he added, "You were on the razor's edge, all right."

"Oh, but don't desp-*hair*," Twelda quipped as she wiped away tears of mirth.

Kal could barely form the words. "We're right... *hair*...behind you."

Rudger huffed his annoyance, but Twelda plowed on. "Hey, Kal. You know the old adage, right?"

"Which one?"

The gnomette managed a semi-serious expression. "There's nothing to fear..."

"...but *beard* itself!" she and Kal finished in unison.

"This isn't funny!" Rudger cried over their hysterical laughter. "Vermis, tell them to stop laughing and help me!"

"Oh, Rudger, it's all in pun," Vermis dared. At Rudger's outraged glare, the bookworm relented. "Okay, you two, cut it out."

"Or 'off,' as the case may be," suggested Wingnut. "Does anyone have a pair of scissors?"

"Oh, yes. I-I think I do," Twelda gasped. She rooted about in her satchel and produced a large silver pair. "Sit on that stool in front of the hearth, Rudger, and we'll get you all fixed up."

Rudger hopped up on the stool and crossed his arms under the beard. "Let's get on with this, okay?" he grumped. "This thing itches."

"All right, all right," Twelda soothed as she opened the scissors wide and nestled a swath of whiskers against its blade. A firm snip sent the long red hairs tumbling into Rudger's lap.

"You know, in some wizarding circles, red hair is thought to contain latent magical properties," Vermis commented.

Twelda turned to look up at the vermitome, the scissors

drooping in her hand. "You don't say."

"I do. I've consumed volumes on the subject."

"So is that why everyone thinks leprechauns are magical?"

"In part. Though there is a debate as to whether their red hair makes them magical or their magic makes their hair red. A sort of chicken-and-the-egg quandary, as it were."

"This is fascinating and all," Rudger broke in, "but I'm kind of lopsided, here." He waggled the remnants of his whiskers with one hand.

Twelda turned back and inserted the scissors around the next section of beard.

"Of course, red *gnome* hair is a heretofore unexplored commodity," Vermis continued.

"I'll say," rejoined Kal. "Can't remember hearing of a redheaded Humdrungle before."

Twelda turned away from Rudger again. "Neither can I," she stated, punctuating her words with a bob of her scissors. "But some *humans* have red hair. Does that make them magical?"

"I should say not," scoffed Vermis. "Humans may do magic, but they are not magical."

"There's a difference? Between doing magic and being magical, I mean."

"Indubitably," Wingnut interjected. "Certain flora are known to possess an inherent magic, like amnesioaks and jawjackle bushes. Some fauna are so endowed, as well. Human wizards, however, have simply learned how to usurp the magic of the Elements and other species and turn it to their advantage."

"Guys!" interrupted Rudger. "Can we *please* finish this?

My face is prickling."

Twelda whirled back around and made a few cursory snips. Then she turned from the task once more. "But what about gnomes?" she asked of Vermis. "If leprechauns are intrinsically magical, why not us other minikins?"

"Your kind might be brimming with innate magic," the bookworm admitted, "but your society's taboo on its practice has made it difficult to investigate."

Twelda's eyes grew round. "So what you're saying is, research needs to be done. *Scientific* research."

"Naturally."

"Augh!" cried Rudger as he scratched at his face furiously. "If you're not going to have done with this, I'm going to rip these wretched riskers out!" He stopped and cocked his head in confusion. "I mean, I'm going to whip these wetched whouskers out. What? No! Rip these roucher, wowp these witched—"

"Okay, okay! Stop before you accidentally spout a Weird Wyrd and make everything worse!" cried Twelda. She sized up the rest of the unwanted whiskers and set upon them with her shears.

Moments later, Rudger gave a sigh of relief. Only a hint of reddish scruff remained on his face.

"But what Twelda said brings up another interesting idea," Kal mused, drawing Twelda's attention once again. "Logomancy. Surely, *that's* one way humans can be magical themselves."

"A point for debate," Vermis conceded. "The source of such magic is as yet unknown. Perhaps it is also seated in the Elements. But most humans cannot cast word spells, so it appears to be a skill acquired by few rather than a characteristic possessed by many."

"Oh, *no*," came a moan from behind Twelda.

As she turned aside, she, Vermis, and Kal watched in amazement as Rudger's beard regenerated with astounding speed. In seconds, it was as long as it had been before its shearing, then longer. It grew with alacrity, never faltering, until it filled the thunderstruck gnome's lap.

Rudger leapt off the stool with a strangled cry, and the beard's ripples straightened to reveal its full length, now down to Rudger's knees.

"Egad!" Rudger shrieked. "It's alive! Get it off! For the love of Helios, *get it off!*"

Twelda was frozen with shock, so Rudger wrested the scissors from her hand and hacked away at the hexed hair himself. Both she and Kal begged Rudger to stop while Wingnut flew in agitated circles around them all, but the gnome was in a frenzy. With every frantic chop, the bewitched beard came back with even greater gusto.

When at last the scissors dropped from Rudger's shaking hand, they all stared aghast at the result: a veritable carpet of coarse red fibers cascading from Rudger's flushed face into a billowing heap at his feet. Rudger gasped in horror and leaned against the stool for support.

Vermis' eyes narrowed as he turned to look up at the human boy. "Was this your intent when you cast your Weird Wyrd?" he accused.

Kal was distressed. "No! Of course not! It was an accident. I'd never do anything to hurt Rudger on purpose."

"You did sic a wereweasel on him," Twelda pointed out.

©2022 Simerlein

"That was before I knew him," the boy said desperately. He lunged forward to catch the tottering gnome before he collapsed into his own beard. Kal then carried Rudger and his extraordinary facial hair to the bed. Wingnut followed, berating the human boy.

"What in high skies just happened?" Twelda asked of Vermis.

"It's like a hydra," Vermis postulated as he watched Kal lower the semi-conscious gnome onto the bed. "Cut off one of its heads, and two grow back. Except in this case, it's whiskers."

"But what does it mean? Will it hurt Rudger? Can we reverse Kal's curse?"

The vermitome shook his head in dismay. "I can't answer any of those questions," he said, "but I do know one thing."

"What's that?"

"Kal's managed to conjure one really weird beard."

CHAPTER FIFTEEN

Princess Hildegarde's arms ached as she held her slingshot at the ready. Her gaze was fixed five yards distant, on a crack between two courtyard flagstones where she knew the black menace lay. The human girl could feel its malign presence, sense its patient vigil for an avenue of escape.

The stand-off had aged a quarter-hour; the effort of stretching the slingshot's puxa-fiber cord was sapping Hildegarde's strength, slowing her reflexes. She needed to act, but advancing on the beastie would surely send it scuttling, rendering it a far more challenging target.

The fourteen-year-old courtier reevaluated her surroundings and felt a nudge of inspiration. Willing her cramped legs into motion, she rose in agonizing increments from her crouched position until she was hampered by a hard stop. A twist of her ankle freed the hem of her velveteen gown from underfoot which allowed her to finish straightening up. The burgundy skirt of the billowing garment made less than a whisper as the huntress edged toward a nearby well. She raised a foot to the brim of the bucket she'd spied there and tipped it over.

Water gushed over the flagstones. By the time the torrent reached her foe's hiding place, Hildegarde had reassumed her archer's stance. The creature was washed out of its flooded haven, and the girl let fly. Her missile, a common stone, connected, cracking the hackerpede's black shell. Its lifeless body drifted aimlessly in the waning trickles of the miniature deluge.

The thin applause of a single observer prompted her to turn about. She consciously forced her knotted muscles to relax as a heavyset man approached.

"Bravo," he praised her, smiling through a close-cropped beard. "Imagine what you could do with a proper bow."

"Proper young ladies do not shoot arrows," Hildegarde informed her Uncle Fabian.

"Ah, but apparently, they do shoot rocks," he observed, still smiling. "Face it, Hildie. You are no proper lady."

A clever comeback was called for, but Hildegarde came up empty. Her uncle's simple statement imputed no malice, only fact. Try though she might, Hildegarde could never quite achieve the air or demeanor of a lady. Her older cousin, Winifer, seemed to have extracted every quality of culture from their collective gene pool before Hildegarde was ever conceived.

"Don't look so glum," Prince Fabian bade her. "There's far more to life than fair features and pretty manners. Though I wouldn't discount those from your future just yet."

"Thank you, Uncle," Hildegarde replied, "but I believe I am a bit old to keep hoping for the impossible."

"Not every flower blooms in the spring," he countered. "And wildflowers know no season."

"Wild or not, I'll never become a great beauty." She looked despondently at the tatty slingshot in her hand. "Nor a great archer, I'd wager. The King will not allow it."

"Kings come, and kings go," Fabian said cryptically. "My dear brother, Emmett, may not always hold such sway over you."

Hildegarde stared at her uncle. For a fraction of a second, he seemed to regret his near-treasonous words. Then his smile returned.

"I come to bring you news. Lendar wishes to see you."

Hildegarde blinked in confusion. "Lendar? The Wayward Wizard? What does he want with me?"

Fabian's expression grew solemn as he rearranged his tunic over his prominent belly. "I'm sure I don't know, but it won't do to have him hear you call him that. He is a master of the magical arts, Hildie. You ought not to provoke him."

She scoffed. "Guess that's my unladylike nature coming out."

"Hildegarde, I am in earnest. You must show Lendar the utmost respect."

"As you advise, Uncle," she said, bowing her head in acquiescence. "When am I to go to him?"

"That is a good question," Fabian replied, at ease once again. "He asked me to send you to him as soon as possible. That was last night, but no one seems to have seen him about today."

"See? Wayward."

"Hildie…"

She pinched her lips in deference to his chiding tone.

"I suggest you go to his tower immediately. He has a habit of remaining therein for days at a time. It's best to answer his summons at the earliest opportunity."

"Summons?" repeated Hildegarde. She tossed her head with pride. "I am a member of the royal court. Who does Lendar think he is to issue such—"

The girl broke off as her uncle leaned forward to stroke her chestnut hair. "My brother, Geoffrey, certainly has a spirited daughter in you," he said quietly. "You must learn to keep that spirit in check. Winsome or not, a sweet woman leaves a better taste in the mouth than a salty one." He lifted her chin and caught her eye. "Remember that."

"I'll try."

Fabian straightened up and clicked his heels to announce his imminent departure. He marched halfway across the courtyard before stopping and looking back over his shoulder. "Oh, and Hildie?"

"Yes, sir?"

"Be sure to dispose of that hackerpede. The guards are unlikely to attend to it, and Lendar becomes agitated when their corpses are strewn about."

"I will."

He turned a bit more and skewered his niece with a shrewd look.

"But, by all means, do keep up your target practice. You never know when a skill like that might come in handy."

He chuckled and turned to exit the courtyard.

Hildegarde stared after him, uncertain as always whether he was jesting…or deadly serious.

Hildegarde growled in annoyance as she battled her voluminous skirts on the way up the rampart staircase. A single hand was proving insufficient to tame the unruly folds of material, but her other hand could not come to its aid. That hand was engaged in keeping the dead hackerpede balanced on the prongs of her slingshot—a task made all the more difficult by the constant threat of stumbling over the problematic petticoats.

The plain-faced Princess was determined not to let the oozing, dripping thing fall. It had been ordeal enough to maneuver it onto the slingshot, and she wanted nothing more than to rid herself of it at the earliest possible opportunity. Down in the courtyard she'd considered expediting her chore by dropping the 'pede into the well. She immediately thought better of it. The possibility of ingesting water laced with hackerpede guts was too horrible to chance.

At last, Hildegarde reached the parapet and tipped the mangled monster over the crenellated stone wall. She watched as it fell forty feet into the moat below. Instantly, the creature that dwelled in its depths surfaced to snap up the morsel in its great toothed maw. *A fitting end for the little brute*, thought Hildegarde, but she did not linger to celebrate. Lendar's tower lay across the courtyard, at the northeast corner of the keep.

Along the battlement she sped, passing a patrolling guard with such swiftness he scarcely had time to salute. Hildegarde knew this was unseemly conduct for a princess—for any lady, truly—but after the extended stand-off with the hackerpede, it felt heavenly to run. She could practically hear her mother's scandalized voice as her feet pounded against the stone blocks. *A lady's gait is her calling card. Dignity above all else.* Dashing into the roofed enclosure that protected the northwest tower's entrance, Hildegarde felt her throat tighten. *If only Mother could say that now*, she thought.

Hildegarde rounded the corner and burst back into the sunlight. The abrupt brightness forced her to squint. She failed to see the oncoming figure in time.

Wham!

A high-pitched scream informed Hildegarde that the other victim of the collision was female. When Hildegarde stopped seeing stars, she found herself looking upon a most peculiar sight.

A young woman, even more elaborately frocked than she, was struggling to pick herself up from the stone path. Despite splayed limbs and a slightly squashed hairdo, the girl somehow managed the maneuver with grace and refinement. Lovely of visage and perfumed to perfection, she radiated a cultured regality which was regularly interrupted by dainty cries of outrage.

"Hildegarde, you oaf!" she scolded through richly rouged lips. "Why weren't you—*ow!*—watching where you were going? And why by the wizards of Lex were you—*ouch!*—running like the banshees were chasing you? *Ow-wouch!!*"

Hildegarde was too stunned by what she was witnessing to manage anything more than, "I- I'm sorry, Winifer."

©2022 Simerlein

"I should hope so," the blonde Princess seethed. "Honestly, a person of such considerable bulk should be—*ouch!*—more mindful of the impact she may have on—*thee-hee-hee!* —slenderer people around her."

Under normal circumstances, the insult about her size might have bothered Hildegarde, but at the moment, it was all she could do to keep from laughing.

"What are you smirking at?" demanded the prettier Princess.

Hildegarde's suppressed giggles gave birth to a snort as she waved an arm at the swarm presently assaulting Winifer. Four sets of false teeth orbited the Crown Princess, each eagerly seeking its opportunity to snap at various aspects of her royal anatomy.

"Don't stand there pointing like a simpleton," Winifer jeered. "Obviously, I am the innocent victim of an evil enchan —*y-y-youch!*"

She shook a set of teeth off her right elbow and grandly swept an errant lock of hair back into place.

"…an evil enchantment—totally random, mind you—which requires immediate magical inter—*arrgh!*"

A set of choppers was locked onto her disarranged coiffure. She pried it off, losing more than a few golden hairs in the process.

"…magical intervention. I was seeking out the aid of Archmage Janusz when—Oh, no, you don't!"

She batted away a set of teeth that had divebombed her pert little nose.

"…when I ran into an *ogre* called Hildegarde! Now, get out of my way-*hey-hey-hey, now!*"

Dislodging a particularly adventurous set of incisors from her posterior, Princess Winifer pushed past her huskier cousin and resumed her flight along the battlement. Even in her distress, she maintained a certain poise, only bouncing skyward on every fifth or sixth step when she suffered further nips from her attackers. Her cries of indignation continued to ring out over the courtyard until she slammed the door of the northwest tower behind her, leaving two sets of teeth behind to gnaw savagely at its wood.

Hildegarde's mirth faded as she considered the source of her cousin's woes. The troublesome teeth were no random enchantment, as Winifer would have had her believe. They were a punishment, compliments of Lendar the Wizard. A punishment which Hildegarde herself hoped to avoid.

Apprehension building, the girl moved into the shade of the enclosure that sheltered the northeast tower's entrance from the elements. She stepped up to the portal and lifted its heavy iron door knocker. She then released it, knowing that in so doing, she was setting into motion an uncertain chain of events.

The door swung open on creaking hinges. Hildegarde took in a shaky breath and stepped through.

She had no idea what to expect inside. Previous visitors had reported a variety of noxious curiosities in the wizard's anteroom. Some had walked into a riot of swirling colors while others had been swallowed by blackest darkness. For some, the anteroom had been silent while others had been forced to plug their ears against a cacophony of screeches and snarls. Still others claimed they had faced exotic beasts of the most fearsome dispositions.

Whatever the wonder—atmospheric, auditory, or animalistic—every visitor had warned her that some sort of mental challenge had accompanied it. It seemed Lendar delighted in testing his callers with riddles and logic puzzles, and he delighted even more in ejecting the unworthy with a variety of humiliating penalties.

Hildegarde edged into the room, braced for a basilynx attack or an ear-splitting chorus of yowls and roars, but her fears proved unwarranted. The anteroom was quiet, and empty, save a small gnarlicwood table bearing an hourglass and a lighted candle. Alert for an ambush, she drew nearer and studied each item, noting the scrolling contours of the tarnished silver candleholder and the shiny metal support arms in the hourglass' casing.

A deep voice seeped from the walls,

Passage barred unless you delve
Betwixt a face's one and twelve.
Speak the name of what is spent
But rarely borrowed and never lent.

Hildegarde swallowed nervously. So it was to be a riddle, she thought. Was it the same one Winifer had failed to solve? Hildegarde pushed the thought aside as sparkling sand began to fall within the hourglass. She couldn't allow herself to be distracted by trivial thoughts.

A face's one and twelve, she mused. Well, a face had one nose and one mouth. But what of the twelve? Twelve eyelashes? Twelve freckles? What lay between a nose and freckles? Or between a mouth and eyelashes? A person's eye, perhaps? She twisted her lip as her line of reasoning reached an apparent dead end.

She switched her focus. *Speak the name of what is spent.* Money, of course. But what did money have to do with an eye? Maybe it wasn't an eye. A cheek, then? But even that had no connection to money that she could fathom.

A series of clicks intruded on her ponderings. The hourglass was tapping one of its support rods against its upper glass bulb. The sand inside was already more than half gone.

Panic blossoming within her, Hildegarde squeezed her eyes shut and covered her ears in an effort to concentrate. What was the last line of the riddle again? *Rarely borrowed, never lent?* Money was often borrowed *and* lent, so she must be on the wrong track again. Had Winifer made this same mistake?

A rapping noise startled her eyes open. The hourglass was hopping about the tabletop in a most impatient manner. It almost seemed to be trying to tell her something. But what? Barely a thimbleful of sand remained. Time was running out.

A flash of inspiration set her lips into motion. "Oh!" she exclaimed. "A clock's face runs from one to twelve, and you can spend time and live on borrowed time, but you can't lend time. So that's the answer! *Time!*"

A horrible grinding noise made Hildegarde stagger backward. Had she failed? Eerie lavender light spilled through an overhead aperture as a hatch fell from the ceiling and pulverized the table before her. The girl stood amongst the splinters of wood, heart thudding in her chest, until a tiny flash of light penetrated the settling dust. It was the hourglass, which had somehow survived the blow and was now bouncing about gaily at the foot of the staircase. She watched as it turned itself end-over-end up the steps. It was almost at the top before Hildegarde could bring herself to follow.

The stone-walled chamber above mirrored the one below except that it was empty. The Princess lingered uncertainly in the pale purple illumination. "Lendar, sir?" she called, striving to keep the shakiness she felt out of her voice. "You sent for me?"

Light drew inward from the circular room's walls and coalesced into an amorphous blob at its center. The blob shifted, gradually assuming the shape of a man. Purple shimmers retracted from the head and hands of the figure to reveal the wizard, now cloaked in a resplendent violet robe that continued to pulse gently with light.

"Princess Hildegarde," the mage said. "We meet at last."

Hildegarde worked to keep her jitters in check. The man, however powerful he may be, was still a servant to the Crown —and by extension, to her as well.

"Greetings," she said. "It appears that I have passed your little test, though, as a member of the royal family, it seems an exception ought to have been made. Now, kindly dispense with these theatrics and tell me why I am here."

The hourglass, which had been hanging close to Hildegarde's feet, gave a little start at these bold words and began to quake. The edge of its circular, wooden cap tilted up toward the wizard as if in fearful anticipation.

The Wayward Wizard remained silent for a tension-filled moment. Then a low, rumbling sound began. As it grew in volume, Hildegarde recognized it as laughter.

Lendar gave his long dark brown beard a downward stroke

and finished the gesture with a flourish of his nimble fingers. Instantly, torches mounted to the curved wall around them burst to life. A circle of chairs with plush purple seats came into view around the chamber's circumference. The hourglass nudged the hem of Hildegarde's gown. It tilted its top toward the nearest chair and then at Lendar who was seating himself in a somewhat grander one in the middle of the room.

Catching the timepiece's meaning, the Princess stepped back to the indicated chair. Instead of sitting down, she slotted a hand between its back and seat and hefted it from the stone floor. Her heels made one, two, three echoing clicks before she set the piece of furniture back down, just two yards from where the wizard waited, his gray-green eyes watching stolidly. Hildegarde took her time perching herself on the padded seat and arranging each fold of her velveteen gown just as her mother would have insisted. She then slowly raised her eyes to meet the magicker's penetrating gaze. "I am now prepared to hear you," she announced, hoping he had not the means, magical or otherwise, to see through her façade of bravado.

Lendar did not respond to her prompt. He continued to regard her unblinkingly, his thin lips pursed and nostrils flared ever so slightly. The wizard seemed much younger than Hildegarde expected; he appeared not to have yet tasted his fourth decade of life. He was surprisingly handsome as well, with prominent cheekbones and a small, sloping nose. His jawline was difficult to assess under its profusion of dark whiskers, but Hildegarde felt sure it must be strong to complement the chiseled architecture of the balance of his face.

The Princess slapped herself mentally. *That's the glamour*

at work, she thought angrily. Everyone knew Lendar had the power to portray youth. She herself had seen his advanced age on days when he was not seeking to beguile. What she saw before her now was a veneer, a ruse, designed to disguise a keen and wily intellect honed by years of worldly experience.

"Princess," he said in a cooing baritone the moment she'd freed herself from his spell. "It warms my heart to find you live up to your reputation."

"Pray, inform me, sir," she replied with neither warmth nor frigidity. "Is this a reputation of worth or shame?"

"Oh, worth, I assure you," Lendar said, revealing a dazzling smile that was likely also augmented by magic. "The denizens of this castle describe you as clever, resilient, and stout of heart. All qualities you have demonstrated in these past minutes we have shared."

Stout. Quite a word her cousin, Winifer, would use to describe her, though in a less flattering context. Hildegarde turned her thoughts away from the emotional quagmire this sort of thinking produced.

"Pretty words," she said with a hint of bitterness. "Have they a purpose?"

The smile faded. "Your Highness, you accuse me of empty flattery, and we've only just met. Let us become acquainted before we cast judgments. Shall we speak of something pleasant? Your parents, perhaps?"

"What about my parents? All there is to know is of public record. My father is a Prince of the realm, after all."

"Yes, that is true. Prince Geoffrey is a fine man and a great leader. His counsel is of great value to King Emmett, I am sure. But, of late, your father seems a trifle…morose. I have known him and your mother to appear together at every royal function over the past two decades. And yet, at the spring ball, Eleanor was nowhere to be found."

If Hildegarde had had her way, *she* would've been nowhere to be found, too. Six hours of Winifer's jibes and flouncing about as she flirted with every eligible prince from miles around was sickening enough, but enduring this without her mother at her side had been torture. And it was sure to be even worse at Winifer's formal presentation ball in seven days' time. Again, Hildegarde pushed her emotions aside to address the mage.

"Mother was not feeling well that evening."

"Or any evening since, I gather," Lendar observed. "I hear her ailment is more serious than anyone has been letting on."

He let the words stand as an invitation for Hildegarde to unload the burden she'd been carrying for a fortnight. She certainly did not trust the man before her, but the temptation to divulge the truth was strong.

The wizard read the conflict on her face. "Hildegarde, you can talk about it. I already know."

A small part of her warned that the wizard's glamour was at work again, but she shuddered and surrendered her secret.

"Mother's been struck dumb."

The whispered words rang horribly through the stone chamber, returning to her with a sharpness that brought tears to her eyes.

Lendar allowed his guest a moment to collect herself. When she had finished wiping away the tears with a handkerchief she'd forgotten to have pressed, he asked, "So Duchess Eleanor has no command of speech?"

"None," Hildegarde confirmed. "She can't talk to us or understand what we're saying. We can't even get her to understand by writing. It's…it's like she's empty inside."

"A pity. I wish your father had confided this to the Guild before. I can tell you your mother is not the only victim in the kingdom. This strange affliction is known to the villagers, as well."

"Really?"

"Yes. In my absences from the court, I walk amongst the common folk. Many have described to me the symptoms your mother displays. They call it the Mute-ation."

"But what is causing this horrid illness? The healers seem powerless to help my mother. And the priests are faring no better."

"This is because the Mute-ation is a magical malady, milady. And magical maladies require magical remedies."

Hildegarde looked up, suddenly feeling a flicker of hope. "Could…could *you* devise such a remedy? You and the Guild wizards?"

The mage spread his hands. "That is difficult to ascertain. I have studied my texts thoroughly, and I am reasonably confident that there exists a countermagic for this plague."

"Oh, that is heartening news!" exclaimed the girl. "We must try it at once."

The wizard grew solemn. "If only I could. Sadly, the artifact that harbors the required magic is inaccessible."

Hildegarde frowned. "Inaccessible? What do you mean?"

Lendar gazed at the Princess. "It is currently in the possession of a dreadful guardian."

Fear prickled the nape of Hildegarde's neck. "What is this artifact?" she asked. "What is it, and who has it?"

"It is a sword," he told her, his eyes seeming greener than before. "An enchanted sword known to few in the human world. It harbors a multi-faceted magic which I believe can be harnessed to cure your mother and the villagers of the Mute-ation. But to acquire it, I need a non-magical champion."

"You mean you can't get it yourself?"

"Nay, I cannot. Nor can any member of the Guild, I fear. This is why I have not mentioned it before. But with your mother stricken, it has become a matter of urgency."

"What would this non-magical champion have to do?"

"Travel south along the River Gush to the caves in the bluffs beyond the Hinterlands. There, he would have to engage a terrible wyvern to liberate the sword."

"A wyvern?" Hildegarde breathed. "A dragon has this sword?"

"Aye. And as you know, dragons are highly attuned to magic. No wizard could draw within a league of the beast without its noticing."

Hildegarde's hand moved to the slingshot hidden in the billows of her gown. A crease formed in her brow.

"Of course, a non-magician might not have to engage the wyvern directly," Lendar went on. "He might best it by stealth and cunning and so steal away the prize."

Hildegarde's mind was a tempest of thoughts. Who could best be trusted with this important task? The King's guard? The Great Knights of Lex? Even a legion of the kingdom's finest warriors would be hard-pressed to defeat such a monster. And Lendar wished to send only one man?

It was as if he could read her mind. "Whoever stepped up to the challenge would not go unarmed. In addition to his preferred weaponry, he could carry magical aid without arousing the dragon's suspicions.

"My hourglass knows the way," Lendar continued. "It could accompany the champion. And, in case of confrontation with the monster, the champion would be wearing this protective amulet." He pulled a glowing green stone set in a golden necklace from his robe.

Hildegarde found herself reaching out to take the proffered charm. Its energy caressed her skin as a transformation ensued before her eyes. The hand holding the amulet lost its stodginess and grew slender and smooth. Hildegarde recoiled in shock, dropping the jewel to the floor. The hand transitioned back to her own again, with its sausage-like fingers and short, lusterless nails. Yet when she picked the necklace up from the stones, it phased again into the elegant hand of a true princess.

For the first time, Lendar seemed nonplussed. "How very extraordinary. That artifact is capable of deflecting the notice of one's enemies and repelling dragon fire, but I've never known it to produce this particular effect. Still, all the better. Beauty soothes the beast, does it not?"

"So they say," Hildegarde replied, taken aback by the dulcet tones of her own voice. Suddenly, she was seized by a fierce desire to gaze upon herself in a looking-glass. She opened her mouth to voice the wish but caught herself just in time.

"You must keep this until the champion is found," she said, handing back the amulet. She experienced a grave pang of loss as it left her fingers.

"With this discovery, I have had a revelation," Lendar told her, his eyes on hers. "Why must our champion be male? Dragons are fond of damsels, are they not? Imagine one wearing this charm. The wyvern would be transfixed. And I know just the lady for the job."

Hildegarde's stomach leapt in anticipation of the wizard's next words.

"She shall be the one who once owned a dragon as her pet. The Princess Winifer!"

"No!" Hildegarde cried.

The impassioned utterance seemed to echo endlessly in the stone-lined chamber. The wizard regarded her in stunned silence until it ebbed away. Then an eyebrow arched above a handsome green eye.

"Have you an alternative to suggest?" he asked with a grin.

CHAPTER SIXTEEN

"Great gobs of doggedness," yawned Vermis as he stretched his segmented body. "You've been at it all night again, haven't you?"

Rudger looked up blearily from a ponderous tome, its binding as dull and dry as its contents. Exhaustion hung in rings under his red-rimmed eyes. A stub of a candle, his third since dusk the day before, was guttering its death throes. He sighed, licked his fingers, and put the taper out of its misery.

"You can't go on like this," the vermitome lectured. "It's been three days now, and you aren't one iota closer to ridding yourself of that beard than when you started."

"No. I think I've got it this time," Rudger contradicted, fatigue robbing his voice of inflection. He placed his fingertips on his temples in an attempt to focus his weary mind.

"Barbibanish!" he cried.

The facial hair didn't even have the decency to twitch.

"You're *really* scraping the bottom of the barrel now," Vermis observed. "What was that? Weird Wyrd number two hundred?"

"And twelve," Rudger moaned as he dropped his forehead onto the table with a clunk. Twin mountains of books pressed in from either side—a monument to his enduring failure.

Vermis tutted his disapproval. "Despair not, Master Rump. Perhaps your morning lessons will turn something up."

"Ugh! That's even worse than poring over these awful old texts," Rudger mumbled, still face-down on the table. "Can't we just wait for Kal to come back? He's way better at Logomancy than you. Maybe he should teach me."

"Surely mine ears deceive me," Vermis bristled. "What has this paragon of scholastic virtue done to earn your vote of confidence, I ask? Was it not he who plagued you with that garish facial plumage in the first place?"

"Snot oomij."

"Beg pardon? I couldn't make that last bit out with your face plastered against the tabletop."

Rudger lifted his head. "I said my beard's not plumage. Plumage means feathers." He waved weakly at the piles around him. "Learned that six books ago."

"I am aware of its meaning," Vermis snipped. "Have you never heard of poetic license?"

"Look, maybe Kal did conjure up this beard, but at least that means he *did* Logomancy. Your lessons are nothing more than endless lists of word roots and prefixes and suffixes and origins and conjugate this and subjunctivize that. And when we finally run out of word scraps in one language, you start in on another!"

"Just because that human boy managed to construct one successful Wyrd does not make him a suitable tutor for your talent. Yes, his Glynt is strong—radiant, even—but that alone does not a Logomancer make. Why, I bet the lad wouldn't know a sesquipedalian if he consumed it."

"Sesquipe-*what*? Ugh! There you go again, trying to rope me in to another vocabulary lesson. Look, I need some practice actually *casting* Wyrds from someone who knows how to do it."

Vermis' spots had dilated to such an extent that he was almost entirely crimson.

"Very well. If my instruction is so substandard, I shall release you to the tutelage of the human child you idolize so. But where is this great sage?" Vermis twisted his upper body back and forth in a dramatic search move. "I see him not. Again, he dallies elsewhere while I do my best to prepare you for the trials ahead. But if you prefer to be ill-equipped when you meet your father's abductor, be my guest. It is of no consequence to me."

"What are you two arguing about now?" asked an exasperated Twelda as she turned over in the bed. She glared at them good-naturedly.

"Oh, Vermis is just being a drama-tome, as usual," Rudger announced, crossing his arms.

"And Rudger is just being an ingrate, as usual," Vermis fired back.

Twelda sighed. Flinging back the covers, she dropped to the floor, fully dressed. She'd slept in her clothes, minus the tan lab smock.

"You two are going stir-crazy, cooped up in this cottage,"

the gnomette told them as she reached up to pull the smock off the seat of a human-huge chair. "What you need is some time apart, preferably outside. I propose we make today a science day."

"A what?" asked Rudger.

Twelda retrieved her shoes and pulled one over a squarish foot. "A science day," she repeated. "Drillwork all day and research all night makes Rudger a very cranky gnome. I say we take a day off from Logomancy and go out to the pond to do an experiment. It won't take long, and maybe Kal and his master will have returned by the time we're done."

Rudger peered at the empty peg where the purple robe once hung. It had vanished, along with Kal, the morning after the beard debacle. Wingnut had assured the three houseguests this was not unusual. But when Rudger questioned the winged newt about the wizard boy's exact whereabouts, Wingnut had gone cagey, flitting here and there to avoid being pinned down. Rudger, Twelda, and Vermis quickly learned not to press the newt for details lest he whiz out a window and go missing himself.

The perturbed gnome pulled his eyes off the peg and redirected them to the mantel where Vermis stood. "Is *he* coming along?"

The question came out harsher than Rudger intended. Vermis put his nose, or rather the greenish nub that passed for one, up in the air and floated gracefully down to the tabletop.

"I could do with some independent fact consumption," he announced. "Even if my amassed knowledge isn't appreciated by certain parties."

Rudger rolled his eyes. "Just don't wipe out anything in the books still on the shelf, okay? I haven't had a chance to plow through those yet."

Receiving no response, the young gnome wound the multitudinous strands of his beard around his left forearm and eased himself off the stack of books he'd been perched upon. It was a long drop from the oversized chair's seat to the floor, and by the time he'd managed it, Twelda was waiting by the door, her noggin-guard secured to her head. He gave the gnomette a leg up to the upside-down world outside.

Rudger hesitated and glanced back at the table. The vermitome was curled up with his back to the door, his body its usual green color again. The gnome sighed. Slinging Twelda's satchel over his shoulder, he shimmied up the door post and left the cabin.

———

"You know, you were kind of hard on Vermis back there."

Rudger tried to ignore Twelda's comment as they sat and gazed out over Bunion Bog. Some gabblers were making a ruckus as they fought over liddlerfish that had unwittingly meandered into the reed-choked shallows. The birds' raucous cries were far less grating to Rudger than the truth of the gnomette's words. Rudger was annoyed at his failure to banish his beard, and it was easier to blame the bookworm for not teaching him enough than to blame himself for learning too little.

"You know, I've been wondering something," Twelda

continued after a pause. “Vermis mentioned something called a Glynt. What is that, exactly?”

Rudger reluctantly hauled himself out of his sulky silence. “From what I’ve read these past few nights, it’s a sort of magical signature.”

Twelda looked at him with interest. “You mean you can identify a wizard by this Glynt?”

“A wizard *and* his works of magic,” confirmed Rudger. “The Glynt appears as a sort of glow around the sorcerer and rubs off on anything his spells touch.”

“Huh,” the gnomette said thoughtfully. “I’m pretty sure some of my scientific instruments back home had previous owners who were wizards. How come I haven’t noticed a glow on them?”

“Glynts wear off over time. And it takes magical talent and training to detect them.”

“Vermis can see Glynts. Does that make him a wizard?”

“I think he’s a special case—a nonmagical being with a random magical skill.”

Twelda considered this. Then she said, “He’s been trying to teach you to see Glynts, hasn’t he?”

Rudger scoffed. “He’s been lecturing me about them, if that’s what you mean. Origins and theories, categories and classifications, not a bit of it practical. He says you have to ‘turn your perception sideways and cast it around a metaphysical corner’ to see them. Whatever that means.”

“So what do they look like? Aside from a glow, I mean.”

“Dunno. Never seen one. Vermis says Kal’s is a violet radiance like a sunset.”

“Do you have a Glynt?”

"Pshuh. Vermis told me mine's gray and grainy. When I asked for more detail, he said to imagine a moth-eaten dishrag."

They fell silent for a time, listening absently to the chorus of avian battle cries.

Rudger suddenly slapped his thighs and stood up. "Well, break's over. What kind of experiment are we doing?" he asked.

Twelda grinned. "We've already done one."

Rudger cocked his head. "Really? No flower juice this time? No peculiar devices?"

"We'll get to that in a minute. I want to check on the results of the first experiment first."

"What was its hippo-cyst?"

"Hypothesis," she corrected with a giggle. "Its hypothesis was that the separation of two clashing personalities might prevent a physical altercation."

"Oh. You mean like me using Vermis as fish bait? I would never do something like that." He gazed out over the pond. "Fantasize about it, maybe. But do it, never."

"Then I suppose it was a successful intervention," Twelda concluded. "So, on to the main event."

The gnomette sprang to her feet and disappeared into a patch of reeds. Rudger picked up her satchel and charged in after her.

"You haven't been the only one doing research in Kal's cottage," Twelda explained as Rudger stumbled after her. "Vermis got me thinking about the nature of magic, and Kal has some heavy-hitting books on the subject in his library. Wonder who his master is, to own so many books. I've never seen so many in one place before." She shook the digression aside. "Anyway, with all that knowledge lying about, it didn't take me long to come up with a hypothesis of my own."

"What is it?"

"I think your magical abilities might be inborn rather than acquired," Twelda said. "And to test that idea, I need to do an experiment on you."

Rudger came to a squelchy halt in the muddy terrain. "Oh, no. Not *that* again."

Twelda stopped and turned around. "Don't worry. This has nothing to do with the jawjackle juice. It's far more fundamental."

Rudger raised an eyebrow at her. "How?"

"The manipulation I've planned will help us to determine if you simply *do* magic or if you are in fact magical."

"What difference does that make?"

"Weren't you listening to our discussion during your barbering session?"

"In case you didn't notice, I had more pressing things to think about." He pointed at his beard.

"Well, Vermis was saying—"

"Augh! Vermis again?" interrupted Rudger. "Can't we have a conversation without bringing up that know-it-all book-worm? I thought you said this was *your* idea."

Twelda stared at Rudger for an uncomfortable moment before replying, "It is. And I'm beginning to get another idea. About *you*. It's not flattering."

Rudger rubbed at his eyes. "Twelda, I'm sorry. Between the lack of sleep and the fight with Vermis, I'm fresh out of manners today. Plus, I'm worried sick about my father. He's out there somewhere in who-knows-what sort of danger, and here we are in the middle of nowhere. I mean, shouldn't we be *doing* something instead of hoping Kal's guardian might show up with information about who gnome-napped Dadders? We've been waiting three days now!"

Twelda smiled sympathetically. "I understand how frustrated you feel, but Kal's master is our best lead right now."

Rudger blew out his cheeks. "You're right, of course. And there's no excuse for me to bite your head off. I'm ashamed of myself."

"Good," the gnomette said with a flick of her eyebrows. "You can make it up to me by doing my experiment."

Rudger sighed. "What do I have to do?"

"Simple," Twelda answered as she started moving again. "You just have to stand where I tell you. Although that might be harder than it sounds."

"Why?"

"Because you seem to fall a lot."

Rudger scoffed. "No, I don't."

"Hmm. Let's see," she said, ticking off the evidence on her fingers. "First, you fell when you missed tackling the human at Gnomister's Knoll. Then you fell down the hill at our campsite. *Then* you stumbled against the stool in front of Kal's fireplace and almost collapsed, though I'll forgive you that one. The appearance of that beard must have been quite a shock. Oh! And didn't you say you fell off a cliff just before I met you?"

Rudger gave a little shrug of embarrassment.

"There you have it. Classic klutz." She ended her analysis

and peered through a shock of tall grizzlegrass. "Ah, here we are."

Rudger tried to work up a counterargument, but it fell apart in his mind as an elaborate contraption came into view.

At its center was a stout pole driven into the sodden earth. The pole rose five full feet into the air and had four long, wooden arms protruding from its top. The arms were fashioned from a springy kind of wood so that they bent under the weight of buckets tied to their ends. Despite their bouncing in the wind, these bucking buckets remained high enough to clear a rope that was looped about the lower part of the pole. The rope extended outward to a large cranking device which had been assembled a short distance away.

A wooden wheel held the other end of the rope in a deep track carved into its edge. This wheel was the first of a series of interlocking cogs that ended in a large winch. Twelda stepped up and worked the crank. The buckets responded by rotating slowly around the pole.

"Behold the Eleminator," the gnomette said proudly. "Pretty scientific, eh? Took me over two days to build this beauty."

"You built this?" Rudger asked in wonder. He could now see that the pole at the center of the action was not a single piece. Apparently, Twelda had hollowed out one wooden pole and slipped it over another so it would spin.

"Those center supports were practically impossible to hoist into position, but persistence won out," she told him. "And now we get to see if my hard work has paid off."

"What's in the buckets?" inquired Rudger.

"Take a look."

Rudger stepped forward and peered into one as it drifted past. "It's empty," he said.

"No, it's not."

He frowned and chased the rotating bucket down to look again. "There's nothing in there."

"I guarantee you, there's something important in that bucket."

"What?"

"The Third Element."

"Air?" the gnome said, quirking an eyebrow. "That's very funny, Twelda. Of course, there's Air in there."

"And Water in the next one, and Earth in the next. And in a minute or two, we'll have Fire going in the fourth."

"Fire?" Rudger yelped as Twelda stopped working the winch and headed toward the satchel he'd dropped at the clearing's edge. "Why do you need Fire?"

"Because we need all four Elements if we're going to determine which one your magic stems from," she said, pulling out the fire-flinger and a handful of tinder. Then she looked at Rudger. "That is, of course, if you are magical by nature."

"What do you mean?"

"I mean that fundamentally magical creatures owe their very essence to one of the Elements," she explained. "Didn't you read *The Nature of Natural Magic* yet? Fairies have Air magic. Kelpies are tied to the Water Element."

"What about dragons?" Rudger asked, thinking about his dream in Aunt Ragna's burrow.

"Well, dragons are a special case. They pull their magic

from *two* Elements—Air *and* Fire. That's why they're so powerful."

"That makes sense, but what does all this have to do with me?"

"Well, I've long suspected that Humdrungle gnomes might be a magical species, even though we're brought up to shun magic. No gnome has ever dared to investigate this, as far as I can tell. So today, we take the first step in finding out."

"What exactly do you have in mind?"

Twelda reached up and caught one of the suspended buckets. Pulling it down, she dropped the tinder inside and then clacked the fire-flinger. Instantly, a blaze took hold.

"All *you* have to do is stand in the middle against that pole, without falling over. I'll do the rest."

"I'm guessing you're going to spin those buckets around me, then."

"Yep. My theory is Humdrungle gnomes are invested with Earth magic. So as I spin the buckets, they should all move away from the pole, like this." She turned the crank to demonstrate. "But when *you're* standing in the middle, my hypothesis is that one of the buckets won't move outward as much as the others."

"The one filled with the dirt?"

"Right. The Earth Element should be attracted to your magic, pulling that bucket closer to you."

"Uh, one question. If dirt's attracted to me, how is it I'm clean now?"

Twelda raised her eyebrows. "You call that clean?"

Rudger looked down at his clothes. They were smeared with muck from tromping through the bog.

He rolled his eyes. "You know what I mean. I don't walk around coated in dust all the time."

Twelda smiled. "That's an excellent point for further research after we get the results from this one." Her smile broadened. "Very good, Rudger. I knew you had a scientific mind."

"Oh, joy," Rudger said sarcastically. "But one of those buckets has real Fire in it. You know I'd do almost anything for you, but I'm not keen on getting barbecued."

"Oh, don't be such a pandypuss. Now, get in there, or there won't be any Fire left."

Rudger quelled his doubts and did as he was asked. Ducking between two of the moving buckets, he took his position at the pole. Twelda increased her effort, and the buckets tilted farther away. Trying to follow their movement made Rudger slightly dizzy.

"Uh, Twelda?" he said after a time. "It doesn't seem to be working. Is there anything else I should be doing?"

"Do your Logomancy thing," she advised between ragged breaths for air. "Maybe that'll bring the Earth magic out."

Rudger looked up nervously as a bank of clouds rolled in front of the sun. "I don't think I can do it on command. With me, Logomancy usually happens accidentally. So it's kind of looking like the experiment is a failure. Maybe you should stop cranking now?"

"No," she panted. "Not until you try."

"I told you. I can't," Rudger said. "And I think a storm might be coming in. Don't you feel the wind picking up?"

"It's just a draft from the buckets, Rudger. Come on! You can do this! Speak a Wyrd! In the name of science!"

Clearly, Twelda was prepared to crank both of her shoulders out of their sockets, so determined was she to make the cockamamie experiment a success. Rudger, for his part, simply wanted it to end, but with the buckets whizzing about, he couldn't slip out of the circle safely. The most expedient way to terminate the experiment was to humor his friend.

Rudger closed his eyes and retreated into his mind. He searched aimlessly for the glowing rip he'd stumbled upon while they were in the Standards Chamber. It did not appear, and no unbidden Wyrd came to him. Rudger finally decided he would have to concoct one to satisfy the gnomette. With his missing father still preying on his mind, he melded two word roots Vermis had taught him. "Paterniloc…"

Rudger choked on the last syllable as a snaggle-fanged zingbat dive-bombed the apparatus. The creature's leathery wing grazed Twelda's cheek as it zoomed past, causing her to cry out. Rudger flinched in sympathy but managed to keep his eyes on the normally nocturnal mammal as it turned in the air. In the course of tracking the airborne threat, he caught sight of something else that made him gasp. The bucket Fire had escaped its confines and was raging its way up its suspensory arm.

Twelda released the crank-handle, allowing the contraption to decelerate as the zingbat came back for a second pass. This time, it ignored Twelda, choosing instead to ram its considerable weight into the bucket containing the Water. It almost seemed as if the monster was trying to douse the Fire with this maneuver, but most of the Water ended up drenching Rudger instead.

The terrified gnome tried to bolt, but as he entered the path of the still-spinning buckets, inertia drove the one containing Earth into his side and sent him sprawling. Twelda yelled and moved to help, but the zingbat somehow managed to cut her off.

No, Rudger abruptly realized. *There are two of them!*

The Fire was spreading fast, now feasting on the pole and questing down the other three arms. Twelda rushed forward again, but a deafening crack stopped her in her tracks. The pole at the heart of the umbrella-shaped blaze yielded to the combined assault of the zingbat pair, toppling it in Rudger's direction. Twelda screamed as her flaming creation engulfed him.

Zephury!

A gale-force wind swept through the clearing, knocking Twelda off her feet. The wind ripped at the flames with such ferocity that the Fire succumbed, blown out like some twisted nightmare of a candle. Twelda reached the beleaguered gnome and gathered him into her lap, wiping away beads of water, mud, and soot. His extravagant beard was curiously intact, though the great wind had disarranged it thoroughly.

"Rudger!" Twelda cried as she patted at his still-smoldering tunic. "Rudger, please be all right. You've got to be all right!"

The gnome gave a little cough and smiled weakly at Twelda.

"You did say to do Logomancy," he croaked.

Twelda heaved a sigh of relief.

"I also said not to fall," she reproached him with a grin.

Heavy footfalls behind Twelda drew Rudger's attention away from his relief. He struggled to see around the gnomette.

"Wow," Kal said with a grin of his own. "*That* was dramatic."

CHAPTER SEVENTEEN

"You're back," Twelda Greeze observed as she looked the wizard boy up and down. "Just in time, it seems."

"For the excitement?" Kal asked, still grinning.

"For the clean-up," Twelda informed him. "We've got two unconscious zingbats, here. Probably deranged since they're almost never seen in the daytime. Luckily, we have you to stop them from attacking again."

"Oh, they weren't attacking," Kal said as he knelt down by Rudger. "They were helping. Under my direction."

"You call that helping? Torching my Eleminator and toppling its flaming remains on Rudger?"

The human's smile faded. "I didn't do that."

"I don't see any other animal-controlling wizards mucking about," Twelda pointed out.

Kal opened his mouth to defend himself but then seemed

to think better of it. "Fair enough," he said. "I sent the zingbats. Well, the first one, anyway."

"Which practically ripped my head off."

"Oh, you didn't appreciate that little aerial stunt?" he giggled. "It was just a warm-up to get you to stop cranking. The real ace of a move came when I brought the zingbat back around to clip that bucket of Water." He mimicked the bat's flight with his hand. "*Nyeeeeer,* splash! Sssssss."

"I hate to burst your bubble, but if you intended to douse the flames, your aim was atrocious," Twelda criticized. "Most of that Water ended up on Rudger."

"Ah, but that protected him from getting burned when your contraption fell on him."

"The Eleminator was not a contraption! And it was your zingbats that knocked it over."

"I told you, only one of those was mine. The other one ruined my maneuvering. Who knew those beasts traveled in pairs, huh?"

"Well, a *capable* wizard could've handled them both."

"Guys!" Rudger interrupted as he struggled to his feet. "Time out, okay? I'm okay; Twelda's okay. Everybody's okay." He looked back at the smoking debris and shrugged. "Pity about your machine, Twelda, but it wasn't really working, anyway."

"I beg your pardon," Twelda said, separating the words for emphasis. "It was working just fine until this dingbat—"

"Zingbat," interjected Kal.

"No, no. I'm referring to *you*, mister," Twelda clarified, shaking a finger at the boy. "The dingbat who rammed zingbats into my scientific triumph and ruined my experiment!"

"Now, Twedna—"

"*Twelda.*"

"Whatever," Kal said dismissively. "I gather this little toy of yours was meant to identify which Element Rudger draws his magic from, but it failed long before I tried to put the Fire out."

Furious at the human boy's condescending tone, Twelda crossed her arms and glowered in the general direction of Rudger. But as her wet, muddy subject coughed up a bit of smoke and tried to detangle his wind-swept beard, a realization hit her.

"All four," she muttered in amazement.

"What did you say?" asked Kal.

Twelda's attention snapped back to the conversation at hand. "Huh? Oh. Doesn't matter. But what *does* matter is where you've been these past three days."

Kal stepped over to a lone canfa tree and leaned his lanky frame against its spindly trunk. He crossed one leg in front of the other, digging the toe of his blunderhide boot into the sodden earth. "I had some business to attend to."

"Well, you could've told us that before you disappeared in the night," Twelda scolded. "We were worried."

The boy shrugged off the concern. "Wasn't Hieronymus around? He's used to my comings and goings."

"He was," Twelda confirmed, "and he was just as stingy with details as you're being now."

"There's only one detail *I* care about," Rudger piped up. "Did your master come with you?"

Kal's jaunty air faltered. "My master? Lendar? Oh, no. He

hardly ever comes here. Too busy hobnobbing with the King and his court."

Rudger's shoulders drooped with disappointment.

"Do you two mind if we move this interrogation up to the cottage?" the boy wizard continued. "I've been walking all morning, and I'm beat. Not to mention starving." He pushed himself off the tree trunk and sauntered to the other side of the clearing. He glanced over his shoulder. "You coming?"

Twelda bristled again at his obnoxious demeanor. "Come on, Rudger. Experiment's over. Time for lunch."

As the gnomes followed the human through the reed-choked bog, Twelda adjusted her gait to put distance between them and Kal. The science-gnomette kept an eye on her woe-begotten friend, but despite his latest trial, Rudger seemed sure-footed and alert. She shot a wary look at Kal. The back of his head could be seen above the reeds some fifty feet ahead.

"Do you think it's a coincidence that Kal's nearly killed you three times?" she whispered to Rudger.

"What?"

"Shh!" Twelda hissed as she grabbed his arm and slowed to a stop.

Kal continued to make his way through the swamp, apparently oblivious to Rudger's outburst.

"I'm serious," she told the gnome. "That human's had it in for you since the moment you met."

Rudger pulled his arm away from the gnomette. "That's ridiculous. Kal's a great guy."

"Oh, yeah? Let's examine the evidence, shall we? First, there was the wereweasel—"

"He explained that," Rudger interrupted. "He thought I was a leprechaun."

"Allegedly. Then he pushed you down a hill."

"He didn't push me! I fell."

"If you say so," the gnomette said, "but that doesn't absolve him of the zingbat attack."

"Attack?" Rudger repeated as he rolled his eyes. "It was an accident, Twelda. Kal didn't have control of the other bat. It made them both crash into the pole, which brought the Eleminator down on me. Kal was trying to *save* me from the Fire. You, too."

"Ugh! You don't see the pattern here?" Twelda asked in disbelief. She faltered, searching for something more to support her case.

"Ah, ha!" she exclaimed. She pointed at the skein of whiskers around Rudger's forearm. "What about that beard curse? Huh?"

Rudger gave her a withering look. "Puh. You call this a curse? I may not like it, but it hardly constitutes a malevolent act. Heck, it wasn't even intentional."

The gnomette crossed her arms over her chest. "Your faith in people astounds me," she said.

"Thank you."

"It wasn't a compliment. And here's another thing I don't trust about Kal." She paused dramatically. "His clothes fit."

Rudger stared at her. "Now you don't like people who have good tailors?" he asked.

The gnomette groaned. "Don't be so daft! This doesn't have anything to do with the cut of his clothes, though I've certainly seen better. What's suspicious is that I'm almost positive he's wearing the same outfit he had on the day we met him."

"So are we," Rudger pointed out. "Twelda, only a snob judges a person by his lack of wardrobe. Are we done here? Because Kal's so far ahead of us I can't see him anymore."

"Rudger, are you really this dense? The pants Kal's wearing now have the same patch as the ones he was wearing three days ago, but three days ago, they were *way too long*. Bunched up around his ankles, remember? Now they're practically the right length."

"Maybe he had them shortened while he was away. Did you think of that?"

"I did, but he's filling out that tunic better, too. No, Rudger. There's no other explanation for it but that Kal's gotten bigger."

"Bigger? In three days' time? Do you know how crazy that sounds?"

Twelda glanced up ahead and saw that Rudger was right; Kal had disappeared from sight. She resumed her trek. Rudger fell in step with her.

"Okay, maybe it does sound crazy, but he's acting differently, too. He was a real sweet kid when we met him—eager to please, you know? But now he's confident. Too confident. Cocky, even. You noticed that, didn't you?"

At last, a troubled expression crossed Rudger's face. "I guess so. A little."

"And now that I think of it, there's something else, too," Twelda continued, scrunching up her eyes as she worked to visualize the wizard boy's face. "It's subtle, but…wait! I've got it. The red dots all over his cheeks. Those weren't there before. I wonder what they are."

"Acne."

Twelda's eyes popped open. "Ew. Is it catching?"

Rudger laughed. "For somegnome so clever, there's sure a lot you don't know," he said. Then he stopped short and considered. "Actually, I wouldn't know this either if I hadn't read it in *Doctoring for All Species* up at the cabin. The red spots on Kal's cheeks are a minor skin affliction humans get when they're teenagers. But don't worry. Acne isn't contagious. Actually, some experts think the pus inside those blemishes might be beneficial for plant-induced maladies." He paused to consider again. "You know, maybe I should ask Kal to squeeze a little out for me. Might help me with my amnesioakia prob—"

"Blech!" interrupted Twelda with a shiver of disgust. "That is beyond gross!" Fortunately, the revolting notion was quickly displaced by another thought. "But there is something interesting in what you said, Rudger."

"What?"

"Humans get acne when they're teenagers."

"And that's interesting because…"

Twelda threw her arms up in excitement. "Kal told us he's only ten years old! Or possibly nine. There seems to be some confusion on that point."

"So what? He could be what they call an 'early-bloomer.'"

Twelda's shoulders fell. "Rudger, that's naïve, even for you. My gut tells me there's something shady about our friend Kal. We've got to be on our guard around him."

"Whatever you say," Rudger replied, clearly unconvinced.

"Hey, look. There's the cabin. And Kal." He squinted, trying to make out a tiny form darting around the human boy's head. "Is that Wingnut? Why's he so worked up?"

As they drew nearer, it became clear the winged newt was indeed buzzing about the boy in an agitated fashion. The annoyed human swatted at his flying assailant, but his hand only met air. Twelda and Rudger arrived at a trot.

"What's the matter?" the gnomette asked.

"It's Vermis," the towering human answered solemnly. "The Mute-ation."

Twelda and Rudger gasped as one. Rudger recovered first and urged Kal to help him up into the cottage. A running start was no longer necessary for the long-limbed human. Kal had only to lift Rudger and Twelda through the doorway and then pull himself in after.

The tiny vermitome was still on the human-huge table. From across the room, Twelda could just make out his limp, segmented body drawing unnatural, heaving breaths.

Rudger charged up a chair, scattering his booster-books as he clambered onto the tabletop. Twelda hurried toward another chair, listening as Rudger labored to evoke a response from the stricken bookworm.

"Vermis!" he cried. "Vermis, wake up! Say something!"

Wingnut alighted on the table as the gnomette began her climb.

"I found him like this," the winged newt reported sorrowfully. "I was only gone for a few minutes, and when I came back…"

Twelda finally achieved a view of the tabletop scene. Rudger was gently nudging the vermitome with a forefinger as he chewed the nails on his other hand. His beard had come unwound from its place on his arm; he was kneeling on a hank of it as he rocked back and forth in agitation. The pinned hairs pulled at his lower lip each time he leaned back, but if this caused him pain, he made no outward sign.

Twelda's heart dropped; it was the first time she had witnessed the aftermath of a Mute-ation. She could hardly bring herself to gaze into the milk-glazed, uncomprehending eyes of her friend's irascible tutor.

"He…he *has* to say something," Rudger said thickly. "It's still Vermis, right? He always has to have the last word."

Twelda's eyes drifted from the Muted worm, seeking respite from the tragedy before her. They scanned over breakfast dishes, still exactly where they'd been left that morning, and came to rest on the ponderous book Rudger had been struggling through, which lay open beside her. As Rudger began to sob, Twelda pulled the tome closer.

"Maybe he did have the last word," she announced. "Look."

Rudger sniffled as he moved to join Wingnut and Kal in their examination of the open book. The first few words at the top of the left-hand page were missing—an artifact of the vermitome's scholarly snacking. But thereafter, the consumption pattern became erratic. Blank swaths meandered through the dense, hand-lettered text, rendering both pages useless. Useless, but for the nimble swiftness of Twelda's mind in stitching together an intelligible message.

"V-I-C," she spelled for the others, tracing the negative-space letters on the parchment page with her finger. "Vic."

She looked at Rudger expectantly. “Does that mean anything to you?”

The grief-stricken gnome frowned. “It’s the name of my family’s sword,” he said slowly. Then he looked at Twelda in bewilderment.

“Why would Vermis write that?”

CHAPTER EIGHTEEN

Life in the Hinterlands was hard.

During the wet season, the marshes overflowed and spilled their putrid waters into the burrow. During the dry season, the garden withered and forced a half-league hike to forage for riverside edibles. In the summer, roving blunderelk were as likely to trample Humdrungles as look at them. And in the winter, gnomes lost in the blizzards risked stumbling across wereweasels eager to part them from their flesh. Oh, yes. Life in the Hinters was hard.

And it was just the way Ragna Riggle liked it.

The middle-aged gnomette was adept at dealing with the hazards of her harsh homeland. Hackerpedes and zingbats, blunderelk and lummoxes—these were vexatious critters she could dispatch with ease. Of late, however, she'd found herself saddled with three pint-sized pests she could not so readily rid herself of.

Rani, Roni, and Roon were presently tearing through the

skunkin patch, shrieking at the top of their lungs. The sisters were fleeing from their brother who was gleefully brandishing a skunkin sprout in each hand. He launched one after the other, but fortunately for Rani and Roni, his aim was poor. Instead of hitting them, each sprout splattered on the ground, releasing a puff of foul-smelling vapor.

Ragna gagged as she drew in the tainted air to reprimand her nephew. “Roon, if you don’t stop terrorizing your sisters with those stink bombs, so help me, I’ll feed you to the arachna shrubs myself!”

The response was another round of shrieks as two more skunkin sprouts missed their intended targets.

Ragna jabbed the trowel she was using into the buffa beet bed and stood.

“Well,” she announced loudly, as she wiped her hands on her bright orange apron. “Guess it’s time to get the supper on. Puxa pods can be mighty tough, you know. Takes a long, hard boil to get them to pop.”

“What?” Roon asked over his shoulder. “What did you say you’re making?”

“Puxa pod stew,” Ragna answered with a tilt of her head. “I believe I have a hankering for it.”

The Terror Trio looked down at their tempered tan jumpers which still bore the marks of their puxa pod war from the week before. The gooey drippings had mostly dried, but they were now acquiring an alarming coat of greenish fur.

“Puxa pod stew?” cried Rani.

“Not again!” moaned Roni.

“That stuff made me puke!” wailed Roon.

Ragna crossed her arms and looked down at the gnomelings. "I scarcely believe my tippy ears. I make you a nutritious meal, and you tell me it made you sick?"

The girls glanced at each other in shame. Roon looked down at his feet and muttered, "Well, it did. In my mouth."

"Oh, balderdash. That was quality mucus broth. And you'll want to be sure to coat your whole mouth with it this time. Makes the husks go down easier."

"*Husks*?" Rani repeated with horror-filled eyes.

"Why, yes," confirmed her aunt. "I thought I'd leave them in this time. For a little roughage."

"Aunt Ragna, no!"

"Well, that's what I always fed your mother and aunts and uncles when they were…How do the leprechauns say it? 'Acting the maggot?'" Ragna paused thoughtfully. "Hmm. Now there's an interesting idea for a garnish."

"*Hurp!*" retched Roni, while Rani turned as green as the spots on her jumper.

Ragna looked at them appraisingly. "I suppose there *is* another option."

"What? What is it?"

"Dringledollop pie. Ah, but your mother would have my head if I served you such an extravagant dessert for supper. She only ever got it as a reward for exemplary behavior." Ragna shook her head rapidly. "It's too much, really. Better go with the stew."

"No, no! We can be good! Please!" chirped the trio.

Ragna could barely suppress a smirk as she drew out their agony for another delicious moment. Then she sighed dramatically.

"Very well. Dringledollop pie, it is. But you'll have to

work together to get the berries from the top of that big bush over yonder. And remember, dringleberries bruise easily. If you let them fall to the ground, they'll be spoiled for sure. You'll find a net on a pole at the base of the burrow stairs. That should help you get the berries down safely."

And just like that, three rambunctious rabble-rousers were transformed into a cooperative berry-picking team. Ragna grinned in the relative quiet as she returned to transplanting the buffa beets. All went well until her trowel slipped as she was trying to coax a particularly portly specimen out of the ground. The beet didn't take too kindly to its treatment. It abruptly unearthed itself and slapped Ragna across the face with its shock of leaves. Then it marched away on its little roots, all in a huff, only to re-embed itself in a skunkin patch two yards away.

Ugh, thought Ragna with disdain. *Buffa beets are* such *divas.*

A double scream ripped the gnomette's attention away from the moody tuber. "By the High Gnome's giblets," she growled. "What now?"

The girls barreled past, running as if their lives depended on it. Ragna called after them, but the panicked gnomelings didn't look back. Even the writhing arachna branches couldn't slow them down as they crashed through and out of sight.

"Aieeeee!"

Ragna's head whipped round as Roon burst into view. The tiny gnomeling's legs pumped furiously as he swatted repeatedly at his scalp. A plume of white-gray smoke stretched out behind him. This time, Ragna was ready.

"Where is your cap?" she demanded as she snagged him by the collar. "And why is your hair smoldering?"

Roon gibbered in response, his eyes bulging with fear.

She lifted him onto his toe-tips. "Speak sense!" she demanded.

"Dr-dr-dr-*dragon!*" he squeaked. Then he twisted loose from her grasp and dove behind her.

Ragna felt the old fighting spirit swell out her chest as the shadow of the great beast's head fell across the buffa beet bed. One hand reached back protectively toward her cowering nephew; the other snatched up the trowel. She eyed the makeshift weapon. Fight a great Wyrm with this paltry garden tool?

Yes, please.

She stood at the ready as the odious beast approached. Backlit by the late afternoon sun, its exact dimensions were difficult to ascertain. Its head was a good five feet above the ground—low for a dragon, but still well above Ragna's own. Its body… well, that was a bit more perplexing. It seemed to taper abruptly at the neck. So much so that it called to mind her…

"Dringleberry net? Your dragon is my dringleberry net?"

The net floated toward them, its wooden handle swinging below it like a comically stiff tail. Without warning, a small gout of flame spurted through the toe of the net. Ragna trained her trowel on the blast, but as it ended and blackened fibers disintegrated, something shot out. The ruined net and pole fell to the ground.

The projectile came at Ragna. She swung at it with her

little shovel and missed. Her orange attacker was six inches to the left of where she'd thought it was.

She made a correction and struck again. Now the thing hung in the air eight inches to the right.

Three more swipes, each a failure to connect. The infernal thing was too quick, even for Ragna's excellent reflexes. It was time for a different tactic.

The gnomette prodded her nephew into motion with a nudge of her foot. Together, they feigned a retreat, taking step after backward step as Ragna kept up the battle.

Roon broke off to the side, and a tickle at Ragna's back let her know she was in position. She had been studying her airborne adversary and had identified a flaw in its advances, a tiny shudder that broadcasted its intent. Presently, it was preparing a direct frontal assault.

Ragna let her trowel drop.

The aggressor charged.

She ducked.

The arachna bush did the rest.

"It's okay," she called to Roon as the undulating branches tightened their grip on the struggling creature. "The little salamander can't hurt you now."

"Salamander?" inquired Roon with a tremor in his voice. "It's not a dragon?"

Ragna looked more closely at the bush's captive. She grinned.

"Bit small, wouldn't you say? I figure it's a fire salamander, what with the flames. But it could be a flying lizard of some sort. Or maybe a skink."

"Madam, please," the creature huffed. "A skink? Surely, you jest."

"Oh. It talks," Ragna remarked with a shrug.

Roon appeared at her side. "It talks?" he echoed. "Isn't that weird for a…" He looked warily at the tiny reptile. "What did you say you are?"

"I didn't," it replied breathlessly. "There are those of late who have deemed me a winged newt. Of course, if you do not secure my release from these branches soon, they will not call me anything other than dead."

"Oh. Right," Ragna said. "I'm sure that's quite asphyxiating. But before I call off the arachna, would you mind explaining why you were attacking us?"

The winged newt tossed its head weakly. "It was not I who attacked, but you, madam. I only came to talk."

"Then why didn't you?" Roon asked. "Talk, I mean. You didn't have to scare everybody like that."

"Having a net dropped over your person is hardly an invitation for polite parlance," the newt replied. "Now, Miss Ragna, Master Roon, if you don't mind…" Its strained speech ended in a gurgle.

"It knows our names," Roon whispered excitedly, pulling on Ragna's dirt-smudged apron.

She looked down at him. "That didn't escape my notice, Roon." She turned her attention to the distressed newt. "Very well. Stand back. This is going to get messy."

Lacking a sword to cut the clutching branches, Ragna charged forward with the only tool at her disposal. It took a considerably increased effort to free the newt from its herbaceous bonds with only a trowel in hand. Roon kept a wary eye on the sneaky shrub, raising the alarm each time its branches sought to ensnare Ragna herself.

The gnomette was drawing air in gulps by the time the tiny reptile was free.

"Well, that certainly brings new meaning to the phrase 'being bushed,'" she panted as she sat down to rest. Her muscles ached, but the workout had been most gratifying.

"Ah," the newt responded as it alighted on a broad bippup leaf. "I see you are your nephew's aunt. Rudger delights in wordplay as well."

"Oh. So you know Rudger," Ragna commented. "He's much better with words than I. Now, you came to talk?"

"Deliver a message, more like," it replied with a touch of acerbity. "That is what I am reduced to these days."

"What's your name?" Roon interrupted. Now that the creature wasn't endeavoring to set him on fire, the little gnome seemed enthralled by the newcomer.

"What's in a name?" it quipped. When it became clear Roon wouldn't except this banal response, it added, "Your brother calls me Wingnut. I suppose that's as good as any moniker."

"Are you a boy or a girl?"

A tiny flame escaped from Wingnut's mouth as it scoffed. "What is it with you hominids and gender? Does it really matter?"

Roon cast his eyes downward. "I-I'm sorry. I didn't mean to make you mad."

Wingnut sighed. "If it makes you feel more comfortable, you may regard me as a member of your own sex."

Roon frowned in confusion. "Huh?"

"It means it's a boy," Ragna clarified. "And that's enough questions from you, young gnome. Wingnut came here to tell us something."

"Yes. First, I am to tell you that Rudger is well and sends his regards."

"How are his parents? And his grandparents on his father's side?"

"I'm not quite sure. When I flew over Old Drungle Town, it seemed very still. My guess is it's still quarantined."

"Quarantined?" Ragna asked. "Gnomes' homes, whatever for?"

"Ah, so you haven't heard. It seems Rudger's grandparents did not suffer simultaneous strokes as originally thought. They are, in fact, among the earliest victims of the Mute-ation."

"The what?"

"The Mute-ation," Wingnut repeated. "A mysterious malady which renders its victims mute and largely unresponsive. Only habitual behaviors seem to remain."

"Oh. Poor Ridna. And Rondo, too. I had no idea. I guess this Mute-ation hasn't reached the Hinters."

"Yet," appended Wingnut. "It seems to be spreading among gnomish circles. The human population is affected, too."

"Wait a minute," Ragna said with a scowl. "You said you flew *over* Old Drungle Town. Does that mean Rudger isn't there?"

"It does," the orange creature confirmed. "He is currently two leagues northeast of the city at a cabin in the woods."

"How did he get there?"

"Through a series of misadventures and mishaps, I gather.

Something to do with his father being abducted and Rudger's unwitting defiling of the True Hues."

"His father's been gnome-napped? Rondo isn't in Old Drungle Town, either?"

"No. Rondo's whereabouts are unknown."

Ragna paused in contemplation. "That's awful, but the news about the Hues isn't. I hate those four shades of brown."

"I noticed. May I compliment you on your robustly vivid apron?"

"You may, although it is something like complimenting yourself. I've always fancied creatures who aren't afraid to show their true colors. Orange, especially."

"In my case, I seem to have little choice. But we digress. During his stay at the aforementioned cabin, Rudger has come to believe that there exists a sword which might be a critical link in curing the Mute-ation, a sword your family is most familiar with."

"You mean Vic?"

"Yes. The sword forged to human scale by your father. Rudger tells me it harbors a most peculiar magical property."

"'Most troublesome' would be more accurate. That sword brought me nothing but grief in my youth."

"Yes, but I am afraid it is imperative we learn more about it. Rudger did not seem to have all the details."

"Well, that's because I don't usually talk about it."

"So what are these troublesome properties, as you put it?"

Still in a seated position, Ragna rocked backward and stretched out her arms to support herself. "Vic—or Vicarius, to use its full name—is a very unusual sword. It bears a charm that renders it unusable in battle."

"Go on."

"As I found out firsthand, anyone who seeks to strike an opponent with Vic becomes subject to a powerful switching charm."

"I'm sorry. Did you say 'switching' charm?"

"Yes. It has the power to drag the spirit out of any wielder and deposit it into his foe's body. In turn, the foe's spirit ends up transported into the aggressor's body."

Wingnut's wings fluttered excitedly, raising him from the bippup leaf. "That *is* a powerful magic." Then he settled back onto the leaf heavily. "But only for one strong enough to wield such a blade."

"Ah, but that is another aspect of its magic," explained the gnomette. "The sword is bewitched to be feather-light."

Abruptly, Wingnut was in the air again, this time zipping about as he had done during their brief battle. "Feather-light? Feather-light? Are you quite sure of this?"

Ragna frowned at the newt's antics. "Well, yes. I daresay just about any creature could lift it. Why is that so important?"

Wingnut seemed to settle down again. "Um, it's not. It's just curious, that's all. Now, Rudger said you gave the sword away. It is imperative we locate it. The fate of the Land of Lex may depend on it. Do you know where it might be found today?"

"I'm not sure. It's been thirty years, but dragons do tend to hold onto things. Especially this particular dragon."

Wingnut's entire body was vibrating before her eyes. "Dragon? Which dragon?"

Ragna's frown deepened. "Are you sure Rudger sent you?"

"Yes, yes! Fifteen-year-old chap. Has a way with words.

Writes them down in that Logofile of his. With a quill he stows behind his ear. Now, what about this dragon?"

Ragna looked askance at the agitated creature. He was so worked up that tiny tendrils of smoke were escaping from his nostrils.

"I think maybe I've said enough," Ragna said slowly. "Maybe you could go back to Rudger and ask him to let you bring me that quill of his. Just to make sure he really… did…send…"

Her voice trailed off as the newt rose from the leaf and drew close. His yellow eyes captured hers; they sparkled like a pair of mystic gems—the kind humans went on great quests to acquire.

"The dragon," the hovering newt said evenly. "His name."

"He's…not a dragon. Exactly. He's a…wyvern."

"Aunt Ragna?"

"His name. Speak his name."

"Aunt Ragna? What's going on?"

Roon was on his feet, hanging close and looking back and forth between Ragna and the newt. Ragna shivered when the orange reptile broke eye contact in order to direct a spurt of fire at her concerned nephew.

"Back off, 'ling," the newt hissed. Then his hypnotic eyes gathered up the whole of Ragna's attention once again.

"You were about to tell me the wyvern's name."

"N-n-no. No, I wasn't," she said weakly.

The winged newt edged in closer. His voice was Ragna's entire world.

"Could it be…*Herald?*" he whispered.

The dregs of defiance holding Ragna's tongue melted away. "Yes."

The cunning creature did a loop-the-loop, breaking his hold on Ragna. The gnomette sprang to her feet and pulled the trowel from her apron pocket. Wingnut flew out of range.

"Thank you for your help, Miss Ragna," he said as he did a victory spiral in the air. "You've done a very great service. I'll be sure to give Rudger your warmest regards."

With one last aerial trick, the winged newt soared up and over the arachna bushes' outstretched branches.

Roon was the first to recover his tongue. "Are you all right, Aunt Ragna?"

The gnomette shook her head vigorously to dislodge the remnants of the newt's compel-spell.

"I think so, Roon," she answered. She looked up into the blue sky at the shrinking dot that was Wingnut. A shudder rippled up her spine.

"I pray to the Five Elements that Rudger will be, too."

CHAPTER NINETEEN

Princess Hildegarde had taken idle pleasure in imagining a glorious start to her maiden quest. A grand proclamation, complete with trumpeting heralds. Throngs of cheering well-wishers crowding her magnificently outfitted charger. A score of attendant knights, oath-bound to protect her royal personage. And, best of all, a bricklebark bow and fine blunderhide quiver presented to her by the King himself.

She sighed miserably as the village baker's rickety cart trundled down the rutted dirt road, tossing her about like a leftover sack of flour. Her stomach heaved with the lurching movement, her queasiness made worse by the heat trapped under the burlap drape that concealed her. It was a merciful relief when the cart at last came to a wobbly stop.

Hildegarde waited while the baker unhitched his donkey and led it away. Rolling out from under the drape, she retrieved her rucksack and flipped its flap open to inspect its contents. The wizard's hourglass was still intact, but its sand was a disconcerting shade of green. As she watched, a plume of the sickly green grains shot from its lower bulb to its upper. The embarrassed hourglass bent one of its three metal support rods like an arm to cover its vomitous indiscretion.

"I know how you feel, Minsec," she said, using the name she'd given the animated timepiece. "Thank Lunira, we've made it to Little Lexicon. Look behind us. There's the…castle..."

Her voice trailed off as she gazed up and over dozens of red thatched roofs at the great stone edifice to the north. In all her fourteen years, the Princess had only left the castle twice, and never without a royal retinue. The alarm her escape would surely cause pressed in upon her.

No, she scolded herself, squelching her burgeoning fear. She would not lose her nerve. For years, she'd craved a chance to prove herself, and at last it was upon her.

So it was with determination, and not fear, that the fugitive Princess looked upon her exalted home.

A gentle metallic clinking drew her eyes back to the rucksack. The hourglass was tapping Lendar's amulet with its support arm.

"We've got a job to do," she told the timepiece evenly, "and I'm going to do this first part without magic." She paused and then lowered her voice to a whisper. "Besides, there may be thieves afoot."

"Better thieves than stowaways."

Hildegarde rounded on the speaker, one hand jumping to the slingshot tucked into the waistband of her brown suede breeches. The rotund man put up two beefy hands.

"Whoa, now, missy," he said as if talking to his donkey. He eyed her with part concern, part amusement. "Don't you folks have jokes up at the castle?"

"What makes you think I came from the castle?" she asked.

The baker quirked a bushy eyebrow. "No disrespect, but I know how my cart rides when it's empty. Ol' Dex had his work cut out for him pulling the pair of us, even if it was downhill."

The man's empathetic grin and self-deprecating tap on his own protuberant belly took the sting out of his words.

Hildegarde returned his smile. "Please thank Dex for his noble service," she said. "My name is Hildie."

"And I'm Crager. The baker. As you can plainly see."

Hildegarde leaned forward and shook hands. "Delighted to make your acquaintance."

Crager's merry eyes flitted over the fringed suede ensemble Hildegarde was wearing. Its newly tanned hide crinkled slightly as she withdrew her hand.

"You a huntress? For the royal household?" he asked.

The Princess felt her heart skip a beat. In her rush to begin her quest, she'd failed to consider how she would represent herself to the commoners. Obviously, she couldn't tell them who she really was.

But a huntress? She was suddenly keenly aware of the poor cut of the clothes she'd commandeered. They had been fashioned for the castle's groundskeeper and so were long in sleeve and leg and tight about the middle. Hildegarde felt like an utter fraud. Who would believe her to be in service to the King?

A cry from the nearest cottage caught them both by surprise.

Crager reacted first, spinning on his heel and dashing into the building with far more speed than a man of his girth should be able to command. Hildegarde hurried after him.

Inside, she found the trappings of Crager's trade. An oversized fireplace dominated the far end of the room. Black-iron pots, pans, and trays littered worn wooden tabletops. Batter-smeared bowls, crusty rolling pins, and dirty utensils lay about, awaiting a wash after the frenzy of the morning bake.

Another high-pitched scream pierced the air.

Hildegarde caught sight of Crager's bulk disappearing through a narrow doorway near the fireplace. The Princess moved to follow but was distracted by something in her peripheral vision.

A black-shelled hackerpede was scuttling amongst large sacks of flour stacked on the floor. It froze as she drew her weapon, staring at her with beady, unblinking eyes.

Revulsion brought a shiver that threatened to spoil the Princess' aim, but it was the angle of the black monster's gaze that put Hildegarde on notice. She took a quick side-step deeper into the room.

Her instinct was sound. A second hackerpede fell from the ceiling, narrowly missing Hildegarde's head as it bounced off her right shoulder. It landed upside-down, providing the split-second the Princess needed to act.

A sickening crunch brought a grin of satisfaction to Hildegarde's lips. The beastie's bodily fluids seeped onto her boot as it writhed in shock. When it grew still, she turned her attention back to the first hackerpede.

It had vanished from sight.

Her eyes scoured the spot where it had leered at her as she worked her way around the large central table. The sounds of distress coming through the narrow doorway were no longer shrieks of terror. They had devolved into whimpering sobs punctuated by the odd thud or clatter.

Hildegarde stepped over the threshold into a common sleeping chamber. Therein, she saw Crager wielding a rolling pin, heroically defending two children against yet another of the black invaders. The little monster splayed its mouthparts aggressively as the man forced it to retreat to a wall beneath an open window.

The hackerpede reared up and flipped itself over. Using its little barbed legs, it scaled the wall with lightning speed. Crager yelled and hurtled his rolling pin at it, striking the spot where the 'pede had been only a second before. The flour-covered projectile ricocheted harmlessly away as the monster reached the sill.

Thock! An airborne stone hit the hackerpede in the side, propelling its glossy body across the sill and crushing it against the corner of the window.

It fell out of sight, and Hildegarde pursued. Her chase was unnecessary. The hackerpede's lifeless body lay in the grizzle-grass outside.

Crager whistled in admiration. "That cinches it," he declared. "You're a huntress, all right."

"So it would seem," Hildegarde replied as her eyes swept the room. They came to rest on the two young girls perched upon a cot, crowding a very still, prostrate figure. "Did the hackerpede do that?" she asked gently.

"No. One of its brothers Muted my poor wife weeks ago," the man reported with regret. "The hackerpede you killed was after my daughters."

"Hackerpedes," Hildegarde corrected as she paced toward the kitchen.

"Beg pardon?"

"Hackerpedes," she repeated. "At least three, though it appears the third has eluded me."

Crager gasped as he laid eyes on the stomped 'pede on the kitchen floor. Hildegarde employed his help to tear the bakery apart, but there was no sign of the escaped hackerpede save a tiny hole between the slate tiles beneath a flour sack.

"How can I thank you enough, dear lady?" Crager asked as he clutched his daughters, one to each side. "Would you accept your fill of dringleberry tarts as a humble reward for your service?"

"I would gladly accept them for later consumption," Hildegarde proposed. "With the battle just ended, I am not hungry at the moment."

"Nor will we be, for some time," Crager agreed. "Allow me to wrap the treats in cheesecloth for your travels."

Moments later, Hildegarde found herself stowing the proffered pastries in her rucksack. A glint of glass sparked an idea. She peered up from the sack's interior and eyed the pale, shaking girls.

"I have something here that might help you forget those nasty old 'pedes," she told them.

They looked at her shyly.

"How often do baker's daughters get to see a real wizard's

familiar, hmm?" Hildegarde continued. "Not often, I'd wager. And certainly never one as clever as this."

She lifted Minsec out of the sack and placed it on the stone floor. With an encouraging nudge of her foot, the sprightly timepiece began to dance a jig for the little girls. When she was certain they were fully absorbed by the hourglass' antics, Hildegarde turned to their father.

"I heard that the Mute-ation was plaguing Little Lexicon, but I had no idea how long." She glanced in the direction of the bedroom where Crager's wife lay. "Weeks, you said?"

"Yes," he confirmed. "Hardly a household has escaped its cursed touch."

"And you think this is linked to the hackerpedes?"

"By all accounts, yes. No one has actually caught the beasts in the act, but the trouble began when they appeared. Surely, this is not a coincidence."

The idea that some filthy hackerpede had caused Hildegarde's own mother's condition only deepened her hatred for them. "And no one has found a cure?"

"Nay. Once a person is stricken, he or she remains unresponsive, unable to speak or understand. I keep telling the girls it's only temporary, but when I see how the light's gone out of poor Della's eyes, I…"

Grief choked off Crager's words. Hildegarde felt for the man, but she forced herself to press on.

"Crager, I have been sent to end this curse, but my mission is a secret. The King would likely stop me if he knew of it."

"Stop you? Why wouldn't the King want you to help us?"

"It's complicated," she told him. "Trust me when I say I have information that King Emmett does not. But I need help to act on this information. Do you think you could provide some?"

The baker pinched his lips in determination. "Anything I have is at your disposal."

"What I need presently is a mount."

"A mount?" he repeated uncertainly. "Well, you're welcome to take old Dexter, out back. He's reliable all right, though not very swift."

Hildegarde placed a hand on Crager's shoulder. "I wouldn't think of depriving you of Dex," she assured him. "You need him to make your trips to the castle. I need a horse, and I was wondering how I might acquire one."

Crager looked troubled. "Well, there's a horse trader lives a scant half-league south of the village. He might sell you a horse for a fair price."

"Might he consider bartering for one?" Hildegarde asked. "I carry no gold at the moment."

"Perhaps," the baker said slowly. "Gedd's a shrewd sort of fellow. But what do you have to barter with? Not your magical hourglass, I hope."

"Oh, no," Hildegarde replied. "I need Minsec as a guide. I have something better in mind. *Much* better."

When at last a small, weather-beaten shack came into view, Hildegarde felt certain she had misconstrued the baker's simple directions. She had, indeed, traveled south on the King's highway, for the castle was little more than a speck behind her, but the wretched hovel she now approached seemed in no way a passable horse farm. And yet, as Hildegarde drew near, she was able to make out nine woe-begotten nags loitering in a fenced pen that was scarcely big enough for one.

Hildegarde trudged through high grasses and thorny patches of duchess-bloomers toward the horse-trader's ramshackle establishment. She carried before her a tray of cinnamon buns which Crager had insisted she take.

"You don't want to encounter Gedd without something to sweeten his disposition," he'd told her. "If there's one pastry I'm known for, it's my schnecken. Just think of these as an invitation to do business with you."

It sounded more like a bribe to Hildegarde, but she took the buns and the advice. Now she found herself balancing the tasty tribute on one hand while she knocked on a splintering door with the other.

"Mr. Gedd?" she called when no one answered. "Mr. Gedd, I wish to bargain with you."

Still no answer came, and with each passing moment, Hildegarde became increasingly tempted to penalize the horse-trader for the delay by reducing his bribe by a schnecke or two. The tantalizing aroma of the fresh buns was becoming harder and harder to resist, but before the penalty could be levied, the battered door swung inward just enough to allow an eye to peer out.

"Begone," its owner ordered. "We ain't open fer business today."

"Ah, but look," Hildegarde said, passing the tray of buns by the narrow crack. "I bring a gift so that we may enter cordial negotiations."

The eye moved closer to the crack and looked her up and down. "What manner of person are yeh?" the voice rasped. "Don't look like a villager, yeh don't."

"I am a huntress in service to the King," she answered, warming up to the persona she'd adopted. "And I am in need of a horse."

"Where's yer bow?"

The persona faltered. "Uh,…my bow?"

"Yeah. Long curvy thing. Shoots arrows."

"Oh, my bow! Well,… I, uh,…I don't have it with me just now."

The eye narrowed. "If yeh don't have no bow, yeh won't be hunting much, will yeh? So I reckon yeh won't be needing no horse, neither."

The door began to close.

On impulse, Hildegarde jammed her foot into the shrinking gap. "Mr. Gedd, you mustn't refuse me," she said quickly. "You *can't*, actually."

"How's that?"

"Well,…I…I am Princess Hildegarde, daughter of Prince Geoffrey of the Land of Lex. And *as* your Princess, I order you to provide me a horse."

This wasn't the tack she'd been planning to use, but Gedd's curt dismissal had forced her to play the princess card.

To her utter bewilderment, he began to laugh at her.

"A princess, is it, now?" he said between guffaws. "Hefty thing like you? That's even crazier than the hunter thing." His demeanor suddenly went dark. "Clear off, 'Princess.'"

Sarcasm dripped from that last word, and Hildegarde found herself pressing the issue.

"I can prove it," she said, trying not to convey the anger and desperation she felt. "I was sent by Lendar the Wizard to beguile a dragon and reclaim a sword from its hoard. If you give me a horse now so I may complete my quest, I shall reward you handsomely with its gold."

"That ain't proof," the man growled. "That's a pack of lies told to get a horse. Now get yer fool foot outta this door, or I'll crush it, see?"

Hastily, Hildegarde withdrew the foot and bent to place the tray of buns on the ground. "I *do* have proof, Mr. Gedd," she insisted as she grabbled about in her rucksack. "I-I can understand why you don't believe I'm a princess looking like this, but I'm under an enchantment so no one will recognize me. And all I have to do to cancel the disguise is to put on this amu —What? Hey! Let go of that!"

Curiosity must have kept Gedd at his door while Hildegarde fought for control of Lendar's amulet. Minsec had hooked a support arm around its chain and was resisting Hildegarde mightily.

"Argh! You little imp!" she cried as she battled to extract the amulet and hourglass as one from the sack. Breathing heavily, she went to work prying Minsec's metallic arm off the amulet's golden chain, only to discover the timepiece had doubled down with its other two appendages.

"Fine!" Hildegarde exclaimed. She jammed her head through the chain, leaving Minsec hanging from it like an enormous pendant.

The peeved Princess felt a peculiar serenity settle over her as the magic did its work. Her hands and arms went slender and smooth just as they had in the wizard's tower. A glance down the length of her body revealed now-dainty feet encased in lovely tan slippers. Her suede hunting outfit had been transformed into a golden-brown gown that hugged her shapely torso and revealed a bit more ankle than her mother would have approved of. A gasp of delight passed through her lips before she remembered her audience.

Gedd, however, seemed equally transfixed. The middle-aged man had opened his door fully and now stood before Hildegarde, his mouth slightly agape. The magic of the amulet had done nothing to improve *his* looks. A squashed-pear nose, yellowed teeth, and ragged scar coursing over his jaw and neck aptly complemented his harsh, gravelly voice. His thick, muscular arms hung loosely at his sides, the left one brushing up against a horsewhip tucked into his waistband. His gray eyes gazed at her in astonishment.

"There you have it," Hildegarde said in her silky new voice. "Instant Princess."

The man jerked out of his stupor. "Uh, yes, Yer Majesty! My apologies, Yer Majesty. If I'd known about that trinket of yers, I would've been more accommodating, I would. Please, please, follow me to the yard. Yer welcome to yer pick of the lot."

Hildegarde could scarcely believe the change in Gedd's attitude as he led the way. She grinned down at Minsec, who was still dangling from the necklace. "See?" she whispered. "The amulet worked. I was right."

The hourglass responded by spewing up vomit-colored sand. Hildegarde rolled her eyes and tucked the peevish timepiece under her arm.

"Nine fine specimens to choose from, Yer Highness,"

Gedd said as he opened the gate and gestured for her to enter first.

Hildegarde made a tiny curtsey as she'd seen Winifer do a thousand times before. Then she stepped into the crowded pen to inspect the merchandise.

All nine horses turned out to be female. By the looks of their teeth, not one of them was as young as Hildegarde herself. A disappointing array, but one would have to do. She was about to announce her choice when a piteous whinny caught her attention.

"What about that one?"

"Which?"

"The white gelding tied to the hitching post."

Gedd chuckled derisively. "Yeh don't want that brute, miss. He's bull-headed, that one."

Hildegarde frowned and gently pushed her way through the mares to approach the gelding. He was clearly the finest horse of the group, young and fit, with a keen intelligence in his nut-brown eyes.

"Yer Highness, please," cajoled the merchant. "Take any of the others yeh please. They'll serve yer purposes well, and yeh won't even have to come back to pay me."

She turned to look at him. "Beg pardon, did I catch your meaning correctly? Are you saying you're willing to gift me any of the mares?"

Gedd smiled. "Would if I could, but I'm only a poor horse-trader. Can't be giving up my stock for free and stay in business, now, can I?"

"Then we are back where we started. I shall have to return and pay you from the dragon's gold."

"Ah, but there's a problem with that," said Gedd, his smile widening to reveal even more of his crooked yellow teeth. "See, what yer asking fer is credit. And me old pap learned me that a good businessman never risks giving credit when he doesn't have to."

A pinch on her side diverted Hildegarde's attention. Minsec's sand had gone bright yellow and was swirling anxiously.

When she looked back up, the horse-trader had moved closer.

"But, sir," she said nervously. "I am a Princess of the realm. I assure you my credit is good. And, besides, I have nothing to offer you as payment at this time."

"Oh, now that just ain't quite true, is it?" the man said, his eyes alight with greed. "Yeh got that necklace there. A magic necklace that would fetch a right nice price, I'd wager."

Hildegarde took a step back. "Y-you misunderstand, sir. I need this amulet to complete my quest."

"Yeh don't say."

"I do, in fact. And it's not even mine to give. I told you Lendar the Wizard gave it to me. Loaned it, actually. He... he'd be very upset if I didn't deliver it back to him."

"Well, ain't that a shame?" the horse-trader said quietly. "Guess yeh'll have to explain yeh had no choice in the matter."

The man's hand shot forward, fingers lacing themselves around the amulet's chain. A hard tug wracked Hildegarde's now-slender neck, but the sturdy links held.

Hildegarde tried to use her one free arm to fend off the attack, but she hadn't the strength to oppose her aggressor. He grasped her arm with his other hand and delivered a second yank on the chain which cut sharply into her delicate skin.

"Now, why don't yeh be a good little lass and slip that necklace off for me? It'd be a right pity to rip yer pretty head off to free it."

Hildegarde continued to fight. A third jerk, the most savage yet, loosed a cry of pain from her throat. She dropped Minsec and used both thin arms to beat at the man's chest and face. A well-placed jab caught him in the eye.

He grunted but did not let go of her. "That there was a mistake, girlie," he declared with an evil grin. "I've been nice up to now, but the gloves are comin' off, see?"

He backhanded the Princess, and she screamed—a shrill sound that spooked the nearby mares. The gelding, however, was otherwise affected.

Quick as lightning, the horse advanced and made a downward slashing motion with his head. A wicked gash opened up on the horse-trader's right shoulder. The man howled in pain, releasing Hildegarde to turn and face his new foe. He drew the whip from his waistband.

"I'll teach you, yeh worthless hack!" he raged, lashing the animal across the nose. "You *will* fear me, yeh hear?"

Hildegarde had fallen; she scuttled backward, crablike, away from the conflict between man and beast. Somehow, the horse opened another wound on his owner's left forearm, though the Princess never saw a point of contact between them. Gedd whipped the horse again and again, cursing a blue streak and apparently forgetting all about his original victim.

Something cool and hard tapped the Princess' elbow. It was Minsec, waving its support arms to urge their escape.

But Hildegarde couldn't let the evil man beat the white horse so cruelly. She sneaked up behind the abuser and, with a high-pitched cry, leapt onto Gedd's wide back.

Her weight encumbered him sufficiently to interrupt the merciless whipping. He twisted this way and that, trying to dislodge the girl, but she held fast. Gedd began to run backward, a move Hildegarde had not anticipated. By the time she worked out his intent, it was too late.

Wham! Hildegarde's back slammed into the withers of one of the mares, knocking the wind from the girl's lungs and the strength from her arms. She dropped to the ground as a tremendous *crack* announced the demise of the pen's old wooden fence. A stampede of hooves rained down around Hildegarde as the mares made good their escape.

"I wasn't planning to kill yeh, missy," Gedd growled with malice, "but now I see I have to." He raised his whip. "What a waste."

His massive arm tensed to deliver the blow. Before it could complete the movement, a terrific metallic pop was heard, followed by a cry of agony as a hole opened in Gedd's broad chest. How the gelding made the puncture was a mystery to Hildegarde, but it had a devastating effect on the man, dropping him to his knees.

The gelding leapt over the wounded horse-trader, but instead of seeking his freedom, he stopped beside Hildegarde. His soft brown eyes regarded her expectantly; his knees flexed with urgency.

The Princess caught his meaning. "You want me to ride on your back?"

The gelding tossed his head in assent, chuffing his impatience. With effort, Hildegarde got to her feet and picked up her hourglass friend and rucksack. Then, wincing with pain, she climbed upon her kneeling mount.

The dazzling white horse rose to his feet and galloped out of the pen into the awaiting forest.

CHAPTER TWENTY

"Kal? Kal, slow down!" Twelda shouted at the receding form in front of her. "Rudger and I can't keep up!"

The long-limbed human paid her no heed, continuing to cover the better part of a yard with each of his gigantic strides. Rudger Rump watched as the towering boy bore down on a fallen canfa tree and vaulted its enormous trunk in a single bound.

"Show-off," Twelda grumbled as the selfsame log loomed high upon their approach. "He *knows* we're going to have to go around this thing." She veered to the right. "Come on. This way's fastest."

But Rudger grasped Twelda's arm.

"I…I…can't," he gasped as he dragged her to a stop. "I have to…rest…a minute."

"You've got to be kidding," she complained. "He'll leave us behind!"

Rudger's response was to stagger the rest of the way to the log and flop his left shoulder and head against it.

"Ugh!" groused the gnomette. "Fine. If you can't run anymore, then do something to stop him."

The exhausted gnome closed his eyes. "What…do you want…me to do?" he panted.

"I don't know! How about whipping up another windstorm and blowing him back here? Or put a trip hex on him. That'd serve him right."

"Twelda, you know I can't call up…magic like that." He drew in a huge breath and exhaled slowly. "And I wouldn't hex Kal even if I could."

"Why not? He deserves it, running off at the crack of dawn without telling us. That wasn't the plan! We were supposed to wait for Wingnut at the cabin."

"In fairness, Wingnut's kind of late getting back," Rudger pointed out as he straightened his head and looked at the gnomette. "He was supposed to return last night. Maybe Kal got so worried about Vermis he couldn't stand to wait any longer."

Twelda scoffed. "Kal didn't seem too worried when Vermis was muted. Why would he suddenly feel compelled to take off and find Vic the sword on his own? Besides, we all agreed we need facts from your aunt before we act. The story she told you is full of holes. Some dragon *might* be living south of the Hinters, and it *may* have a sword called Vic which could *possibly* have great magical powers to heal Vermis. That's not much to go on."

Rudger set his hands on his hips. "It's all I could remember," he said defensively.

Twelda started to pace.

"But do these supposed powers include un-Muting magic? Maybe we *should* try my jawjackle juice on Vermis. And where exactly is this dragon's lair? What if it's relocated in the past thirty years? Wingnut might be able to answer these questions, but we didn't wait for him. And *why* are we assuming the consumption trail Vermis left on that page has anything to do with this sword? The letters V-I-C could stand for a hundred other things!"

"Like what?" Rudger asked.

Twelda stopped pacing and jerked her eyes in the direction of the wizard boy's disappearance. "How about, 'Very Irritating Companion' for a start?"

Rudger half-giggled, half-snorted. "Better not let Kal hear you call him that. He might zap you."

"What, and give me a beard to match yours? I'm not too concerned." She craned her neck to peer over the trunk. "*Because he's leagues away by now!*"

The frustrated gnomette dropped into a cross-legged position and lapsed into a sulky silence.

Rudger took the opportunity to check on his passenger. He looked down at Vermis, who was cradled in a sling Twelda had cleverly woven into Rudger's profusion of whiskers. The young gnome was glad to see that the little bookworm had secured himself by embedding his legs into the hairy hammock. It was the first sign since Vermis' Muting that he was even vaguely aware of the events transpiring around him.

Rudger was trying to figure out how to seat himself without disturbing the bookworm when Twelda's shoulders fell and she let out a noisy sigh.

"I'm sorry for being such a troll about this," she apologized. "It's just what we're doing here is illogical. I get irritable when things aren't planned out."

Rudger laughed. "Try living with triplet siblings. You get used to chaos."

Twelda got up and sighed again. "Guess there's no going back now. We're a really long way from the cabin. I just hope Wingnut will be able to find us—preferably before we find that dragon."

An hour passed as Twelda and Rudger hiked through the forest in search of their human acquaintance. None of their calls had reached Kal's ears, or if they had, he'd ignored them. And since neither of the Humdrungles was a skilled tracker, they had turned up no trace of the boy's flight through the forest.

"Are you sure we're going the right direction?" Rudger asked for the umpteenth time. "I thought we were supposed to be heading southwest."

"We *are* heading southwest," Twelda chided. "How many times do I have to tell you to use the sun for guidance?"

Rudger squinted as he looked up at the great glowing orb known as Helios. "It's directly overhead now," he observed. "Without any shadows, how can you be sure we haven't gone off course?"

"Because I can hear the river. Can't you?"

Rudger concentrated and found that he could.

"Well, that proves we've gone west," he admitted, "but not

necessarily south. Shouldn't we have reached Old Drungle Town by now?"

"You aren't very observant, are you?" Twelda said. "We passed the jawjackle bush near my burrow twenty minutes ago."

Rudger halted abruptly. "What? Why did you say anything? I want to see my mother. And my grandparents."

Twelda stopped and faced him. "And I would've liked to stop at my burrow for more supplies, but that isn't wise with the Mute-ation running rampant through the city, is it?"

"It'd only be a quick trip through the tunnels, Twelda. That couldn't do any harm."

"I told you before we left Drungle Town—your grandparents' burrow is quarantined; you couldn't get in if you tried. And don't forget there's a very angry Sergeant Sartorio who would love to get his hands on us after that fracas in the Standards chamber."

Rudger was crestfallen, but it didn't dull his logophilia. He pulled his quill from behind his ear and carefully circumvented his beard to fish the notebook out of his jerkin pocket. "Fracas," he said experimentally. "That's a cool word. What does it mean?"

Twelda rolled her eyes. "Ever the wordsmith, huh? It means a fight or a debacle."

"Oh, I've got that word here somewhere," he said, quickly turning the pages. "Ha! 'Debacle, a violent commotion or upheaval.' Now, I'll write 'fracas' right beside that." He hesitated, the quill hovering over the parchment. "Um, how do you spell that?"

"F-R-A...uh,...Gosh, what was that?"

"What?"

"I thought I saw a blunderelk through those shrubs. We'd better get moving."

Rudger looked where she'd indicated. He hurried after her. "I didn't see anything."

"You wouldn't. Blunderelk are sneaky."

"How sneaky can they be?" Rudger challenged. "They're almost as big as Kal's cabin."

"You're exaggerating."

"Well, you're making things up." He thought a moment and then put two-and-two together. "You don't know how to spell 'fracas,' do you?"

"Don't be ridiculous."

"Then why won't you tell me how to spell it?"

"Because I'm the navigator of this quest, not a dictionary! Ask Vermis how to spell it. *He's* supposed to be your tutor."

Rudger stopped, hard hit by her words. He looked down at the vermitome, who seemed utterly oblivious to the conversation.

A moment later, Twelda placed a comforting hand on his shoulder. "You can't keep blaming yourself," she said gently. "It would've happened whether you two fought or not."

"Maybe," Rudger said dejectedly, "but if we hadn't fought, Vermis might have come with us, and then…"

"Life is full of might-haves, but we're powerless to change the past. We can, however, affect the future, which is why we're on this cockamamie quest. So let's get on with it and help poor Vermis." Twelda paused for effect. "What do you say?"

Rudger flipped a couple of pages in his Logofile.

"I say, how do you spell 'cockamamie?'"

Twelda shook her head. "You're incorrigible, you know that?"

"That's three in a row! I can barely keep up!"

Twelda groaned and walked on.

Ten minutes later, they were both standing on the east bank of the River Gush. Rapidly flowing water lay between them and the marshlands of the Hinters which contained Rudger's aunt's burrow. His longing to see Rani, Roni, and Roon was tempered by imagining his poor aunt's plight. She may have raised eight of her younger siblings, but that was a walk in the swamp compared to babysitting the Terror Trio.

Twelda broke in on his musings.

"If you look way to the north, you can see the cliffs near the sea," she told him, pointing to their right. "Those dots above the treetops are the towers of the King's castle. Beyond them is water as far as the eye can see."

She directed him to look the other way. "A little less than a league south of here, the landscape starts to rise again, forming bluffs that are riddled with caves and grottoes. It's dragon country. If that dragon of yours has Vic, it'll be there."

Rudger looked at Twelda. Her profile was strong and assured as she gazed at their ultimate destination.

"Twelda, how do you know so much about the Land of Lex?" he asked, suddenly a bit in awe of her.

She looked back with a smirky smile. "You'd be surprised how much a scientist like me gets around."

Embarrassed by the closeness of the moment, Rudger

averted his eyes and made a show of scanning the river in both directions. "I don't see Kal anywhere around. Do you suppose we've beaten him here?"

"Hard to say," Twelda replied. "He sure was running fast when we last saw him. Too fast, I've been thinking."

"What do you mean?"

"I mean, I think Kal really *was* trying to ditch us up at his cabin. And when we caught him trying to sneak away, he lost us by using magic."

"Magic? How?"

"Probably by casting some sort of speed charm on himself."

Rudger stroked a few loose strands of his beard as he considered what she'd said. "Hmm. I figured he was so fast because he's got really long legs."

"So do other humans, but I've never seen them run so fast for so long. We Humdrungles can't beat them in a sprint, but we usually have better endurance."

Rudger shrugged. "I wouldn't know. Aside from Kal, I've only ever encountered two other humans in my life. One was chasing me, and the other was being chased *by* me, but I can't remember either one."

Twelda looked thoughtful. "You know, that old wizard you tackled at Gnomister's Knoll was huge. And Kal seemed every bit as tall as that this morning, even if we did only see him from a distance." She grinned with satisfaction. "I *told* you he seemed bigger yesterday than the day we met him. And he was definitely bigger than that today."

"Is that normal for humans? To shoot up several inches in a day, I mean?"

"It doesn't seem scientifically plausible. But we *are* talking about a wizard boy, here. And speaking of wizardry, do you happen to have any tricks for getting across this river?"

Rudger looked again at the racing currents before him. "I don't know," he said slowly. "Vermis told me I somehow stiffened the water to get across last time, but I can't remember because of the amnesioak fracas." He grinned at Twelda.

"Cute," she said cocking her head. "But 'debacle' would've been better there."

"Anyway, I guess I'm capable of some sort of Water magic, but I have no idea how I did it."

"Well, did Vermis tell you what Weird Wyrd you used?"

Rudger slapped his forehead. "Of course, he did. I wrote it in my new notebook."

He pulled the Logofile back out of its pocket and scanned through dozens of real words and their roots to find the Wyrd.

Twelda peered over his shoulder and made a tutting noise. "Don't you organize your notes at all?" she asked.

"Hey! This is wizard's work. No scientists allowed."

"Whatever. But if it were my file, I'd at least alphabetize my entries. And maybe put asterisks by the magic Wyrds that worked for me in the past."

"Well, it's not your file. I happen to have my own system here, and I'll thank you not to criticize it."

"Why should I criticize? I mean, it obviously works so well."

Several minutes passed as Rudger continued his search.

Twelda forced a yawn. "You know, if this were an emergency, we'd be dead by now."

"Ah, ha! Here it is. Should've known it would start with *hydro-*. That means 'water,' by the way."

"I know what it means," Twelda said scathingly. "Science-gnomettes know all about hydrology. There's hydrostatics, and hydroponics, and hydrodynamics, and hydrokinetics—"

"Twelda—"

"—and hydrometamorphism, and hydrolysis, and hydroplaning, and—"

"Twelda, please—"

"—and hydrotherapy, and hydrophobia, and hydrocephalus, and hydrops fetalis, and—"

"Twelda, pinch 'em!" Rudger shouted in frustration. "The Wyrd isn't any of those!"

The gnomette pursed her lips in irritation. "Well, excuse me for trying to help. What is this precious Wyrd, anyway?"

"I can't tell you. The more people who know it, the less power it will have."

"Fine," Twelda said, insulted. "Give me your notebook for safekeeping and go meditate on your special Wyrd. I'll just sit over there."

"Fine," Rudger said as he hunkered down at the water's edge. When the negative energy of the spat had passed, he closed his eyes and probed his mind for the elusive window to the font of magical power.

Hydroscleros, he thought with intensity, imagining the Wyrd boring though the fabric of his mind. *Hydroscleros. Hydroscleros*.

But the weft of his mind would not be warped. It remained as tightly woven as the Gnomister's fine suit clothes.

"Sorry, Twelda," he said in defeat. "I can't—"

A powdery substance assaulted him, and a firm shove sent him tumbling into the shallows. He rose, water streaming from his eyes, and prepared to express his outrage. Before he could, he heard a loud click and the heat of a flame held close to his right cheek. He also heard a puffing noise accompanied by a stream of air striking his left cheek.

"Why in the Fifth Element are you blowing on me like that?" he cried as his vision cleared.

Twelda was brandishing the fire-flinger and puffing out her cheeks.

"Ugh!" Rudger went on. "And *what* did you have for breakfast? Your breath stinks!"

Twelda stopped blowing long enough to speak. "Try it again. The Elements—I think you need all four!"

Suddenly, he remembered her Eleminator experiment—Water in the buckets, Air in the form of storm wind, Earth pouring over him, Fire everywhere. He settled his mind into its mental search once again. This time, he felt the Source.

Hydrosceros!

As the water about his feet grew firm, he flung the image of a boat at the Source. The skiff of solid water expanded, its edges a constant blur of construction and erosion. The effort of shaping the spell brought sweat to Rudger's brow, but the beads of moisture he provided seemed to strengthen the magic. The mass of solidified water turned up at the edges, droplet coalescing upon crystal, over and over, until the form of a translucent boat was complete.

Straining to maintain the spell, Rudger risked a glance at his friend. Twelda had fled from the Water and was now standing some twenty feet away, frozen with awe.

"Get in!" Rudger urged her. "I don't know how long I can keep this thing together!"

Twelda gave a start and came rushing toward him. She hesitated slightly as she tested the bottom of the impossible boat with her foot. It held.

"We don't have any oars," she said as she climbed the rest of the way in.

"We don't need them," Rudger told her through gritted teeth. With a willful surge of mental energy, he pushed the hydroboat off the shore.

The ride was rocky, but sound. The raging currents slammed the port side of the boat, but any damage done to the writhing water-glass hull was instantly repaired as the offending waves solidified and became part of its structure. Twelda breathed heavily as Rudger guided the boat past the midpoint of the river.

"We're drifting north," Rudger reported as the marshlands before him slid to his left. "We'll have to walk back up the bank a bit."

"Don't talk!" Twelda cried in a strangled sort of way. "Just concentrate!"

Gradually, they bested the current, inching ever closer to the riverbank. Rudger was just daring to feel a sense of victory when he heard Twelda scream.

He turned, struggling mightily to keep the inconstant boat

intact. A tentacle of a most shocking apple-green hue had thrown itself over the tiny boat, its suckers endeavoring to attach themselves to Twelda's forcefully retracted legs.

The hideous appendage slid backward into the water, allowing its end to be dragged up into the boat. To Rudger's disgust, the mottled thing ended in seven slender tentaclettes, giving it the disturbing appearance of a mangled green hand with too many digits.

Twelda screamed again, and the combined visual and auditory distractions shook Rudger's tenuous hold on the Source. The beast tossed a second and third tentacle over the vessel, at bow and stern, and began to squeeze. The magically adherent water droplets lost their cohesiveness as the tentacles slid through. The boat disintegrated.

Again, Rudger found himself fighting for air as the wicked currents of the River Gush dragged and dunked him—but this time, there was the added peril of the marauding river monster. Its terrible tentacles ensnared him, its suckers pressing sickeningly against the bare skin of his arms and neck. The muscular green limb dragged him underwater, toward a gaping maw he could scarcely make out through the rushing water.

Then, suddenly, he was coughing, water draining away as he took in glorious gulps of air. The tentacle had pinned his arms to his sides, but its grip had loosened enough for him to twist about. When his sight cleared, his heart leapt in tenfold terror.

The green leviathan was airborne, catapulting both Twelda and himself into the Second Element along with it. Did the tentacled beast have wings? The answer came as Rudger's eyes picked up on violet scales pressed into the apple-green flesh of his captor. The gnome craned his neck to look above the bulbous head of the creature that held him. He and Twelda were not the only captives at the moment.

The great, green monster was hanging from the talons of an even greater purple dragon.

CHAPTER TWENTY-ONE

Princess Hildegarde was uncommonly adept at horsemanship. When astride, her bulky, awkward form seemed to melt into the rhythm of any horse's stride. But her equestrian skills availed her not as she was whisked, league after league, through the forests of Lex on the back of the white gelding. Try as she might, she could not settle herself into his peculiar gait, and without saddle or rein, it was all she could do to stay atop the runaway steed. Indeed, Hildegarde was faced with something she'd never encountered before, a horse with such strength and stamina that it could gallop farther than she could ride.

"Please," she begged as the young stallion powered on, "please, stop. I feel I may fall."

Incredibly, the horse responded, his pace gradually slackening to a halt. Her legs and back on fire, Hildegarde gratefully slid off the magnificent creature's back to the ground. Though she'd intended to stand before the great horse, her weary limbs refused to bear her weight. She collapsed into a clump of fairy's-breath ferns.

The young stallion stepped forth, nickering his concern as he nuzzled her cheek.

"Oh, I'm all right," she assured him, stroking his pearly mane. "Especially since you saved me from that awful man."

That was no man, dear lady.

Hildegarde's eyes widened as she peered into the equine's. The intelligence therein left no doubt about the source of the unspoken comment.

Still, the Princess found herself seeking confirmation. "You can talk, noble horse?"

The stallion made a scoffing sound.

I am no horse, he stated without speaking. *And, yes, I can communicate in human words, though to call it 'talking' is a simplification.*

Hildegarde felt herself go slightly faint.

"Purest white coat," she muttered to herself. "Stronger and swifter than any common horse, communicates telepathically…"

The haze of her fatigue suddenly cleared. She looked at the creature's forehead. "But no horn. Why don't you have a horn?"

Because I am not a unicorn, he explained.

"Then…what are you?"

Well, at the moment, I consider myself an un-*corn.*

Somehow, the fantastic creature managed to convey a whit of irony in his unspoken statement.

"An *un*-corn?" Hildegarde repeated. Then she gave a

weary smile of comprehension. "I understand. *Un-*, because you have no horn."

I sensed from the moment you stepped into Gedd's horsepen that ours would be a most enlightened acquaintance.

Hildegarde shivered as the memory of the gruesome assault flashed through her mind.

Take heart, milady. That creature of artifice shall trouble you no more.

"Creature of artifice?"

A changeling, the un-corn went on. *A creature which draws its magic from the darker aspects of the Earth Element. The real Gedd, I fear, was consumed in the process that generated that foul abomination.*

"I'm confused," admitted Hildegarde. "Why would such a creature want to impersonate a simple horse-trader?"

Gedd was more than a horsemonger, dear lady. He was a wizard, and a good one at that. 'Good' insomuch as he was kind—not powerful. He wielded no more magic than a common Earth wizard, or the changeling could not have overcome him.

"If the real Gedd was only a First-Element wizard, how did he manage to bind you?" Hildegarde asked. "I am no expert in magic, but it seems that Fourth-Element Fire magic would be required to hold a uni…" She stopped to correct herself. "...an *un*-corn such as yourself."

The fabulous beast snorted. *Who said I was being held against my will? I was there undercover.*

"Undercover?"

Certainly. I was investigating who was behind the dark magic.

"And did you find out?"

Alas, no. You forced me to blow my cover, remember?

"Oh. Right," Hildegarde said, looking down at her hands. "I'm dreadfully sorry about that."

Hush, dear one. There was a great profit in this turn of events. I, at long last, have found my maiden.

Hildegarde was slow to process the un-corn's declaration.

"Wait. *Me?*" she eventually laughed. "A uni-…I mean, an un-corn's maiden? Oh, no. You jest, surely."

The great beast dropped to his knees in an unmistakable gesture of reverence.

It is you, milady, for a creature of greater beauty I have ne'er encountered.

It was Hildegarde's turn to snort at the absurdity of the idea.

"You're crazy," she said with a dismissive flick of her wrist. "No one in his right mind would *ever…*"

Her protest died on her lips as she caught sight of her raised hand. Elegant and slender-fingered, she drew it slowly to her neck where Lendar's amulet lay.

"Oh, no," she began again in a completely different tone. "You don't understand. I…I'm not normally like this. I'm not fit to be your maiden. Not in the slightest."

The un-corn's nut-brown eyes regarded her mournfully. *Am I not the best judge of the maiden of my pledge?* he asked.

"Well, yes, I suppose so. But I told you, I *can't* be your maiden. I'm simply not maiden material."

You spurn me, then? I, who am unworthy of your affection?

"No! Look, you've got this all wrong. You're certainly worthy of any girl's affection. She'd be a fool to reject you."

Then I ask to lay my head in your lap, dear one. 'Twas a tiresome flight from your place of rescue.

"You…my…Oh, Helios! This is all wrong."

Let me assure you, nothing shall make my world more right.

The glorious un-corn lowered himself deftly to the ground and nestled his head into the folds of Hildegarde's golden-brown gown. With a combination of guilt and embarrassment, the Princess moved one hand to caress the magnificent beast's temple. His sigh of contentment pierced Hildegarde's troubled heart.

Her distress suddenly spawned a giggle. "Uh, you know, I generally prefer to be introduced to magical creatures *before* they use my lap as a pillow."

Fred, dear one. My name is Fred.

"Oh. Uh, okay. Fred. It's nice to make your acquaintance, Fred. I'm Hildegarde."

The un-corn did not respond as he reveled in the delights of Hildegarde's affections. At length, his breathing grew shallow, his head a bit heavier against Hildegarde's legs. The Princess looked down at the slumbering equine and blew out her cheeks.

"Hildegarde the Uncomely, and Fred the Un-corn," she muttered in bemusement. "Elements, what a pair we make."

We do, indeed, said Fred.

CHAPTER TWENTY-TWO

"EEEEeeeeEEEEeeeeEEEEeeee!"

"Twelda, *please*," Rudger Rump cried as he fought his own urge to scream. "How can I think up a Wyrd to save us with you making all that noise?"

"Bogs and boggarts, don't you think I have any dignity at all?" the gnomette yelled back as she dangled a short distance away. "*I'm* not making that awful racket!"

Rudger popped an eye open. Twelda was right. The shriek was emanating from the apple-green river monster whose tentacular grip on the two gnomes was the only thing preventing them from plunging a hundred feet into the river below. By the sound of it, the monster was every bit as terrified as Rudger.

"Uh, excuse me?" he shouted uncertainly over the thing's incessant wailing. "Could you just…stop that, please? I can't concentrate with you—"

"Ah. That explains it," interrupted a deep, rumbling voice.

The young gnome squeaked with fright and twisted about in the river monster's grip. A pair of yellow eyes set in a reptilian head regarded him with interest. The enormous purple cranium was suspended from a sinuous neck which arced upward to join the body of the dragon above.

"I was certain the Glynt I detected couldn't possibly belong to this polydactopus. Now, I see it's yours."

"P-poly-...dac-..."

"Polydactopus," the dragon repeated genially. "Or dactopus, for short. And there really isn't any point in trying to address it. A good-sized boulder has more sense than it does."

Rudger was straining to make out the dragon's words. The dactopus' screeching had amped up to a skull-cracking volume.

"My, but it does go on," the dragon tutted. "This is no way to carry on a civilized conversation. Allow me to put an end to its caterwauling." The head flicked briefly toward Twelda and then back to Rudger. "You folks wouldn't mind a little aerial maneuver, now, would you?"

The Humdrungle gnomes shot each other an anxious look.

"Pardon me," Twelda called out in trepidation, "but what kind of aerial maneuver do you have in mi-I-I-I-I-I-I-ND?"

Her question ended in a shriek as the dragon performed a barrel-roll and a half before launching dactopus and gnomes into the sky above. The river monster's tentacles loosened their grasp on Rudger and Twelda, sending them flying toward opposite riverbanks. The dactopus' scream continued as it began to fall.

A back-bending loop-the-loop centered the purple dragon under the plunging polydactopus. With a squelchy snap of the dragon's mighty jaws, the blood-curdling ululation ceased.

This allowed two smaller screams to be heard as Rudger and Twelda plunged toward the earth a field's-width apart. The dragon swallowed, flipped over, and banked right, executing a dive that positioned it perfectly beneath the plummeting gnomette. Her cry cut off as she dropped neatly onto the dragon's neck.

Rudger barely registered the impressive save, so occupied was he with the construction of a Wyrd of salvation.

"*Scleros*-air! *Scleros*-air! Air-*scleros*?" he cried in desperation. When the atmosphere failed to thicken and slow his descent, the would-be Logomancer cast out whatever Wyrd fragments his frantic mind could seize upon.

"*Ala generatum!*" But he sprouted no wings.

"*Gravitinverto!*" Gravity's pull did not reverse.

"Please, please! Anything!" he begged the Source as the cliffs rushed up to meet him. At last, he felt the faintest tug of inspiration. "*Barbanimus!* **Barbanimus**, I say!"

But the Wyrd held no power to stop his fall; the ground was close enough to make out the individual rock-spires that would spell his demise. He screamed anew, throwing his forearms over his eyes.

Fwizz!

Rudger's body slammed against a leathery surface. His hands clutched reflexively, catching the leading edge of the dragon's wing. The sharpness of its scales bit into his flesh, but the gnome held fast.

Together they spiraled, dragon and Humdrungles, as they searched for a place to land.

"There! There!" Twelda cried as a clearing fifty yards from the cliff's edge came into view.

"I shall have to make another pass, or we risk a crash landing," the dragon told them. Its head appeared in front of Rudger. "Can you hold on a bit longer?"

"Yes," Rudger replied through gritted teeth, "but, please, hurry!"

The punishing airstream over the dragon's wing threatened to rip Rudger's abused hands free, but the young gnome squeezed his eyes shut and thought of his mother, his siblings, his grandparents—all his kinfolk who were depending on him to return to them. Then he thought of his father, held by a human wizard in parts unknown with Rudger himself his only hope of rescue. Determination welled in the muscles of the young gnome's short arms. He found he had strength to spare as the great dragon's clawed feet at last touched the ground.

"Rudger!" said Twelda, now standing over him on the dragon's wing. "Rudger, you can let go now. Lunira's love, what a mess."

Rudger dared to relax his grip and opened his eyes to see fingers and palms streaked with blood. He stared at the wounds but felt no pain.

Twelda dug through her satchel, which she had somehow managed not to lose.

"Bilgreed root," she said as she used a canfa leaf to wipe away most of the blood. "A layer of this will take the sting out of those cuts."

"They don't hurt," Rudger informed her.

"They will if we don't cover them thoroughly." She rubbed the crushed root over Rudger's lacerations. "There. And these steamed canfa leaf bandages will speed up the healing process. You'll be much better by tomorrow."

"I must say I feel a certain culpability in your injuries," the dragon said to Rudger once the gnomes had hopped to the ground. "I felt sure you would conjure yourself to safety, so I concentrated my rescue efforts on the young lady."

"Oh, I'm Twelda, by the way," the gnomette broke in. "Twelda Greeze of Old Drungle Town. And all that matters is that you managed to keep us both alive. We thank you for that."

"You are entirely welcome."

She gave the dragon an appraising look. "You are an impressive aerialist, sir. But I must admit I feel much better being back on the ground. Guess I'd make a lousy dragon."

"As would I," the winged serpent replied. It flexed its magnificent purple wings one at a time and then stomped each of its two clawed feet. "Four appendages, not six. That makes me a wyvern, in the technical sense. A subspecies of the greater dragon family, but I prefer precision, whenever possible."

"Who wouldn't?" Twelda agreed. "I'd hate to be mistaken for an imp."

"And now to complete our introductions," said the wyvern. "It is an honor to make your acquaintance, Twelda Greeze of Old Drungle Town. My name is Herald."

"Herald!" interjected Rudger, slapping his forehead with a bandaged hand. "*That's* the name I couldn't remember before." He looked up at the great beast. "Are you the purple wyvern my aunt speaks so highly of?"

"How many purple wyverns do you suppose there are in

the Land of Lex?" the beast asked in reply. "And if I may inquire, who are you?"

"Oh, right. Introductions," the young gnome reminded himself. He looked back up at Herald and suddenly felt a certain shyness. "Uh,...I'm Rudger Rump, sir. Of the Hinterlands. I think you know my aunt, Ragna Riggle?"

"Bless my claws and scales! You're Ragna's nephew? How extraordinary. Though I do see the family resemblance."

"Really?" Rudger asked, pulling on a lock of his red hair.

"Oh, not in hair color," Herald said, chuckling mildly. "What I mean is, you seem to share her daring spirit."

"What makes you say that?"

"You took on a fully grown dactopus with nary a weapon. That borders on suicidal for a fellow your size. And Ragna? Well, let's just say I remember her performing more than her fair share of derring-do."

Rudger blushed. "Thank you, sir, but the way I recall it, there was a lot more screaming than derring-do going on back at the river."

"One does not necessarily preclude the other," Herald said obtusely. Then he frowned. "But as I recall, Ragna was not magically inclined. Nor are any of the Humdrungle gnomes, as far as I know. So where does that remarkable Glynt of yours come from?"

"I don't know," Rudger said with a sigh, "but it can go right back where it came from. Ever since it showed up, there's been nothing but trouble. I can't control this magic I've supposedly got. That's why I couldn't save myself up there."

The wyvern nodded knowingly. "A novice, I gather. Air magic is fairly advanced stuff. I am not a practitioner, of course, but I understand from others that it takes time to develop control. But that *was* a pretty fancy Water trick you did back there. Stiffening a liquid without the advantage of cold, and then fashioning it into a useful form. Water magic may be your niche."

"Perhaps, but Vermis keeps telling me that Logoman-… Oh! We forgot to introduce you to Vermis. He's a vermitome and a great scholar, though it's hard to tell these days. You see, he's been Muted."

"An awful affliction, that," sympathized the wyvern.

"Rudger's grandparents have been Muted, too," Twelda added.

"Which is why we've been trying to find you," Rudger explained. "Actually, it's funny you mentioned us not having a weapon because Vermis, here, left us a clue about…" The gnome's voice trailed off as he looked down at his sodden beard.

"Rudger? What's wrong?" asked Twelda.

"It's Vermis," he replied, still staring at his whiskers. He shoved them about clumsily with his wrapped hands before looking up at Twelda.

"He's not here," Rudger reported with dismay. "Vermis is gone."

CHAPTER TWENTY-THREE

Rudger Rump gazed down upon the River Gush as twilight settled over the Land of Lex. The sky had turned purple in the rapidly fading light, and the moon Lunira, flushed pink with anticipation, was peeking over the eastern horizon before him. Her entrance onto the panoramic stage would be cued by the appearance of her seventh sister star, which, at that very moment, was blossoming into brilliance overhead. Despite this pomp and circumstance, the celestial players failed to garner the interest of their audience of one. Rudger's eyes were fixed, unseeing, on the ever-darkening river waters as they coursed by.

The search had gone on for hours, one set of wings supporting three pairs of eyes which scoured the riverbank to the east and the precipices to the west for the tiniest speck of green. It had been a lost cause from the start, but Rudger pressed on, refusing to give up until the light had failed him. Twelda and Herald had done their part to help, but the young gnome couldn't seem to feel the appropriate gratitude. The entire spectrum of his emotions had been swallowed up by despair.

Presently, Rudger's keen ears picked up on the sound of scraping footsteps over the gurgle of the dark, distant water. He knew this intruder upon his misery, but he lacked the will to acknowledge her arrival.

"Herald's still looking for the sword," Twelda Greeze said softly. "We'll have the object of our quest soon."

It took Rudger a long moment to coax his tongue into motion. "The object of our quest," he repeated bitterly. "That's funny."

Twelda crouched next to her friend. The faint sound of the water closed in around them.

Rudger sighed. "It's pointless," he said. "Vermis…Vermis is gone."

"We might still find him," Twelda countered, her tone cautiously optimistic. "Herald's going to take us out at first light to continue the search."

"That's sporting of him, but what's the use? Our chances of finding Vermis were slim today. By tomorrow morning, they'll be practically nil."

"Oh, I don't agree. Vermis is a plucky little fellow. He'll come up with some way of signaling us where he is."

Rudger turned to look at Twelda. Her facial features were inscrutable in the gathering darkness.

"How, Twelda? How could he possibly do that? He was Muted, practically catatonic. You saw that."

"Well, maybe you'll be able to locate him by casting a Wyrd."

"Don't you think I've tried, over and over?" Rudger lamented. "There's nothing left. I burned up everything I had making that stupid water boat."

"Still, we might spot Vermis if we keep circling long enough."

"Twelda," Rudger said, his voice rising, "didn't you see all the wurblebirds nesting in these cliffs? Even if Vermis did survive the fall, he's surely been gobbled up by now."

"But when Herald finds the sword—"

"What good will that do? What can we do with it? Slice open every wurblebird from here to the Icon Sea, hoping against hope that Vermis will still be alive inside one of them? We have to face facts. Vermis left me that clue about Vic. He trusted me to work out what it meant and to get the sword to un-Mute him. And what did I do? I lost him during a fight with a dactopus! Or maybe it happened while we were in the air; it doesn't matter how. I lost him, and now he's dead. And it's all my fault."

The distraught gnome's throat had closed up while making this speech. Now his suppressed emotions surged forth in a torrent of ragged sobs.

When at last he grew quiet, Twelda placed a sympathetic hand on his slumped shoulder. "It's not your fault," she reassured him. "We were under attack. There was nothing you could do."

She stood before continuing. "But there's something you can do now. You can get the sword like Vermis wanted and take it back to Drungle Town. And there, you can use it to end the Mute-ation, starting with your grandparents."

"We don't even know if Vic has the power to do that,"

Rudger said quietly.

"We won't know until we try. I think we owe it to that little vermitome to do that much, don't you?"

A thunderous crash rang out from the cave behind them, accompanied by a hair-raising roar. Twelda didn't wait for Rudger to answer her question. She scurried toward the source of the commotion. Rudger hesitated for a bit. Then he grudgingly called his legs into service to convey him into the cave.

The gaping mouth in the cliff's wide face opened into an expanse too great for its half-dozen torches to illuminate. Shadows danced along jagged crests and craggy spires, lending a sinister air to the dragon's lair.

Wyvern's lair, Rudger reminded himself. He scanned the empty cavern in search of the beast and the gnomette.

More metallic clangs and clatters resonated through the chamber, apparently originating from a huge, rocky corridor to Rudger's left. Moving toward the source of the noise, the gnome's sensitive hearing picked up on a high-pitched voice. It was Twelda, offering scathing commentary on the wyvern's housekeeping skills—or lack thereof.

"...colossal mess! It's no wonder you haven't been able to find Vic yet. How can you find anything is this disarray? And what about this heap of junk in the middle? It doesn't leave any workspace at all. Really, Herald, I'm surprised at you..."

An image of the overburdened table and cabinets in Twelda's burrow-lab popped into Rudger's mind as he continued down the corridor. He had just about decided to expose Twelda's hypocrisy when he was confronted with so surreal a scene, it chased every other thought from his head.

There his friend stood, hands on her hips, bawling out a

stupendous wyvern who stretched from floor to lofty ceiling. The beast stared down balefully at the tiny gnomette while he employed his bent wings as makeshift arms to stabilize a teetering tower of metallic torsos—hollow and apparently dismembered from suits of armor, human-sized. A pile of arms and legs, gauntlets and helmets, and a bewildering assortment of human weapons littered the floor between them.

Twelda's critique had continued throughout Rudger's flabbergasted inspection of the wyvern's arsenal. At the moment, she was appraising the value of a helmet half as tall as she was.

"...and why are you keeping this helmet? It's far too small for you to wear. What other purpose could it possibly serve? There seems to be some writing on it, but it's too dark in here to make it out. Really, Herald, if we're ever going to exact some semblance of order over this disaster area of yours, couldn't you at least provide an adequate level of illumination? Three torches just aren't cutting it."

With each subsequent poke, Rudger had watched the wyvern swell up more and more with indignation. Now, the great yellow eyes flashed as smoke rolled out of the outraged wyvern's flared nostrils. With an exasperated roar, he jerked his wings away from the torso-tower, allowing it to fall. A titanic tumult assaulted Rudger's ears as torsos toppled higgledy-piggledy onto the heap of metal artifacts. Several rolled off the pile, clattering their way into the farthest recesses of the chamber. One came to a stop just a few feet from the entranceway where Rudger stood.

"Well, that was mature," commented Twelda. "Now you've dented them all."

Rudger dashed for cover behind a pile of shields as the wyvern spewed fire over their heads. Herald turned in a circle, scorching the entire circumference of the room. When the blast ended, Rudger peeked over the shields to find that eight additional torches had been lit. Nine, if you counted Twelda. Still standing in the open, she slowly removed her brown pointed cap, licked her fingers, and extinguished the flame dancing at the top.

"Wyverns have *excellent* low-light vision," Herald stated testily. "Unlike certain half-blind hominid species."

Rudger scampered to Twelda's side.

"Well, that was impressive, Mr. Wyvern. Yes, sir," he said in a tremulous, over-loud voice. "Thanks for saving our lives earlier today, but I think we should be going now." He caught Twelda's eye and spoke in an undertone. "You know, before he changes his mind."

"We're not going anywhere," the gnomette stated flatly.

"Uh, I'm thinking you ought to rethink our position here. Gigantic, terrifying, fire-breathing wyvern. Tiny, helpless Humdrungle gnomes. See my point?"

"Herald's not going to hurt us. He wouldn't dare."

Rudger's high-pitched laugh was laced with fear. "I really don't think you're striking the right tone, here, Twelda. Little heavy on the aggression, little light on the groveling. You know what might be perfect just about now? An apology. What do you say?"

"Not until this overgrown lizard says he's sorry."

"Ohhh-kaaay," squeaked Rudger. "Looks like it's up to me to do the apologizing. We're sorry. And now, we're out of here."

"Wait."

The wyvern's booming command stopped Rudger in his efforts to usher Twelda out of the chamber. Both Humdrungles turned to look up at the winged beast.

"Twelda is right. I have behaved abominably. I am sorry."

Rudger's knees went out from under him. Twelda kept him upright.

"Thank you," she said. "And I apologize for criticizing your…whatever you call this."

"My collection."

"Your collection?" she said in disbelief. "A bunch of human armor?"

Herald shrugged. "I like to save the containers my food comes in."

Rudger scanned the hundreds of artifacts littering the room. "You ate…*all* of these?"

"Alas, no," said the wyvern. "The Land of Lex doesn't produce this many knights with a death wish, more's the pity. Hence my diet of dactopuses. Disgusting, rubbery things. Give me a young man in fine fettle any day of the week. But most hominids have the good sense to stay away from wyverns, so they're rather the delicacy."

Rudger felt his knees go weak again as the beast regarded them like swampkunks on a spit. It was a fortunate thing Herald had dined that afternoon.

"At any rate," the winged reptile continued, breaking eye contact to gesture around him, "I've acquired the majority of these pieces of war paraphernalia through other means."

"Hoarding," said Twelda, scanning the chamber anew. "It's a classic case of hoarding."

"Ugh. '*Hoarding*.' What an ugly word," Herald grumbled, a puff of dragon-smoke emphasizing his distaste.

"Well, it *is* what dragons are known for," Twelda said reasonably.

"Yes, for hoarding gold and jewels and other such sundries, but I am a wyvern, as I believe I have mentioned before, so I *collect* objects of interest and historical importance. Like that helmet you were examining earlier. It was part of my very first acquisition. Did you notice that it's twelfth-century Arcedonian? Probably meant for ceremonial use since it contains far too much silver to provide any real cranial protection. That's why the dent on the vertex is so pronounced. One good conk on the noggin, and the bloke was a goner. Silly humans. Oh, and then there's that adorable mace right in front of you. Now, *that* piece has an especially fascinating history—"

"Yes, yes, I'm sure it does," interrupted Twelda, "but we're here because of another weapon, remember? A sword called Vic?"

"Of course. I haven't forgotten. Vicarius is the most important piece in my whole collection. It's just so vexing I can't find it in all this clutter." The wyvern shrugged his wings in a helpless gesture and proceeded to upset a barrel filled with quarterstaffs.

"Well, you've got two motivated volunteers ready to take over the search and turn this chaos into a first-rate museum at the same time," Twelda said. "How does that sound?"

"Great, but I do wish I could assist you. Only this sort of work is difficult when you don't have hands." The great wyvern paused a moment. "I did have hands once."

"Really? When?" asked Rudger, joining in the small talk now that he was fairly confident he and Twelda would not be burnt to a crisp or eaten.

"When I went questing with your Aunt Ragna thirty years ago. I occupied her body for a day. What an experience *that* was."

"Occupied her body?" Twelda asked, looking up from some gauntlets she had begun to stack. "What do you mean by that?"

"Well, you folks want Vicarius because you think it might cure the Mute-ation, and perhaps it can," said Herald. "But I am more familiar with a different aspect of its magic, a most peculiar property that enables it to switch spirits."

"Switch spirits?" asked Rudger. "Like wine for ale?"

"No, no. Not 'spirits' as in alcohol. 'Spirits' as in a person's essence or soul. You see, if you strike someone with that particular sword, your spirit ends up in their body, and theirs in yours. It renders Vicarius quite useless in battle, I'm afraid. I believe Ragna said this was done because most of her family are strong believers in pacifism."

Twelda considered this. "Sounds like pretty potent magic."

"It is," Herald confirmed. "So potent it managed to yank my spirit out of my wyvern body and deposit it into Ragna's. Curious, since wyverns are typically immune to such enchantments."

"So you spent time as a Humdrungle gnome," Twelda said. "But why did you stay that way, even for a day? Why didn't you just switch back immediately?"

"Ah, that's another aspect of the curse," Herald answered. "No two bodies can be involved in its magic twice. But the same two *spirits* can. So, if you involve a third party and are clever about it, you can get switched back." He sighed wistfully. "But that single day rather ruined me, I'll admit. I never envied hominids for their hands or my dragon kin for their foreclaws, but since then, I've been painfully aware of what I'm missing."

"Well, I don't know about Twelda, but if we find the sword, I don't mind switching bodies with you for a while," Rudger offered.

"Oh, no," Herald said firmly. "That will never do. Not to sound pompous, but only a wyvern can control a wyvern's body. For any length of time, I mean. Because our bodies are so highly magical, they tend to be overwhelmingly seductive to hominid spirits. Poor Chauncey du Shayne managed to survive a number of hours in my body, but it was a close-end thing. And Prince Emmett was driven out of his mind with power-lust. Though, if the truth be told, that young man was corrupt before the switch ever happened."

"Prince Emmett?" Twelda asked. "You mean King Emmett, King of the humans? He was inside your body, too? For how long?"

Herald flexed his wings uncertainly. "Well, *Prince* Emmett's spirit resided in this body for a few minutes. that much is true. But as for *King* Emmett, that becomes a bit too complicated for the telling. Uh, Rudger, my boy? How are you making out with those shields, there?"

"They're heavy, but I can manage them one at a time. The problem is there isn't any space to lay things out."

"Well, I guess I shall take my leave, then," Herald said. He plowed his huge, clawed feet through the pile of armor, forcing the two Humdrungles to scurry out of the way. When the wyvern reached the entrance to the chamber, he turned.

"It really is a pity I can't help," he said regretfully. "You *will* take good care of my treasures, won't you? Fortunately, these aren't as delicate as my other collectibles."

"Oh, you hoard…I mean, *collect* other things, as well?" inquired Twelda.

"Oh, yes! Music boxes."

"Music boxes?" Rudger said in surprise.

"A passion I discovered just a few decades ago. Come to think of it, I haven't heard any of my music boxes play their tunes for…over three years, I'd say. Not since my dragon friend up and disappeared. Bit of a shifty sort, but he was always happy to wind the mechanisms for me."

"Well, maybe after we've found Vic and cleared up this mess, we can wind them for you," Rudger offered.

"Would you? Oh, that would be most excellent!"

Herald turned and shuffled happily into the corridor, still talking to himself.

"My favorite one plays 'Waltz of the Wyverns.' Such a sweet little tune. But a ridiculous notion, truly. I mean, how could wyverns waltz? You need arms and hands to stay in hold. Still, it's a lovely sentiment. Ah, me."

Rudger and Twelda looked at each other for a long time, struggling to process the abrupt change in the wyvern's mood.

"Barmy as a boughbrat, that one," Twelda said. "But I think he's harmless."

"Except for the fire-breathing," Rudger replied. "And the teeth. Let's just find the sword and get out of here."

The gnomette grinned. "Rudger that!" she said.

CHAPTER TWENTY-FOUR

"Minsec? Minsec, where are you?"

Hildegarde pushed her way through a drape of hanging vines to emerge from the hollow in which she'd spent the night.

"Minsec?" she continued to call, scanning the dewy woods around her. "Where have you gotten to, you naughty…Oh! Fred."

The stately un-corn stepped forward, his hooves stirring up a patch of mist that hovered near the ground between two gnarlic trees. Their boughs were covered with lush, flowering vines whose ivory-colored blossoms paled in comparison to the un-corn's brilliant white coat.

"You…you're still here," Hildegarde stuttered, her hand darting to her neck to verify the amulet's presence. "I rather thought you'd be gone, like a dream." Her brow crinkled slightly. "Did you stand guard over me all night?"

Naturally, Fred told her. *I am your sworn protector.*

"Oh," she said, a swirl of emotions plaguing her. "I…I wish you hadn't. I wouldn't want you to lose sleep over me."

When you are near, sleep loses its allure, Fred replied.

Hildegarde scoffed at the sheer ridiculousness of the statement, but it quickly became clear that the un-corn was quite serious. Embarrassed, the Princess cleared her throat and changed the subject.

"Uh, did you happen to see Minsec this morning? He seems to have wandered off."

The hourglass left your side just before dawn.

"Really? You didn't try to stop him?"

I did not wish to risk disturbing your slumber.

"Oh. Well, we need to find him. We have to reach dragon country as quickly as—"

A sudden growl interrupted her. She blushed and pressed a hand against her belly until the gastric complaint stopped.

I had forgotten humans require regular nourishment, commented Fred. *My apologies for not procuring your breakfast.*

"It's okay," Hildegarde replied. "Truth be known, I could do with a little less nourishment."

The un-corn regarded her seemingly svelte form. *I wholly disagree. Now, if you'll kindly follow me.*

Hildegarde watched as the magnificent beast strode through the green undergrowth and disappeared into the trees. Released from the thrall of his beauty, she shook her head, bent to retrieve her satchel, and hurried to catch up.

Soon, worry began to gnaw at her.

"We really mustn't stray too far," she told the equine. "Minsec won't know where to find us."

And does that matter?

"Well, yes. Minsec is our guide."

Un-corns such as myself have a highly developed sense of direction, Fred told her as he pressed on. *I have every confidence I can find the bluffs unassisted.*

"That's good to know, but we still have to go back for Minsec."

Why?

"Because we can't abandon him in the forest."

Why not?

"Why not?" Hildegarde repeated in disbelief. "Well, he'd never find his way out on his own. He might die."

Does the hourglass have a soul?

"What?"

Does the hourglass have a soul of its own?

Hildegarde stopped walking, so stunned was she at the implications of the question. "I…don't know. I hadn't thought about it."

It does not breathe; it has no heartbeat. Therefore, it is not alive. If it is not alive, it has no soul and cannot die.

"Wow," Hildegarde said. "That's a heartless thing to say."

At last, the un-corn halted. He turned his elegant head and regarded her with one soul-searching eye.

Forgive me, dear one. We un-corns are anchored in a more existential plane than most creatures. I only broached the subject because you seem fond of that soulless object, and its Glynt disturbs me.

"I'm sorry. Did you say 'glint?'"

Yes, but not with the meaning you think. A Glynt is a signa-

ture a wizard leaves on anything his magic touches. And the Glynt on that hourglass is...ominous.

"I didn't see anything."

That is not surprising. Most humans are Glynt-blind. But trust me when I say it is in your best interest for us to distance ourselves from the hourglass and whatever wizard is responsible for animating it.

Fred resumed his walk, and Hildegarde fell in step behind. Her mind was abuzz with thoughts of the wizard Lendar—so much so that she jumped when her stomach afforded her a reminder of their current objective. Embracing their foraging activity for the first time, it wasn't long before she spotted her breakfast.

"Oh, Fred, look. Piprum pods! I can scarcely believe our luck." She moved toward the vines which held the spindle-shaped fruit.

Milady, I advise you to keep your distance.

"See the blush of purple on their skins? And how fat they are in the middle? That means they're ready for eating. Oh, we get piprums so rarely from the fruit vendors who visit the castle. And here, we stumble upon enough for both of us."

Even so, we must leave that fruit be.

"But why? They're right there for the taking."

We can't eat them for the simple reason that we don't wish to be eaten ourselves.

"I don't understand."

Look at those vines with your eyes rather than your stomach, and you will.

Hildegarde did as her protector advised, setting her hunger aside as she scrutinized the scene. Three canfa trees stood on a rise before her, supporting the fruit-bearing vines of her desire. As she looked more closely at the vines, she at last identified the peril.

Intertwined with the pod-laden vines swinging so tantalizingly in the breeze were thin, dark tendrils with short, narrow, blade-like leaves. She traced the invasive shoots down to the ground where they blended in with the mosses of the soft forest floor. With a little effort, she managed to follow the tendrils back to their source—a shaggy green-black bush some ten feet away.

That is an arachna shrub, Fred informed her. *It is dormant now, but the moment you lay a finger on those piprums, it shall endeavor to bind you with its runners like a spider traps a fly. It's a tactic the arachnas in the Vale of the Vines employ all too often. Hence the reason your piprum pods are such a delicacy, milady. I imagine many a forager has perished in his efforts to procure those precious pods for your royal table. Now, let's please move on.*

Shame superseded Hildegarde's hunger, but the un-corn's lecture also kindled a spark of defiance. Instead of joining Fred, Hildegarde unshouldered her rucksack.

The un-corn seemed to sense her intent. *Milady? Milady, I beg you: do not engage the arachna. A few measly piprums are not worth the trouble such action is sure to bring upon us.*

The Princess did not heed the warning. She had already sighted in on her target—a particularly plump piprum pod hanging at shoulder height twenty feet away. She pulled her slingshot from the folds of her golden-brown gown and a stone of pleasing weight from a hidden pocket.

Zzzzz-tip!

The projectile crossed the space, striking and severing the piprum's short stem. The pod dropped to the forest floor and rolled down the rise until it came to rest a yard from Hildegarde's feet.

Scanning the immediate area for arachna tendrils, she stepped forward and retrieved the fruit. The arachna shrub did not stir.

She turned toward the un-corn and took a juicy bite. Her raised eyebrows invited his commentary.

Impressive, Fred admitted, *but gravely unwise. And not a feat likely to be successfully repeated. Shall we press on, then? I believe there are some wild dringleberries over the next rise.*

"Hold on. Did I hear you correctly, Fred?" Hildegarde asked in a mischievous tone. "I believe I heard you dare me to repeat my shot."

Milady, you misinterpret my words. Having found my maiden at long last, I have no desire to lose her so quickly.

"No, no. I'm pretty sure that was a dare. And I never turn down dares."

One by one, the piprum pods fell, some rolling within reach of the Princess and others getting stuck in the niches of the canfas' intertwined roots. Hildegarde took perverse pleasure in the increasingly dire warnings from her audience. *Milady, I beg of you. Milady, I beseech you. Milady, I implore you to desist!*

The eighth piprum pod suffered an awkward bounce as it fell, catapulting it directly toward the arachna shrub. Girl and un-corn alike held their breath as the fruit thumped against the bush's stout base. The only movement from the arachna was a harmless flutter of its tiny leaves, the only sound a sigh in the breeze.

Hildegarde exhaled first.

"Do you suppose it's dead?" she wondered aloud.

Perhaps, but let us not press the issue. Just pick up your peck of piprum pods.

"Partial peck."

Pardon?

"Partial peck. There's not enough for a proper peck."

How many piprum pods comprise a proper peck? asked Fred. Then he paused. *Wait. Why does this sound familiar? 'Princess picked a peck of purple piprum pods. How many purple piprums did the peckish Princess pick?'*

Hildegarde gave the un-corn a withering look. "Seriously? We're doing tongue twisters now? That's not playing fair. You don't even use your tongue to speak!"

And you do not use caution when you forage. Now, for the last time, gather up the fruits closest to you and let us begone.

"No," Hildegarde said stubbornly. "I worked hard for those piprums." She pressed a finger against her cheek as she thought. "If the arachna shrub is dead, it would be a shame to leave that lovely piprum there to rot. But it might not be dead, in which case it's luring me into a trap. Perhaps tagging it with a couple of stones would be a good test to see if it's alive."

Fred snorted and tossed his mane in agitation. *Milady, you are making my job as your protector most challenging.*

"Then go get your dringleberries while I work out how to…" She stopped short. "Did you hear that?"

Hear what?

"Shh!" she hissed. "Something's coming this way."

The sound grew louder as the Princess and the un-corn readied themselves for an encounter. The noise was a cross between a rustle and a scrape—not intermittent like footsteps, but constant like wheels rolling through leaves on the forest floor. And yet, there was no carriage to be seen.

Movement attracted Hildegarde's eye. She drew in a sharp breath.

"Minsec!" she cried.

The little hourglass was on its side, using its top and bottom discs like wheels as it rolled toward them. Upon hearing Hildegarde's voice, it righted itself and struck a hero's pose, complete with bent support arms perched on its tiny glass waist.

The Princess began to rush to its side.

Milady! The arachna!

The un-corn's sharp warning stopped her just in time. The timepiece had unwittingly set up a diamond with itself and Hildegarde at opposite corners and the plants of interest at the other two. A straight run across that diamond would have brought Hildegarde within range of the arachna.

Confused by the Princess' apparent change of heart, Minsec shrugged and tipped onto its side to close the distance between them.

"No!" Hildegarde cried. "Stay where you are! There's a dangerous bush there!"

Minsec righted itself again and began to hop about, gesticulating at the arachna shrub and the piprum pod with all three of its metal arms. Hildegarde tried to persuade the timepiece to back away from the bush, but her efforts only seemed to agitate the hourglass further.

"What's he trying to tell us, Fred?" the Princess asked desperately. "Why won't he just back away from that awful thing?"

It seems to me it wishes to retrieve the piprum for you.

"Forget the piprum! It doesn't matter."

The maneuver may not be as dangerous for the hourglass as it would be for you or me, Fred said. *The hourglass is not alive, and so it may not trigger the predatory instincts of the shrub.*

"I don't care. I started this quest with Minsec, and I'm not going to lose him over a stupid piece of fruit."

Now you know how I was feeling, the un-corn stated drily. *And like the object of my protective efforts, it seems that yours is not listening, either.*

Minsec had edged its way up to the base of the motionless arachna, still gesturing forcefully at the plant and piprum pod.

"Yes, yes," Hildegarde encouraged the brave timepiece. "Just get the pod and get out of there."

Minsec cocked its top disc questioningly. Reaching out an arm, it poked the piprum pod.

"That's it," Hildegarde cooed. "Pick it up and come over here to me."

Minsec's sand suddenly turned bright orange as it threw all three of its arms into the air in exasperation. Punting the pod out of the way, it seized some of the tendrils wrapped around the bush's base and began to rip them away.

"Minsec! What in the Elements are you—"

Hildegarde didn't have a chance to finish her question as arachna tendrils shot upward from the forest floor like a hundred enraged snakes. She screamed as they grabbed at her slippered feet and ensnared the skirts of her gown. She managed to launch a rock from her slingshot, but its impact only stunned the aggressive branch for a moment. Desperate to fend off the plant's attack, she began to strike the wriggling runners with the handle of her weapon.

"Fred! Fred! Help us!" she cried.

She included Minsec in her plea because the little hourglass was in even more dire straits than she. Closest to the arachna, it was rapidly becoming mummified in the plant's twining shoots.

Fred, however, had his hooves full dealing with marauding branches of his own. With a fierce battle cry, he slashed down with his head, chopping the runners in two as quickly as they advanced. Being the farthest from their source, the branches were not as dense, and soon they had been reduced to a pile of piteously twitching fragments.

"Fred, please! They've got my wrist! They…Aaaugh! Fred!"

The un-corn did not pause to rest but raced to his maiden's rescue, slashing with even greater zeal. As the equine severed the tendrils, they lost their strength, and Hildegarde hurried to strip them away. Fred whinnied angrily as several tendrils wrapped themselves around his hindlegs and tail. He bucked and reared as Hildegarde struck these branches with the slingshot. In moments, they were both free.

Come on! cried the un-corn as he knelt to permit Hildegarde to mount.

"But Minsec—"

Nothing doing. It's too great a risk to save the hourglass. Now, get on!

©2022 Simerlein

Tears sprang to Hildegarde's eyes as she contemplated the horrible fate her hourglass friend would suffer. She looked at where Minsec had been a moment before. All she could make out was an hourglass-shaped mass of runners dragging their prize toward the heart of the shrub.

But enough of the tendrils had been severed by Fred's efforts that the base of the bush was no longer solid green with the thin wrapping branches. Glimpses of a human-like anatomy could be seen—a foot there, a strip of tunic there, a shock of dark hair above.

Hildegarde gasped in horror.

"Fred! There's a child in there!"

Rules. The little boy's existence was fraught with them.

From the moment he awakened to the moment he went to sleep, the Never Man's rules controlled him. If he awoke in the safe place, he was to stay there. If he woke up anywhere else, he was charged to go to the safe place. If he could not, he had to stay where he was and hide. No one could be allowed to see him; he could speak to no one. He had to stay put until the day was over and it was time to sleep. With luck, the next day might be a better one.

On those better days, his Tutor would be with him in the safe place. Tutor made him learn hard, boring things he didn't always understand, but that was much better than hiding all day long in a scary place he didn't know from people who wanted to hurt him. He'd learned to dread the Hide days.

And today was to be one of them.

He'd awakened, cold and alone, in a part of the forest he didn't recognize. It had weird trees and too many vines, and that meant he could be almost anywhere in the Land of Lex. Panic started to well up inside him, but he forced it down with a deep, calming breath. He had his big boy pants on. Literally. Their extra-long legs fell in circular folds around oversized boots as he struggled to stand. He caught the trousers before they fell off his hips, cinched them up by making a roll of the extra material and tucking it in. The ludicrously long sleeves of his tunic kept swamping his hands as he did so, but he didn't let it frustrate him. The clothes were unimportant; he had a job to do. He stepped out of the enormous boots he was wearing and began to walk.

He couldn't go too far; that was another Never Man rule. He mustn't ever leave the boots behind. So he only went a hundred paces. That was far enough to be sure the safe place wasn't close by.

He returned to the boots and set out in another direction. Then another. And another. Nothing looked familiar. The panicky feeling returned, accompanied by dread. It really was to be a Hide day.

On his final check-trek, he heard it. A woman's voice a short distance ahead. Caution dictated he back away and find a hiding place immediately, but there was something strange about the way the lady was speaking. She would say something and then pause. When she spoke again, it was as if in answer to an unheard person's comment. It was peculiar and fascinating.

She suddenly started moving toward him.

He ran, high-stepping to avoid tripping over the pant-legs, the moss-covered ground muffling the impact of his stocking feet. He spotted a large, dark green bush up ahead —a perfect hiding place. But the moment he touched it, it came alive, grabbing at him with sharp-leafed branches. He tried to scream, but the writhing branches laced across his chest and tightened, squeezing the air out of him. They made a horrible sucking noise as they pricked the skin on his face and hands, injecting something that made him dizzy and weak. He lost the will to resist, succumbed to a venom-induced oblivion.

And then he was coming to. The horrible branches had fallen away, and he gasped for air. It was the same day. He knew this because he was still in the weird forest, and the lady he'd heard was talking again, but this time, she was talking to him.

"Are you okay, pipkin?" she asked, using the same pet name his own mother had once used. "Did that plant hurt you?"

He realized his face and hands did hurt, but the Never Man's rules kept him from saying so. He was supposed to get away from the lady, but as his vision cleared, he saw she was very beautiful. She had lovely chestnut-brown hair that hung in curls around a pale face with a tiny nose, cupid's-bow lips, and eyes the color of honey. It was those luminous eyes which captivated him. They reminded him so strongly of his dead mother's, he began to cry.

"There, there," the lady said, drawing him into an embrace. "That nasty bush can't hurt you anymore. We made sure of that."

She held him close a moment longer. She smelled of

sunspray blossoms and sniggleswort and all things comforting and safe.

"I suppose that's true," she said upon releasing him. "You did do most of the rescuing."

The boy frowned. Woozy as he was, he recognized that this statement didn't make sense.

The lady seemed to acknowledge his confusion; her eyebrows rose, her lips puckered slightly. But there was a delay before she spoke.

"Of course, you're right," she seemed to reply to no one. Then she focused fully on him.

"Pipkin, the nice horsie told me you can't hear him. He says he's very happy you are well."

The boy turned his head and saw a stunning white stallion standing a short distance away. He knew most horses didn't communicate, vocally or otherwise, but the intense intelligence in this equine's eyes led him to believe what the lady was telling him.

"Now, my name is Hildegarde, and the horsie's name is Fred. Can you tell me what your name is?"

Tutor had pounded this Never Man rule into him. *Never* speak to strangers.

"No?" Hildegarde said in response to his silence. "Well, are you out here all alone, or are your parents somewhere about? Can you tell me that?"

Again, he bit his tongue.

She looked at the white horse for a long moment.

"Yes, Fred, he could be in shock," Hildegarde said after the pause. "Or worse, he might be Muted. But whoever this little boy is, we can't leave him out here all by himself. I think we should take him with us."

As Hildegarde and the telepathic horse discussed the feasibility of her plan, the boy took the opportunity to look around. He and his rescuers were at the bottom of a heavily forested valley. A wide stream meandered there, flowing languidly over a rocky bed. The terrain rose steadily on either side of it, eventually touching the pearl-gray sky overhead. The boy saw that the only reasonable route of escape from the lady and her horse would be to plunge back into the trees. But which way should he go? He had no idea where his boots were.

"Yes, I realize having a youngster with us might make it harder to escape the wyvern, but I don't see any other option," the lady told her horse. "I wouldn't leave Minsec to the dangers of this forest. What makes you think I would leave a little boy?"

Hildegarde paused again and then nodded. "I appreciate that, Fred," she said before she turned to the boy. "Okay, we've worked it all out. You're going to come with us. There's a little something we have to do on the way, but you and Minsec can wait somewhere safe while Fred and I attend to that. Then we'll all head north to the castle, and we'll see what can be done to help you."

The boy knew he should run from the strangers and hide, but the kindness in Hildegarde's eyes was difficult to resist. Hide days were so scary, and here was a lady who genuinely wanted to help him. But Tutor had always insisted all strangers were cunning and evil. How could he trust them?

A gentle nudge on his knee pulled the boy's attention away from the pretty lady. An hourglass rested there when a moment before there had been none. Suddenly, the timepiece sprang to life, using one of its metal arms to doff its top wooden disc like a hat. The boy was delighted, but Tutor's warning still niggled at him.

Then he remembered a trick Tutor had worked hard to teach him. The boy narrowed his eyes and quieted his mind. Flipping a mental switch revealed a strong indigo light swirling like storm clouds around the outlines of the hourglass.

Then he turned his Glynt-sight on the lady. She was smiling warmly at him, but it wasn't her expression that made up his mind.

Her necklace had the indiglow, too.

CHAPTER TWENTY-FIVE

Herald took wing just after daybreak, carrying his Humdrungle passengers up into a gray and dispassionate sky. Its damp, drear touch leached away any bits of optimism Twelda's pep talk had managed to instill in Rudger the night before. The young gnome fought against the hopelessness, staying alert as he and the others patrolled the river basin below.

Early on, trailers of mist billowing off the river hampered the search party's efforts. Rudger could barely catch a glimpse of the riverside between rolling banks of fog as he soared through the chilly air.

Helios eventually took pity on the trio, emerging through his veil of clouds to dispel the troublesome mist. But hours passed, and no trace of the lost vermitome was found. By the time the sun god had reached his zenith, even tenacious Twelda was forced to admit defeat. She twisted around on the wyvern's neck to comfort Rudger behind her.

"Vermis would have wanted us to go on," she told him. "He started this quest with you to stop the Mute-ation, and using Vicarius to do that would be the best way to honor him."

The weight of Rudger's guilt and regret limited his response to a simple nod.

Twelda turned to face forward again. "And we thank you for your excellent help, Herald," she said to the wyvern. "You've been more than understanding, considering the circumstances."

"When you have lived as long as I have, you become a master at delaying gratification," Herald replied.

The great wyvern banked sharply, forcing Twelda and Rudger to clutch at the loops of knotted rope that served as a makeshift dragon saddle. When Herald's wings leveled out, the Icon Sea was at their backs and the Malgrieve Mountains loomed in the distance before them.

"Yeshirumon's lair is at the base of those mountains, four leagues distant," Herald said. An angry thrum rumbled through his cavernous chest, vibrating the gnomes in their seats. "By my fabled ancestors, that odious thief had best be in residence."

"You know, I still can't believe you didn't know Vicarius was missing," Twelda remarked. "I thought dragons could sense if even the tiniest trinket was taken from their hoards."

"Dragons can," confirmed Herald, "but I am a wyvern, as you seem to keep forgetting."

"Oh. Sorry," Twelda apologized. "No offense intended."

"None suffered. And in answer to your question, I don't have a running inventory of my treasures in my head. And I don't sleep on my collection, as dragons do. A peculiar habit, if you ask me. Seems like it would be dreadfully uncomfortable."

As they flew on, Rudger took the opportunity to wrestle with his emotions. The blackness he felt was real, but it was also counterproductive. Twelda was right; Vermis *would* want him to continue their quest. And in a crazy sort of way, Rudger felt that a part of Vermis was still with him. He forced himself to push aside the grief and join the conversation.

"Herald," he asked, "what makes you so sure this dragon friend of yours has the sword?"

"Simple deduction, Rudger. Yeshirumon is the only individual who has had access to my trove since I last laid eyes on Vicarius three or four years ago. Come to think of it, that was about the time he stopped showing up to curate the collection."

"'Curate'? What does that mean?"

"It means taking care of the artifacts, keeping them safe, clean, and organized. Yeshi convinced me to let him maintain my collection since I lack forelimbs. Did I tell you he can use his foreclaws to wind music box keys designed for human fingers?"

"Yes, you did," Rudger reminded him.

"Extraordinary! Anyway, over the past half-century or so, every time I acquired a new piece, Yeshi would find a place for it in my treasure cave. I paid him with whatever jewels or gold my would-be slayers had on their persons when they met their ends, but I never offered him a sword, and I never even *showed* him Vicarius." The wyvern paused and then suddenly breathed a gout of fire. "That *snake!* I should have known not to trust someone with so many aliases."

Rudger perked up. "Hey, that's another new word! 'Aliases.' What does it mean?"

"An alias is a pseudonym," Herald explained.

"A 'pseudonym?'"

"A nom de plume. A false name."

"Whoa. This is great stuff. Twelda, give me your satchel, will you? I gotta record this in my Logofile."

The moment she'd lifted the strap over her head, Rudger started rooting through the contents of the blunderhide bag.

Twelda scoffed at him. "You know, if I hadn't insisted on carrying your notebook in there, it would've been ruined in the river like your first one. Maybe you should show me a bit more appreciation."

"Thanks, Twelda," he said absently as he turned the pages of his Logofile. He reached for the quill on his ear and discovered it was gone.

"I lost my quill," he said as he tucked the file under his left arm and dove back into the bag. "Do you have one in here?"

Twelda sighed. "Yes. Hand it back to me, and I'll find you one."

Rudger pushed the satchel toward her backwardly directed hand. At the same moment, his Logofile slipped out from under his arm.

"Oh! Oops."

"What 'oops?'" Twelda asked. "What's going on back there?"

Panic rose inside Rudger. "I, uh,…I kind of lost your satchel, Twelda."

The gnomette twisted around.

"What?" she demanded. "What do you mean you lost it?"

Rudger swallowed hard. "It was an accident. It just slid over Herald's side." He gestured helplessly toward the ground.

"Rudger, that bag has everything in it!"

"Not everything," he said sheepishly. He lifted the Logofile in front of her face.

"That's just great!" she cried. "You saved your idiotic notebook and lost everything that matters! The fire-flinger is in that satchel. And my scientific equipment. And all of our provisions!"

"Ooo. What are 'provisions'?" Rudger asked with a glance at the Logofile.

"*Gah!*"

"Children, children," Herald intervened. "No need to come undone. We're flying slightly inland from the bluffs at the moment. I'll just circle around. Surely, we'll be able to spot Twelda's rather ponderous bag."

"We'd better," the gnomette growled. "Or I might be chucking something *else* overboard."

"Sorry to keep bringing this up, but Minsec is most insistent," Hildegarde said from her seat astride the un-corn's back. "Are you quite certain we haven't veered off-course?"

Fred snorted in annoyance. *As I have told you before, this stream necessarily empties into the River Gush, and that is where we will find the wyvern's lair.*

"I get that, I really do. It's just that Minsec is saying we're going north instead of east."

We are. The stream courses north here for a short distance.

Your navigator ought to understand that it is better to follow this bend to the cliffs than to hike up and over that wooded slope.

Hildegarde shrugged at the timepiece, which was balancing itself on the un-corn's back in front of the Princess and the rescued boy. Minsec had removed its top disc and was jabbing a support arm emphatically at a compass set into its underside.

"Yes, I see the compass says north," Hildegarde said, "but Fred assures me that following the stream is the best route to the wyvern's cave. Your input is totally appreciated, but why don't we let Fred navigate for a while?"

Minsec's sand turned an irate red as it slapped its top disc back onto its upper glass bulb. It thrust all three of its metal arms downward in an expression of outrage. Hildegarde extended a hand to soothe the frustrated timepiece, but it crossed two of its arms in a huffy manner and turned its back on her. At least Hildegarde *thought* the side now facing her was Minsec's back. It was hard to tell. The hourglass looked the same all the way around.

"Well, now Minsec's feelings are hurt," the Princess announced.

That is not possible, Fred commented. *Soulless objects have no feelings to hurt.*

Hildegarde rolled her eyes.

A few hundred yards later, the streambed did in fact curve back to the east. It became narrower at this point, and with the addition of water from a tributary brook, its current increased noticeably.

We are less than a tenth of a league away from the cliffs,

Fred reported. *This stream becomes one of several small waterfalls feeding the river from its western side.*

"How far are we from the wyvern's lair, then?"

That is hard to say. We are about a quarter-league from the foothills of the Malgrieve Mountains, and there are quite a few caves suitable for dragon occupancy there. Plus, the cliff's face is riddled with caverns all along the southern half of the River Gush's tract. Your wyvern could have its lair in one of those. We may need to consult the hourglass to identify the exact one.

"Well, I hope Minsec will be in a more helpful mood by the time we reach the cliffs," Hildegarde said as the timepiece continued to pout. "I'm not wild about stealing into *one* lair. There's no way I'm playing Door to My Love with half a dozen bloodthirsty dragons."

Door to My Love? said the un-corn. *What is that?*

"Oh. Just a silly children's game," Hildegarde explained. "Winifer made us play it all the time when we were kids."

Who is Winifer?

"My bossy cousin. She's going to be Queen of Lex someday," Hildegarde said with distaste.

What are the rules?

"Well, the boys hide behind a bunch of doors in a hall, and the girls are blindfolded, and they take turns opening the doors and kissing and identifying the boy behind each one until they get one wrong."

I have heard of kissing. It is not an equine custom.

Hildegarde giggled. "That's because you need lips."

Un-corns have lips, contradicted Fred. *It's puckering them that presents the problem.*

Hildegarde laughed, much harder and longer than the humor in the remark called for. It was a wonderful release after the tensions of the previous two days.

I am glad I amuse you so, milady. But at the risk of spoiling your mood, I do have a concern to express.

"What concern?"

When we find the wyvern's lair, just how do you plan to best it?

"Oh. Didn't I tell you? The amulet I wear around my neck was given to me by a wizard."

The same wizard who gave you the hourglass?

"Why, yes," Hildegarde answered. "How did you guess?"

The Glynt is the same.

"Right. I keep forgetting about that. Anyway, Lendar—that's the wizard's name—he told me the amulet will conceal me from the wyvern and protect me from its fire." She stopped short of mentioning the amulet's third magical effect, beautification of the wearer.

Claws.

"Beg pardon?"

The amulet protects you from a dragon's fire, but what about its claws? And its teeth?

"Well, I guess I didn't think about those."

Perhaps you should.

"But I'm not going to *fight* the wyvern," Hildegarde explained. "I'm just supposed to find a magic sword in its lair and take it."

And you don't think the beast will put up a fuss?

"With any luck, it won't even know I'm there. And if it does threaten me, I'll have you to come to my rescue."

The un-corn tossed his mane as he continued to walk. *I have sworn to protect you, dear one. But while I can readily overcome an arachna shrub, a wyvern may pose a more serious challenge.*

"I've seen you do battle twice," the Princess said. "I have every confidence in you, though I must admit your method mystifies me. You never seem to touch your foes, yet they sustain injury just the same."

I am an enigma, so it would seem.

Hildegarde laughed. "Don't be obtuse, Fred! Tell me how you do it."

Nay, milady.

"Well, at least give me a hint."

Nay, milady.

"Nay, nay," the girl mocked the un-corn good-naturedly. "You sound like a common horse. Wait. Is that a hint? Neigh? But you are not a simple horse, clearly. Ah, but I wonder what your nature is."

That is my secret, Fred replied smugly. *But I daresay you will discover it soon enough.*

Hildegarde grinned. "Is that an official dare?"

You may depend on it. And I expect you will ignore this warning, but I must give it all the same. Desist in this quest, dear one. No sword is worth your life.

"I can't, Fred. My mother's life depends on it. And the lives of countless subjects to the Crown—like this poor boy, here. The Mute-ation must end, and if Lendar can use the sword to do this, I must help in whatever way I—"

WHUMP!

A sudden percussive thud spooked the un-corn. He whinnied and skittered to his right, forcing Hildegarde to grab a hank of his mane with one hand while she stabilized Minsec and the boy with the other.

"What was *that?*" she asked as she tried to pinpoint the source of the noise. Leaves and twigs cascaded through the branches of a gnarlic tree partway up the ridge to their left.

Apparently, something fell out of that tree, Fred observed. *Perhaps it was a boughbrat that missed its footing?*

"Boughbrats aren't big enough to make that kind of impact," Hildegarde remarked. "Must've been something heavier." She paused, considering. "Think we should investigate?"

No, answered Fred, but Hildegarde was already dismounting.

"We need a break from riding," she said as she helped the boy down after her. "This will give us a chance to stretch our legs."

And to satisfy that sense of curiosity you humans can't seem to resist. 'Curious as a human,' my dam always says. It gets your species into no end of trouble.

"Oh, pooh," Hildegarde said in a fit of eloquence. "Where's your sense of adventure?"

Fresh out of it, grumbled Fred. *I used it all up on that arachna shrub back yonder.*

In spite of the un-corn's surly reticence, Hildegarde proceeded to tuck Minsec into the crook of her arm, hike up her skirts, and begin the climb. Fred chuffed his disapproval but was soon following behind.

Offering verbal encouragement to the boy she had dubbed Pipkin, Princess Hildegarde led the foursome up to the spot where the debris had settled. She drew in a sharp breath as she identified the cause of the disturbance.

"It's a suede bag. Like the one I'm carrying," she announced. She looked in every direction, including up into the twisty branches of the gnarlic tree. "I wonder whose it is?"

No one we need to meet, groused the un-corn. *You'd probably try to recruit them, and this questing party is too big as it is.*

"How in the Five Elements did a satchel end up here?" Hildegarde continued, ignoring Fred's snide remark. "It must have been dropped from above. But what tree-dwelling creature carries things in a bag? Oh, Pipkin, no! That's not ours."

The boy had opened the bag and was pulling items out of it.

Hildegarde looked at the un-corn and shrugged. "Finders keepers?" she said apologetically, though to whom she didn't know. Then she bent down next to the boy who was examining a two-armed contraption with sparkling stone teeth at one end.

"What strange devices," the Princess commented as she rummaged about in the bag. "I wonder what they are for. Oh! There's food, too! Bread and mushrooms and some sort of root vegetable, I think."

She looked up at the un-corn. "It's been such a long time since the piprums, Fred. Do let's go up to the top of the rise and have ourselves a picnic."

Hold on, said Fred. *Are you telling me you've already eaten that entire peck of piprum pods?*

"Partial peck, remember? And I didn't eat all of them. Pipkin ate two."

So, to summarize, Pipkin pinched a pair of purple piprum pods from the pretty, peckish Princess?

"Bite your tongue," Hildegarde chided the un-corn playfully. "We're not starting *that* up again."

Another thirty feet of climbing brought the party out of the vale to a narrow, rocky plain that denied the trees footing. Twenty feet out, the strip of plain fell away to form the face of a cliff. Although she couldn't see it, Hildegarde heard the water of the stream they'd been following crashing down into the River Gush somewhere to her right. Farther in that direction loomed the mighty Malgrieve Mountains.

The Princess looked back at the rock shelf's granite surface, sparkling so invitingly in the sunlight. It promised a breathtaking view of the Lexiconian river country if only they edged closer.

"This is perfect for our picnic," she announced to the others. "We can sit in the sun and chase the dampness of the woods from our bones."

Out in the open? the un-corn asked dubiously. *I'd prefer to keep the forest's canopy over us, milady. One never knows what might be coming from above.*

As if on cue, a huge shadow fell over the rock shelf, darkening its glittering appeal. The sound of enormous flapping wings accompanied a colossal, descending form. Hildegarde gripped Pipkin's shoulders protectively and drew him deeper into the shade of the trees.

"I'm pretty sure it fell somewhere around here," an unfamiliar voice said.

Hildegarde didn't know who was speaking, but she felt

sure the child-like voice couldn't belong to the enormous purple dragon before her.

"You'd better hope it's here," snapped an even higher-pitched voice. "I just remembered the auriculator's in there, and it's a prototype. I don't even want to *think* about trying to rebuild it from memory."

Hildegarde managed to wrench her eyes from the great winged marvel and redirect them to two tiny figures sliding down from its neck. At first, she took them for human children like Pipkin, but as their feet hit the ground, she realized they were much too small—not even half Pipkin's height.

"Are those…gnomes?" she whispered to Fred. "I've never seen one before."

Humdrungle gnomes, to be precise, he confirmed, *but I believe it is the wyvern you should be concerned with.*

"Wyvern?" she echoed.

As the titanic creature pushed itself upright, she made a quick inventory of its appendages and found it to be true. She whispered excitedly to her un-corn companion.

"You don't suppose it's the wyvern we're looking for, do you?"

Wyverns are *rather rare beasts,* Fred said pointedly.

"So, should we approach it?" Hildegarde asked, nervous about the implications of the suggestion. "I mean, can wyverns be reasoned with? Are they intelligent?"

A great deal more intelligent than human beings, Fred intoned. Then he seemed to reconsider what he'd said. *A thousand apologies, milady. I meant no personal offense.*

"None suffered. But we'd better stop chatting and figure

out what to do. Those gnomes are getting closer. Look at the crazy red beard on that one!"

May I suggest we leave the satchel here and retreat? My instincts tell me that approaching the wyvern would be risky. If the gnomes find their bag, it is reasonable to assume they and the wyvern will resume whatever activity they were engaged in. That will keep the beast away from its lair for a time, and provided the hourglass can, in fact, lead us to the wyvern's cave, our chances of getting out alive will be greatly enhanced.

"Good plan," Hildegarde whispered back. She pulled gently on the boy's shoulders. "Come on, Pipkin. We're backing up now. Where's Minsec?" The little hourglass was no longer standing in the patch of grass where she'd put it down. She looked left and right. "Minsec?" she hissed urgently. "Minsec, where are you?"

Then she looked in front of her.

"Oh, *hackerpedes*," she cursed.

"Hello. What's this?"

A flash of light reflecting from some unknown object caught Rudger Rump's eye. He moved closer to get a better view.

"Twelda! Check this out! There's an hourglass over here."

She came to his side. "An hourglass? Well, foosh. I thought you'd found my satchel."

"No. Just this so far," Rudger replied. "Did it come out of your bag?"

"No. I didn't pack an hourglass, Rudger. It was probably left here by some irresponsible, littering human who...*jumping jawjackles!*"

Twelda's exclamation directed Rudger's attention back to the timepiece. To his astonishment, it was moving.

Both Humdrungles backpedaled as the glass-and-wood device hopped out from behind an isolated clump of grizzle-grass. Half the gnomes' height, the hourglass bounced around in agitation, waving its three metal support rods wildly. It seemed particularly fixated on Rudger, for every time he backed away from the crazed timepiece, it pursued him.

"Uh, Herald?" the young gnome asked as he dodged this way and that. "What do I do?"

The wyvern bent down and blew a bit of dragon smoke at the advancing hourglass. It reacted by dropping onto its side and rolling backward several feet. When it righted itself, it seemed to be quivering.

"Magically animated," commented Herald. He paused a moment and then added, "It has a powerful Glynt around it. Bit off-putting, actually. Perhaps I should torch it to be on the safe side."

"No!"

The cry came from the trees. Rudger's heart stopped as he saw a human girl in a golden-brown gown hurrying toward him. His instincts screamed at him to run. Then he remembered the six-ton fire-breathing wyvern backing him up.

"Please don't hurt Minsec," the girl begged. "He isn't dangerous. I don't know why he's acting this way."

It was clear, even to a Humdrungle gnome like Rudger, that this girl was beautiful by human standards. Rudger personally preferred a stouter female, but if he overlooked her gangly limbs and peculiar five-fingered hands, he found her tempered tan tresses and honey-colored eyes rather appealing.

The hourglass came out of hiding and edged closer to Rudger. Now the gnome could see he'd mistaken the timepiece's excitement for aggression. It was gesticulating emphatically between Rudger and itself, the sand in its bulbs flashing back and forth between mudpud brown and a deep purple.

"That's his way of communicating," the girl explained. "I think he's trying to tell you something."

"Doesn't mean anything to me," Rudger admitted. When the hourglass' sand turned an angry red, he added, "I'm sorry…Minnick, was it?"

"Minsec," corrected the girl. "And I'm Princess Hildegarde." She turned to address Herald. "I left Castle Happenstance to find you, Mr. Wyvern, sir." She made an extravagant curtsey.

"It is heartening to see that some humans still observe the niceties of good breeding," commented the wyvern. "You may call me Herald."

Suddenly, the girl seemed distracted. Her hand touched the necklace she was wearing. "Yes, it *is* strange the wyvern can see me, but we can worry about that later," she said to no one in particular. After a pause, she added, "I know this isn't the plan, but sometimes you just have to improvise."

She seemed to notice the peculiar looks she was getting from the wyvern and gnomes.

"Beg your pardon," she said, blushing. "I was conversing with my questmate." She turned and called into the woods behind her. "Fred! Pipkin! You might as well come out."

Rudger experienced a thrill of awe as a stunning white horse emerged from the forest. A small human boy in baggy clothes accompanied it.

"Say hello to Herald," the Princess began. Then she flicked her eyes questioningly between the gnomes. "I'm sorry. I didn't catch your names."

"We didn't throw them," Twelda said flatly.

When the pause that followed grew awkward, Rudger spoke up.

"I'm Rudger Rump, and she's Twelda Greeze. Nice to meet you all." He held out his elbow to Hildegarde in the traditional Humdrungle greeting.

The Princess looked at it in befuddlement. "Oka-a-ay," she said uncertainly. "It's nice to make your acquaintance, too. Anyway, you'll have to excuse Fred, here. He communicates telepathically, and only with me, it seems."

And wizards, Rudger heard in his head. *Salutations to you, Rudger Rump.*

The startled gnome tried to think back a polite response.

No, no. It only works one way. You'll have to speak out loud.

"Oh. Well, in that case, salutations to you, Mr. Fred."

"Wait," Hildegarde said, turning to look at Fred. "The gnomes can hear you, too?"

"*I* can't," Twelda said tersely. "And who's that boy with you?"

Princess Hildegarde shrugged. "Frankly, we don't know his name. We rescued him from an arachna shrub this morning, and he hasn't said a word to us. We think he's been Muted."

Flashes of his siblings ensnared by arachna runners and of Vermis writhing on Kal's table stabbed at Rudger's mind. Preoccupied with these memories, Rudger regarded the boy before him vacantly at first, but then with slowly dawning recognition.

"Wow," Twelda said coolly. "That's dramatic. But we'd expect nothing less since we know that kid. Don't we, Rudger?"

"I think so," Rudger replied in confusion. "But isn't he… too young?"

All this time, the hazel-eyed lad had been distancing himself from the introductions and the conversation concerning his identity. He seemed to be staring blankly to his right, but Rudger abruptly realized the boy's eyes were moving incrementally to the left, toward Herald, as if tracking the movement of something.

"Herald! Watch out!" Rudger shouted.

The warning came too late. While everybody else was talking, the boy had been quietly watching a sword floating through the air.

Except it wasn't floating—at least, not of its own accord. A tiny orange blur was holding the sword aloft by its hilt.

Herald whipped his reptilian head in the direction Rudger was pointing. To the young gnome's horror, this brought the wyvern's purple snout perfectly in range.

Bink!

The mildest of sword strokes brought about the most devastating of effects. The sword dropped to the ground, and without warning, the wyvern began to beat his immense purple wings, catching everyone in their powerful backdraft.

As Rudger and the others fought for their balance, Herald snatched the sword up in his talons and launched himself into the air.

"Tutor's coming for you, Kal!" he roared.

Fire erupted, but not from the wyvern's maw. The white stallion called Fred suddenly sprouted a flaming horn upon its forehead—one which did not singe its own gleaming fur. The unicorn, for that is what Fred had become, charged as Herald's claws closed around the arms of the boy he'd called Kal and lifted him from the ground.

"Fred! Fred! Save Pipkin!" screamed Princess Hildegarde.

The unicorn's fiery horn struck the dragon's leg—with no effect.

Rudger quickly deduced why: *Dragons are fireproof.*

Fred apparently deduced this, too, because a gleaming ivory horn replaced the flaming one. The wyvern was swift; it had already ascended out of range, but the unicorn's forceful slash with its new horn caught the folds of the boy's baggy pants, pulling them off his legs. As the trousers hit the ground, a metal object flew free, clattering against the granite surface.

"Herald! Herald, what are you doing? Come back!" Twelda shouted as the great wyvern winged its way over the river with both the sword and Kal.

The orange blur darted after it, but before anyone could recover from the chaos, it was back.

"I'm sorry," it panted, looking left and right. "I…These tiny wings just can't keep up."

"Wingnut, what in the Elements have you done?" demanded Rudger.

The winged newt cocked its head. “I’m not Wingnut,” it said.

“Hieronymus, then,” growled Twelda.

“Nope. Wrong again. And I’ll give you a hint. I’m not Yeshirumon, either.”

Rudger made a horrifying connection. “Herald? Is that you?” he asked, looking aghast at the tiny flying lizard.

“You got it, kid. Vicarius the Switching Blade has struck again.”

CHAPTER TWENTY-SIX

"Here it is! Lair, sweet lair," announced the flying orange newt. He flitted about the expansive cavern, igniting torches with his tiny plume of exhaled fire. Whizzing past Hildegarde's shoulder, he added, "The place seems so much more spacious now that I've been miniaturized."

The human girl, who was rather inexperienced with the vagaries of magic, shook her head in bewilderment. Having spoken little and listened much on the league-long trek here, she at last ventured a query. "It doesn't bother you, then? That your rightful body's been stolen, I mean."

To her dismay, the little lizard darted toward her head and then hung in the air inches in front of her nose.

"Well! Will you look at that," he said, turning his head to take a gander at his wings. "I'm hovering! Always wished I could do that. Wyverns have to keep powering forward to stay aloft, you see. Elsewise, we drop like boulders. Most inconvenient, really.

"Ah! Rudger! Twelda! Come in, you two," the creature called to the gnomes, who were just arriving at the mouth of the cave after climbing down the cliff. "You know your way around. Make yourselves comfortable. Plenty of room for everyone.

"And to answer your question, Princess," he continued, abruptly turning his focus back on her, "it *is* rather irksome to have one's body spirited away, but it's nothing to get in a tew about. Admittedly, this particular bodily form is 'newt' to me —Ha! See what I did there?—but it's not the first time I've suffered corporeal eviction."

"It's not?"

"Elements, no! Why, I was telling Rudger and Twelda only last night that a mere three decades ago, I spend a rather gratifying day in Rudger's aunt's body. And a brief stop-off in a human boy's body, too, as I recall. Gnomette, human, and now this. It's quite educational, if you ask me.

"Ancestors! What am I blathering on about? Sit, sit, you three. I'm so unused to having company! I'm sure I have some victuals lying about someplace. You must be famished after our journey here. If you'll excuse me…"

The quivering ball of energy shot deep into the cavern and veered around a corner.

Hildegarde heaved a sigh of relief, feeling as though she'd suffered a form of mental whiplash. "Is Herald always that enthusiastic?" she asked, looking down at the gnome called Rudger.

"Well, he's talking a lot faster than usual," Rudger stated

uncertainly. He then turned to the gnomette named Twelda. "Do you suppose he got into your jawjackle juice?"

She looked in her satchel. "Nope," she replied, pulling out a vial of blue liquid. "It's still here. Lucky thing—the noggin-guard must've saved it from breaking when you dropped my pack." Then she regarded the vial more closely. "Hmm…I thought maybe…but, no. Guess there was only enough for one more dose."

Twelda exhaled slowly and looked at Rudger. "You know," she said, "I regret not trying this on Vermis."

"I do, too," Rudger replied. "Maybe it could have un-Muted him."

"But I suppose we can't be too hard on ourselves," reasoned the gnomette. "Vermis' message *did* imply that he believed Vicarius was the cure. So who are we to experiment on him with an unproven potion?"

Twelda shook her head sadly and slipped the vial back into her satchel. Then she cleared her throat. "Anyway, getting back to the cause of Herald's hyperactivity, I have a different hypothesis. I think it's an effect of his abruptly reduced size." She looked up at Hildegarde. "Speaking of size, could we all bump a rump like Herald suggested? I'm going to get a crick in my neck talking up at you like this."

Hildegarde's brain choked on the gnomette's jargon. "Noggi-…hypothe-…bump a rump?" she said, utterly mystified. Then the last one clicked. "Oh! You mean you want to sit down." She swept her gown's skirts aside and seated herself on the nearest rock. She let the knee-high gnomes do the same before she continued. "Now, at the risk of being indelicate, I want to ask something that's been bothering me ever since we met out on the cliffs. Have I done something to offend you?"

"You mean other than being human?" Twelda mumbled.

Rudger gave the gnomette a sharp look. "You'll have to excuse Twelda's rudeness," he told Hildegarde. "What she means is we Humdrungles are naturally wary around members of your species. In fact, we avoid humans if we can. You're only the second one she's ever met."

Hildegarde breathed a sigh of relief. "Well, you are the first gnomes I've ever met," she told them. "And I do want us to be friends. Especially since we seem to have a common goal."

"What's that?" asked Twelda.

"Finding the sword Vicarius. That is why I left Castle Happenstance, and from what I've gathered, it's why you started your quest, as well."

"Technically, this is Rudger's quest," Twelda stated. "We're after the sword because his grandparents have the Mute-ation, and we're hoping Vicarius can cure it."

"I hope that, too. My mother suffers the same affliction."

"Who told you about Vic?" Twelda asked.

"Oh. Um, a wizard. One who's in service to my uncle, the King." Hildegarde turned to Rudger. "Who told *you* Vic can cure the Mute-ation?"

"Vermis," Rudger answered. "We were talking about him earlier. He was a bookworm friend of ours. Then he got Muted."

"So it's spreading," Hildegarde concluded. "And not just amongst humans."

"We minikins are susceptible, too," Twelda confirmed.

"And other intelligent creatures like Vermis. So we need that sword, but Wingnut took it when he flew off with Kal."

A faint whinny interrupted the conversation.

"Lunira's luster, that's Fred," Hildegarde said. "I forgot all about him." She turned her attention inward to listen for her protector's telepathic voice, but there was only silence. A second whinny was heard, louder and more insistent than the first.

"Could you excuse me, just for a moment?" she asked the gnomes as she rose and walked to the mouth of the cave. Outside, she turned her eyes up the cliff's face. Fred was peering down at her from thirty feet above, his elegant white head gleaming in the moonlight.

Milady! Are you well?

"Yes, Fred," she told him, shouting slightly so he could hear. "Everything's fine. There's no need to fret."

I cannot help but fret with you so far away. Why have you ignored my inquiries concerning your welfare?

"I didn't receive them. I guess telepathy doesn't work through rock."

All the more reason for you to stay up here with me.

"No offense, but I'm not keen on spending another night out in the open. I'll feel safer with a roof over my head."

Then I shall find a way down to you.

"No, you will not," Hildegarde yelled to him through cupped hands. Her throat was beginning to hurt with the effort of generating sufficient volume. "You'll break a leg trying to climb down, or worse. And even if you managed it, how would you get back up again? Unless you have a pair of invisible wings you haven't told me about."

I detect a twinge of sarcasm in that statement.

"Well, that's what you get for keeping secrets from your maiden, Mr. Unicorn."

I told you. I am not a unicorn. I am a quadricorn.

"Yes, yes. Four horns, not one." Hildegarde had to stop to cough. "You've got one for each of the Standard Elements."

You question my veracity?

"Let's see. I saw your Earth and Fire horns when you battled the wyvern. And, supposedly, you used your invisible Air horn on Gedd and the arachna shrub. By my count, that makes three, which means you're *still* holding out on me regarding the fourth one."

You wish to see my Aqua-horn? Is that what this little snit is about?

"Yes! And I'm not having a snit. I just don't think there should be secrets between a maiden and her quadricorn."

A sudden stream of liquid spattered her upturned face.

"Fred, you *child!*" she shouted in outrage. "I…*glup*…*glurk*…This had *better* be water!"

Furious, Hildegarde wiped the mystery liquid out of her eyes. When her vision cleared, she saw Fred still standing above her, moonlight illuminating a horn of rippling fluidity on his forehead.

Satisfied? he asked smugly.

Hildegarde's exasperated growl devolved into a fit of coughs. When at last she'd recovered, she looked back up at Fred, shielding her face with a hand lest he drench her with water again.

"I can't talk to you when you're like this," she yelled at the quadricorn. "And I'm screaming myself hoarse. Or screaming *at* a horse. Whatever! Look, I'm going back inside. Just go bed down somewhere, and I'll see you tomorrow morning. Okay?"

Fred snorted loudly and pulled his head out of view.

"Ugh!" Hildegarde cried as she returned to the cave, wringing out her hair. Herald was back, and he'd lit a brazier which he and the gnomes were now gathered around. They each held a skewer with bits of meat impaled upon it.

"Dactopus-kebabs!" the newt announced cheerily. Then he cocked his tiny head. "Is it raining, Princess?" he asked.

"No," she said testily, "but I may need to *rein* a certain somebody in."

"Fred doesn't like being up there all alone," Twelda surmised. "I don't blame him. He's missing all the action."

"What action?"

"We're making plans."

"Indubitably," agreed Herald. "Rudger's keen eyes and quick wits have procured for us an item that fell out of the boy Kal's pants."

Curiosity quelled the Princess' irritation. "Really? What is it?"

"We're not quite sure. It appears to be some sort of magical device. At least, it has a Glynt on it. One that coincidentally matches that of your necklace and hourglass."

"Hourglass? Oh, no! I forgot about Minsec, too," Hildegarde exclaimed, hurrying to retrieve the rucksack she'd dropped near the entrance. Opening its flap, she extracted the timepiece. Its sand went black as it crossed two of its support rods in a disgruntled manner.

"Lunira help me, I can't seem to please anybody tonight,"

she lamented. "I'm sorry, Minsec. And I apologize to you, too, Herald. Please continue."

"Well, as I was telling Rudger and Twelda, this artifact, whatever it is, is constructed of metal."

"Is that important?"

"Yes. Because in addition to my many other attributes and skills, I happen to be a first-class Ferrie."

The newt waited for oohs and ahhs, but the significance of his statement was lost on his audience.

"Didn't you hear what I said? I'm a Ferrie!"

Rudger coughed uncomfortably.

"Well, you *do* have wings, and you're the right size now, but I've never heard of a fairy with scales and a tail before."

"Oh, you hominids!" the newt cried. "Not *that* kind of fairy. It's spelled *F-E-R-R-I-E*."

Rudger looked at Twelda.

"Nope," she said curtly. "Never heard of it."

"I know it's a rare talent, but surely you've heard of metal-urging before."

"Metallurgy?" asked Rudger. He pulled a notebook from his pocket and a quill from behind his ear. "What's that?"

Herald rolled his eyes. "You really are your aunt's nephew," he said ruefully. "She made the same mistake, so I've been told. But this isn't about metallurgy; it's about metal-*urging*—the art of coaxing secrets out of metal objects."

"Huh. Can you coax the secrets out of a quadricorn?" Hildegarde asked drily.

Herald blinked at her. "No. It only works on metals like bronze or iron. Actually, the latter is where the word *Ferrie* gets its derivation. *Ferrum* means iron."

Rudger's quill darted across the page of his notebook.

"What kind of secrets can a hunk of metal hold?" asked Twelda.

"That depends entirely upon the hunk," Herald said. "Personal items sometimes reveal quite a lot. But knowing the name of the artifact helps the process. Rudger, when you're done with that entry, could you hold the object of interest at arm's length, please? There's a lad."

The gnome set down his quill and produced from his pocket a small, rectangular box that gleamed gold in the firelight.

Herald rose from his rock and flitted about it. After examining it from several angles, he settled on Rudger's shoulder. "Is this as strange for you as it is for me?" the flying lizard asked him off-handedly. "If I had landed on you like this yesterday, you'd have been a grease spot."

"Well, at this size, you're welcome to perch on me anytime you'd like," Rudger said genially. "Wingnut and Vermis did it all the time."

"How kind. Now, to business. There is no name inscribed on the artifact, so we must assume it has none of its own. That forces me to resort to its owner's name, Kal. Place the artifact on that rock, Rudger, and I will see what I can do."

The gnome did as he was instructed, and the winged newt circled the object, speaking a language Hildegarde had never heard before. The words seemed heavy with age and history, but they produced no effect on the artifact.

Herald returned to his rock and sighed.

"It's no use," he said. "I was confident I would succeed, but 'Kal' doesn't seem to be the right name."

"Maybe the box doesn't belong to Kal," suggested Twelda.

"Or maybe that boy on the cliff wasn't Kal at all," Rudger said. "I know we've argued about this, Twelda, but how *could* that little boy be Kal? Kal's ten years old; he told us himself. And Hildegarde said the boy she rescued couldn't be more than six or seven. She's a human. She should know."

"And I keep telling you there's something very peculiar about our friend, Kal," Twelda replied. "Sure, he and Wingnut *claimed* Kal was ten when we met him—or possibly nine, they couldn't seem to agree. But then a few days later, Kal seemed taller and older. Maybe fourteen, if I'm any judge. And then, just yesterday morning, we saw him running away from the cabin. You can't tell me he didn't seem even older than fourteen then."

"But assuming all that is true, it would mean Kal is aging super-fast," Rudger pointed out. "So it stands to reason he should be an adult now, not a six-year-old child."

"That's the part I'm still trying to work out."

Herald interrupted their debate. "I may have an answer to your dilemma, but I'm not entirely sure. Let us pursue our other lead. The Glynt on the artifact is identical to the one on the amulet. Who gave you that necklace, Princess?"

The human girl hooked her thumb around the amulet's chain, nervous they might ask her to remove it and thus expose her true appearance. "Um, it was a wizard. The same one who told me about Vicarius. But he's a court wizard. He couldn't have anything to do with this."

"I'm not convinced of that. What is his name?"

Hildegarde felt an uncomfortable pressure build in her

chest. For some reason, she didn't want to divulge the man's identity.

"Princess," the newt said gently, "I really must have the wizard's name, if you know it."

"Lendar," she finally said. The pressure dissipated as if a valve had been turned. "The wizard's name is Lendar."

"Thank you."

Herald took to the air again, orbiting the metal box and muttering in the archaic tongue. But again, he settled back on his rock.

"Still no good," he reported. "This is exasperating! With each of the names, I felt a certain give in the metal's resistance, a certain inclination to speak. But the names don't seem to have full power—as if they're incomplete." He paused for a moment and then lifted his tiny reptilian head sharply. "I wonder…"

For the third time, he flew in a circuit, whispering to the artifact in the age-old language. Suddenly, the box glowed with a light that did not come from the fire. Herald glided to a landing on the floor, his little head bobbing in an unnatural way. Without warning, tintinnabulous words fell from the entranced newt's lips.

Tock and tick, tick and tock,
He bears the weight of the disordered clock.
I manage the punishment for his crime,
A Chronocurse from the Beast of Time.
His prison boasts no bars or cages,
But imprisoned he is, this Mage of Ages.

The eerie recitation ended, and the otherworldly gleam on the artifact faded. Herald's eyes came back into focus, and he collapsed, clearly exhausted by his Ferrie efforts.

"Herald?" Rudger inquired as he hurried to the newt's side. "Are you all right?"

"No need to fuss," he assured his visitors. "Took a lot out of me, that's all. There was a powerful barrier to overcome."

"But was it worth it?" Rudger asked. "What did we learn?"

"Something important, possibly," Hildegarde said. "The owner of this box, this 'Mage of Ages', is cursed."

"Right. A Chronocurse, whatever that is," Twelda stated thoughtfully. "And there was something about a disordered clock." She fell silent for a moment, and then her expression changed. "Do…do you suppose Kal *is* the owner of this golden box? Could that explain why we keep seeing him at different ages? He is a mage, after all."

"But why would Lendar want to put such a horrible curse on a little boy?" asked Hildegarde. "What crime could a six-year-old commit in order to deserve that?"

"No, no," Twelda said, shaking her head. "You're assuming Kal is actually six years old. He might not be six. Or ten. Or fourteen. We're just seeing the effects of his disordered clock. Kal might really be any age at all."

"What if," Rudger began. Then he stopped and swallowed hard. "What if Kal is a *man* sometimes? What if *that's* why he disappears from the cabin so often?"

"And Wingnut is in on it," Twelda said, shaking a finger with increasing certainty. "That would explain why he cut off what Kal was saying."

"When?" asked Rudger.

"At tea on the day we met Kal. I remember because it was so odd. Kal was saying something like, 'My parents died before I was cur—' And then Wingnut got all excited and blurted out the word 'weaned'. It didn't make sense at the time, but it does now. I think Kal was going to say 'cursed.'"

"But I still don't understand why Lendar the Wizard would want to curse a boy way out in the woods," Hildegarde persisted.

"He didn't," stated Herald with uncharacteristic gravity.

"He didn't?" repeated the Princess. "But you said the Glynt on the artifact matches the one on my necklace. And Minsec. And both of those items belong to Lendar."

"And so does this box," Herald replied.

"Wait," Twelda said. "We heard what the box said. It belongs to the Mage of Ages, and that has to be Kal."

"It is," agreed Herald.

Twelda frowned at the newt. "What are you saying, Herald? That this cursed artifact belongs to both Kal *and* Lendar? How can that be?"

"Because of the name that successfully urged the artifact," he told them.

"What name was that?"

Herald raised his head and chest from the ground and looked at each of his three guests.

"Kal-Lendar. Kallendar. The boy and the wizard are one and the same."

CHAPTER TWENTY-SEVEN

Lunira had exited her nightly stage, leaving her seven sister stars behind to bathe the small lake with their muted light. At the water's southern edge, a rocky ridge sheltered the wurblebirds roosting in its recesses. To the north, an upside-down cabin balanced itself on its crooked fieldstone chimney. And through that cabin's window, the meager light of a candle spilled, softly illuminating the hulking form of a giant at Giant's Foot Pond.

It was Hieronymus the wyvern, who, in his stolen form, now matched the cottage in size. The human boy he'd brought there was sleeping inside on a bed that, from Hieronymus' point of view, appeared to be suspended from the cabin's ceiling.

The wyvern tutor had been standing guard over his pupil all night, anxiously awaiting the change to take place. As fond as Hieronymus was of the little human, he knew how urgent it was for the boy's alter ego to emerge. Lendar the Wizard had been absent from the castle too long, and their great undertaking—the one that might end Kallendar's double life—was in jeopardy. Everything hinged on the age the wizard boy was about to manifest.

But the Chronocurse was fickle. It rarely obliged its victim, or his tutor. This night, it chose to toy with Hieronymus, stringing him along until the cusp of dawn. Only then did the wyvern finally sense the transtemporation energy as it gathered around his charge. The six-year-old moaned softly as his day's tenure finally drew to a close.

Hieronymus first noticed the change come over the boy's limbs, each of them beginning to lengthen, pushing hands and feet outward, away from his trunk. Kal's shoulders grew broader; his hips followed suit. Muscles all over the boy's body stretched and swelled in response to his rapidly expanding frame.

The wyvern focused on the boy's candlelit face. Kal's childish features were falling away—the button nose elongating, the delicate cheekbones spreading and thickening, the tapered chin growing heavy and square. But when the skin on the boy's jawline sprouted dense brown whiskers, Hieronymus knew he could relax at last. The coming day would belong to Lendar.

The wizard's still-lengthening feet jutted their way over the end of the bed, dragging with them his linen coverlet. The exposed chest widened a bit more, and then the transformation was complete. Where once lay a little boy now lay a fully grown man.

Hieronymus found himself unable to wait for his companion's natural wakening. "Lendar?" he inquired. "Will you wake?"

The man inhaled through his nose and stretched languorously. He opened green-tinted eyes and dully considered the rafters above him.

"Good morning," said Hieronymus.

The man twisted his neck to the left. Upon seeing the upside-down head of the great purple wyvern in the window, he yelped and conjured forth a ball of yellow Fyre.

It struck Hieronymus squarely in the face. "Gah!" complained the wyvern. "Is that any way to treat your faithful familiar?"

"Hieronymus? Is that you?" Lendar asked shakily. The wyvern nodded, and the wizard cleared his throat to continue. "You…you must take care not to startle me like that. The last time I remember seeing you, you were small enough to fit in the palm of my hand. Where in the Elements did you get *that* monstrosity of a body?"

Hieronymus chuckled. "You could not de-miniaturize my natural one, so I took matters into my own claws," he answered. The wyvern raised his eye-ridges expectantly. "Can you remember how?"

Lendar rubbed his face. "I am not yet awake enough for your games, Hieronymus," he grumbled. "Give me a hint. How old was I yesterday?"

"About six, I'd say."

"Six? By Helios, that's young. And today?"

Hieronymus sized up the man. "Old enough to be Lendar, thank the ancestors, but a few more years would've been better."

"Perhaps, but there's no help for that," the wizard replied. "Very well. On to your irksome memory test. You say I was six yesterday. That's what? Two decades ago for me?" He fell silent, appearing to be sorting through his memories.

"Need another hint?" Hieronymus offered after a few moments. "Come to window and gaze upon me in all my splendor."

Lendar scoffed but did as his familiar suggested. Hieronymus flexed his expansive wings to catch the dawn sunlight on his glittering purple scales. The man seemed duly impressed.

"My compliments on your choice of body," he said. "I seem to remember little orange you wielding the Switching Blade and striking this poor creature."

"That I did," Hieronymus admitted. "I couldn't tolerate being tiny enough to bed down in one of your shoes any longer." A shudder of disgust rippled the wyvern from head to tail. "Blech! I can't believe I actually did that."

"It was far more distressing for me. Shedding those sharp scales of yours into my footwear these past…" Lendar frowned in concentration and then shook his head. "Oh, it's not worth the figuring. You tell me. How long were you lizard-sized in this timeline?"

"Three years," Hieronymus replied with a dramatic sigh. "Three long, mortifying years of tininess, and I am *so* glad they're finally over. To think, a chance encounter with some random magic-worker could strip me of my dragonly magnitude, and all because that bozo thought he was saving Princess Winifer from me! Ugh!" The wyvern paused and turned his head top-for-bottom to regard Lendar with his imploring yellow orbs. "You…you *do* think she'll accept me now. Like this, I mean."

The wizard rolled his eyes as he stood and donned his tunic. "As I've told you countless times before, Winifer was devastated by your sudden disappearance in that field. I'm sure she'd welcome you back in any form. But truly, it would have been kinder to let her see what had become of you than to vanish without a trace."

"Oh, no," Hieronymus said resolutely. "I could never have let her see me in that pathetic, shrunken state."

"Ah, but you had no problem letting *me* see you as a flying newt, it seems."

The wyvern blinked. "Well, of course not. I had every expectation you could restore my grandeur. But you couldn't."

"Ugh! You're not going to grind those bones again, are you?" cried the sorcerer. "I've told you a dozen times, that magician worked a most potent incantation on you! If it had been based in Earth, Water, Air, or Fire magic, I would have had you fit to terrorize the peasantry before you could stoke your fire! But any hex cast upon a dragon such as yourself *couldn't* be based in Elemental magic because your natural resistance would have repelled it. No, a successful curse on you would have to be steeped in the art of Logomancy. And as you very well know, I do not have willful access to the Source of that magic. It…it's a matter of some embarrassment to me."

"Well," said Hieronymus, "I am happy to report that in my present form *I* have no further call to be embarrassed. And soon, neither will you."

The wizard's eyes brightened. "What? Do you mean to say the

Logoleech has finished its work? That my Chronocurse is at last lifted?" Then his face darkened again. "But, no. This cannot be, or I would remember it, no matter what age I was yesterday. And we certainly wouldn't still be hiding out in this wretched cabin."

"Regretfully, you are correct," said the wyvern. "The Chronocurse is still in place, and the Logoleech continues to spread its Mute-ation plague. I was referring to the fact that you have likely amassed enough eloquys to end the curse —*and* depose Archmage Janusz in the bargain. You only need one more thing to set our plan in motion."

"Vicarius," Lendar said, casting his eyes about the room as if in search of the magical sword. "But the last time I saw it was decades ago on the day I was a boy and got ensnared by that awful arachna shrub in the Vale of the..." He stopped abruptly, his eyes sliding to one side as if trying to jog a memory. "Wait," he said. "Wasn't that the same day you struck the wyvern with Vicarius and took its body?"

"It was," Hieronymus confirmed with a reptilian grin.

"And that was yesterday in your timeline, right?" Lendar asked, staring avidly at his familiar. "I...can't remember. It was too long ago for me. Did you manage to retain Vicarius in that debacle on the cliff top? Do you have it today?"

The wyvern's head disappeared from the window and promptly reappeared. His words were slightly garbled as he spoke around the sword he held in his mouth.

"Would you believe it's been in my own lair for almost four years now? I stole this sword from Herald the wyvern's hoard just because it had an intriguing Glynt. I had no idea until quite recently it was Vicarius." Hieronymus chuckled.

"Poor Herald. First, I stole his sword, and then I used it to steal his body. What a dirty trick to pull on my old mentor."

"Great Elements!" exclaimed the wizard as he eagerly took the sword in hand. "Hieronymus, we must return to the tower at once and investigate the properties of this fabled blade. But first thing's first." Lendar abruptly dropped to all fours and began to scrabble beneath the bed.

The wyvern stuck his head through the window in an effort to see. "Is something the matter?" he asked.

The bewhiskered man's head popped up from behind the mattress. "Yes. You forgot a second crucial thing we need to set our plan in motion."

"Oh? What is that?"

"My pants. Wherever could they have gotten to, I wonder?"

Hieronymus laughed. "A funny thing happened on the way off the cliff," he began.

CHAPTER TWENTY-EIGHT

"I'm sorry, Your Highness," Rudger Rump blurted, "but this just *can't* be the way to your castle."

The young gnome made his declaration atop Fred the quadricorn, sandwiched between the human Princess and Twelda Greeze. The foursome, plus Herald the flying newt and the hourglass called Minsec, had set out for Castle Happenstance at the crack of dawn. But shortly after leaving the rock cliffs and entering the marshy terrain of the Hinterlands, Rudger had begun to distrust the directions being doled out by the enchanted timepiece.

"It's not?" the Princess asked Rudger from behind. "I don't see how we could have gone wrong. We've followed Minsec's directions to the letter."

"But we can't see the river anymore," Rudger pointed out. "Isn't the castle on the river? And that brook we just crossed. I'm pretty sure I've seen it before. Back when my mother and the triplets and I were traveling to my Aunt Ragna's burrow. I think the hourglass is leading us there, Your Highness."

"How could Minsec possibly know the way to your aunt's home, Rudger?"

"I'm not sure, Highness, but we're practically there."

"Well, I may not know these parts, but there's something I do know," the Princess said.

Rudger turned in his seat. "What's that, Your High—"

"Uh-uh!" she chided good-naturedly. "I *know* I've had my fill of this 'Highness' business. So for the duration of our quest together, I ask you and everyone else to call me Hildegarde."

Rudger and Twelda were quick to agree. The human girl smiled and then addressed her steed.

"What do *you* think of Rudger's topographical concerns, Fred?"

Rudger heard no response to the question, and for a worrisome moment, he thought he'd lost his ability to detect the quadricorn's thoughts. But when Hildegarde repeated her query, Rudger realized the equine had simply failed to answer. It took yet a third inquiry to elicit Fred's acerbic reply.

Oh, I'm sorry. Are you speaking to me? You're soliciting my opinion now?

Hildegarde seemed taken aback. "Well, of course I am," she said. "Why wouldn't I?"

It's just that after the way you stabled me above Herald's cave last night, I've been re-evaluating my status in this questing party.

"What? Whatever are you talking about, Fred?"

Lowly beasts of burden such as myself should never

presume to provide input, madam. My role is simple: to convey you and your companions on my unworthy back to your self-decided destination.

"Lunira's luster, Fred! You're sulking, and it doesn't become you. We may have had a disagreement last night, but that doesn't mean I don't value your input."

Herald suddenly swooped down from his aerial reconnaissance. "Tsk, tsk," said he. "Sounds like there may be dissention in the ranks, Your Highness."

"Hildegarde," the girl corrected him, "and we're fine. Fred is just feeling a little underappreciated at the moment."

"Underworshipped, more like," the wyvern-turned-newt snipped. "Unicorns have an epically overinflated opinion of themselves. Pretentious ponies with horns, if you ask me. And quadricorns, by extension, are *four* times as bad."

"Herald, will you please stay out of this?" Hildegarde snapped. "Fred's already being a handful, and you're only making it worse."

A handful, am I? cried the outraged quadricorn. *If this pretentious pony is too much to handle, perhaps you and your hoity-toity hominid friends would prefer to walk!*

"Fred, I swear you'd better rein in your ego before I—"

TWEEE-uh-EEEEET!

The piercing whistle made everyone wince.

"That's enough!" bellowed Twelda Greeze as she lowered her fingers from her lips. "I may not be able to hear Fred's contribution to this catty conversation, but it's clear all this bickering has got to stop! We have to work *together* to get Vicarius back from Kallendar and his hench-dragon, Wingnut, or Hieronymus, or Yeshirumon, or *whatever* he's calling himself these days. So let's grow up and get on with this quest!"

The gnomette's outburst seemed to hit home with most of the questing party. It instantly silenced the quarrel between girl and quadricorn. Even the centuries-old wyvern backed off, his little blurred wings lifting him back up into the sky without so much as a snide parting shot.

But Rudger felt maligned by Twelda's scolding. "*I* wasn't bickering," he mumbled.

"Noted, but beside the point," Twelda replied. "Now, since we're so close, I suggest we check up on Rudger's aunt and his siblings. We can rest at the burrow for a few hours and then resume our trek to the castle. Agreed?"

No one seemed particularly keen on arguing with the sharp-tongued gnomette, so in just over a quarter-hour, Rudger felt the comfort of familiar surroundings for the first time in a very long week.

The dirt trail they were following wended its way past the puxa-pod bushes where the Terror Trio had waged their little war under the disapproving auspices of their beleaguered mother. It felt to Rudger this had happened a lifetime ago, and it suddenly occurred to him that his mother had been right. He *would* have been a negligent babysitter, taking off on a grand adventure at the behest of a strange little vermitome. A twinge of sadness struck Rudger for neither Vermis nor his mother would be found at the burrow, but his heart lightened as he drew breath to call to those loved ones who would.

"Aunt—"

The abrupt *twang!* of an unseen mechanical device cut Rudger's salutation short. A moment later, the *whump!* of an impact somewhere above them made Rudger cringe and throw his arms over his head lest a falling something bean him on the noggin.

"Gotcha!" cried a distant, high-pitched voice. "I *knew* you'd be back, and this time, you won't be escaping by burning a hole through our net! Ha!"

"Roon?" Rudger called as he scanned the marshland from his vantage point on the quadricorn's back. "Roon, is that you? Where are you?"

"Rudger?" came the disbelieving reply. The tip of a gnome's tan cap circumnavigated a scraggly bush and parted the sea of tall weeds that carpeted the area. "Rudger, is that you?"

"Yes, yes! Over here!"

"Cool! You've got a beard!" the bobbing cap exclaimed. "I want one, too!"

Rudger barely noticed the long drop to the ground in his haste to dismount and embrace his little brother. The Humdrungling burst out of his weedy cover wearing the biggest smile Rudger had ever seen on his tiny face. But an embrace was impossible, for Roon's arms were full. Tucked under his left arm was a bulky device constructed of sticks and puxa-fiber cord. And pinned under his right arm was a bedraggled orange creature slathered in slime.

"Herald!" Rudger cried. Then his voice took on a scandalized tone. "Oh, *Roon*. What have you done to him?"

The younger brother frowned at the elder. "'Herald?' I thought you called this varmint 'Wingnut.' That's what it told me, anyway."

"Wait. You've already met Herald?" Rudger asked in confusion.

"Couldn't have," Twelda stated as she came up on Rudger's right. "He must have met Wingnut when he was in that body." She took another step forward and jutted out her elbow. "Hello, Roon. I'm Twelda. It's nice to finally meet you."

The gnomeling did not return her gesture of greeting. His saucer-like eyes were transfixed on a point far above Twelda's head. "Hu-…hu-hu-…hu-hu-hu…," he babbled.

Rudger turned to see an amused look on Hildegarde's face. "Oh, don't mind Hildegarde," he assured his brother. "She's all right. Turns out all humans aren't evil, after all."

"I should say not," the Princess remarked as she gathered up her skirts to kneel. "I'm pleased to make your acquaintance, Master Roon." Taking a cue from Twelda, she proffered her elbow in greeting.

Roon regarded her with amazement as several seconds ticked by. Then a shy grin tugged at the corners of his mouth. He bent his arm and tapped elbows with the human.

Ahem.

Hildegarde's eyes widened suddenly. "Oh, I beg your pardon, Fred! Roon, meet Fred. He's a quadricorn."

Roon promptly dropped both the device and his captive newt as his mouth fell open. The colossal equine seemed one shock too many for the little gnome.

"A lot has happened since I left home," Rudger explained with a shrug. "As if meeting a human princess and a quadricorn weren't enough, I also made friends with a wyvern." He gestured toward the orange blob at their feet. "That's him."

"B-b-b-but, Rudger," stammered Roon. "That flying lizard...it *attacked* us."

"He's not a lizard, Roon. He's a newt. Well, actually, he's not a newt, either. He's a wyvern magicked into the body of a newt. And it seems it was the other newt that attacked you, not this one. Well, it was this *body* that attacked you, but with a different spirit inside. It's all very complicated." A second glance at the weakly struggling creature prompted Rudger to address the quadricorn. "Oh, Fred, that slime's got poor Herald in distress. Do you mind?"

The white stallion closed his eyes and summoned his Aqua-horn. It was just as Hildegarde had described it—a sparkling semi-solid spear. A few squirts of its pristine water washed the slime away and roused Herald with a spate of spits and sputters.

"Now, *that* was a humbling experience," he said between coughs. "A mighty wyvern nearly done in by a gnomeling's snotball."

"Actually, it was a glob of puxa-pod pus," Roon admitted sheepishly. He pointed at the device he had dropped. "I launched it with that. And I'm sorry."

Twelda picked up the launcher. "You built this yourself?" she asked Roon as she examined it from every angle.

"Sure," he said with a shrug. "No big deal."

"He's always tinkering with something," added Rudger. "Come to think of it, that's something the two of you have in common." He shifted his gaze to his little brother. "Where are Aunt Ragna and your sisters?"

"Gardening in the back. That's all those three ever do around here. Come on, they have to meet all of you! Just be sure to watch out for Auntie's arachna shrubs. They're extra grabby today. Haven't had a decent meal in a while."

As Roon scampered off, Rudger heard Fred scoff telepathically. *Arachna shrubs. Ugh.*

Hildegarde caught Rudger's eye as she stood.

"You know, Rudger, I'm famished," she said with a wink. "Might a peckish Princess procure a peck of purple piprum pods in this particular patch, perchance?" She risked a sly look at her steed.

Fred blasted her with horn water.

Everybody laughed.

CHAPTER TWENTY-NINE

Hieronymus soared through the crisp morning air, reveling in his newly regained size and power. His gleeful exuberance tended to make him forget he had a rider.

"This…flying, it's…totally unnecessary," Lendar gasped as his trembling legs gripped the base of Hieronymus' long neck. "I…I could have made it to the castle perfectly well on foot."

The wyvern laughed. "Don't be absurd! We only have twenty-two hours before you transtemporate again, maybe less. You'd waste two whole hours of it walking into Lexicon City, crossing the river, and climbing the Stonesculpt Steps. No, no. It's much faster to fly. And besides…"

Hieronymus turned his head to eye his nervous passenger.

"…flying is to *die* for!"

The wyvern tilted his wings to execute a glorious spinning spiral up into the clouds. Lendar let out a strangled cry and seized Hieronymus' neck in a choke-hold of terror. When they leveled out at a higher altitude, the wizard gasped in a singularly undignified manner.

"Hieronymus!" he scolded in a shaky voice. "Don't you *ever* do that again!"

"Do what? This?"

The wyvern performed a killer barrel roll.

"Yes! That!" Lendar cried. "Stop doing that, or I'll hex you!"

"Can't," Hieronymus teased. "I'm immune to Elemental magic, remember? And you're rubbish at Logomancy."

"Then I'll reap some Logomagic from the urn and turn you into a chitterbug!"

Hieronymus' mirth met an abrupt end. "Boy, you're a grouch today," he said petulantly. "You're way more fun when you're a kid."

"Oh, yes," the wizard agreed. "And I'm a barrel of laughs when I'm not in mortal peril. Look, there's the river now. Just deposit me on the other side. I'll climb the Steps and sneak into the—"

"Why don't I just land on the tower, and you can pop down into the lab through the star-gazing hatch? It'd be a lot easier."

Lendar paused. "You think that's safe? You're no lightweight anymore."

"Puh. I did that sort of thing all the time when I was Princess Winifer's companion."

The wizard snorted. "What *is* it with you and that girl, anyway?" he asked. "I've seen her at court. She's a prissy little brat, if you ask me."

"She is not a brat," Hieronymus said defensively. "She's just...misunderstood."

"It's hard to misunderstand the way she mistreats that cousin of hers."

"Who?"

"Hildegarde. Winifer bullies her relentlessly."

"Well, *you're* one to talk," Hieronymus fired back. "You certainly didn't have Hildegarde's welfare in mind when you sent her on that ludicrous quest."

"Beg your pardon?"

"You know, the quest you sent her on to get Vicarius from Herald's lair? To save her poor, Muted mother? And then you bribed her with an amulet that casts a glamour on the wearer?" The wyvern chuckled. "Actually, that was one of *my* more diabolical ideas. Does any of this ring a bell? It happened just a few days ago."

"No, I do not remember," Lendar said irritably. "How many times do I have to remind you I'm chronologically challenged? I can't remember things that happened on days when I was older than I am now. How old *was* I when I did all this?"

Hieronymus' own irritation manifested in a puff of dragon smoke. "How should I know? You expect me to keep track of everything that happens around here *and* your constantly changing ages when they happen? Isn't that what your little golden box is for?"

Lendar sighed. "The Chronologue's gone missing. Along with my pants. *And* my favorite boots. I've been racking my brain, trying to put the puzzle pieces of my life together without the record the Chronologue provides. Like, what in the Elements was my younger self doing in dragon country so he could be trapped by that arachna shrub? You're supposed to keep Kal safely ensconced at the cabin on days when I'm that young. What happened?"

"Beats me," answered the familiar. "I was away in the Hinterlands, mesmerizing Ragna Riggle for information. I was shocked to see cute little you with Princess Hildegarde above my waterfall."

"I am not 'cute.'"

"Not now, you aren't," Hieronymus agreed. "Right now, you're a cross between an ogre and the wrong end of a blunderelk. But when you're six or seven, you're downright adorable."

"Enough!" growled the wizard. "The point is my six-year-old alter ego couldn't have traveled four leagues south and crossed the river all by himself. So it only stands to reason *I* must have made that journey."

"A logical deduction, but how old were you the day before yesterday? Can you remember making the journey?"

"I think so. It was about a year ago, in my timeline. I started out by ditching a couple of gnomes at the cabin, so that must have been Rudger Rump and...What was that gnomette's name again?"

"Twelda Greeze."

"Right. Most of my interactions with those two Humdrungles were years and years ago by my reckoning, when I was Kal. But in this more recent memory, I was outpacing them on my way to your lair to retrieve the Chronologue. I can't remember why it was there and not in my pocket, where I usually keep it. Ugh! Everything gets so muddled when I don't have that device!"

"So you keep telling me," commented the wyvern.

"I do remember eventually finding it," Lendar continued, "but it was well past sunset, and you weren't there, and I went out to look for you and lost my way in the dark. I tried to stay awake all night, but I must have dozed off just before dawn."

"And you woke up as six-year-old Kal," Hieronymus surmised. "Then you wandered into the clutches of the arachna shrub, got saved by Hildegarde and that quadricorn, showed up on the cliff, and lost your pants with the Chronologue inside it during my rescue operation."

"I guess so," Lendar agreed uncertainly. "I don't remember most of that. Just the part when a pretty lady freed me from the arachna."

"That was Hildegarde. Wearing the glamour-producing amulet you provided."

"Oh, this accursed curse!" the man suddenly wailed. "How can I be expected to function with my timeline in perpetual chaos?"

Hieronymus peered at the terrain below through a breach in the cloud cover. They were over the River Gush, but he saw no sign of the Stonesculpt Steps. He veered north toward the sea.

"You know," he said, "things might be a lot simpler if you just told people about your curse. Especially Kal. You owe it to yourself." The wyvern cocked his head as he processed what he'd just said. "Whoa. Talk about your double meanings."

"Absolutely not, Hieronymus," Lendar said firmly. "No one can know. If anyone at the castle caught wind of my magical affliction, I'd be expelled from the Guild. And above all others, Kal must be kept in the dark."

"Why?" asked the wyvern. "He's…I mean, you're pretty tough. Even as a child. You could handle it."

"Hieronymus, we've been through this! Everything that happens to Kal threatens to change *me*. *His* experiences alter *my* memories. *His* feelings color *my* perceptions. And Helios forbid he should ever sustain a serious injury—or be killed! No. When Kal manifests in this timeline, he must be kept safe and ignorant of the identity of his mysterious Never Man."

"He's going to figure out it's you eventually," Hieronymus ventured.

"I know. And when he figures something out in your timeline, it changes what I remember in mine. One day, I'll have a certain set of childhood memories and impressions, and on my next day, by my own chronology, there are new ones! I can still remember when I *didn't* have those memories. Half the time, I feel like I'm losing my mind! So, please. I just need Kal sequestered and studying magic as hard as you can push him when he's here. It all adds to my knowledge and power on the days when I'm Lendar."

"Whatever you say," the wyvern acquiesced, though he was unconvinced. "But there's one thing I'm not agreeing to."

"What's that?"

"Dropping you on the riverbank. Because there's the castle now."

Hieronymus went into a sharp dive.

"No, no!" Lendar yelped. "The guards! They'll shoot us down with their crossbows!"

"Oh, balderdash. They're used to Winifer having a dragon around."

"But that was three years ago in your timeline. And you were an orange dragon then, not a purple wyvern!"

"You'd better make fancy with the magic, then, because I'm going in for a landing."

Hieronymus approached the northeast tower's roof, which at his present size seemed disconcertingly small. As he took aim, he glanced at the two sentries patrolling the battlement walkway below. Fortunately, neither challenged his approach.

"They must have seen my purple wizard robe," Lendar said once the landing had been accomplished. "That's why they didn't fire. I'll go speak to them to ensure they don't have second thoughts."

Lendar dismounted, took one step, and leaned out over the tower's edge. Meanwhile, Hieronymus worked to arrange himself more securely on his little stone pedestal. It was a challenge to keep his various body parts from covering the hatch door which led to the laboratory below.

"There," the wizard announced as he turned around. "Those men won't disobey a direct order from me, so you'll be fine up here." He paused and then added, "Think you'll be able to reach?"

Hieronymus was looking over the edge of the tower at an opening in the wall below. "It's a good thing your laboratory is close to the top," he stated. "It's going to be a bit of a stretch."

"You'll manage," the wizard replied as he lifted the hatch door.

Once the man had disappeared inside, Hieronymus braced himself with claws and wings against the stone merlons that crested the tower. Extending his head over the side, he found his new neck was just long enough to let him peer through the window at the inverted lab within.

A profusion of beakers and flasks covered the gnarlicwood workbenches which abutted the western wall of the circular room. Overburdened bookcases crowded the eastern wall, holding twice as many volumes as were housed in the cabin at Giant's Foot Pond. A vast clay urn rested on a stone plinth in the center of the lab. Coils of glass tubing wrapped its circumference, some filled with water and others with air. A single copper fitting boasting multiple nozzles was affixed to the great vase's midsection. Hieronymus remembered that the copper tubing contained lamp oil.

"You know," he commented as Lendar descended the staircase leading down from the hatch, "I'm getting awfully tired of looking at things upside-down."

"You should have thought of that before you absconded with that ridiculously huge body."

"Oh, no. No regrets there," Hieronymus informed the wizard. "Dragons are meant to be large and in charge."

Lendar scoffed as he placed Vicarius the sword in the only space available on the benches. He then checked the progress of his various experiments, uttering an oath wherever he discovered one ruined by his extended absence. While watching the sorcerer, Hieronymus caught a bit of movement in his peripheral vision.

It was a hackerpede, high on the wall next to the window. The miniscule monster extended its bristled mouthparts at the dragon's head.

Hieronymus spat a jet of dragon fire from the corner of his mouth, roasting the tiny challenger on the spot.

"Hieronymus!" chided the wizard, who was now fiddling with copper valves on the urn. "You know those are critical conduits for the eloquys."

"I'm aware of that," the wyvern admitted, "but, *yech!* They're so darn creepy! Couldn't you have used something more pleasant to steal the words from people's minds? Flufferbunnies, for instance?"

"Don't be daft. What self-respecting wizard would employ flufferbunnies as his minions?"

"A clever one?" suggested Hieronymus. "No one would see it coming."

"Stop your prattling and do something useful," Lendar growled. "Like double-checking my settings. I devised this eloquary collection vessel when I was older than I am today, so I'm relying on what you've told me about it rather than on firsthand experience."

Hieronymus sighed and did as he was instructed, watching as two more hackerpedes emerged from the shadows and scaled the sides of the urn. Without a moment's hesitation, the little black beasts hurtled themselves into the vessel.

"Everything seems fine to me," the wyvern reported. "Shall I light the burners for you?"

"From that distance? With my luck, you'd miss and crack the tubing. It took that glass-blower ages to get it right."

Lendar raised one hand and encircled the strands of his dark brown beard with the other. As he stroked down the length of his whiskers, a small ball of Fyre formed in his free hand. A flick of his wrist directed the Fyreball around the urn, lighting the burners.

"*Eloquin reveliat*," he intoned. If Hieronymus hadn't seen him do this so many times before, he might have been impressed by the glowing azure cloud that mushroomed out of the giant urn.

"Tuh," Lendar grunted. "Still not enough eloquys. But perhaps…"

He stepped to the workbenches and retrieved the sword. Advancing on the urn, he reached up and dropped Vicarius point-first into the vessel. Both wizard and familiar awaited a change, but none came.

"The cloud's *still* blue," Lendar announced with frustration. "We can't act until it's silver!"

"Now, now," soothed Hieronymus. "It's at least a little paler than before. You must have nearly enough Logomantic power collected. And I have an idea where we might acquire an uncommonly large amount of it all in one place."

"Where?"

"Right under our noses, really. You mentioned Rudger Rump earlier. What do you remember about him?"

"*More* memory games, Hieronymus?" Lendar groaned. When Hieronymus continued to stare at him, the wizard gave in. "Pleasant enough chap. Red hair. Long beard. Wait. Did I have something to do with that?"

"You tried to work Logomancy on him, and it backfired," Hieronymus reminded him. "Have you ever checked out Rudger's Glynt?"

"Glynt? No. Why would I? Humdrungle gnomes don't do magic."

"This one does. Remember that contraption the gnomette, Twelda, built at the cabin? The one with the rotating buckets?"

"Oh. Right. The one I set the zingbats on. Yes. Now that I think about it, Rudger used magic to call up a gust of wind to extinguish himself, didn't he?"

"That's what you told me. And if I know my Glynts, Rudger Rump is capable of much more. Logomancy at its highest echelon, I suspect. Now, if you took *his* eloquy and added it to what you already have, you might really have something."

"Yes, but he's such a nice, little..." Lendar suddenly slapped his own cheek. "Ugh! See what I mean? I'm wrestling with warm, fuzzy memories of that gnome which were never there before! They must have been generated by Kal since the last time I was this age."

"Well, perhaps this will help ease your spotty conscience," Hieronymus said. "Rudger Rump is on a quest to save his grandparents from the Mute-ation. You know where that will lead."

"To me."

"And here's a bonus. I saw him pick up something that fell out of your pants back on the cliff."

Kallendar thought hard. "I think I saw that, too."

"Therefore, it's reasonable to believe if you find Rudger, you find your Chronologue. And even if his eloquy isn't enough to break the Chronocurse and overthrow the Arch-mage, at least you'll get your life's history back."

The wizard stood still, pondering for a moment. "How do you propose we find this Rump?" he asked.

"Well, if you're too young to remember orchestrating

Princess Hildegarde's quest, you probably don't remember what you sent with her."

"The amulet?"

"And something even more useful."

"What?"

"An hourglass."

"An hourglass? Why would I do that?"

"To guide her to Herald's lair."

"Well, that would mean it was Enlivened, right?" He raised his eyebrows in surprise. "That's very advanced magic. I'm able to do that when I'm older?"

"Yes, but more importantly, you can use that magical link now to track the hourglass and spy through it. With any luck, Hildegarde and Rudger might still be together."

"But Enlivenment requires a living soul. Whose did I use?"

"See for yourself."

Lendar moved to the spot his familiar indicated. A satin drape covered something large and square set on the floor. He pulled back the drape.

Underneath was a cage, and inside lay the tiny, curled-up form of a gnome dressed in a tan shirt and brown pants. The unconscious Humdrungle's pointed tan cap had fallen from his head, revealing auburn locks with distinct ginger highlights.

"You nabbed that gnome during a minikin gathering," Hieronymus reported. "Thought he was a leprechaun that might enhance your Logomantic prowess with a bit of Blarney. Another dead end, but you repurposed him well."

Lendar looked down at the helpless gnome. He pulled his robe's sleeves back from his raised forearms, placed his palms on either side of his beard, and closed his eyes. "Seek out the hourglass, reap the Humdrungle eloquy!" he cried. A quick downward jerk of his hands sent a crackle of energy through the cloud above the collection urn.

Droves of clacking hackerpedes spilled from its bowels.

CHAPTER THIRTY

"My compliments, Miss Riggle, on this delicious stew," Rudger Rump heard Hildegarde say as he tipped the last few drops of his portion into his mouth. "It possesses a most unusual quality. I'm not sure how to describe it."

"An *ebullience*, perhaps?" supplied Herald. Rudger's ears perked up at the unfamiliar word. He made a mental note to ask the miniaturized wyvern about it later.

"Something like that," Hildegarde said uncertainly. "It…it feels like my belly is being tickled from the inside."

Ragna Riggle grinned. "That'd be the buffa beets, Your Highness. First harvest's always the liveliest. The trick is not to boil all the zest out of them. Gotta let 'em strut in your gut, I always say."

BRA-A-A-AP!

Roon slapped a hand over his mouth. Seven pairs of eyes stared as the gnomeling turned red *as* a beet.

His aunt made a flourish in his direction.

"There you have it," she declared. "Zest!"

Rudger laughed as hard as anyone at Roon's gaseous gaffe. It was wonderful to be in Aunt Ragna's garden again, enjoying a gnome-cooked meal with family and friends. So wonderful, he'd almost managed to forget the plight of his father and grandparents and the urgency of his quest to save them.

Ragna slapped her knees and sprang to her feet. "Reckon this meal's over," she announced. She pointed at the triplets. "Let's go, you three. I'll lug the pot inside while you clear up the bowls and spoons."

Rudger was amazed at how quickly Rani, Roni, and Roon acted on their aunt's orders. Somehow, Ragna seemed to have tamed the Terror Trio in the one short week they'd spent together. The only glimmer of noncompliance Rudger noticed was in their behavior toward Hildegarde. The threesome had been watching the human warily throughout the meal, and now they balked at approaching her to collect her dishes. When the Princess suddenly stood up, the skittish triplets seemed of a mind to bolt.

"Please allow me to help, Miss Riggle," Hildegarde said, apparently unaware of the panic she was inspiring in the gnomelings. "I'd be more than happy to carry that pot for you."

"Oh, pish," Ragna said, scanning the girl from head to toe. "Don't get me wrong, Highness; it's a kind offer, but how do you propose to carry the pot down into the burrow? You'd never be able to squeeze into my kitchen."

"*I'll* help," Twelda said with a sideways glance at the

towering Princess. The science-gnomette scrambled to her feet and snatched up the iron pot.

"Great gobs!" Ragna laughed. "The way you're all fussing over me, you'd think I hadn't survived fifteen years alone in the Hinters! Very well. Mollycoddle me if you must, but step smartly. There's work to be done. Hup-hup!"

In two minutes' time, Ragna had driven her kitchen brigade to the edge of the garden. Rudger was keen to see how she would best the arachna shrubs this time, but Herald commandeered his attention.

"There's a subject I need to broach while our hosts are out of earshot," the wyvern-turned-newt said. "I'd rather Twelda were present, but she can catch up later. Everyone must be made aware of the problem with that hourglass."

Rudger, Hildegarde, and Fred turned to look at Minsec. The timepiece was tipped on its side, rolling around in the skunkin vines with no discernible purpose.

"Problem? With Minsec?" asked Hildegarde. "What do you mean?"

"I mean that its Glynt has undergone a disturbing change."

"Its Glynt?" repeated Rudger. He screwed up his eyes and tried again to make out the hidden magical aura. "Nope," he conceded with a disgusted grunt. "Still can't see it."

Well, I can, said Fred. *And Herald's right. It's a very bad sign.*

"Why is everyone so against Minsec?" Hildegarde complained. "He's been nothing but helpful to me, and he's taken a real shine to Rudger and his family. He's been gesturing and flashing sand-colors all over the place since he got here. Look! He's doing it now."

"But we don't know what that means, Hildegarde," Herald said. "Meanwhile, Minsec's Glynt has changed from a purple billow to a pitch-black vortex. Glynts don't intensify like that unless active magic is afoot."

"Well, Rudger's the only wizard-type here," Hildegarde said shortly. She looked down at the gnome. "Have you been casting spells on Minsec?"

"Me? Heck, no," Rudger said. "I can't do that. And even if I could, why would I?"

"You misunderstand, Princess," Herald explained. "The spell is not being cast *upon* Minsec, but *through* it. Someone is working magic through the hourglass, and a sorcerer of any appreciable ability wouldn't have to be nearby to do it. All he or she would need is the proper magical link."

Rudger made a sudden connection. "You told us Minsec has Kal's Glynt on it," he said to Herald. "Could *he* be responsible for the change?"

Fred snorted disbelievingly. *The little boy Hildegarde and I rescued? This magic is too sophisticated for a mere child to perform.*

"Oh, but Fred," interjected Hildegarde, "didn't we tell you? Herald urged a metal artifact that belongs to Kal. It turns out the boy we rescued is a powerful wizard suffering from a Chronocurse. He lives the days of his life out of order. Kal may have only been six years old yesterday, but he could be any age today."

Fred flicked his ears in irritation. *Clearly, I was not privy to this information since I was treated like a dray horse last night.*

Hildegarde heaved a sigh. “How many times do I have to apologize for—”

“Please, you two!” interceded Rudger. “Am I going to have to get Twelda to referee again? Look, I have an idea. Herald, why don’t you do your Ferrie thing on Minsec so we know what we’re up against?”

Hildegarde beat Herald to the response. “Because metal-urging only works on metal, Rudger. Herald’s already told us that.”

Rudger gazed up at the perturbed Princess. “But does the object have to be made *entirely* out of metal?” he countered. “Minsec is constructed mostly of wood and glass, but his support arms are metal, aren’t they?”

The hourglass leapt at Rudger’s suggestion, its sands turning a tickled pink. At the same time, Herald slapped his own forehead with one of his newly acquired forelimbs. “Great ancestors!” he exclaimed. “Why didn’t I think of that myself?”

The newt took wing and began to circle the hourglass, which was positively vibrating with excitement. Herald’s ancient urging words permeated the air, stilling the breeze coming down the rise and quieting the ever-present thrum of the marshland insects. The entire garden seemed to hold its breath as the little orange oracle spoke.

Eloquy leached is not its own,
Encased in glass in lieu of bone.
Pulled and planted by wizard’s power,
It yearns return to the wizard’s tower.
Schism begets such heartsick woe

For this fractured Suppli—

Herald's wings jerked violently as if he'd been struck. He broke out of his spiral pattern and cut a wide, weaving circle around the group of onlookers.

"Herald?" inquired Rudger. "Are you all right?"

The newt shook his head forcefully before answering.

"Something broke my concentration," he said dazedly. "Never had that happen before." As he glided past the young gnome, he seemed to pull himself together. "Never fear, Rudger. I'll get the rest."

But when the flying newt closed in on the hourglass for a second go-around, a burst of energy sent Herald spinning backwards through the air.

Rudger cried out as the miniaturized wyvern dropped into the skunkin patch. The horrified gnome moved to help his friend, but a dazzling green flare stopped him in his tracks. The eerie light hovered over Minsec, and as Rudger watched, it coalesced into a thick glowing ring. A black space formed in the ring's center, giving the impression of a pupil surrounded by a shimmering green iris.

A spy-eye, reported Fred.

A deep, resonating voice filled Rudger's ears. "We meet at last, Rudger Rump," it boomed. "You have something that belongs to me."

The gnomelescent fought to swallow a lump that had formed in his throat. "Wh-what have you done to Herald?" he asked.

"Who? Oh. The wyvern. I brushed him back for prying into my secrets. Ferries are a meddlesome lot, always nosing about in other people's business. But theirs is a minor magical talent, easily dispatched. Rather like swatting a fly."

"Oh…oh, yeah?" Rudger stammered. "W-well, *this* fly's gotten the better of you,…*Kallendar.*"

The voice was quiet for several heartbeats.

"So you've discovered my name," it finally rumbled. "I gather that means the wyvern urged it out of my Chronologue. No matter. I *am* Kallendar. You, however, know me best as Kal, the poor, forsaken ward of Lendar the Great, who also happens to be me. We are two incarnations of the same convoluted timeline, Kal and I. What he learns, I remember. What he experiences enriches me. And so, I am the Mage of Ages, both young and old. But, unfortunately for you, it is Lendar the elder you face today…"

As the wizard continued his boastful monologue, Rudger found himself battling a growing bubble of indignation. He knew the less he revealed to this enemy the better, but as the words Herald had extracted from Minsec festered in his mind and their meaning became clear, the mental blister containing his anger swelled ominously.

And then Kallendar was laughing at him—a raucous, condescending guffaw that cut away all caution and reason. The blister ruptured.

"You *fiend!*" Rudger cried. "You *monster!* You took my father!"

Again, a pause. Rudger heard only his own ragged breathing, a sound soaked up by the stunned silence hanging over the garden.

And then a throaty chuckle.

"*This* is the crime you accuse me of?" the disembodied voice queried. "The paltry kidnapping of a no-account Humdrungle gnome?"

"He's the Supplico!" Rudger argued.

"Poor little Rudger," the wizard said, clucking his tongue. "So desperate to see his dadders as a big, important gnome. Even *I* know the Supplico is a toady. A joke. Why should I bother to kidnap such a pathetic underling?"

Tears of fury rolled down Rudger's cheeks.

"Oh, enough of this charade," Kallendar went on airily. "I admit it. I abducted your father. And quite by mistake, I might add. I thought him a leprechaun. Reddish beard, you see. Much like that ridiculous one Kal gave you."

"Let him go," Rudger seethed, his voice barely above a whisper. "Let my father go and give Vicarius back. It's rightfully ours. My grandfather forged it."

"Well, now, that's a bit greedy, don't you think?" Kallendar jeered. "Your father's eloquy has proven most useful to me, and I have great plans for the Switching Blade. And you demand them both?"

Rudger Rump closed his eyes and worked to block the wizard's callous voice from his mind. He wrestled with his racing thoughts, subduing them in pursuit of the Source. *One Wyrd,* he asked of it. *Just one Wyrd.*

Seconds passed. Kallendar scoffed.

"I see words have escaped you," said he. "I speak in the figural sense, of course."

One Wyrd, Rudger thought fiercely. *Reveal it to me. Please.*

"And that is a delicious irony, for very soon the words shall escape you in the *literal* sense, as well. I take my leave, Rudger Rump. I have more pressing matters to attend to. Oh, and make no mistake. I intend to have my Chronologue back."

Rudger's eyes fluttered open at the sound of Minsec toppling to its side. The giant green iris was gone. The young gnome gave a frustrated groan at his continued failure to wield Weird Wyrds at will. Then he remembered his questmates. He spotted Hildegarde rushing to Minsec's side. Fred was standing a short distance away.

Are you well? the quadricorn inquired of him.

"Not particularly," Rudger replied as he began to search the skunkin patch. "We've got to find Herald and get to Castle Happenstance immediately. Kallendar has my father imprisoned in a tower there, and I have to rescue him."

We heard.

"You did?" Rudger asked. "Oh, that's right. You were here. When that eye was on me, I lost track of everything else."

I thought it best not to attract Kallendar's attention, Fred explained. *That is why we did not participate in the conversation.*

Hildegarde approached with the hourglass cradled in her arms. "Good news," she said. "Minsec's okay."

Fred gave a disgusted whinny. *Why do you persist in coddling that hourglass, milady? You just saw how dangerous it is.*

"Maybe so, but Minsec is linked to Rudger's father's... What did Lendar call it? His eloquy? Anyway, we have to keep the hourglass safe."

Well, it can't go with us, Fred argued. *Kallendar can spy on us through it.*

"Wait," Rudger interrupted. He stopped his search for Herald and turned his head this way and that. "Do you hear something?"

The three questmates stood in the garden, straining their ears. At first, Rudger only made out the rustle of the breeze through the skunkin leaves and the occasional, tentative chirp of a chitterbug hoping to strike up the usual chorus. But then he picked out something else—a harsh, clicking noise. Hildegarde's face went pale.

"Hackerpedes," she whispered.

In the distance, Rudger's family screamed.

CHAPTER THIRTY-ONE

"Find Herald!" Rudger urged the Princess and her steed as he took off up the rise. "Aunt Ragna and the others need me!"

The words had barely escaped his lips when a hackerpede ambushed him.

He nearly ran into the nightmarish thing, which clung to a dringleberry branch that bobbed before his eyes. Its revolting, bristly mouth-feelers writhed under unblinking obsidian eyes. Its mandibles clacked gratingly. Dozens of creeping, barb-tipped legs bunched themselves up under its shining, chitin-shelled body. With a hair-raising hiss, the creature launched itself at Rudger's face.

And missed, tangling its plethora of legs in Rudger's knotted beard. Crying out, the young gnome beat at his attacker, each blow producing a painful yank at the roots of his whiskers.

A stab in his leg jerked his attention away from the beard-burrowing 'pede. One of its brutish brethren had latched onto his breeches, digging its needle-like mouth parts in deep.

Rudger flailed about, realizing to his horror that a dozen of the six-inch-long monstrosities had surrounded him. They advanced, ripping at his clothes and gouging his skin as they climbed. He let out a garbled cry.

Zzzz-tip! Zzzz-tip! Zzzz-tip!

Three quick impacts left blossoms of pain in Rudger's leg, hip, and chest, but the subsequent oozing he felt was not his own blood. It was bodily fluids leaking from the shattered hackerpede carcasses still embedded in his clothes and beard. Disgusted, he tore at the dead 'pedes, desperate to dislodge them.

"Leave them!" Hildegarde shouted at him, her slingshot still in hand. "Just get over here! I'll keep the others at bay!"

Rudger did as he was bid, leaping over his swarming foes as he lurched his way toward the girl and his salvation.

"That's it," she encouraged him. "You're almost in the—wait! Come back! What are you doing?"

"Getting Herald!" he shouted, veering into the skunkin patch. He swiped at leaves as tall as he was. "Herald! Herald! Can you hear me?"

Zzzz-tip! Zzzz-tip! Two more black-shelled pursuers crumpled at the hand of the hunter-Princess. A third landed on Rudger's back. He did a somersault to crush it.

"I'm out of ammunition!" Hildegarde hollered. "You gotta get up on Fred! He can get us out of here!"

Please, please! thought Rudger. *Helios, Lunira, Terreste—anybody! Help me find Herald!*

A flash of bright orange shone through green foliage

dotted by black-and-white skunkin sprouts. Rudger jammed his heels into the earth, preparing to double back.

Ploof! Ploof! Ploof!

An overpowering stench assaulted his nasal passages; his eyes began to water. The released gases of the smashed skunkin sprouts rose in a blinding cloud.

"Hildegarde!" Rudger coughed. "Stop launching those sprouts!" He gagged as he grabbled in the vicinity where he thought he'd seen the splotch of orange. "I can't see anything. I think Herald's here."

Something snagged the back of his tunic, jerking him upward. "Gotcha!" he heard Hildegarde say.

He rose above the gas; his eyesight cleared. Twisting around, he discovered he was hanging from Fred's teeth. The mounted Princess extended a hand to him.

Rudger grasped it gratefully. "Herald's right around here," he repeated as he straddled Fred's backbone. "He's somewhere in all that haze."

A rippling, crystalline horn materialized on the quadricorn's forehead. Fred bowed his head and began to spray the area with water, washing the skunkin gas from the air.

"There! There!" Rudger cried.

Fred advanced, mangling half a dozen hackerpedes under hoof and shaking off the ones so bold as to scale his legs. The gas from the skunkin sprouts he was unintentionally stomping threatened to re-conceal what Rudger had spotted, but Fred had a fix on his target.

"Let me get him," Rudger implored the quadricorn. "Your teeth could hurt him." The gnome slid down Fred's lowered neck and scooped up the winged newt's limp body.

Then Rudger was being lifted again. He scrambled for a stable position in front of Hildegarde on the equine's broad back.

"Here's Herald," Rudger said as he handed the newt to Hildegarde. "Now let's get up to the burrow."

Fred's long, powerful legs carried them up the hill and away from the hackerpede horde. The screams Rudger had heard had ceased; the only sign that his family and Twelda had been this way was a rumpled tempered tan cap caught in the grizzlegrass outside the burrow. As the rescue party drew closer to the burrow's entrance, Rudger's heart dropped. The soil around its closed flaphatch was riddled with small round holes.

"High Helios," Rudger said, cold prickles playing up and down his spine. "They went underground. Twelda *knows* hackerpedes can tunnel. Why didn't she keep them topside?"

He didn't wait for an answer. Leaping recklessly from Fred's lofty back, Rudger grunted as his ankles bore the brunt of the long drop. He raced toward the hatch and threw it open.

"Rudger! No!" Hildegarde cried. "We can't follow you down there!"

The young gnome plunged into the darkness.

Rudger skidded down the first few steps of the burrow's staircase, grabbing wildly at the earthen wall to his left. His feet found no purchase, and he stumbled down the rest of the flight, landing clumsily at the bottom. He braced himself for another attack by the black beasts. None came.

It occurred to him, too late, that he'd charged into the hackerpedes' stronghold without a weapon. He crept slowly into the kitchen to avail himself of the knife block he'd seen there seven nights before. The fungus-glow was dim, and Rudger's heart pounded with every step he took. He ran his four-fingered hand along a barely visible counter until it dropped into a metal basin. Set into the wall behind the basin was a hinged metal door that opened into the side of a stone-lined well. Above that door was the crank which raised and lowered the bucket within the well itself. He remembered the knife block was only an arm's-length farther down the counter.

CHOP!

Rudger shrieked and pulled his hand back just fast enough to avoid dismemberment.

Chop-chop-chop-chop-CHOP!

A faintly outlined figure beside him had produced this volley of knife blows. Rudger gathered his wits to speak.

"Aunt Ragna?"

SWIPE!

The broad, scraping stroke across the countertop might have delivered chopped vegetable bits into the basin before him—if there had been any vegetables to chop.

The knife returned to its work, producing a clamor that filled the small, dark underground room. Rudger tried again to speak to his aunt. Her only response was another grating swipe with her knife.

Rudger retreated to the hall to find a candle. He intended to dig through the ashes in the kitchen fireplace for a cinder to light it, but his foot caught on something as he reentered the room. He crouched down and discovered it was Twelda's satchel.

Immediately, he inserted his hands into the pack. They fumbled over a small, conical object—the vial containing the remaining jawjackle juice. Questing farther, his fingers closed on the handles of the fire-flinger. He pulled the device out and clacked it once. A flame sprang to life on the candle's wick.

Aunt Ragna was still at the counter, chopping air. She turned her head toward the light and regarded him with dull, milk-white eyes.

Rudger gasped.

His poor, Muted aunt went back to her mindless chore.

A faint sobbing noise diverted Rudger's attention. It wasn't coming from the now-passionless gnomette who had once battled her arachna bushes in spectacular fashion before his very eyes. No, these sobs seemed to echo eerily from somewhere beyond the kitchen.

A sudden rattling noise made Rudger jump. It was the well-crank, jiggering about in its seating. With a wary look at his aunt, Rudger crawled up into the basin and pulled on the well door. A tiny squeal of fear came from the damp, dark space beyond.

"Hello?" Rudger whispered, his voice magnified by the well's stone walls. "Is somebody in there?"

"Rudger!" came the hushed cry of his sister Rani. "Rudger, we're down here!"

The gnome scooted forward in the basin so he could stick his candle and head through the aperture. He peered downward and spotted his sisters balanced on a bucket hanging ten feet below.

"Rani! Roni! Are you okay?"

"We're scared, Rudger," said Rani.

"Are they gone?" whimpered Roni.

"I don't know," Rudger told them.

"Is Aunt Ragna there?" asked Roni.

"We want Aunt Ragna," clarified Rani.

"Uh…yes. She's here. She's here, and she wants you to stay where you are until we make sure those baddies are all gone."

"It's cold in here," complained Rani.

"This bucket's too small," whined Roni.

"I know, I know. But you're safe where you are. The 'pedes can't tunnel through the rocks, see? It'll only be for a few more minutes. I promise. Okay?"

"Okay," they said in unison.

"Oh!" Rudger said suddenly. "Where's your brother? And Twelda?"

"We don't know," answered Roni.

"They stayed inside the burrow," replied Rani.

"Okay. I'm going to shut you back in now. Be brave."

Rudger climbed down from the basin and, with a mournful look at his aunt, exited the kitchen. He stole across the narrow hall and peered into the hearth-room.

The soft, yellow glow from his candle revealed that the room was empty. The few sticks of furniture that graced the small chamber were either disarranged or overturned. Rudger stepped quickly to the fireplace and picked up the metal poker. Having a weapon in hand helped to bolster his courage.

He entered the bedroom wing tunnel. No gnome was in the first bedroom he came to. Its bed and wooden nightstand were undisturbed; it seemed the struggle had not touched this room. A second look revealed gaudily colored garments hanging in the open wardrobe. *Aunt Ragna's room*, he surmised.

Rudger moved down the dark, musty corridor to the next doorless opening. It was the room Aunt Ragna had evicted him from after the scary story he'd told the triplets. He clung to the memory of what she'd said afterward—one of the last things he could remember before the amnesioaks cut a gash in his memory.

That's not what you said in there...words the likes of which I've never heard before... 'Gnomelings fear their endless slumber, corporsapiensi spell.'

Then he'd had his recurring dream about the tart-tongued human girl and the villainous dragon who had captured her.

After that, nothing. Nothing until he woke up in the Standards Chamber and met Vermis, for the second time.

Rudger moved back into the hall and negotiated a sharp bend to reach the most distant room of the burrow. This was the room he'd slept in on the night it all started. There was no opportunity to reminisce here. The room was occupied.

A small form stood with its back to Rudger. As he watched, it reached out and drew back a blanket on the bed. It paused, as if looking for something. Then it replaced the blanket and repeated its actions.

"Roon?" Rudger ventured.

The figure neither responded nor interrupted its sequence. His chest tight with apprehension, Rudger went to the nightstand where the oil lamp he'd used still rested. Tipping the candle inside, he lit its wick. Then he reached out to grasp his little brother's shoulder.

Roon turned to look at him with placid, white-glazed eyes.

Rudger clamped a hand over his quivering mouth. *Not Roon,* he thought in despair. *Not him, too.*

The silent gnomeling went back to his repetitive tic, unmoved by his elder brother's anguish. Rudger leaned heavily against the nightstand, squeezing his eyes shut against tears that threatened to flow. When he reopened them, they fell upon a different part of the room.

Where Twelda lay deathly still.

It was a third stab to his broken heart. Now, the tears did flow; sobs racked his small, stocky frame. It was simply too much; practically everygnome he loved had been taken from him. He lamented the bleary image of his friend which swam before his eyes.

A sudden realization cut through his grief. Taking an angry gulp of air, he rushed forward, pausing only to snatch a lost pointed cap from the floor.

The hackerpedes' work was not yet complete.

One of the black menaces was still perched on its victim's chest, dragging Twelda's eloquy out through her voice box. The language-intelligence emerged in a long, thin, glowing ribbon which was consumed inch by inch by the hideous hackerpede. As it did so, the outlines of its shell glowed brighter and brighter.

Rudger pounced, trapping the parasitic beast under the hat against Twelda's chest. He jerked the monster away; its needle-like legs ripped Twelda's blouse as it came loose. The hackerpede writhed in the hat, fighting to escape, but Rudger kept it shut tight.

"Twelda? Can you hear me?" he asked, prodding the science-gnomette's arm. "Come on. You gotta wake up."

Twelda failed to respond, and a crackling sound stopped Rudger from inquiring a second time. Horror plucked at the hairs along his neck. It was in that moment the Humdrungle gnome recognized his mistake.

He'd neglected to look *up*.

A torrent of hissing, clacking hackerpedes descended from the ceiling upon him. Their sheer weight pinned him to the ground, allowing their cruel, barbed legs to rip at his clothes and tear at his skin. His screams were muffled by squirming legs and hard chitin shells; the beasts were obstructing his mouth and nose, subduing him through suffocation.

Then, through a swarm of bodies passing over his eyes, he saw a hackerpede take up a position on his chest. Its mouth-parts splayed outward; its mandible retracted. The extraction of Rudger's eloquy was about to begin.

Rudger's mind screamed in terror, but a kernel of reason remained. That kernel dug deeply into his mindscape, scouring and drilling as never before. The Source of Logomancy suddenly opened to him. Its power filled his chest, gripped his abdomen, vibrated his limbs. His head swam as the energy demanded release. Rudger gabbled the only Wyrd he could think of:

Corporsapiensi!

Instantly, the walls closed in, jamming his head into his

shoulders, his knees into his chest. The hard-shelled monstrosities tumbled off him in the wake of the magical blast; the pricking pains they had been inflicting ceased.

He tried to get up and rammed his forehead into the ceiling where a few straggling hackerpedes were tunneling to make good their escape. Moaning, Rudger brought his right hand to his throbbing forehead. He froze when it came into his line of sight. It had too many fingers.

Confusion battered his mind, but this was no time to sort things out. The hackerpede he'd captured was in the hat he still clutched in his other hand. Twelda was up against a wall near his left thigh. Energy still crackling through his limbs, he reached over his torso and dragged her up onto his chest. So light was she that he reached out in the other direction and added tiny Roon. Hugging both of his passengers to his breast, Rudger hitched up one shoulder and then the other while digging his heels into the floor.

In this way, he painstakingly propelled himself out of the room, down the narrow corridor, across the hearth-room, and into the entrance hall. Carefully setting his passengers aside, he crawled up the short, narrow staircase and poked his head out into the sunlight.

"Rudger!" Hildegarde cried joyfully as he emerged. Then her tone changed to one of confusion. "Ruh-…Rudger?"

The young gnome worked to dislodge himself from the confines of the flaphatch opening. His shoulders and hips proved the most troublesome, each breaking away clumps of packed soil as he forced them through the small hole. At last, he tumbled out onto the grizzlegrass, his breathing heavy and ragged.

"Twelda's down there," he said in a daze. His voice sounded thick and deep. "Roon and Ragna, too. They… they've all been Muted."

"Rudger," Hildegarde said, turning pink. "Rudger, what's *happened* to you? Where are your *clothes?*"

It slowly dawned on Rudger the only thing he was wearing was a coat of dirt. He tried to preserve his modesty with the hackerpede hat he still held.

"I have to get them out," he told Hildegarde. "The satchel, too. There might be a chance to save them."

Rudger turned and inserted his free hand back into the burrow. His fingers closed around Roon, and he lifted the gnomeling out with startling ease. Roon still clutched the blanket from the bed he'd been making and unmaking. Rudger released it from his brother's impossibly tiny fist and wrapped the small rectangle of cloth around his own waist.

Twelda proved only slightly heavier to extract, and soon Rudger was straining to reach the satchel at the foot of the stairs. When at last he managed to get it out, he saw that Hildegarde had begun to tend to Roon and Twelda.

Rudger, said Fred. *What's going on down in the burrow? Where are Ragna and your sisters?*

"Sisters? Oh, right. Sisters!" Rudger exclaimed. He stood up and had to check his balance. The ground seemed so far away. Turning unsteadily to face the quadricorn, he suffered a thrill of shock. He was looking the great equine straight in the eye.

"Uh, Rani and Roni are okay," he reported distractedly. "They're hiding in the well. We just have to find the opening up here so we can fish them out."

©2022 Simerlein

What about Ragna? You said she's been Muted.

"Yes. She was in the kitchen before the hackerpedes attacked me. I think she's still there."

"The hackerpedes did this to you?" Hildegarde asked as she came to his side.

His brain did a flip. How could he be looking down at the human-huge Princess? "N-no," he said slowly. "I…I'm pretty sure I did this to myself. Somehow." He shook his head. "Look, I'm kind of wigging out right now, but it's Roon, Aunt Ragna, and Twelda we need to focus on. I think there may be a way to bring them back to us that doesn't involve Vicarius. I-I think I can use the jawjackle juice."

"The jawjackle juice?" Hildegarde repeated. "You mean that blue potion Twelda showed us in Herald's cave?"

"Gnomes' homes, I forgot all about Herald," Rudger blurted. "Is he all right?"

"I shall survive," the little orange newt said from his resting place on Fred's back. "But if you've devised another method to revive those who have been Muted, I implore you to act quickly."

"Right," Rudger agreed. "We need to get Aunt Ragna up here and then we can divide the juice three ways."

"*Three* ways?" interjected Hildegarde. "Rudger, I'm pretty sure Twelda said there's only one dose left."

"What?"

"Twelda told us there's only enough juice left for one person," the Princess repeated. "You'll have to choose who to give it to."

"Choose?" Rudger echoed. He felt a creeping horror. "Choose between Aunt Ragna, Roon, and Twelda?"

Better to maximize your chances of success with one victim than to portion the potion out three ways and risk saving no one, reasoned Fred.

Flashes of each Muted gnome played through Rudger's fractured mind. Roon coming out of the weeds to embrace him. Aunt Ragna battling the arachna shrubs in her shining crimson chemise. Twelda smiling as she cranked up her Eleminator. It was an impossible decision.

"Rudger, what is it you have there?" Herald asked.

Rudger looked at his huge, five-fingered hand. "It's a hackerpede," he said flatly. "In a hat. It's the one that Muted Twelda."

"Then that has made the choice for you," Herald stated. "Having the beast in hand means you have Twelda's eloquy, too. Your chances of reviving her are greatly enhanced by that fact."

Rudger looked down at the tiny gnomes lying in their tamped-down grizzlegrass nests before him. His eyes lingered on his little brother, who was now as still as Twelda.

Herald went on. "I know it's hard, but there's no time to waste. Twelda is the best equipped to aid us in the quest to recapture Vicarius and liberate your father. Not to mention she was the one who distilled the juice in the first place. There really is no choice."

Tears began to sting the corners of Rudger's eyes as the soundness of Herald's logic sank in. Handing the squirming hat to Hildegarde, he retrieved the vial from the satchel and knelt beside the Muted gnomette. He removed the cork and gently pried her lips apart to pour the blue fluid into her mouth. He accessed the Source, now fading from his mind, and uttered a Wyrd.

De-eloquarantine!

An iridescent, gossamer ribbon emerged from the cap. Hildegarde hurried to hold it close to Twelda's mouth. Rudger gently directed the Princess' hand down to the gnomette's voicebox. The ribbon passed inside.

Twelda Greeze coughed and turned her head. Her sea-green eyes fluttered open and locked on Rudger's face. He smiled.

"Hi, Twels. Remember me? Rudger?" he said to her, trying to sound upbeat. "Looks like your jawjackle juice works after all. Just say something, and you're an official genius."

The gnomette's brow crinkled as her lips strained to form the words.

"Rudger?" she rasped. "W-why are you a…human?"

CHAPTER THIRTY-TWO

Twelda Greeze's mind was broken.

Throughout Rudger Rump's chaotic quest, the science-gnomette had prided herself on being a bastion of reason in a realm gone mad with magic. But ever since the hackerpedes had extracted her eloquy, Twelda had not been her nimble-minded self. Her language intelligence may have been restored, but her thoughts were scattered and askew. Even after a full night's rest, she was finding it a challenge to focus on the present conversation.

"Don't get me wrong," Rudger was saying to Hildegarde from his place on the quadricorn's back behind Twelda. "I totally appreciate the shirt and britches you made me out of Aunt Ragna's blankets last night. It's just that I feel weird breaking the Gnomister's law by wearing maroon."

"It's against the law to wear red?" Hildegarde asked incredulously.

"Yes," Rudger replied. "Humdrungles can only wear four shades of brown."

"Well, you're a human now," the Princess pointed out. "You can wear any color you want."

"Really? *Any* color?"

"Yep."

"So I can wear green?"

"Yes."

"And yellow?"

"Yes."

"And pink?"

"Sure."

"At the same time?"

Hildegarde laughed. "I suppose so. But I'm wondering about your aunt. Doesn't she care about your laws? She was sporting a lovely pair of teal blue bloomers during supper yesterday."

"Oh. Well, that's Aunt Ragna for you," Rudger told her. "My mother says she's 'eccentric.'" He paused and added, "Want to know a secret?" Rudger twisted in his seat. "I want to be eccentric, too," he whispered to the Princess.

Hildegarde giggled. "That settles it. When we get to Little Lexicon, we're getting you a proper suit of…Oh! Twelda, you're slipping."

The gnomette pulled away from the Princess' steadying hand. "I'm fine," she said gruffly.

"Are you sure?" Hildegarde asked. "You've been through a lot. Maybe we should stop and let you rest a while."

"I said I'm fine," Twelda insisted. "We don't steed to nop."

An awkward pause led Twelda to turn around and stare at

Fred's other two riders. Hildegarde and Rudger were looking down at her with bemused grins.

"You did it again," said Hildegarde.

"Mixed up your words," clarified Rudger.

Twelda groaned. "Whoa sut?" she asked. Then she frowned. "Er, I mean, so what? We've got a quest to get on with. Kallendar isn't going to postpone his plans just because I'm out of sorts. We've wasted too much…Wait! Aren't you listening to me?"

They were not. Fred had come to a halt next to the River Gush just before its western bank began to rise to form the northern stretch of bluffs. Rudger dismounted and helped Hildegarde down. Then he plucked Twelda off the quadricorn's back and deposited her on the ground. The gnomette glared up at him.

"How dare you gnome-handle me like that!" she snapped. "Just because you're big now doesn't mean you can throw me around like a sack of beeffa butts…er…I mean buffa beets. Ugh!" She yanked angrily at the strap of her satchel and marched away. A hundred paces later, she sat down to sulk.

Twelda had fought hard to keep her place in the questing party. After her Muting, the other members of the group had been ready to discard her. When she proved she was not a mindless liability, the discussion had turned to leaving her behind to watch over Rudger's family. This was harder to argue against. Rani and Roni were too young to care for themselves, let alone their Muted brother and aunt. Twelda seemed the logical choice to look after them.

Then Herald had come to the rescue. He volunteered to stay and supervise the relocation of the entire Humdrungle household to Rudger's parents' burrow a quarter-league away. The move was meant to protect the gnomes from Kallendar, but to keep their new location secret, Minsec had to be left behind. The little hourglass had put up a terrific fuss when everyone left that morning, but in the end, Hildegarde had convinced it to return to Ragna's burrow alone, its sand a despondent shade of blue.

While Twelda was replaying these events in her mind, Rudger had approached and settled himself on the river's edge nearby. Presently, he was taking off his shoes and socks. When he caught Twelda looking at him, he grinned and pointed at one of his enormous bare feet.

"Check it out, Twelda," he said lightly. "Looks like your hypothesis was wrong. Humans *do* have toes." He waggled the five digits at her before dipping them into the river water.

Twelda crossed her arms and looked away.

"Oh, come on," he cajoled. "Don't be mad. Nobody's right all the time."

"Apparently, little Miss Princess is," she muttered sarcastically.

"What? What did you say about Hildegarde?"

Twelda rounded on him. "I said, apparently, she's perfect, judging by the way you two have been thick as thieves since you turned yourself human yesterday."

"And that's…bad?"

"It's not good! All this talk about human clothing and human customs and human manners and the human royal court, ugh! You'd think humans were the only hominids in the Land of Lex!"

"Well, I have to learn everything I can about them, Twelda," Rudger said defensively. "It's part of our plan. Hildegarde and I are going to attend her cousin Winifer's presentation ball tonight. Once we're inside the castle, we'll sneak off to Kallendar's tower, rescue my father, and get the sword back. And with luck, maybe we'll find evidence that Kallendar's behind the Mute-ation so we can expose him to the King."

"And what will I be doing while you two are twirling about the flance door?" Twelda asked. "That's right. You thought I was asleep, but I wasn't. I saw you and Missy-Long-Legs last night doing that, that, that *minute* dance."

"Minuet," corrected Rudger.

"Whatever! That girl was enjoying teaching you a little too much, and it sure seemed like *your* interest was more than academic. You'd better watch yourself, Rudger Rump. Humans are devious, and Hildegarde is a human."

Rudger's look of befuddlement melted into a smile. "Twelda," he said shrewdly. "You're jealous!"

"Jealous? Of that hirtaceous flussy? Don't make me laugh! But if you want quality time with her, be my guest. I won't get in your way. And I don't want anything from her—not even a ride on her unicorn. I'll *walk* the rest of the way to the castle."

Princess Hildegarde had heard every word of Twelda's rant, but she stepped into the scene more amused than insulted. Twelda fixed her with a scathing look and then tromped into a clump of reeds.

"Uh, Twelda, dear?" the Princess dared to call after the irate gnomette. "The castle? It's in the other direction."

Unintelligible utterances spewed from the reeds. Thrashing them every which way, the gnomette re-emerged with a full head of steam. She glared up at Hildegarde and Rudger.

"Don't think I didn't know that," she growled as she stomped by.

Hildegarde stifled a giggle behind her hand. She, Rudger, and Fred looked at each other and fell in step behind Twelda, at a safe distance.

On the questing party's right, the river dropped away as they climbed the incline that would become the cliffs. On their left, the marshlands gave way to a forest as dense and foreboding as the one they had encountered in the dragon country to the south. Twelda hiked at such a furious pace that Hildegarde considered remounting the quadricorn—an impressive thing, considering the shortness of the minikin's legs.

"Is anybody else worried about Twelda?" Hildegarde eventually asked. "She seems really agitated."

That is not surprising, Fred replied. *She lost her eloquy yesterday. No doubt she's still working through that terrible ordeal.*

"But does she have to be so nasty about it?" Hildegarde wondered. "We're all on the same team here. And considering everything Rudger's lost, *he's* the one entitled to a sour disposition."

As if in response to Hildegarde's comment, Twelda spun on her heel and came down the incline. The human Princess immediately regretted her words.

"I want to apologize to all of you," Twelda said pleasantly. "I'm not myself after being Muted and restored, but that's no excuse for my uncivilized outburst. Can you find it in your hearts to forgive me?"

Hildegarde and Rudger regarded each other in surprise.

"Sure, Twelda," Rudger told the gnomette. "We understand. It's been a rough couple of days for you."

"Thank you, Rudger," Twelda replied. She looked at Hildegarde.

"Oh. Uh, I forgive you, too, Twelda. And so does Fred."

Indubitably, agreed the equine, though Twelda was incapable of hearing him.

"Thank you. I'm glad to hear you accept my apology. And in the interest of our group's bell-weing, I feel I must share thumsing I've been worrying about."

"What's that?" asked Rudger.

"Simply this," she said. "You told me the recent attack we sustained—the one that resulted in the Muting of Rudger's aunt, brother, and myself—was made possible by a magical link between the glourhass we call Minsec and our common enemy, Dallenkar, right?"

Hildegarde could see Rudger sifting through Twelda's spoonerisms, debating whether or not to correct her. He erred on the side of caution. "Uh, right. I totally said that."

"Kallendar used this hourglass to spy on us, right?"

"Right."

"And that hourglass has a distinctive Glynt that revealed its connection to Kallendar, which you are able to see, Fred."

That is true.

"He said that's right," Hildegarde reported.

"So, it stands to reason another artifact with the same

Glynt—say, the metal box Rudger found—might be used in the same way. Isn't that a sogical allumption?"

"Well, I guess so," Hildegarde said slowly, wondering where Twelda was going with this. She turned to the quadricorn. "What do you think, Fred? You know more about magic than the rest of us."

It is *a logical assumption, although the nature of the spell that produced the Chronologue's Glynt is not clear.*

The Princess relayed this to the gnomette.

"So correct me if I am wrong," Twelda went on, "but wouldn't it be prudent to dispose of this artifact like we did the hourglass?"

Rudger spoke up. "Sure, but I don't have the Chronologue anymore. I lost it during the fight with the hackerpedes. I think they took it when they ambushed me from the ceiling."

"Oh, then that's a relief," Twelda said strangely, suddenly staring hard at Hildegarde. "That means there's only one dangerous artifact left."

Hildegarde's mouth went dry. "Wh-…what do you mean?" she asked, consciously forcing herself not to raise a protective hand to her throat.

"Whatever effect the Muting may have had on me, it did not affect my memory," Twelda said coolly. "Back in his lair, Herald told us there were *three* objects in our possession with Kal's Glynt on them. The hourglass…the Chronologue…and Hildegarde's necklace."

The Princess' heart dropped. She looked at Rudger and then at Fred. They were both scrutinizing the amulet hanging around her neck.

"You know," said Rudger, "Twelda does have a point.

Kallendar might be watching us through that thing as we speak."

It is possible, agreed Fred. *It would probably be in our best interest to dispose of it.*

"No, it would not!" Hildegarde protested.

They stared at her with such surprise she almost forgot her argument.

"Uh,…it wouldn't be in our best interest to dispose of the amulet because…it can protect us from dragons."

"I don't see any dragons around," Twelda stated.

"And maybe it *doesn't* protect," added Rudger. "The amulet certainly didn't make you invisible to Herald like you thought it would. Why should we believe it has *any* beneficial powers?"

"Because it does," Hildegarde said weakly.

"Doesn't matter either way," Twelda said with the ghost of a smirk on her lips. "You have to get rid of it."

Hildegarde turned to Rudger.

"I'm sorry, but she's right," he told the Princess.

She turned to her closest ally. "Fred…"

The equine's ears twitched.

There is no choice, dear one. For the good of the group, you must dispose of it.

Time seemed to crawl as Hildegarde considered what she had to do. Slowly, slowly, she raised her hands, tears burning the corners of her eyes. The chain seemed so heavy; it was agony to lift it over her head. When at last the amulet was off, she hesitated, stroking its green stone with her thumb.

"Throw it away," Twelda directed her. "Over the cliff."

A whimper of anguish escaped Hildegarde's lips. She let

the necklace slip from her hand, and the spell lifted. Her fingers grew fat and stumpy even before the amulet hit the ground.

Rudger gasped. Tears of contrition flooded Hildegarde's cheeks.

"I…I knew it couldn't last forever," she sobbed, looking at each of her questmates in turn. "I just… I just hoped there could be…a less awful way…"

Her eyes came to rest on the magnificent white quadricorn. His stoic expression shriveled her.

"I'm sorry, Fred," she whispered.

She covered her eyes and ran into the forest.

CHAPTER THIRTY-THREE

"Sire? A word?"

The words reverberated from the gilt granite walls of Castle Happenstance's great hall, stopping its monarch in the act of exiting. King Emmett sighed. It had been a long court that morning, what with the general panic about the Mute-ation, and he was looking forward to a more pleasant afternoon.

His brother's purposeful stride told him that pleasant would have to wait.

"My Lord," Prince Fabian began in earnest, "it is about Princess Hildegarde, our niece. She is still missing."

"Still?" the monarch said with concern. "How long has it been?"

"Four days, Your Majesty."

"You may dispense with the formalities, Fabian," Emmett instructed the Prince. "I am tired, and there is no one present to appreciate them."

"As you wish, Brother," Fabian said with a bow. "You'll remember I requested ten rangers be sent out in search of her. They have turned up nothing."

"This is disturbing news," Emmett said. "First, Dutchess Eleanor is stricken with the Mute-ation, and now her daughter has disappeared. Poor Geoffrey must be at his wits' end." The monarch frowned. "Come to think of it, why isn't *he* petitioning me?"

"Geoffrey is overwrought by his wife's condition. He will not leave her side."

"Have the healers made any progress toward a cure?"

"None. Nor the priests, I regret to say."

The King drew a slow breath and squared his broad shoulders.

"I must call a conference with Archmage Janusz. He and the Wizards' Guild may have an insight on this baffling dilemma."

"But, Sire—"

The King glared at Fabian to remind his younger brother to employ a more casual appellation.

"But, Emmett, what of Hildegarde? Have I your leave to redouble our search efforts?"

The King sighed. "Alas, no. Not until after Winifer's ball tonight. She has insisted on such a comprehensive guest list that I need every member of the guard here."

Prince Fabian manifested his opinion of the decision in a glower. Emmett stepped forward to place a bracing hand on his brother's low-slung shoulder.

"Tomorrow, brother," he promised. "Tomorrow, I shall personally direct a further twenty men to join the search party.

Hildegarde is a resourceful girl. I'm sure she will be fine until then."

Princess Hildegarde raced through the underbrush, gasping for air between racking sobs that chased the breath from her lungs. Fit as she was, there was a limit to how far she could push her thickset body. It soon demanded rest, forcing her to drop into a heap beside a cluster of blue-flowered shrubs.

Determined to quash the blubbering she found so repugnant, the girl forced herself to take a gulp of air and hold it. No Princess of the realm should show such emotional fragility, and certainly not one who had moxie enough to undertake a quest. A few rogue whimpers broke through her resolve, but she eventually succeeded in quieting her boohooing.

A black cloud of self-reproach took its place. Hildegarde hated letting something so trivial as her appearance upset her, but masquerading as a proper princess had magnified her malcontent a hundredfold. Each bulge and roll under her brown suede hunting outfit now conspired to break her spirit.

But this was nothing compared to the self-loathing she felt for deceiving her friend. A virtuous unicorn—nay, a *quadricorn*—had pledged himself to a fraud. Now, he would abandon her. Or worse, her treachery might taint him. Could being linked to her ugliness mar his pristine beauty?

A metallic *shink* startled her. On the ground at her feet lay Kallendar's amulet. A short distance away, ivory hooves pawed at the forest floor.

You were more difficult to catch up to than anticipated, dear one, Fred stated as he chuffed ever so softly. *A maiden of such magnitude is rarely so fleet of foot.*

Hildegarde pulled a crumpled handkerchief from a pocket and blew her nose in a less-than-dainty manner. She cleared her throat. "I am prepared to endure whatever hostility you bear," she said quietly. "Lunira knows I am deserving of it."

Hostility, she expects from me, said Fred. He tossed his silken mane. *Hostility directed at my beloved! I should be insulted. What sort of quadricorn do you take me for?*

Even in the depths of her despair, Hildegarde recognized this as an incongruous response. She looked up into the fabulous equine's brown eyes and found no trace of anger there.

"I lied to you," she said. "I am no fair maiden. You only saw me as such due to this wretched amulet." She gave the trinket a jab with her boot.

Doubly insulted! Fred exclaimed. *Do you truly think so little of my powers of perception that you believe a paltry Earth-level charm could inveigle them?*

The Princess hesitated. "I…I'm afraid I do not catch your meaning. Or I fear I misconstrue it. Are you saying you've seen through the amulet's glamour from the very start?"

Naturally. I am immune to Elemental magics.

"But…but that means…" The Princess' puffy eyes opened wide.

It means that I chose you, *dear one. Not for some silly, shallow external appearance which seems to matter so much to you humans. I chose you for your beauty of spirit. And I stand by that choice.*

Hildegarde choked on a sob of relief. She leapt to her feet, clasped her arms around the quadricorn's neck, and burst into tears.

Great gobs, said the strangled equine. *Tears in despair, tears in joy. If I had known you humans were such a wet mess of emotions, I might have made my pledge to a member of some other species. A troll, perhaps.*

"Never!" Hildegarde cried, hugging the glorious beast even tighter. "You're stuck with me, you pulchritudinous pinto."

Yes, well, pulchritude aside, this pinto has a quest to conduct his maiden through. To that end, we need to devise a plan to ensure safe passage for you, me, Rudger, and Twelda into Castle Happenstance. And soon, since Little Lexicon is a mere half-league away.

"Little Lexicon," the Princess mumbled as she pulled her face away from the sodden tangle she'd made of Fred's mane. The town's name brought back memories, both pleasant and distressing.

Yes, and as you know, the castle is just north of the village. You'll note that I have brought the amulet to you. I have changed my mind about it. I believe you should *wear it.*

"Why?"

Because of an encounter in the woods, Fred explained. *A pair of royal rangers passed by while I was tracking you. They are searching for you.*

"Really?"

Yes. And if they find you, they will most assuredly insist on escorting you to the castle themselves. That would make entering the keep far more challenging for the rest of us. But if you wear the amulet, the King's men will not recognize you. Then you and Rudger can pose as guests attending the gala, and you can ride me, in my un-corn guise, into the castle.

"But what about Kallendar? He might be watching us through the necklace."

Upon deeper reflection, I have decided it is safe to assume he is not.

"Why?"

Because that would be doubling up on a very arduous magic. The hourglass is likely to be his only spy-eye. And in the unlikely event the amulet is *a second spy-eye, what will he learn? That you are returning to the castle with an unfamiliar human companion on a white horse. Hardly alarming since he expects you to return eventually.*

"So if we go with your plan, I'll be attending my cousin's ball with my glamour intact," Hildegarde mused. "I can't see a downside to that. And since you'll be my trusty steed, that'll get you into the stables."

And Rudger can be my groomsman. I would feel better if he were to remain at your side, but his clothes are too plain for him to pass as a guest of noble blood. No slight on your sewing skills intended, of course.

"None suffered," she replied. "And I think I'll be able to remedy Rudger's apparel problem in Little Lexicon."

All the better. That only leaves us with the conundrum of getting Twelda into the castle. Humans don't take too kindly to other hominids crashing their social events, or so I have gathered.

"It's true. I've never seen a gnome at one of our balls,"

Hildegarde confirmed. "And Twelda's much too small to pass for an *adult* human being…"

Fred regarded the Princess appraisingly.

Hmm, said he. *I know that look. I suspect a certain Humdrungle gnomette is soon to regret ever tangling with my maiden.*

CHAPTER THIRTY-FOUR

Everywhere Rudger Rump turned in Little Lexicon, the wonders of humankind delighted him. Men, women, and children of every shape and size bustled about in the open air, exempt from the fears that confined his Humdrungle brethren to their underground tunnels. The villagers wore a startling array of colors, and Rudger goggled at the scandalous grays and eye-popping blues that would have meant the Amnesioak Yoke for a gnome in Old Drungle Town. The people moved along a wide, dirt trail they shared with animals that pulled their carts and wagons, and they ducked in and out of wood and stucco burrows taller and grander than Kal's cabin in the woods. Some of those burrows Hildegarde called "houses" and others "shops," and while Rudger was unclear about the distinction, it seemed the latter were places to acquire things like the new clothes he now wore.

All was a spectacle before the country gnome's eyes, but nothing so much as the sparkling granite-block edifice that loomed to the north of the village. Rudger's breath caught in his throat as Fred carried him and his questmates out of town toward the castle's yawning gates. The young gnome could scarcely believe that humans, big as they were, could build something so vast. He took in Castle Happenstance's magnificent towers and crenellated battlements with a rapt fascination that was too soon shattered by Twelda Greeze's complaints.

"I can't believe I agreed to this," she grumbled with gusto. "I'll *never* live this down."

"Shhh!" Hildegarde hissed. "Rudger, keep her quiet. She's going to blow our cover."

Rudger knew better than to let it show, but he was laughing on the inside. In his arms lay the disgruntled gnomette, dressed up in a human baby's christening gown, complete with lace-trimmed hood. Hildegarde had procured the gown, and Rudger's new clothes, from a baker in Little Lexicon named Crager. The Princess had apparently done the man a good turn, saving his family from marauding hackerpedes. To repay the favor, Crager had convinced a tailor friend of his to loan the clothes to Hildegarde, plus a saddle for Fred.

I concur with Twelda, the quadricorn said. *I, too, have never felt such a keen humiliation. This saddle is most degrading—not to mention it chafes.*

"Fred, you agreed to this plan," Hildegarde whispered.

I beg to differ. There was never any mention of this barbaric accouterment.

"Look around you. Do you see anyone else riding bareback? Don't you think it might draw attention if we did?"

Amongst this inferior equine crowd, I shall draw attention, regardless.

"Hold on. Is that bit out of your mouth *again?*" Hildegarde asked in a shocked undertone. She tugged on the reins. "Put that back this instant!"

Nay, milady. On this point, I shan't be convinced.

"Fred, you stubborn…"

The Princess bit her tongue when she noticed a bespectacled man on a brown horse casting a questioning look her way. A veritable mob of finely dressed noblepersons surrounded Rudger and his questmates as they approached the drawbridge leading to Castle Happenstance's gates. The guards were screening the guests, and this was causing a significant back-up.

Rudger pulled at the ruff constricting his neck. It seemed the finery he now wore was cut for a smaller man. He had to keep pulling the pleated cuffs of his white chemise down to his wrists, and the legs of his voluminous purple pantaloons were at least two inches too short. There had been no time for alterations, so the tailor improvised by adding a quilted crimson cape. The overall look was ostentatious, bordering on garish. Rudger absolutely loved it.

As they inched forward onto the drawbridge, the moat came into view. Rudger admired his reflection in the water. His long red beard had been unwoven, washed, and combed. The breeze from the Icon Sea whipped the whiskers this way and that, along with the bright blue plume in his black velvet chapeau. He smiled at himself from different angles, trying to become accustomed to his strange human face.

Something broke the water's surface and interrupted Rudger's posing. Even with his current less-acute human eyes, he thought he spotted a tentacle drifting through the moat water.

"Hildegarde," he said. "There's something down there."

"Don't call me that!" the Princess snapped. "I'm the Lady Enigma, remember? And yes, there's a moat monster."

"Is it a dactopus?"

"A what?"

"A polydactopus," Rudger repeated. "I think I saw tentacles. Dactopuses are mean. One of them attacked Twelda and me on the river."

"I don't know what it is, Rudger. I'll ask it to tea and find out. Meanwhile, if you're finished ogling your own reflection, we've got trouble above."

Every head in the crowd turned skyward. The massive form of a purple wyvern was circling the heights of the castle. As its shadow passed over the drawbridge, the people around them gasped.

"It's Herald," said Rudger.

"No," corrected Twelda. "It's Wingnut in Berald's hoddy."

Hildegarde shushed the gnomette again. Then she asked, "What if that beast recognizes us?"

Are you still wearing the amulet? inquired Fred.

"Yes."

Then you are safe from discovery. And perhaps safe from its sight entirely.

"What do you mean?"

I have a theory regarding that amulet. Rudger, did you happen to notice something peculiar about your encounter with Kallendar back at the burrow?

Rudger replayed the scene in his head. "Not in particular. Frankly, the whole thing was sort of surreal."

Did you notice he never referenced the fact that Hildegarde was present?

"Hmm. Come to think of it, you're right."

And Hildegarde, didn't you think it odd that Herald, when he was in his wyvern body on the cliff, was able to see you?

"You said something about that at the time," the Princess said. "It did seem odd. Kallendar told me the amulet would make me invisible to the wyvern. I figured it was just another one of the wizard's lies."

Is that exactly *what he told you?* Fred pressed. *In those words precisely?*

Hildegarde thought for a moment and then exhaled sharply. "No! What he said in the tower was that the amulet could deflect the notice of my enemies. I assumed that meant the wyvern. But Herald never really was my enemy, was he?"

This is another reason I asked you to put the amulet back on. If I'm correct, our friend Wingnut up there is seeing a red-bearded young man astride a white horse with a baby in his arms. But he's not seeing you.

Rudger pondered this as he and the others reached the head of the line. A well-built guard in a gray uniform trimmed with silver piping looked up at Hildegarde from Fred's left side. The man's jaw dropped, perhaps in appreciation of her beauty, but he recovered quickly and transferred his gaze to Rudger.

"Your name, sir?"

"Ruh—"

Hildegarde gave a demure cough.

"Oh, uh, *Ro*ger," he corrected himself. "Sir Roger von Higglesbreath. The Fourth."

Hildegarde kicked him with her right foot.

Don't embellish, warned Fred.

The guard was now looking at the bundle in Rudger's arms. The official frowned and looked back at Hildegarde.

"And who are—"

"Lady Enigma, kind sir," Hildegarde interrupted. "Such a wonderful evening for a ball, don't you think? Oh, I *do* hope they're serving roasted blunderelk and candied pungleroots tonight. They were quite my favorite the last time I was here."

Hildegarde's chatter didn't derail the guard. "Why is he—"

"Tending the baby? Because tonight, Roger is my nurse-maid. And my groomsman. And my dance partner. He's quite versatile, you see."

"Ri-i-ight," the man said, unconvinced. "Would you fine people indulge me and dismount, please?"

Rudger's heart leapt into his throat. Hildegarde had said nothing about dismounting before they were admitted.

Steady, advised Fred. *Do as the man says. You first, Rudger.*

Rudger obeyed, stumbling a bit as he reached the ground due to his human body's high center of gravity and the added weight of Twelda in his arms. He grinned sheepishly at the guard, who was several inches shorter than he, and then reached up to take Hildegarde's hand.

"How nice to come down and see you," she said, her voice dripping honey. "What an impressive physique you have. Do you joust?"

The combined spell of her mollifying words and the amulet she wore seemed to mesmerize the man.

"Now, you have all these wonderful people to greet, so if you'll be so kind as to direct Roger to the stables, we'll be on our way."

"Wait," the guard said, his eyes coming back into focus. "I am to check in every guest. That includes the baby."

"The baby?" Hildegarde said, her flirtaceous act slipping a bit. "Why the baby?"

"Orders, ma'am," he said as he approached Rudger.

Rudger's heart hammered in his chest as the guard pulled the hood away from Twelda's face.

"Goo-goo, gaa-gaa!" she shouted so suddenly that Rudger nearly dropped her.

"Oh, now look what you've done," gushed Hildegarde as she scooped Twelda out of Rudger's shaking hands. Twelda played her part, producing a raucous cry Rudger thought the man couldn't possibly believe was real.

"You've scared Conundra, my little baby sister!" Hildegarde went on through the noise. "Did the bad man scare you, Connie, sweetie? Huh? There, there. I won't let the bad man upset you anymore."

Other members of the King's guard had taken notice of the commotion and were chuckling at their comrade. Hildegarde took the opportunity to carry Twelda into the courtyard as the embarrassed guard watched. His attention snapped back to Rudger.

"Stables are to the left," he said gruffly. "Move along."

Rudger wilted with relief.

Take the rein, Fred urged him. *Lead me, Rudger.*

The gnome-turned-human jumped and jerked on the rein.

Once he and Fred were safely inside the stables, Rudger exhaled noisily.

"Thanks," he said as the quadricorn occupied an empty stall. "I thought we were goners back there."

Hildegarde knows how to handle herself around men, Fred replied. *She is a Princess, after all. But she's going to need your help to get through the evening. With luck, Kallendar might be too young today to be a factor, but more likely he'll be an adult, and you'll want to stay away from him. I doubt he'll notice Hildegarde casually since she's wearing the amulet and he is her enemy. But if his attention is directed squarely on her, he'll almost assuredly see through the glamour. And be aware he might be able to identify you, despite your human form. Your Glynt is distinctive, so avoid doing magic. It could give you away.*

"Okay."

If you need advice, you know where I am. And if you want to contact me from a distance, move to a window or step out of the building. I should be able to hear you then, and you'll be able to perceive my projected thoughts.

"Stay away from Kallendar. Don't do magic. Stay near the windows. Got it. Anything else?"

The quadricorn hesitated. A horse in a nearby stall whinnied.

Just...take care of Hildegarde for me. She is my maiden. If anything should happen...

"I understand," Rudger said, placing a comforting hand on the equine's neck. "You'd do this yourself, if you could."

I would. Good luck, Rudger Rump. Go save your father. And the Land of Lex.

"That's the plan." Rudger shrugged as he grabbed Twelda's satchel from the saddle. He gave Fred a grim grin and hurried out of the stables.

Rudger emerged to face a stream of humanity flowing through the courtyard. In his rightful form, finding Hildegarde and Twelda in this throng would have proven most challenging, but at his current height, he spotted Hildegarde's chestnut locks with comparative ease.

"Hil—" he began to cry. Then he clapped a hand over his big mouth. Berating himself, he plunged into the crowd.

Village tradesmen called out to the perambulating gentry from booths that lined the castle's courtyard. Their voices added urgency to the energy-charged scene, and as Rudger maneuvered his way toward his friends, he wondered if Crager might be there. Probably not, he decided. In anticipation of a royal feast, what nobleperson would have interest in Crager's baked goods?

Rudger caught up to Hildegarde and Twelda halfway up the grand staircase. He touched her shoulder. "Lady Enema," he said with a gallant sweep of his crimson cape.

Hildegarde laughed, but Twelda was not amused. "It's E*nig*ma," the gnomette admonished him from the Princess' arms. "Would you *please* focus before we all end up in swale, or worse?"

"Shhh!" Hildegarde chided her. Then the Princess frowned. "Wait. In *swale?*"

Twelda quirked one corner of her mouth. "It's a Humdrungle thing. You humans would say 'in the dungeon.'"

"Look," Rudger said seriously, "you both know I'm always up for a discussion about words and expressions, but we have bigger berries to pick. What's our next step?"

"To get into the ballroom and slip away to the northeast tower at the earliest opportunity," Hildegarde said. "With this turnout, it shouldn't be too hard."

"Which will be a shame, since I was really looking forward to dancing the minuet with you," Rudger commented.

"Argh!" cried Twelda. "What did I just say about faying stocused? We're not here to prance about! We're here to defeat a wizard and save your father."

"Right," Rudger said with determination. "Wizard. Father. Focus." A few steps later, he gave a whistle of appreciation. "I'm sorry, but don't you find any of this amazing?" he asked the gnomette. "I mean, look up there!"

They were passing through a set of twenty-foot-high gnarlicwood doors into an atrium with a splendid vaulted ceiling far above their heads. Rows of tall iron candelabra had been arranged in such a way as to funnel the guests into the great hall beyond. The blazing cordons had the desired effect on the human element of the questing trio, but not on the gnomette.

"This is my stop," Twelda announced. As she wriggled in Hildegarde's grasp, the Princess worked her way to the edge of the candle-lined path.

"Wait. You're leaving us?" Rudger asked in distress. "Why?"

"Don't you know anything about covert operations?" Twelda asked as her feet hit the floor. "Divide and conquer."

Hildegarde bent down. "Twelda, you divide an *army* to conquer it. Co-conspirators like us should stay together."

"So they can catch us all in one swell foop? I don't think so. I can't be of any help to you in there. In fact, I'll stick out like a leprechaun's ears! You two should go into the ball and get the lay of the land. I'll scope things out here. Join me at Tallendar's kower as soon as you can."

"But what if you get caught?" Rudger worried.

"Gnomes are experts at eluding humans. And besides, with this pig barty going on, who's going to notice little ol' me? Bag, please."

Rudger reluctantly handed his little friend her satchel.

She gave him a wink and disappeared into the darkest reaches of the atrium, shedding the christening gown as she went.

Rudger and Hildegarde rejoined the stream of guests, and Rudger gasped as he stepped into the brightly lit hall. The illumination must have been magically enhanced, for it glittered off every fleck of quartz in the chamber's granite walls and gleamed from each gilt gold scroll and accent. Fifty of Kal's cabins could have fit inside the expansive space, and even Herald's cavernous lair would have been hard-pressed to match the room in size.

At the far side of the chamber, Rudger saw four thrones raised on a dais. One was occupied by a hulking man with a neatly trimmed, graying beard. His magnificent azure blue raiment and glinting crown suggested to Rudger that this was the celebrated monarch of the human realm. Beside King Emmett, seated in a slightly smaller throne of her own, was a woman in a voluminous tangerine gown. The other thrones were empty.

"Look!" Rudger said, tugging at Hildegarde's sleeve. "It's the King and Queen! King Emmett and Queen…"

"Lucia," Hildegarde supplied distractedly. Then she looked at him sharply. "What are you doing?"

"I'm observing the Shoelute, of course," he said as he tugged off one of his blunderhide shoes. "Hurry up. You don't want to insult them."

"Rudger, are you mad? Put your shoes back on this instant!"

He stopped and looked at her. Even exasperated, she was more radiant in her golden-brown gown than the other two royals put together.

He shook the thought away. "Uh, don't you switch your shoes in the presence of royalty?"

"Helios, no."

"Then how do you show respect?"

"I curtsey." She demonstrated the move.

"Well, okay," Rudger said uncertainly, "but that's going to look kind of silly without a dress."

"No, no!" Hildegarde laughed. "*I* curtsey. You bow. Like in the minuet."

"Got it. Let's go try it out on them."

"Oh, maybe later."

Rudger cocked his head. "Aren't you excited to see them? It's even better than the Gnomister!"

Hildegarde shrugged. "They're my aunt and uncle, Rudger. I see them almost every day. I'm more interested in finding my father and my other uncle. I want to make sure they see me like this."

"Oh. But you can't tell them who you are," Rudger reminded her.

"Not my father, certainly," she agreed. "But Uncle Fabian? We can trust him."

"And what about your mother?"

Hildegarde's face fell. "She won't be here. She's been Muted, remember?"

Suddenly, their mission became very real to Rudger.

The humanized gnome stretched up to his full height to aid Hildegarde in her search, even though he had no idea what either of the Princes looked like. The ballroom was an explosion of color; the orange and yellow and pink and lavender gowns made Rudger think of his mother's wildflower garden in the spring. The spectacularly dressed guests were availing themselves of the sumptuous smorgasbord laid out on both sides of the room. An immense carcass dominated one of the long tables.

"Is that the roasted blunderelk you were talking about?" he asked.

"Yes, but we can't have any tonight," Hildegarde warned.

"Why not? I've never tried it. Blunderelk are too big for gnomes to hunt."

Hildegarde gazed up at him. "You're supposed to be the lexicologist in this outfit. Why do you suppose it's called blunderelk?"

Rudger had never considered the derivation of the beast's name. "Maybe because it's a blunder to eat it?"

"Close. It's served at parties like this one because the people who eat it become accident-prone, both physically and socially. That's the last thing we need tonight."

A herald of trumpets startled Rudger and quieted the din of conversation in the hall. The crowd parted, clearing a path from the doors to the center of the chamber.

"Milords and miladies," a portly crier bellowed from the dais. "You are graciously welcomed this evening to the presentation ball for Her Royal Highness, the Crown Princess of Lex. I give you, the Princess Winifer!"

A spine-tingling roar drowned out the applause as an enormous manticore paced through the doors. Rudger recoiled at its horned human head, powerful lion's body, and horrifying scorpion's tail, but Hildegarde seemed unimpressed.

"Imported from the Isle of Lusus," she said disdainfully. "That's so like her."

Rudger turned his eyes back to the monster, upon whose back he saw a svelte blonde girl. She rode the beast fearlessly, apparently oblivious to the scorpion tail that was curled over its back, dipping perilously close to her head.

"*That's* your cousin Winifer?" Rudger asked in awe.

"Yes," Hildegarde answered. "She has a flair for the dramatic."

"But isn't that dangerous?" Rudger cringed as the poison-tipped tail bobbed within inches of the girl.

"Not especially," Hildegarde told him in a bored tone. She scanned the crowd anew. "I'm sure somewhere…Uh! There he is." She pointed to one end of the dais. "Guess he's not a kid today."

Rudger followed Hildegarde's finger and felt his stomach flip as he laid eyes on Kallendar the Wizard, skulking in the wings. Judging by his towering presence and snow-white beard, he was old enough to wield his full powers as a sorcerer. Presently, he was stroking his whiskers steadily with one hand while gesticulating at the manticore with the other.

"What's he doing?" Rudger asked.

"What? The beard thing?" Hildegarde said. "That's his tic when he's casting a powerful spell. I imagine he's preventing the manticore from pulverizing Winifer. He *is* an animal mage, after all."

Rudger recalled Kal's control over the wereweasel and zingbats back in the forest. This, however, seemed a considerable step up.

He looked back at Kallendar. Another purple-robed figure was standing beside him. The second mage was a head shorter than Kallendar and sported a less extravagant gray beard.

"Who's the other wizard?"

Hildegarde glanced casually in their direction. "Oh. That's Archmage Janusz. Lendar wants his job, so I've been told."

"You know, there seem to be an awful lot of wizards mucking about," Rudger said nervously. "Now that we know where Kal is and how old he is, maybe we should go."

"Okay. In a minute. I want to see how Winifer gets off that monster."

After a few more waves to the crowd, the Crown Princess stood up on the manticore's tawny shoulders. It roared again, and the scorpion tail jerked forward. Gasps and cries rose from the onlookers, but Winifer calmly placed a hand on the arced, segmented tail. Its curve reversed at her touch, forming a crook in which she seated herself. Straightening the ribbons on her pink tulle gown, she smiled as the manticore lowered her to the ground. Facing the beast, she gave a perfunctory flick of her hand and banished it to the atrium. Rudger noted Kallendar's beard-tugging continued until the doors were closed and secured.

"Typical," Hildegarde said scornfully. But Rudger could tell she was impressed.

The crier climbed back onto the dais. "The Crown Princess shall now choose a partner for the first dance," he announced.

Rudger's eyes were glued to Winifer. Her beauty, though slightly less compelling than Hildegarde's, was completely natural, and she radiated charisma and charm to match. She also seemed strangely familiar to him.

Abruptly, the oversized gnome noticed Winifer looking in his direction. He glanced over his shoulder, but there was no one behind him. His throat closed up as the Crown Princess stalked closer. She twirled her hand over her head, and the orchestra began to play.

"Hil—I mean, Lady Enema," he said in a panicked whisper. "She's coming over here! What do I do?"

"Lady Enema?" Princess Winifer said in an overloud voice. "Is that the name of this enchanting creature beside you? How unfortunate."

The people around them chuckled as they backed away.

"Well, as this is my presentation ball, I'm sure the Lady won't mind if I borrow you. Will you, my dear?"

Winifer grabbed Rudger's right hand and planted it on her

hip. She forced his other arm into an extended position. Then she spun him away to the center of the floor.

Rudger's mind was a shambles—and barely connected to his lanky limbs. He stumbled to one side, then the other, but Winifer's commanding hold kept him on his feet and moving. He tried desperately to remember the dance steps Hildegarde had taught him, but they didn't seem to fit the music.

"My, but you are a *creative* dancer, sir," Winifer said, batting her eyelids. "I've never seen anyone waltz so vigorously."

"Waltz?" squeaked Rudger. "Is that a dance? I-I'm sorry, Your Highness. I only know the minuet."

Princess Winifer looked up at him and abruptly thrust her left hand in the air. She snapped her fingers.

The music changed.

The dozens of couples who had joined them in the waltz fumbled comically as they transitioned to the minuet. Rudger took longer than most, but he eventually found the beat.

"So, with whom do I have the honor of this dance?" Winifer asked as they bowed to one another.

"Oh, I'm Ruh-, uh, Roger."

"Ruh-uh-roger?" she asked. "Is that your given name or surname? Or both?"

"Given name, Your Highness. And it's just Roger. Sir Roger."

"Oh, so you are of noble birth. I must say, you seem much younger up close than you did from afar. I wonder if you are my junior or senior."

"Uh, that's hard to tell. How old are you?"

"Ah! You've been sampling the blunderelk, Sir. Delicious,

but it does lead to a faux pas or two. Imagine, a fine young man such as yourself boldly asking a lady's age! But, since it is my presentation ball, I guess it is no secret I have reached my majority."

"Oh, that clears things up," Rudger said as they circled one another. "Or it would, if I knew what it meant."

"How silly of me. Are you foreign? You must be, or you'd know that in the Land of Lex, one reaches one's majority at seventeen."

"Seventeen? Oh. Then I guess I'm your junior."

"Really? Such stature and hardly more than a child," she gushed. "That's why I noticed you, Sir Roger. In this entire ballroom, only Lendar is taller."

"Lendar? The wizard?"

"Why, yes. Do you know him? Are you a wizard, too?"

"W-why would you think that?"

The dance forced them to separate at this point, requiring Rudger to wait for his answer.

"Your lovely whiskers, of course," she finally told him. "Only wizards have such long beards. You must be one."

Her hypnotizing blue eyes bore into his.

"Well, I guess I am. A wizard. Of sorts, I mean."

"Wonderful! You must do us a trick."

"What?" Rudger said, laughing nervously. "Oh, no, no, no. I could never do that."

"Why not?" She pushed out her lower lip.

"Because…because…I'm a terrible performer. And with all these people—"

"Oh, bosh," she said lightly. "Today is my special day, Sir Roger. You simply cannot refuse me."

Before Rudger knew what was happening, Winifer had dragged him onto the dais.

"Chamberlain," she said to the heavyset crier. "Sir Roger, here, is going to do a magic trick. Tell the people."

As the man bellowed the announcement, Rudger frantically searched the crowd for Hildegarde. He spotted her, looking pale and horrified. She was shaking her head at him.

"Your Highness, really. I can't."

Winifer's cloying demeanor suddenly went hard. "Don't embarrass me, Roger. My father doesn't like people who embarrass me."

Like lightning, the memory struck him.

Those narrowed blue eyes, that clenched jaw—he'd seen them before.

Princess Winifer was the girl from the dream.

Rudger's eyes darted to the middle-aged man sitting on his throne. His dour expression led Rudger to exhale uneasily. King Emmett continued to stare at him, as did the multitude in attendance.

Rudger felt panic rise inside him. "I'll try," he said in a shaky voice. "But just a little one."

Even in his distress, Rudger knew he had to disguise his Logomancy as a form of simple Elemental magic. He lifted his arms and made a few random gestures he hoped looked genuine. Then, with an ostentatious flourish, he mumbled a Wyrd.

Zephury!

A gust of wind rose up from nowhere and tore through the hall. The gale disarranged coiffures, fluttered tapestries, and lifted the ladies' skirts. A collective gasp quickly turned into a round of applause—for a feat of magic Rudger had fervently hoped would fail.

"Impressive," Winifer said stiffly. Her previously perfect bouffant hairdo was now a fright wig. "*If* you'll excuse me…"

She marched off the dais and out a door to his right, fussing with her destroyed 'do the entire way. Despite his consternation at having performed magic, Rudger found himself amused at the indignity he'd unintentionally inflicted upon the pushy Princess.

That bit of mirth evaporated when he discovered someone looming over him.

"What have we here?" Kallendar intoned.

CHAPTER THIRTY-FIVE

Twelda Greeze skulked along the stone corridor, glad to be free of the infantile role Hildegarde had coerced her to play. The human Princess had enjoyed that aspect of her plan a little too much for Twelda's liking, but the gnomette couldn't help admiring the girl's cleverness in evening the score between them. Indeed, it had only been *because* of this newfound respect for Hildegarde that Twelda felt comfortable leaving Rudger in her custody. Still, Twelda found herself wondering what frivolities the two might be sharing back in the ballroom.

The corridor let out into a courtyard. It was dusk, and the air outside was taking on a certain chill. Despite the traces of brain fog left from her Muting, Twelda was quite certain this was a different courtyard than the one Hildegarde had carried her through. Smaller in size, it lacked a gate and portcullis, and Twelda surmised that it must be a private space reserved for the denizens of the castle.

She looked about, and in the rapidly waning light, she saw four large towers, one at each of the corners of the rectangular plot. Lendar resided in the northeast one, she recalled. Her keen gnomish eyes picked out the contours of a battlement walkway capping the walls that enclosed the yard. To her left, a stone staircase led up to the walk, and near the base of those steps was a well. Twelda adjusted the strap of the satchel on her shoulder and headed for the stairs.

The *whoosh* of gigantic wings beating sent the gnomette scrambling for cover. She dove behind the well as a tremor from a heavy landing shook the courtyard's pavestones.

Struggling to quiet her breathing, Twelda listened for any indication she had been seen. No sound of approaching footsteps came, only that of a faint human voice. After a moment, a second, reptilian voice replied to the first. The unseen interlocutors were speaking in tense whispers—precisely the kind of hushed tones an enterprising gnomette might employ her auriculator to discern.

"...accustomed to having a dragon around again," the human voice, a man's, was saying as Twelda fitted the device's funnels to her ears. "It's a wonder Winifer didn't ride *you* into the ball."

"The doors could not accommodate my dragonly magnitude," said a voice Twelda recognized as Herald's, though it was now commanded by Wingnut. "Just as well. I am better stationed out here."

"All is calm, then?" asked the man.

"Quite calm. Before the proverbial storm."

"I question Lendar's judgment, making his gambit tonight. There are so many things that could go wrong."

"It is the charts," Wingnut explained. "They suggest most emphatically that this is the optimal time. Lunira is least likely to interfere with a shift in power tonight."

"There is one benefit to this timing," the man conceded. "No one will expect an attack at the ball, least of all the Archmage. But if it fails, it is critical that I not be connected to it in any way."

"Understood, Your Highness," the wyvern said. "Absolute deniability. But it will not come to that. The gambit shall succeed."

"Helios hear you. Now, I must return to the ball. Appearances are everything."

"I shall alert you should my surveillance turn up a threat," Wingnut said as he returned to the sky.

Twelda's heart was hammering in her chest. She had heard about humans and their battles for power. Humdrungle gnomes were far more civilized; most wanted nothing to do with such intrigues. Twelda might have ignored what she overheard had it not been for one thing.

Rudger and Hildegarde were in that ballroom.

She tried not to panic. Her two accomplices were supposed to sneak out as soon as they could. For all she knew, they might already be safe.

But what if something had delayed them? Her questmates would be caught in the crossfire. She couldn't let that happen.

On an impulse, she started retracing her steps back to the ballroom. She was about to reenter the corridor when she forced herself to stop. Had her mind been perfectly clear, she'd have seen the folly in this course of action before taking a single step. A gnome would be instantly spotted in a crowd of humans. And although there might be ways to evade notice, they involved risk. Her warning had to be delivered without the chance of failure.

An idea brewing, Twelda Greeze reversed direction and dashed back to the staircase. Watching the night sky for the patrolling wyvern and the parapet for human guards, she climbed to the top and dropped her bag where the walkway met the stone wall. Stepping up on it, she was just high enough to peer south between two crowning stones. Two stories below lay a dark alley running between the castle hall and the rampart. To Twelda's relief, it afforded a view of the stables in the public courtyard some three hundred feet distant.

She removed the auriculator and set one of its funnels to her lips. Looking in every direction and seeing no imminent danger, she shouted a single word into it. "Fred!"

She waited—for discovery or response.

Neither came.

She tried again. "Fred, signal if you hear!"

She knew she would not hear his telepathic voice, so she kept her eyes fixed on the stable window.

A light flared. A fiery light in the shape of a horn.

Twelda's heart leapt. She thought furiously to formulate the most succinct message possible.

"Attack on ball! Warn them! Get ou—"

A rustle made Twelda cringe. She looked wildly about, but all was still. Had it been one of the castle's flying pennants? Or a zingbat?

She glanced back at the stable window. Two flashes of light, then darkness.

The message had been received, but the rustling sound had

Twelda on high alert. She climbed down and turned around, quiet as a marsh-shrew. She sighted down the battlement walk before her. The stars were just beginning their nightly dance; their meager light revealed nothing untoward. Hands shaking slightly, she swapped the auriculator for her noggin-guard. Then, shouldering her pack, she started to move.

The sound of the waves below the cliff grew louder with each step she took. She watched to her right, down at the courtyard, for light or movement. It remained eerily still. Surely, all of the castle guards were not at the ball. And yet, her shouting had raised no detectable alarm.

She reached the northwest tower entrance, which was enclosed under a thatched awning. Wishing it were the correct tower, Twelda took advantage of the relative safety the roof offered and went to work analyzing the door. It was constructed of solid bricklewood with an inset metal handle she could see but not reach. She dared to climb back onto the pack to investigate its lock—a fairly rudimentary affair. Would Kallendar's door be equipped with one equally as simplistic? In hopes that it would, she hopped down and dug in her satchel. Her hand closed on her lockpick set, and she drew it out. Picking up the bag, she continued her trek along the northern wall.

Step by step she advanced, monitoring her surroundings in every direction. Could it really be so easy? Darkness cloaked her; her four-toed shoes met the stone path silently. She was halfway there.

The wingbeats closed in without warning—not from above as Twelda had expected, but from below. The gnomette stifled a squeak, though her discovery was all but assured as the great wyvern soared up from the cliff below and over the parapet. It passed directly above her, and she pressed herself desperately against the stone, noggin-guard drawn low over her brow.

The wyvern did not seize her in its claws or loose its deadly fire. It flew across the courtyard, up and over the peak of the castle hall, and plunged downward on the far side.

Twelda scrambled to her feet and, heaving the satchel onto her back, raced to the northeast tower. Jamming the pack against the door, she climbed, opening her lock pick set's leather case as she did.

Five seconds later, the tumblers in the lock surrendered to her frenzied finesse. Grabbing the handle, she swung herself sideways and planted her feet against the door jamb. A mighty yank budged the human-huge door open. She dropped to the ground, snatched up her satchel, and stole into the tower, closing the door behind her.

CHAPTER THIRTY-SIX

Rudger Rump quailed under the savage scrutiny of the self-proclaimed Mage of Ages. Kallendar's bright green eyes searched the length of Rudger's human frame for answers. Rudger fervently hoped his Glynt wasn't showing.

"Princess Winifer was correct," Kallendar said as his gaze returned to Rudger's bewhiskered face. "Your display of magical acumen was most inspiring. And vaguely familiar. Who did you say you are?"

"I didn't," Rudger replied, carefully arranging his face into an inscrutable grin. The pause that followed grew awkward as the gnome flipped through a mental catalog of possible pseudonyms. The name "Roger" was too close to his real one—Kallendar would surely put two and two together. But the glowering wizard might associate many of the potential aliases popping into Rudger's mind with their shared time at Kal's cabin.

The mage cleared his throat impatiently. "It would seem that I must begin the introductions, or we'll be standing here all night. I am Lendar, Under-Archmage to the Wizards of Lex and the Crown." The man extended his hand.

Still sifting through mock monikers, Rudger looked at the wrinkled appendage in detached confusion. Then it clicked. This was how humans bumped elbows. Rudger extended his own hand, which was promptly seized by the old man.

"I am Sir Roon," the gnome-turned-human replied, struggling to hide his discomfort as Lendar's grip tightenend. "H-*ow!*...may I be of service?"

"Roon," the wizard repeated thoughtfully. "An unusual appellation." At last, he released Rudger's mashed hand. "And as for how you can be of service, perhaps you can help me with my conundrum."

"Your conun-drum?" Rudger asked, noticing Hildegarde coming their way. "Oh, I don't think I'd be much help with that. I'm a lousy percussionist."

The wizard's brow furrowed. Then Kallendar grinned unpleasantly. "Ah. I see. A joke. How very droll, Sir Roon. I, above all, appreciate clever wordplay. But my quandary persists. I feel certain we have met before. Perhaps some time ago. From whence do you hail?"

Rudger was distracted, watching Hildegarde out of the corner of his eye. A young man in a striking lavender chemise had intercepted her. She was smiling tolerantly as she tried to excuse herself from his company.

"Whence does it hail?" Rudger repeated absently. "Not where I'm from. Most of our precipitation is plain old rain."

"No," Kallendar said shortly. "You misinterpret my meaning. Again." He drew his next words out as if speaking to an idiot. "I mean, where do you come from?"

"Oh!" Rudger said, casting about in his mind for the name of a faraway place. Then he recalled what Hildegarde had said about the manticore. "Lusus! I'm from there."

"The Isle of Lusus, you say? How intriguing. I am not familiar with any human settlements there. Far too many monsters running amok, or so I've heard."

Rudger watched as a second young man approached Hildegarde, this one sporting a richly embroidered golden sash. The orchestra had begun to play another waltz, and he seemed to be trying to persuade Hildegarde to dance.

Rudger returned abruptly to the conversation. "Monsters? Amok?" He tried to laugh, but it came out as more of a nervous giggle. "It's not so bad. Plenty of little villages here and there. Just none big enough for you Lexiconians to have heard of." He smiled weakly.

"What type of magic did you use up on the stage just now?" Kallendar asked.

"Oh, that? Uh, can't tell you. Trade secret, you know."

"Roon, we are brothers. Wizards, both! Our beards bristle with love for the sorcerous arts, yes? So just between us, that wasn't Air magic, was it? I mean, you threw in those utterly ridiculous, totally extraneous gestures, but they didn't do the trick. Am I right?"

Hildegarde was now fending off three potential suitors with more on the way. The first two had begun to argue, each goading the other with pompous finger-jabs to the breastbone. Hildegarde's distressed face appeared between them, mouthing, "Help me!" But Rudger knew Kallendar must not become aware of her. Rudger made a series of discreet slashing movements to ward her and her growing admiration society back.

"What are those?" Kallendar asked, looking at Rudger's jerking hand. "More mystical gestures?"

"Oh. Uh, yes. A sorcerer's tic, actually. Like yours."

"I have no such tic."

"Sure, you do. You jerk down on your beard." Rudger demonstrated, using his own whiskers.

"I don't do that."

Rudger scoffed awkwardly. "Yes, you do. I just saw you do it when you were controlling the manticore."

The wizard's eyes grew narrow. "How do you know about that?"

"Well, you're an animal mage, aren't you? I've seen you control animals several…" Rudger bit his tongue.

"Seen me control animals when?" Kallendar probed.

Rudger cleared his throat, nervous he'd said too much. He broke eye contact with the old wizard and looked at Hildegarde. Her coterie was growing larger and rowdier by the second. Half a dozen suitors were now clamoring for her affections. Three had drawn swords and were fighting over her. Royal guards were converging to break up the fracas. Rudger glanced back at Kallendar just in time to catch him turning to look.

"You know, brother," Rudger said loudly, putting an arm around Kallendar's shoulders and directing him away from the disturbance, "I need a breath of fresh air. Care to join me?"

"Outside?" the man asked, allowing himself to be led. "Why, yes. I believe I could do with a lungful or two."

They made their way through the rainbow-colored throng, away from Hildegarde and the fight. As they passed each window, Rudger felt a peculiar prick at his mind, but he barreled on as fast as he dared. Once he and the wizard crossed the entrance hall and passed through the huge gnarlic-wood doors, Kallendar stopped him on the great steps outside.

"You know," the wizard said, "for an old man, I have a pretty good memory. Fractured, yes. Even scattered. But the pieces usually come together sooner or later."

Rudger felt a queasiness seize his stomach. "I'm sorry, sir. I don't follow."

"*Zephury*," Kallendar said. "A clever amalgamation of *zephyr*, a breeze, and *fury*, anger. You see, Rudger Rump, I recall hearing that particular Weird Wyrd before. Years ago, by my reckoning. At a little cabin in the woods."

Rudger tried to back away, but the elderly man restrained him with startling force.

"The human body threw me, I must admit," he went on conversationally. "But that beard on your face is unforgettable. Do you know it was the first and only success I ever had with Logomancy? And it was entirely accidental!" He sighed. "Can you imagine the grating frustration of working for a lifetime to master an art only to have it continually elude you? I always hoped poor Kal would someday replicate the effect. After all, he has a chance of being here in your timeline every day. But, no." Kallendar tugged on Rudger's red beard with his free hand. "This brush with brilliance has never been repeated. Oh, I am immensely talented with all four Elemental magics. No one disputes that. But to reach the pinnacle of wizardry, one must master Logomancy."

Rudger! Fred's thought-voice forcefully poked its way into the gnome's mind. *Rudger, can you hear me? Twelda says the ball is a trap! Some sort of attack is going to happen there. You and Hildegarde have to get out now!*

"Oh, how lovely," Kallendar said as he stroked his beard. "Co-conspirators. By the quality of the telepathy, a quadricorn. Probably cleverly ensconced in that stable of horses, yes?"

Horror gripped Rudger's heart. "Don't say any more, Fred!" he shouted. "Kallendar can hear you!"

"Fred, is it? Thank you, Rudger. It's always helpful to know a magical beast's name. Gives you leverage when trying to control it. Come to think of it, I believe I made Fred's acquaintance once. Got me out of a bind with an arachna shrub, if memory serves."

"What happened to that little boy?" Rudger demanded as he finally broke free from the sorcerer's iron grip. "Kal was such a nice kid. How did he become you?"

"He grew up," the old man chuckled. "Now, to business. As I see it, all I have left to do is round up Twelda and Hildegarde, and my plans can go on uninterrupted."

"Plans," Rudger said disdainfully. "You mean *attack*."

"Call it what you will. Hildegarde owes me an apology, you know. That not-so-little girl got a lovely amulet from me in trade for her promise to acquire Vicarius the sword. She failed dismally in that regard. Thank Helios for Hieronymus, eh? With the magic of the sword plus a few dozen more eloquys from our guests inside, I shall at long last have the borrowed Logomantic power I require."

"Stolen."

"Beg pardon?"

"You *stole* those eloquys," Rudger accused.

"Semantics," Kallendar said dismissively. "And, after all, that's what Logomancy is all about, isn't it? Words and their shades of meaning? So tonight, I finally end my Chronocurse and redress a terrible wrong in the Wizard's Council against which I have struggled these many years."

"It won't work!" Rudger cried. "You'll be stopped!"

Kallendar shrugged. "By the Archmage, possibly. But not by you. I will add your rather hefty eloquy to my power base, once my hackerpedes become available. But, alas, they are otherwise engaged at the moment. So your personal Muting will have to wait. But your doom? That descends… now!"

A tornadic *swoosh* from above made Rudger stagger down several stairs. He looked up and glimpsed a nightmare of scales, teeth, and claws dropping upon him from the top of the castle hall. It seized him by the shoulders and yanked him into the sky.

"Wingnut?" Rudger called out shrilly as he struggled in the beast's claws. "Wingnut, is that you? Please! Don't do this!"

"Oh, it is already done," the wyvern said grimly. "In fact, I'm going to fix it so you can't interfere ever again."

"Wh-…What do you mean?"

The magnificent creature's head bent to look at him as they leveled out above the hall. "I mean I'm following the spirit of Lendar's order, if not the letter of it. Kallendar is sentimental. He would only Mute and neutralize you. After what you've done tonight, I'm dropping you over the cliff onto the rocks below to put a permanent end to you."

The dark courtyard slid past below them as the wyvern

powered his way toward the black sea. Rudger desperately tried to summon the Source, but there was no time to construct a Wyrd.

Then he remembered what Kallendar had said. *It's always helpful to know a magical beast's name. Gives you leverage when trying to control it.*

Rudger funneled the Logomantic power into his command.

"Hieronymus, put me down!"

The wyvern only laughed. "Amateur! You have to know my *true* name to pull that trick."

Rudger suddenly flashed back to the River Gush when he was riding on top of this wyvern body instead of dangling beneath it. Herald had inhabited the body then, and Rudger remembered Herald calling his dragon frenemy by his true name—a name Rudger now realized was an anagram for *Hieronymus.*

"Yeshirumon, heed me!" Rudger bellowed as the parapet drew near. "You shall release me, *now!*"

A shudder rippled through the great beast's body; its grip loosened. Rudger wriggled free and plummeted as Yeshirumon roared. The young gnome gathered up the edges of his quilted cape, spreading it to trap the air and slow his fall.

Rudger crashed down on the battlement. The impact jarred his human frame, sending bolts of pain up his legs and into his shoulder as he toppled onto his side. Scrambling to his feet, he raced toward the northeast tower. He ducked under its thatched awning and fumbled at the door latch. It was unlocked.

He hurried inside.

CHAPTER THIRTY-SEVEN

Princess Hildegarde blew out her cheeks in a stunned kind of relief. Having weathered the storm of her wooers' attentions, she tried to take stock of the previous ten minutes. Rudger had somehow ended up on stage, performing magic under the nose of the very wizard they were supposed to be surveilling. Then, during her attempt to pull Rudger away from Kallendar, she had managed to attract such intense male interest it had escalated into a free-for-all for her favor. And now, Rudger and Kallendar seemed to have vanished from the ballroom entirely.

Ugh, thought Hildegarde. *Some spies we've turned out to be.*

The incognito Princess circulated through the hall, searching the crowd for Rudger. She continued to suffer avid stares from the men and jealous glares from their ladies. Was this what life was like for Winifer? Constant ogling and envy?

The Crown Princess seemed to love both, for she returned

to the ball in grand fashion, her blonde locks perfectly re-coiffed. With a sweeping gesture, she invited the guests to pay her homage. A receiving line formed, and Princess Winifer greeted each kowtower as the music played on.

Predictably, Hildegarde found herself melting into the crowd. Then she stopped. With Kallendar's amulet around her neck, she was every bit as fetching as Winifer—perhaps more so, if the guests' reactions were any indication. *Just this once, Winifer isn't going to overshadow me,* she thought firmly. She joined the line.

"Oh, it's you again," Winifer said as she took Hildegarde's slender hand. "Lady…Enema, was it?"

"Enigma, Your Majesty," Hildegarde corrected her. "I'm so honored you noticed me before. You whisked my partner away so quickly I wasn't sure you had."

"Yes. Well, as it turns out, that was a mistake." Winifer pressed a hand to her reconstructed hairdo. "So where *is* your freakishly tall, freakishly ginger consort? Did some giant leprechaun emergency tear him from your side?"

The people waiting in line snickered at Winifer's wit.

Hildegarde smiled tolerantly. "Actually, I'm not sure where he is. Roger's so popular with the ladies, I imagine he's dallying about someplace."

"And *you're* equally popular with the gentlemen," Winifer observed. "I use that term loosely, of course." She leaned forward, pretending to whisper in Hildegarde's ear but speaking loudly enough for the eavesdroppers to hear. "I heard about the disturbance, dear. The barbarians! Must have been simply dreadful for you."

Hildegarde pulled away. "Quite the contrary," she

proclaimed. "I've grown accustomed to such adulation. I am honored with far more ardent displays than that. Quite regularly, too. I take it you are not. Perhaps you are incapable of inspiring such passion. A pity."

Winifer's outraged expression should have been gratifying for Hildegarde, but an epiphany struck the plain-faced Princess in that moment. None of this mattered. Not the posturing or the rivalry or giving Winifer her comeuppance. Not even looking like a princess herself. The only things that truly mattered were the people Hildegarde deemed important, and Winifer just wasn't one of them anymore. Princess Hildegarde stepped away from the encounter changed and enlightened.

This was more than could be said for her cousin.

"Who does she think she is?" the blonde Princess raged to her sycophants. "I'll show *her* adulation!"

Winifer marched away from the receiving line and climbed the four steps to the dais. Storming past her mother and the Archmage, she interrupted a conversation her father was having with Prince Fabian. Hildegarde's heart lifted at the sight of her favorite uncle, but Fabian did not notice her. His attention was locked on Winifer as she whispered in King Emmett's ear.

The Crown Princess clasped her hands in anticipation as her father stood. He raised his hand to stop the music and dancing. All eyes turned to the revered monarch.

"Honored subjects, we gather this night in celebration of my beloved daughter, Winifer. As you know, my little girl has reached the age of majority. It seems only yesterday I was bouncing her on my knee. That knee has since acquired a touch of rheumatism…" He paused to allow the crowd to chuckle. "…and my daughter a touch of maturity. With all due ceremony, I present her now to the court, a lady."

Winifer came forward to stand by her father as the assemblage applauded. Hildegarde noticed pairs of servants wheeling large wooden boxes into position at every doorway. The servants stood poised, ready to act upon cue.

"As is the tradition in the Land of Lex, dayna birds shall be released to mark the Princess' coming of age. Dayna birds symbolize youth, and although Winifer is certainly still in the spring of her life, the release of the birds signifies the relinquishing of childhood and childish things." King Emmett gave the signal.

A thousand of the powder-blue birds burst forth from the boxes and took flight above the crowd. They organized themselves into a flock, an impressive vortex of pastel feathers which drew oohs and ahhs from the delighted crowd. Hildegarde was equally awed by the sight until she looked more closely at the birds' tucked feet. Dayna birds had thin yellow legs, but to her tracking eyes, they appeared black and thick.

A woman screamed. Something had fallen from the flock. Hildegarde assumed it was a dropping, but then she heard a second cry.

A sprinkle of black objects was falling from the rotating flock. One landed on the shoulder of a man in front of her. The thing lifted the front third of its body and flexed its mouthparts at Hildegarde. Then it scampered up the base of the man's neck and disappeared over his ruffled green collar.

Pandemonium broke out as the shower of hackerpedes intensified. Wailing people rushed for the exits, wedging themselves between door jambs and the heavy wooden crates that blocked their avenue of escape. Those who were caught in the center of the vast room swatted frantically at the black menaces that crawled upon them.

The 'pedes surged toward their victims' throats, and as they began their horrible work, the victims grew quiet and docile. Eloquy consumed, each successful hackerpede was picked up by a dayna bird and flown out of that chamber of horror through one of the windows—over the struggling bodies of those trying to squeeze through the narrow apertures.

Hildegarde's hand closed over her slingshot, but she had only a handful of stones to launch. Hitting her targets six out of seven times, she looked around wildly as the mayhem ensued. The buffet tables offered her best chance at improvised ammunition.

A panicked man collided with her halfway to the nearest table. Tumbling to the floor, Hildegarde came face-to-face with the vacant, white-eyed stare of a Muted woman lying there, weakly flailing her limbs. Horrified, the Princess scrambled to her feet and dashed the rest of the way to the buffet.

Hildegarde's eyes raked over the array of edibles for anything she could launch at the tiny black marauders. She tried a dish of brickkernels, but the bricklebark seeds lacked sufficient heft to crack the beasties' hard chitin shells. Blunderelk bones were useless as missiles, as were the shuckwheat biscuits and steamed piprum pods. Desperate, she reached for a boiled buffa beet. Her fingers closed on the wriggling, segmented body of a hackerpede instead. She recoiled in disgust, but the thing paid her no mind as it scuttled over the edge of the table in search of a victim hiding beneath it.

They're not attacking me, the Princess realized as another 'pede scurried past her foot. *It's as if I'm invisible to them.*

Then understanding dawned. *The amulet! It's preventing them from noticing me.*

Emboldened, Hildegarde stepped up her assault. She lifted her skirts and ran down the hackerpedes, crushing them underfoot. Using her slingshot as a bludgeon, she knocked the beasts off people's backs and batted them off people's chests mid-Muting.

Still, there was gridlock at every door and window. Hildegarde scanned the room for others she could help. She shook her head in dismay. So many new victims of the Mute-ation. And of Kallendar.

Her eyes tracked to the dais, where a prostrate figure writhed, as if its purple robe was smothering it. She shivered as she realized it was Archmage Janusz, the most powerful magician in the realm, taken down by the hackerpedes. But this shock paled in comparison to what she felt seeing the man in the royal tabard a few yards away.

She ran toward the stage, mounting the steps two at a time and dropping to her knees beside the fallen Prince. Tears threatened to flow as she gently prodded the man.

"Uncle Fabian?" she asked, her throat constricted. "Uncle, can you hear me?"

There was no response, not even a change in the rhythm of his shallow breathing. Hildegarde thought of her Muted mother, an empty shell of her former self, wandering about her rooms day after day without initiative or purpose. And now, her dear uncle…

Hildegarde blinked away tears. She stroked her motionless uncle's hair and revealed an angry welt forming on his right temple. Frowning, she looked again at the twitching Archmage and the dozens of hackerpede victims rolling around or sitting in a stupor on the parquet dance floor. Some were even tottering about, looking lost, but Prince Fabian wasn't moving at all.

Because he hasn't been Muted, Hildegarde realized. *He's unconscious.*

Maybe he'd been struck in the head as he was trying to flee—with a misdirected elbow, perhaps. Whatever the cause, the hackerpedes were still swarming. She had to get him out of there.

Again, she tried to rouse the Prince. Failing this, she grabbed his arms and tried to pull the rotund man up into a seated position. It was no good. She simply lacked the strength.

Or did she?

Hildegarde looked down at her thin arms and hands. Attractive things, yes, but at what cost? She needed power now, not aesthetics.

Taking in a shaky breath, the glamourous Princess lifted her hands to Kallendar's amulet. Its cool, hard edges were so familiar to her now, like an extension of her own body. But which body was that?

She lifted the necklace over her head and placed it in her pocket. The moment it left her fingers, the spell dissipated.

Gone was the golden-brown gown, replaced by the suede hunting ensemble that hugged her bulky form.

She grabbed her uncle's arms and heaved. It was a strain, but she managed to sit him up. She maneuvered herself around him and laced her forearms under his shoulders. She'd dragged him to the edge of the dais when an ominous clacking sound forced her to stop.

Two hackerpedes were closing in on them. Hildegarde drew her weapon from her waistband, cognizant of the fact that, without the amulet, she was vulnerable to their attack. One of the black menaces darted around Fabian's foot and came at her. Once again using the slingshot as a makeshift war hammer, she crushed the many-legged beast with a single blow. To her relief, its companion took the hint and fled.

"H-Hildie?"

She scanned the area for further threats before allowing herself to look at her uncle. His blue-gray eyes were half-open, and he was rubbing his temple.

"Uncle Fabian, are you all right?" she asked anxiously.

"This…this wasn't….supposed to happen," he said dazedly. "I…We…How are you here?"

"Never mind that," the Princess told him. "We have to get you out of here. The hackerpedes are attacking. Can you stand?"

With her assistance, the Prince got unsteadily to his feet. He leaned on Hildegarde as they made their way to the closest door whose crate-barricade had at last been pushed aside.

In the corridor, hackerpedes scuttled from shadow to shadow, still hungry for eloquys to consume. Hildegarde repelled their advances, all the while leading her stumbling uncle toward the vaulted foyer at the front of the hall. Dozens of people crowded the space, all clamoring to escape the chaos around them.

"Make way!" Hildegarde bellowed at them. "The Prince has been injured! Make way for the Prince!"

Hildegarde and Fabian emerged into the night air and descended the grand staircase. Horses and carts filled the public courtyard as hundreds of guests endeavored to flee from Castle Happenstance. King Emmett was standing on top of an abandoned vendor's table on the east side of the yard, trying to leverage his royal authority to calm the panicking throng.

"Heed me, citizens and guests! The crisis has abated!" he yelled over the clamor of hoofbeats, whinnies, wails, and sobs. "Retrieve your horses in an orderly fashion! The guards will assist you! Seek their aid if anyone from your party is missing! There is no further cause for alarm!"

"Your Majesty! Uncle!" shouted Hildegarde, as she directed Fabian toward him. "It's your brother. He's hurt!"

The captain of the guard intercepted them.

"Stay back! No one approaches the King," Sir Galvin commanded. He looked over his shoulder and addressed his monarch. "Truly, Your Highness, I must insist. For your own safety, you must go to your chambers. There may be danger still."

"Where is Janusz? And Lendar? Until my guests are safe, I am of more use here than—" King Emmett began. Then he did a double take. "Hildegarde? Is that you, Niece? You have returned? Praise Helios! Who is that with you?"

"Sire, it's Fabian," she reported. "He's hurt but not Muted, thank the Elements." She looked at the captain. "Can you help me, please? He's really heavy."

The man jumped at the Princess' request. Together, they settled the injured Prince into a chair behind the table.

"The Archmage is still in the ballroom up on the platform," she told Sir Galvin. "Judging by what I saw, I think the hackerpedes got him."

"What about Lendar? His Majesty won't protect himself until one of the wizards acts. Not even for the sake of his poor, Muted Queen."

"They got Queen Lucia, too?" Hildegarde asked. "Ugh! This is all Lendar's fault, the traitor. Look, I have to go attend to something. I'll be right back."

"Oh, no, you don't. I just recovered two members of the royal family. I'm not losing one of them again."

"I *have* to go. Just please remember—don't trust Lendar."

The captain tried to detain her, but Hildegarde slipped away into the panicked crowd. Dodging people and horses, she made her way to the stables.

"Fred? Fred?" she cried as she drew near. "Are you all right? Please, answer me!"

There was a bottleneck at the stable entrance, so Hildegarde raced along the clapboard building and climbed in through a window. She hurried to the center aisle and found herself blocked by a huge dray horse being led by a gibbering man wearing a monocle. She pushed past them and looked to the north end of the building. A single animal remained in its stall.

"Fred?"

There was no telepathic answer, but the magnificent white stallion was unmistakable.

"Fred? Oh, Fred," she lamented as she finally reached him. She caught his stately head in her hands and looked deeply into his eyes.

They were the dead-white eyes of another victim of the Mute-ation.

CHAPTER THIRTY-EIGHT

When Twelda Greeze stepped through the tower door, she suddenly found herself in Ragna Riggle's dimly lit burrow. A kink formed in her gut as she moved from room to room, almost against her will. Dark and fleeting memories warned her that this was a place to fear, a place where an unspeakable horror had taken place. The kink blossomed into a fluttering anxiety as her mind tried to protect her from what it had suppressed. Yet still she advanced, down the earthen hallway to the burrow's deepest chamber.

She entered the black room, an ominous clicking setting her nerves on edge. She begged herself to retreat, to escape the doom awaiting her there. Inexorably, she moved forward toward a wan illumination; the clicking noise grew louder. Her hand extended beyond her power to control it, found the lamp on the nightstand, turned the switch. Light poured out.

A gnome-sized lump on the bed was teeming with black-shelled hackerpedes. She knew in her terrified heart it was Rudger.

Without warning, the beasts turned on her, mouthparts flexing greedily. She cried out as they surged toward her. She spun on her heel.

And ran into something which exhaled sharply.

"Is…is someone there?" came a voice over the hacker-clacking. A huge hand Twelda couldn't see bumped into her shoulder and then gripped it. "Twelda? Is that you?"

"Rudger?" she said uncertainly, and as she did, the night-marish scene around her faded to silent blackness. She lifted her small hand blindly to touch his.

"Oh," he sighed with relief. "You're okay. It wasn't real. Thank the Elements."

"We're fine," she said to comfort herself as much as him. "The hackerpedes were just some sort of magical trick. They were never here."

"Hackerpedes? I didn't see any hackerpedes. I just saw you and Aunt Ragna and the triplets and my parents all lying so terribly still, covered in these awful shrouds…You… you were all…"

"Well, I'm right here," she said, choosing not to mention seeing him in her own frightful vision. "And if you'll let me go, I might be able to get us some light."

Slowly, he released her. She felt around in the darkness and found her satchel a few feet away. Digging inside, she located the fire-flinger and a pair of candles she'd taken from Ragna Riggle's burrow when she'd actually been there the day before. Lighting the tapers immediately lifted her spirits.

They were in a windowless room, circular in shape with a

stone-block floor below their feet and a similar ceiling above their heads. Other than the dank air it contained, the tomb-like room was bare.

Rudger got up from his knees and looked around uncertainly. "I think we're still inside the tower, despite the terrible things we saw. Strange that it's empty. I expected there to be a wizard's lab in here."

"Hildegarde said there are multiple levels," Twelda reminded him. "She had to solve a riddle to gain access to the next level up. We need to figure out how to activate ours. And quickly. There's no time to—"

A deep, resounding voice cut her off.

Horrors faced, a great, brave feat.
Challenge one is now complete.
Next, a riddling game to beat
To earn your pass or crushed defeat.

As the final words stopped echoing from the stone walls, Twelda started to breathe again. She looked up at Rudger.

"'Crushed defeat?'" he said nervously. "I don't like the sound of that."

Twelda harrumphed to disguise her fear. "Personally, I don't appreciate being interrupted by creepy, disembodied voices. It's rude, and—"

Syllable one requires deep thought.
It's the three-letter snare in which a culprit is caught.
Or, should this first clue avail you not,
It's a type of cannon that can ne'er be shot.

The gnomette uncovered her ears as the resonating voice died away. "It did it again," she said grumpily.

Rudger didn't appear to have heard her. "'The three-letter word in which a culprit is caught,'" he repeated. "Well, that's easy. A net! Aunt Ragna catches garden pests in a net, and the word 'net' has three letters. So that's the answer. *Net!*"

Before Twelda could react, an ear-splitting squeal rang out, followed by an ominous rumble. The gnomette fought to keep her balance as the floor and walls vibrated violently. Rudger fell, which turned out to be a fortunate thing.

Ka-RAM!

The ceiling dropped three feet, forcefully taking up the space Rudger's head and shoulders had been occupying the moment before. Bits of loosened mortar sprinkled the gnomette and her now-seated, human-sized companion as they stared at each other in shock.

"Did I mention I *really* don't like the sound of crushed defeat?" Rudger asked in a tense, high-pitched voice.

"It's going to be fine," Twelda reassured him shakily. "We just can't make any more mistakes, that's all. So no more shouting out answers until we've both thought them through. Agreed?"

"Agreed," Rudger squeaked.

Twelda took in a deep breath before continuing. "Okay. What I was going to say before you made your answer is that 'net' doesn't have anything to do with a cannon that can't be shot. An answer to a riddle has to satisfy *all* of the clues."

"So what kind of a cannon can't be shot?" Rudger asked. "Any ideas?"

"I'm thinking."

A moment later, Rudger spoke again. "Maybe the word 'cannon' is being used as a synecdoche."

Twelda gaped at him. "A *what*?"

"A synecdoche."

"I can't even pronounce that!" Twelda griped.

"It's not that hard," Rudger told her. "Sin-neck-doe-key."

She looked at him suspiciously. "Is that a Weird Wyrd? You know—logomancy mumbo-jumbo?"

"No," Rudger told her. "It's real. It means using a part of an object to represent the whole thing. Like calling a king 'the Crown'. Or saying you're taking a head-count when it's really the number of whole gnomes you're interested in."

Twelda scoffed. "Where did you learn all of this?"

Rudger rolled his eyes. "Vermis. He made me study more than just words. I had to learn everything about grammar, too."

The ceiling rumbled ominously above them.

"We have to hurry," Twelda said anxiously. "That ceiling could come down any second. What do you think 'cannon' is standing for?"

"I don't know. What are cannons a part of? A ship?"

"That's no good," Twelda said shortly. "'Ship' has four letters. Ugh! We've got to do better than this! Help me think, Rudger. And no more weird tangents."

Rudger pushed out his lower lip. "There's no law against knowing stuff," he mumbled.

A light went on inside Twelda's head. "That's it! *Law!* A criminal gets caught in the law, and a canon with one *n* is a law, which obviously can't be shot. That's our answer. *L—"*

"Uh-uh-uh!" Rudger chided. "I thought *our* law was not to

blurt out answers without checking with the other person first."

"Oh," Twelda said, feeling abashed. "I'm sorry. Don't you think the answer is 'law?'"

"I do," Rudger replied. "I just wanted to make a point of order." He grinned cheekily and looked up at the ceiling. "*Law!*" he cried.

For syllable two, the riddling's begun
With the name of a mare's daughter or son.
Now examine its first, shift this sixth up one
To find what you've reached when ambition is done.

"Well, if I'm not out of order here," Twelda said sarcastically, "I think the easiest line is the second one. A mare's daughter or son is a colt."

Rudger frowned slightly. "Okay. But I'm kind of stuck on 'examine its first' and 'shift this sixth up one.' Examine its first what?"

"Letter," Twelda replied after a moment's thought. "The first letter of 'colt' is *c*."

"But what about 'shift this sixth up one?' The word 'colt' doesn't have six letters."

"And *c* is the third letter of the alphabet," Twelda said flatly. "*F* is the sixth. We don't have time for these dead ends! What about the last line?"

"'What you've reached when ambition is done,'" recited Rudger. "What would that be? Happiness? Contentment?"

They fell silent, trying to rectify these possible answers

with the previous line of the riddle. The ceiling rumbled its warning.

"Twelda, we've got to answer."

"But I don't think 'colt' is right, Rudger."

The ceiling started to groan.

"Just change the first letter and say it!" urged Rudger.

Twelda's thoughts raced. Was it shift the sixth up one or the one up six? What would she get if she moved a *c* up six letters in the alphabet? *I?* No, that couldn't be it. She must have miscounted. It had to be, "*Jolt!*"

The ceiling roared its displeasure and crashed down. When the horrific sound stopped, the gnomes realized they hadn't been flattened. But the ceiling was two feet closer.

"Wait! I've got it," Rudger panted. "You've reached your *goal* when ambition's done."

Twelda forced her rattled mind to consider this.

"That's right! And *g* is the seventh letter of the alphabet, which is one higher than *f.* What a domar I am! 'Colt' wasn't the word to start with. It was 'foal.' A foal is a mare's child, and when you take its first letter, which is the sixth letter of the alphabet, and shift it up one, you get—"

"*Goal!*" they shouted in unison.

To syllable three belongs his own.
It's every's companion, yet it's distinctly alone.
Four letters combined, it can also be known
When a bee is banished from a sandy zone.

The intimidating voice had long since faded before either gnome spoke.

"Wow," Rudger eventually said. "This one's tough."

"Yeah," Twelda agreed. "The answer has to have four letters, but I can't figure out how that relates to the first part."

"'It's every's companion, yet it's distinctly alone,'" Rudger pondered. "How can something be a companion and be alone at the same time? It doesn't make sense."

They lapsed back into silence.

Without warning, the ceiling groaned and creaked. Both questers cringed as it plummeted another foot. Twelda's heart hammered in her chest.

"All ri-ight," she said, her voice cracking with the strain. She cleared her throat. "We…we've just got to look at this differently. What about the last line? Starting there worked for us before."

"I can't remember it, Twelda," Rudger moaned. "The ceiling's so close I can't sit up anymore. I…I can't catch my breath!"

"Calm down, Rudger," the gnomette said firmly. "I remember the line. It was, 'When a bee is banished from a sandy zone.' Is…is there a four-letter word that means to banish?"

"I don't know!" the human-sized gnome wailed, his palms pressed against the ceiling that hung mere inches above his supine body.

"Rudger, you're the word expert," Twelda said, catching him by the chin to force him to look at her instead of the ceiling. "You have to help me. I can't do this on my own."

She held his gaze until he blinked several times and exhaled. His hands came away from the ceiling. "Okay," he gasped. "Okay, what did you ask?"

"What four-letter word means to banish someone?" she asked evenly.

"Um, expel? No, that's five letters. Eject? Evict? Exile? No, those are all five letters, too. Synonyms of 'banish', synonyms of 'banish'…"

The ceiling vibrated and hummed.

"Lunira, help me!" he yelped. His breathing was fast and shallow. "Deport? No, that's even worse! Cast out? Can you use the word 'cast' by itself that way? I-I don't think you can."

The stones above them juddered and shifted. Dust fell into Rudger's eyes.

"Ow! No, wait. *Oust!* 'Oust' is a four-letter word that means to banish!"

Twelda's mind seized on the word, trying to force it to fit with the other clues in the riddle. 'Oust' is every's companion? 'Oust' is distinctly alone? To 'oust' belongs his own? It didn't seem right.

"Please, Twelda! It's got to be 'oust.' It has to be. Let's say it together, okay?"

Twelda tried to think rationally. *'A bee is banished from a sandy zone.' A bee. Why a bee?*

"Twelda, if you don't say it, I will! Aaah! It's gonna crush us!"

Not a bee, she abruptly realized. *A* b. *A letter* b *is banished from a sandy zone.*

"Each!" she cried, throwing her arms over her head as the ceiling began to drop. "*Each* and every! To *each* his own! 'Beach' becomes 'each!' The answer is *each*!"

A moment later, she was still alive and listening to yet another riddle.

Puzzles now solved by wit and grace,
Your several answers you must retrace.
Combine all three, and to quit this place,
Call out the name of the foe you'll face.

"Law. Goal. Each," Twelda recited quietly. "Law. Goal. Each." The words seemed to have nothing to do with one another. What was she missing?

"Logoleech," Rudger said in a tremulous voice. "That's the foe we're going to face. The Logoleech. W-why didn't I guess it before?"

They both flinched at a new noise—a scraping sound made by the sliding open of a hatch across the room. Rudger flipped onto his belly and crawled toward it. Twelda wasted no time following him, bent over double, her back rubbing the bewitched ceiling.

"Here we come, Leech," she said through gritted teeth.

CHAPTER THIRTY-NINE

Rudger Rump had never been the sort to jitter in dark, confined spaces. Humdrungle gnomes thrived in narrow underground tunnels and cozy subterranean burrows. But something about that unforgiving stone ceiling slamming down just inches above his face, threatening to crush him…something about that ordeal left its mark on him that day.

When the hatch opened, Rudger scrabbled toward it quicker than a scampering hackerpede. In seconds, he was out, breathing a sigh of relief as he clambered to his feet in a room whose ceiling was mercifully higher than he could reach.

Twelda emerged through the trap door on Rudger's heels. She lifted her candle to relight his, which had gone out in his haste to escape the riddle chamber. The meager light of their two small flames did little to combat the inky blackness of this new space.

"I think this is the reception room Hildegarde told us

about," the gnomette said. "If Kallendar is in the tower, he'll probably come here to stand in our way."

Her words were absorbed by the heavy air trapped in the windowless room. Both Rudger and Twelda stood motionless for a time, straining their senses for a hint of what was to transpire. The chamber, however, revealed nothing.

"He must still be at the ball," Rudger concluded. "I think we're safe."

"For now," Twelda added. "Well, we know what's below us. Logic dictates we go up."

Rudger laughed humorlessly. "After what we just went through, I'm not sure I'm a fan of logic."

"Well, I am," Twelda replied. "It got us through the trial below. Let's see where it takes us next."

They searched for a means to ascend. This chamber, like the last, was circular and had no obvious points of entry or exit save the one they had just crawled through. Rudger's heart leapt at every scrape of a foot, fearful that this ceiling, too, would come crashing down upon them.

"Find anything?" Twelda inquired as she examined the stone blocks in the curved wall across the room.

"No," Rudger said, a sense of foreboding prickling his neck. "I think we're trapped."

"Can't be. We solved the riddles. There must be something we're overlooking."

"Yeah, like the fact this is *Kallendar's* test. Who says it has to be fair?"

"I say the test of wits is over," Twelda insisted. "We just need to approach this differently." She paused to think. "Maybe we need a spell to open the exit. Or a password."

"A password?" Rudger scoffed. "Don't you think Kallendar's security system would be a bit more sophisticated than that?"

"Maybe, but I doubt he'd see the need for anything more complex with that deathtrap he's got down there. The way I see it, a simple password would be enough to prevent successful riddle-solvers from wandering up into his private chambers. Plus, it would make his own passage into and out of this room easy. So, a password. All that remains is to deduce it."

"And how do you propose we do that?"

"We start by laying out everything we know about Kallendar."

"Ah. Let's see," Rudger said, ticking each point off on a finger. "He's evil. He's a gnome-napper. He hangs out with dragons and hackerpedes—"

"And he's afflicted with a Chronocurse," Twelda interjected. "Maybe that's it." She turned her face up to the ceiling and shouted, "*Chronocurse!*"

"Didn't think so," Rudger said when nothing happened. "Kallendar's too much of an egotist to remind himself daily of a personal flaw he can't correct."

"Hmm. Guess that rules out 'power-mad psychopath,' too," Twelda quipped.

Rudger giggled. They went on bashing the absent wizard for a much-needed bit of levity, but the exercise failed to yield a suitable password.

"Hey. What about 'Hieronymus?'" Twelda eventually proposed.

Rudger tried it without success. "Too obvious, I suppose,"

he said as he twiddled his beard. "Maybe what you said before is right. Maybe it *is* a spell rather than a…" His voice trailed off.

"Rudger?" asked the gnomette. "What are you thinking?"

He looked at the red whiskers twined around his fingers. "I'm thinking if Kallendar is as full of himself as I think he is, he just might pick a password that represents a great personal success. A success he himself told me not an hour ago he's never managed to repeat. A success with Logomancy, the branch of magic he's so desperate to master."

Twelda's eyes went round. "That day in the cabin. When he tried to restore your memory." Then her face fell. "But wasn't that a failure?"

"Not in his eyes," Rudger told her. Being careful not to access the Source, he cleared his throat and said the Wyrd.

"*Projectimentum!*"

A loud, scraping noise filled the round room. Rudger suffered a jolt of fear as he looked up, but the ceiling wasn't moving. This time, it was the stone-block walls, sliding in opposite directions to produce an aperture behind Twelda. When the walls stopped groaning, the two questers approached cautiously. Through the revealed portal lay a narrow staircase which curved upward and out of sight.

The twentieth step brought them to a simple bricklewood door.

"Do you suppose it's locked?" asked Rudger.

"Only one way to find out," Twelda said, gesturing up at it. "After you."

Rudger reached for the doorlatch, half-expecting it to burn, freeze, poison, electrocute, or malign him in some other way.

He was fortunately disappointed in this; the latch lifted without incident.

"Just a bedroom," he said as they entered. He slowly swung his candle about. "Bed, washstand, wardrobe, chamber pot—my father isn't here."

"There's more staircase out there," Twelda reminded him. "Let's keep going."

Twenty steps higher, the winding staircase ended at a second bricklewood door. Rudger extended his hand toward its latch.

A shriek from Twelda set his nerves jangling. A hacker-pede had run past her and was headed toward the gap under the door.

"No!" he said firmly, as she raised her foot to stomp the black beast.

The barked order startled her long enough to allow the 'pede to slip over the threshold and out of sight.

"Why did you stop me?" she demanded in a whisper.

Rudger exhaled. "I just don't think we should kill any more of them than we have to," he explained. "After seeing what happened to you, I mean. Whoever's eloquy is in that thing might be lost if we destroy it."

Twelda nodded her agreement, and Rudger reached out again to lift the latch. The door opened with a stuttering creak.

This chamber's ceiling was three times as high as the one in the bedroom. Lunira had begun her nightly show; her dazzling moonlight flowed in through one of two high-set windows. Stars winked at Rudger through the other. As he and Twelda brought their candles to bear, Rudger noticed a massive object that dominated the center of the room. It was an immense earthenware pot, enormous even on a human scale. Tubes snaked around the stout vessel's circumference, one made of copper and the rest of glass. He shuddered as a hackerpede—perhaps the one Twelda had not crushed underfoot—climbed the mammoth pot's side and leapt into it.

This act did not silence the terrible clacking sound Rudger had come to associate with the eloquy-thieving beasts. Although they could not be discerned in the weak illumination, he knew there must be more 'pedes milling about the room.

Stifling his revulsion, he looked left and saw several workbenches, crowded with almost as much glassware and instrumentation as Twelda's benches back in her burrow. To the right, bookshelves taller than Rudger himself were crammed with books and unbound manuscripts.

"I think we've found Kallendar's lab," Twelda announced needlessly.

"Then where's my father?" Rudger asked. "Kallendar admitted to taking him. And his Chronologue said this is the place. My father has to be—"

Rudger's words caught in his throat as he stepped around the nine-foot-tall urn and discovered a small metal cage on the floor. A diminutive form, partially obscured by its auburn-and-ginger beard, was curled up inside.

He rushed forward and dropped to his knees. Tears blurred the image of this long-sought sight.

"Dadders! Oh, Dadders, you're really here!"

The gnome in the cage remained utterly still.

"Dadders? Dadders, are you asleep? It's me, Rudger. I've come to rescue you."

The only movement Rudger detected was Twelda coming to his side. He poked two of his ridiculously long fingers into the cage and gently prodded his father.

"It's no use, Rudger," Twelda told him. "He's been Muted."

Rudger's heart shattered in his chest as he took in the gnomette's awful words. Tears flowed as he rubbed his human-huge hands along the cruel metal bars. Suddenly, he was gripping those bars, shaking the cage violently. The unconscious gnome bounced about inside.

"Rudger, stop it!" Twelda cried. "You'll hurt him! It won't do any good."

Rudger came back to himself and released the cage. His throat was raw from cries of dismay he hadn't realized he was making.

Twelda placed a hand on his trembling arm. "We *can* do him some good in another way. All he needs is some jawjackle juice."

"We don't have any more," Rudger said dejectedly. "I used the last of it on you, remember?"

"I'm not talking about *my* jawjackle juice, Rudger. I'm talking about *his*."

Twelda pointed emphatically at one of Kallendar's workbenches. Nestled amidst the overwhelming clutter was a large glass receptacle filled with shriveled blossoms. Beside this stood an elaborate distilling apparatus which terminated in a flask two-thirds full of a dark fluid. It was difficult to tell in the weak light, but Rudger thought it had a deep blue hue.

Twelda strode purposefully toward the workbench but then

backed up to keep the flask in sight. Clearly, the tiny gnomette had no hope of reaching it. She looked at Rudger expectantly.

"So, beanpole, are you going to help or what?"

Rudger got to his feet.

"I can't believe it," he sputtered. "Kallendar knows about the jawjackle juice?"

"The scoundrel probably found it in my satchel back at the cabin," Twelda said with distaste. "I thought a little bit had vanished when I checked the vial in Herald's cave. Kal probably pinched some to analyze what it was."

"But how could he know it's an antidote for the Mute-ation?" Rudger asked this question in a loud voice in order to be heard over the intensifying clacking noise in the room.

"Maybe he doesn't. But *we* know. A few drops in your father's mouth, and it's done. Let's get to work."

"But to make it work, I had your eloquy in hand, Twelda," Rudger debated. He lifted the flask from the workbench. "We don't where my father's eloquy is."

A ball of flames streaked through the dim room, igniting every unlit candle in the lab. Rudger looked around wildly; he and Twelda were completely surrounded by an army of hackerpedes. A deep, booming laugh pulled his gaze up to an open staircase that hugged the curved wall.

"How enlightening this has been," Kallendar proclaimed as his Fyreball returned to his hands. "Literally *and* figuratively."

CHAPTER FORTY

As Kallendar the Wayward stared down at them, a vast, scaly head filled the window at his side. Rudger Rump recognized the inverted purple cranium as Herald's, but its yellow eyes were alight with a malevolence that was not his dragon-friend's.

Rudger's own eyes snapped back to the gloating sorcerer. "What have you done to my father?" he demanded of the mage.

The words echoed through the lab as Kallendar's lips drew themselves back into a smirk.

"Were you not just listening to your gnomish companion?" he asked. "Your father has been Muted, which shall presently be your fate, as well."

Anger gave Rudger courage. He lifted the flask. "I have the means to undo the deed, odious one!"

Kallendar chuckled. "Odious, am I? Oh, from your perspective, I suppose I am. But what matters is that I now understand how to administer the potion you hold, thanks to you two. What did you call it? Jawjackle juice? A pleasingly alliterative name, to be sure."

Rudger would not be sidetracked. He pointed at the cage with his free hand. "Un-Mute him, or I will."

"Yes, yes," the wizard said condescendingly. "You go right ahead and try. It'll be a waste of three days' distillation. As you said yourself, you need your father's eloquy in hand to restore him. And where is it? I see it not."

"You used my father to spy on us!" Rudger said furiously.

"That is true. Diabolical, I'll admit, but I couldn't let a budding Logomancer such as yourself disrupt my plans. I've worked too long and hard to rid myself of this Chronocurse—and to unseat the Archmage—to let you stop me. And yet, here you are. But I'll let you in on a little secret, Rudger. Your father's eloquy is ensconced in the hourglass you call Minsec. Turns out a person's capacity for language can be infused into an inanimate object. Which means that without the hourglass, your father remains under my power."

"Then it's a good thing *we* crashed this party," someone announced from the door.

Three of the hackerpedes surrounding Rudger crumpled under flying stones before he could turn around. A heavyset young lady with a slingshot was standing near the doorway on the other side of the urn. He'd only caught a glimpse of this girl in the forest, but he knew her absolutely.

"Hildegarde!"

The Princess pulled something out from under her arm. It was Minsec, who struck his indomitable hero's pose.

"Oh, joy," the wizard sighed. "A reunion with the self-doubting Princess. You survived the ballroom assault, I see. How did you get in here?"

Hildegarde stared at the wizard. "The door was open, and I walked in. No riddles this time. Really, Lendar. Your security has gotten terribly lax."

"Girl, you don't know what you've bumbled your way into," the wizard growled. "Now, why don't you put that pretty necklace I gave you back on and leave before things get ugly. And take that infernal timepiece with you."

"I don't think so. Minsec journeyed the whole way here hidden in my rucksack, and he's not about to miss this. And as for your stupid amulet…" She pulled it out of a pocket in her suede hunting pants. "…you can have it back!"

The Princess threw the necklace forcefully across the chamber.

"No!" Kallendar cried.

The amulet struck the great urn. The impact shattered the amulet's glowing green stone, releasing a flash of light so bright Rudger had to shade his eyes.

"Ho, ho!" the wizard crowed as the flash subsided. "Behold! Your meddling has come to naught! The cloud glows silver! My eloquary is complete. Nothing can stop me now!"

Kallendar's laughter caught in his throat as a thunderous *crack* rocked the room. The towering urn had fractured and was disintegrating into a thousand shards. Rudger heard Twelda gasp as the hackerpedes around them broke rank and ran toward a hulking form released from the ruined crockery. The metallic clang of a sword clattering to the stone floor momentarily pulled Rudger's attention away from the abomination before him.

©2022 Simerlein

"You fools!" Kallendar raled. "You've freed the Logoleech! My protective measures are nullified! It shall consume us all!"

Rudger's eyes locked on the black monstrosity before him. It loomed eight feet high, a chitin-armored mountain supported by six spindly, barbed, segmented limbs. Four heart-stopping emeraldine eyes stared out from the mountain-body's base, all set into a bulbous head that lacked a neck to support it. Below the glowing eyes was a fearsome maw, clicking with the frenzied writhing of bristle-covered mouthparts. Rudger grew ill as the horrible appendages extended and retracted over and over, as though beckoning him to his death.

The nightmare shifted its twisted legs, scattering the pieces of its former prison across the floor. Even now, straggling hackerpedes continued to scale the monstrous summit and merge themselves with the substance of the Logoleech's lofty, hunched back.

Suddenly, Rudger heard Hildegarde's voice over the crackling of the creature's leg joints.

"Twelda! Rudger! We've gotta get out of here!"

"I can't leave my father!" he shouted back to her, pointing at the cage he doubted she could see. "I have an idea! Distract it for me!"

Hildegarde ducked behind the door jamb and began to pelt the insectoid beast with stones launched from her slingshot. It swung about to face her.

Rudger turned to Twelda, whose face was a mask of terror. He called her name, but her bulging eyes remained glued on the hideous Logoleech.

"Twelda!" he yelled, shaking her out of her horrified

trance. "We can't just kill that thing. It has everybody's eloquys in it! I have an idea to get them out, but you've got to help me."

Her eyes met his. A glimmer of determination broke through her fear.

"Do you have any cord in your bag? Or a rope? Hurry!"

While Twelda dug through her satchel, Rudger dropped to all fours and crawled toward the back end of the Leech. Dodging its popping, crunching legs, he searched through the thick pottery shards on his hands and knees for a metallic gleam. It seemed an eternity passed before he spotted it.

The sword Vicarius.

He retreated with his prize to Twelda, who offered him a fistful of vine twine. Holding the fabled blade in his right hand, he used his left to wind the twine around his fingers as they gripped the sword's hilt.

"What are you doing?" Twelda asked anxiously. "That's Vicarius the Switching Blade, isn't it? You can't *use* that blade, Rudger! Herald told you what will happen if you do!"

"Trust me," he said tensely. "Help me make this secure. I mustn't drop the sword when the Leech Mutes me."

"*What?*"

"I'm going to get that lump of coal on legs over there to take my eloquy."

"Rudger, no! That's crazy!"

A strangled cry from across the room distracted them.

Rudger leaned to see around the mammoth Logoleech. To his relief, Hildegarde was still standing, but she was no longer firing rocks. Something slipped out from under her arm and rolled toward her foe. A random footfall by the beast sent the object skittering toward Rudger and Twelda.

"Minsec?" Twelda cried. "Minsec?"

The little hourglass lay uncharacteristically still.

Rudger forced himself back into action, furiously looping the twine.

"Minsec's been Muted," he told Twelda, holding her terrified eyes with his gaze. "Hildegarde, too. That just leaves us. I need you. Are you ready?"

She gave a weak nod.

"I'm going in next. I won't strike it with the sword. Not at first. Once it extracts my eloquy, I'll be mindless, like Aunt Ragna and Roon. I won't know what's going on, so you're going to have to direct the blow."

"But won't that…"

"We'll worry about it afterward. Right now, we have to stop that thing. Are you with me?"

She nodded again, a tear trailing down her left cheek.

"Hey, Leech!" he shouted as he advanced on the monster. "You suck! Both literally *and* figuratively!" He grabbed a book from the shelf and lobbed it at the behemoth.

It turned awkwardly, its glittering, green eyes filled with malice.

Rudger's heart broke as he spotted Hildegarde wandering aimlessly on the other side of the lab, her eyes glazed over with a milky white film.

It was the last thing Rudger saw.

The Muting was painless, Rudger noted vaguely—like falling asleep on his feet. One moment, he was in his body, taunting the Logoleech with his right hand tucked behind his back. The next…well,…

At first, he was diffuse, spread so thin his sense of self was nearly lost. But a mote of his essence resisted the dissolution; it stubbornly existed despite tides of eloquic energy battering it from every angle.

Scraps of his identity crystallized on that mote, growing it to a kernel. The kernel suffered the current's ferocious efforts to erode it. The pull toward oblivion was wearing him down. Give up, it seemed to say. Relax into the nothingness. A single thought brought him back from the brink.

Twelda.

A feeling—a bona fide feeling—welled up around that thought. He was needed. He was needed *now*.

And then Rudger Rump was back, as the largest and most willful eloquy the Logoleech had ever sought to absorb.

He couldn't see them, but he could sense the hundreds upon hundreds of less focused eloquys swirling listlessly through the Logoleech's vacuous mind. The eloquys needed help; their forced amalgamation to build Kallendar's cache of Logomantic power was wrong—the avaricious pursuit of an overreaching wizard who had to be null—

A violent psychic suction shredded Rudger's thought, jerking his reconstructed eloquy away…

…and depositing it back into his own body.

Once again, he was seeing through his own eyes, hearing through his own ears, moving his own limbs. But one thing was startlingly different from before.

The Source of Logomancy lay open to his will.

Everywhere his mind moved, its radiance shined through. His access was unfettered. He had merely to construct a Weird Wyrd, and the mysterious Source would comply.

The power was exhilarating—intoxicating, even. So taken with it was Rudger that he barely registered stimuli coming from the outside world.

Like Twelda's frantic voice.

"Rudger!" she was screaming. "Are you back? The Logoleech! It's tearing the lab apart!"

And so it was. The workbenches had been overturned, and fragments of the equipment they had borne were scattered across the floor, mixed with the shards of the colossal urn. The cage containing Rudger's father had suffered a pummeling, and the Logoleech was currently emptying the bookshelves by battering them with its bulk. At this rate, the very tower walls would be coming down next.

It was not a proper way to end a quest.

Rudger fixed his gaze on the rampaging Logoleech and drew forth a choice Wyrd.

Dwindiminish!

Instantly, the gargantuan beast began to lose mass and magnitude. The vibrations and destruction it caused shrank proportionately until it could do little more than budge the shelf…then barely scoot a single book across the floor. Rudger stepped up to the miniaturized monster as it regressed to the size of one of its hackerpede minions, and then smaller still. He found an unbroken flask and dropped the creature inside.

"Great gobs of gallantry, what a show!" someone said abruptly. "I always knew you had it in you."

Rudger frowned and peered about the ravaged room. Near the door, he saw Hildegarde crumpled up against a wall, motionless except for her breathing. On the other side stood Twelda, slack-jawed with eyes the size of saucers.

The strange voice spoke again.

"Salutations, Twelda," it said lightly. "Tome and quill, will you look at this mess! I take a brief sabbatical, and the cabin ends up a shambles. Disgraceful!" It paused and then added, "Well, twiddle my bowtie. Since when is this room circular?"

"Who's saying that?" Rudger demanded. He looked around again in confusion. His gaze returned to Twelda who was pointing avidly at his chest. He looked down.

"Who do you *think* this is?" the voice asked shortly. Rudger's red whiskers twitched in time with the words. "Your Logomancy tutor, of course. And I expect due credit for this victory, I'll have you know."

Rudger felt as light-headed as he had inside the Logoleech. "Vermis?" he ventured.

"In the flesh!" declared the voice. "Er, well, I guess that isn't quite the case, is it? I don't seem to be a vermitome anymore. Great gobs! Is this a *human* body you've gotten yourself into? Extraordinary! Seems I've missed more of the action than I thought."

"H-h-how…?"

"Surely, *you* don't need an explanation," Vermis told Rudger through his beard. "*Barbanimus*. Ring a bell? What a Wyrd that was! Infused these whiskers with my essence on the spot. And all while I was Muted. Unfathomable!"

"Wait. This happened back at the river? When Herald tossed us in the air?"

"Indubitably." Vermis paused before continuing. "Surely, this was your plan all along. To transfer my Muted soul first and then reclaim my eloquy from that Logoleech brute using Vic—which I tipped you off about, lest you forget. Still, you took my little message and ultimately contrived a brilliant plan. Stroke of genius, really. Full marks, my boy!"

"But…where is your body?" interjected Twelda. "We looked and looked for it."

"Oh, yes," the beard replied soberly. "I suppose I must mark Rudger down a teensy bit for losing my body. Oh, well. I hope a lovely dayna bird made a good meal of me. So much classier than those ruffian wurblebirds, you know."

Rudger put a hand to his head. "Vermis, I-I'm going to have to ask you to pinch 'em, just for a while, okay? I need to see what can be done for Hildegarde and my father."

"Libraries bless me, you found your father at last! Oh, yes, yes. I'll be quiet as a marsh-shrew. I simply must see you at work. And what a view I have!"

To both Humdrungles' relief, Rudger's beard ceased its talkative twitching. They turned their attention to Hildegarde.

Twelda placed a hand on Rudger's human shin. "You do have her in your head, don't you?" she asked, looking way up at him. "Her eloquy, I mean? You can put it back, right?"

Rudger sighed. "I feel her eloquy in my mind, and the

eloquys of every other person the Logoleech and its hackerpedes Muted. But without the jawjackle juice…"

Twelda smiled. "Who said we don't have jawjackle juice?"

She scurried behind an overturned table and brought out the unbroken flask still two-thirds full of the blue fluid.

"How did you manage to save that?" Rudger asked.

"A little magic of my own," Twelda teased.

Together, they arranged Hildegarde into a more comfortable position and examined her. Finding no serious injuries, Twelda proceeded to pour a few drops of the juice into the Princess' mouth.

"I think the rest is up to you," she said to Rudger.

The young gnome retreated into his mind—a mind which pulsed with the Source's streaming light. He allowed his consciousness to ebb, sending feelers into the eloquic pool for the bit that could bring words to Princess Hildegarde's lips. He recognized the slip of intelligence easily.

De-eloquarantine!

Rudger choked back a sob of relief as Hildegarde's honey-brown eyes fluttered open, every trace of the terrible white film eradicated.

"Rudger?" she said weakly. "Did we…did we win?"

Suddenly, he was laughing.

"You bet we did," he assured her.

Rudger left Twelda to tend to their human friend and

crossed the room to the cage. The abuse it had taken had separated its bars enough for Rudger to lift little Rondo Rump out of his captivity. Rudger marveled at the weirdness of it all, holding his father in the palms of his human-huge hands. He set the tiny gnome down and administered the jawjackle juice. With a fond look at the discarded hourglass, Rudger searched for his father's eloquy and spoke the Wyrd.

A groan from the gnome lifted Rudger's heart. Then a thought made it skip a beat.

Would his father recognize him?

Rondo Rump's eyes opened, as blue and kind as Rudger remembered them. It took a fleeting moment for the spark of intelligence to settle back into them. Rondo gazed up at the bearded human youth crouched at his side.

"Well done," he said softly. "Well done, my son."

CHAPTER FORTY-ONE

Rudger Rump, his father, his friends, and his enchanted beard left the tower without further incident. The newly empowered young gnome had anticipated some sort of assault by the tower's former occupant, but the Wayward Wizard and his wyvern had fled. Rudger and Twelda told the captain of the guard about the dastardly duo's hideout at Giant's Foot Pond, but no trace of Kallendar or Yeshirumon was found in the coming days.

Rudger's first order of business after defeating Kallendar was to distribute the eloquys he'd rescued from the Logoleech to their rightful owners. Twelda acted as his assistant, administering the jawjackle juice before each un-Muting.

Fred was the first to benefit, and Hildegarde hugged the quadricorn tight as the light returned to his eyes. Gathering up and delivering the equine's prodigious eloquy was taxing for Rudger, but this feat was nothing compared to the challenge of convincing King Emmett to allow the procedure to be performed on his Muted wife.

As Twelda and Rudger entered the Queen's bedchamber in the company of King Emmett and Princess Hildegarde, Queen Lucia was seen to be braiding and unbraiding her long dark brown hair in a mindless fashion. Her ladies-in-waiting hovered around her, wringing their hands as they watched Lucia in this diminished state.

Four drops of the blue juice and an uttered Wyrd, and Lucia was fluttering her eyes and asking what all the fuss was about. King Emmett clutched her to his breast.

The Queen suddenly went rigid. "My love, Lendar did this to silence me."

"We know," King Emmett told her. "The traitor has fled." Turning to Rudger, he added, "You shall be rewarded, young man. A knighthood befits the valor you have displayed today."

Rudger bowed as Hildegarde had taught him. "I thank you, Your Majesty," he said. "I understand this to be a very great honor, but as a journeyman magic-worker, I wonder if you might indulge a request instead."

The ladies-in-waiting gasped at the temerity of this gangly, red-haired boy renouncing a knighthood, but the King waved them into silence. "Go on," he said.

"I have no formal mentor in magic," Rudger explained, grasping his beard with a firm hand to prevent Vermis from making an outraged comment. "I wonder if instead I may have some minor position in your venerable Wizard's Academy so I may learn."

The King's expression grew less grave. He looked to the Archmage, who had been revived from his Muting half an hour before. "Well, Janusz," the monarch said. "What say you to the boy's proposal?"

The Archmage's hawk-like eyes scrutinized Rudger in his torn purple pantaloons and shredded red cape.

"Sire, I believe young Roger will make an excellent protégé. I shall be honored to school him in the mysteries of Logomancy myself, should that please the Crown."

"It does, Janusz. It does," King Emmett replied. His eyes flicked to Rudger and Twelda. "And now, if you are not too tired from your trials this evening, perhaps we can undo more of the damage Lendar and his hackerpedes have done. Many victims of the Mute-ation await you in the great hall."

"It is an honor to serve, Your Majesty, but…" Rudger began.

The ladies gasped again.

"…perhaps we could begin with someone else," he continued, turning his gaze upon Hildegarde. "There is someone your niece is eager to be reunited with."

Upon restoring Dutchess Eleanor and the afflicted guests of the Hackerpede Ball, Rudger, Vermis, Twelda, Rondo, and Fred left Castle Happenstance. It took another day's work to cure the wife of Crager the baker and the scores of villagers who had been touched by Kallendar's villainy. This task accomplished, Rudger found himself eager to return to his parents' burrow where Aunt Ragna and Roon still awaited his help.

They arrived in the early afternoon, at a spot that was more woods than marsh and a scant twenty-minute hike to the River Gush for sprightly gnomish feet. The five came bearing a mound of flowers, not to comfort the stricken, but to serve in the distillation of more jawjackle juice, for their supply was greatly depleted. Fred had enabled them to acquire the precious flowers by conveying them to the clearing where he'd comforted Hildegarde amongst a profusion of the blue blossoms two days before.

Rudger stepped up to his family's flaphatch, a peculiar mix of emotions coursing through him. He cleared the lump that had formed in his throat and announced their presence.

"Gnome a'home?"

Instead of receiving the customary response, the hatch burst open. Rani and Roni attached themselves to Rudger's still-human shins, but only until they noticed Rondo standing nearby.

"Dadders! Dadders!" they cried in joy as an orange blur zipped up and out of the burrow.

"Well," Herald commented, as he hovered eight inches in front of Rudger's face, "it seems you've managed to survive. Felicitations!"

"And felicitations to you for surviving those two," Rudger replied, tilting his head toward his sisters. "How are Roon and Aunt Ragna?"

"Soon to be much more loquacious, I imagine."

"Hmm. 'Loquacious.' An excellent word," Rudger judged with a smile. "If only I had my Logofile handy."

Twenty minutes later, Ragna was insisting on preparing tea for all assembled, and Roon was sitting on his father's lap, vowing never to be separated from him again. Rudger looked upon his friends and family and took comfort in their happiness and safety. He was chuckling at Twelda playing Four-Toes-and-Go with Rani and Roni when Herald alighted on a sapling beside him.

Rudger sighed contentedly. "Do you have any family, Herald?" he asked.

The orange newt flexed his tiny wings. "I do. Far from here, on the Isle of Lusus. Haven't seen them in decades, but in the face of all this reveling, I have a particular urge to reconnect."

"You should do that," Rudger encouraged him. "Family is what it's all about."

"Yes, but such a journey is quite impossible. The perils are multitudinous for a creature of my magnitude."

Rudger looked at him. "I'm really sorry we couldn't get your wyvern body back. In the heat of the battle with the Logoleech, Yeshirumon took off with it."

"It's not all bad," Herald observed. "As I've said before, I have a fondness for forelimbs. Great for turning music box keys, remember? I would be most aggrieved to lose these clever appendages." He flexed his foreclaws appreciatively.

Rudger frowned and absently stroked his beard. Vermis gave a disgruntled snort that suddenly reminded Rudger the vermitome was there. "Oh! Beg your pardon, Vermis."

"Vermis?" said the newt in surprise. "You mean the vermitome for whom we searched high and low? You recovered him, too?"

"So to speak," the beard said. "Rudger saved my spirit, if not my body. Ah, me. It wasn't much, but I've found I do miss it. And my shoes. And my spectacles."

"Bless my scales," Herald said in return. "It's good to make your acquaintance, Vermis."

"Likewise."

"Do you suppose I still have enough?" Rudger asked, interrupting the introductions.

"To whom are you speaking?" inquired Vermis.

"Enough what?" asked Herald.

"Sorry," Rudger said. "I was asking Vermis. Do you think I still have enough borrowed eloquys at my disposal to reverse the shrinking?"

"Ah," said Vermis. "You're referring to that dream you had the night we met."

"Oh. Did I tell you about that?"

"Certainly. I am your confidant."

"It's just that I still can't remember those couple of days—"

"Well, *I* remember them. *I* wasn't foolish enough to dive into a grove of amnesioaks."

Herald flew in an agitated figure-eight in front of them. "Would one of you please elucidate what you're talking about?"

Rudger quieted his beard using his fist. "Herald," he said, "you're going to need a lot of room. How about flying over there into our meadow?"

The confused newt did as Rudger suggested, landing on a shock of unclipped grizzlegrass. Rudger reached inside for a connection to the Source.

De-dwindiminish!

A deafening *pop* startled the wurblebirds from the nearby bricklebark trees.

Rani and Roni started to scream; Fred reared up in fright.

Roon made an awestruck comment. "*Cool.*"

"It's all right. It's all right," Rudger reassured everyone. "It's Herald…just bigger."

The glorious orange dragon looked himself over, testing each of his wings and all four legs.

"Rudger," he said, flabbergasted. "I-I don't quite know what to say. I know you are a Logomancer, but *this?* This is sorcery of the highest degree."

"It's nothing."

"Rudger, you don't understand. Dragons are immune to all but the most potent of magics. To produce this effect, you must be—"

"Please," Rudger interrupted. "You're embarrassing me. I'm only able to do it because of the extra eloquys inside me right now. Once they're back where they belong, I won't have this power anymore."

"Don't be so modest," Vermis piped up. "You shrunk this dragon body in the first place, when it was occupied by… What was that scoundrel's real name again?"

"Yeshirumon," Rudger supplied. "And I didn't know what I was doing back then. The whole thing was an accident."

"Yes, but you did it, regardless, without any training at all. I've always said you're something special."

"Well, that remains to be seen," Rudger said. He cracked his knuckles and looked up at Herald. "Now, about your original color. Would you say you were an outright purple or closer to heliotrope?"

"No!" the colossal reptile cried. "Er, I mean, no thank you, Rudger. I'm quite satisfied just the way I am. I…I find that orange suits me these days."

Rudger wasn't sure he believed this, but he didn't press the issue. "Well, okay. Just remember I'm happy to give you a makeover, if you ever change your mind."

"I appreciate that. I really do. And since my gnomeling-sitting duties are at an end, I believe I shall take my leave. I have urgent matters to attend to, and a trip to plan."

"Really? You have to go? Before lunch?"

"At this enhanced size, I doubt anything your aunt could serve would be very filling."

"Okay, but wait a minute," Rudger said as he crossed the field and approached Fred. "I have something for you."

The gnome-wizard pulled Vicarius from a scabbard attached to Fred's side. "This is yours," he said to the dragon. "Thanks for letting us borrow it."

Herald shook his enormous head. "No, Rudger. That belongs to your Aunt Ragna and your family. It was wrong of me to confiscate it all those years ago."

"But you're a collector," Rudger pointed out. "It belongs with you."

"Then consider it on loan to you," the orange dragon said. "I have a feeling you may be needing it. And now, I bid you all farewell, my friends."

The backdraft of Herald's immense wings stirred Rudger's hair and beard as the resplendent winged reptile rose into the air. As he watched, the young gnome felt a gentle probe into his mind.

I believe I shall go as well, Rudger, Fred told him. *I've been away from the herd too long. I am most eager to tell them about my beloved Hildegarde.*

"Oh. I understand. Thanks for everything, Fred. I hope to see you again soon."

I trust you shall. You'll be able to get to Old Drungle Town on your own?

"Certainly. My folks make that crossing all the time."

I hope you find your mother and grandparents well. Goodbye, Rudger Rump. You have my greatest regards. The magnificent quadricorn trotted across the meadow and disappeared into the woods.

"Lunch!" Aunt Ragna called from the flaphatch. She stopped climbing one step from the top, a tray in her hands. Her hot pink apron flapped in the breeze. "Wait. Where did the unicorn go? And that newt?"

"They had to leave," Rudger said simply.

"Well, I was going to lug everything out here, but the only one too big to come inside is you, Rudger. Haven't you played human long enough?"

"I guess so," the young gnome said slowly. "Why doesn't everyone go inside, and I'll bring up the rear."

"You heard what the man said," Aunt Ragna told the others. "Hup-hup! Before the skunkin cakes get stinky."

Rondo and the triplets trailed after Ragna, with Twelda close behind. Rudger reached down to tap her on the shoulder, indicating that she should hang back.

"What's the matter, Rudger?" she asked, squinting as she looked up at him.

He accessed the Source.

Dehumanifest!

Returned to his rightful size, Rudger looked the gnomette straight in the eye. “Twelda, did it seem to you that Herald and Fred were a little too eager to leave? That they were almost *relieved* to get away?”

Twelda glanced up to where Rudger’s head had been a moment before and back down again. “Well, you *are* one scary gnome these days,” she said bluntly, and she sauntered off toward the burrow.

Rudger stood there, digesting the comment. Then he shrugged, set Vicarius over his shoulder, and headed off after his scientific friend.

CHAPTER FORTY-TWO

Rudger Rump felt uneasy the moment he, Rondo, and Twelda set foot above Old Drungle Town the next day. The Entry Entreaty was met with anxiety and suspicion at flaphatch after flaphatch; it was clear word had not yet reached the Humdrungle gnomes that the Mute-ation was over. A part of Rudger was relieved each time they were turned away, but in the end, his father managed to gain entry to the underground tunnels by identifying himself as a government official. As the threesome passed from the accom-modating gnome's burrow to the narrow, twisting tunnels beyond, the earthen walls seemed to press in on Rudger. His riddling experience in Kallendar's tower had taken a claustro-phobic toll on the young gnome.

Ridna Rump nearly came undone when she opened the burrow door and found her husband back from the dead.

"They said a *human* gnome-napped you," she sobbed, clutching Rondo on the threshold. "And *you*," she chided, snagging Rudger and pulling him into an embrace fiercer than any arachna shrub could produce. "Nognome knew what happened to you until the Sartorio announced you'd broken into the Standards Chamber and defiled the True Hues! They're calling you a criminal! No wonder you're wearing that ridiculous fake beard.

"Oh!" she exclaimed, releasing her kin and barreling between them to hug a very flummoxed Twelda Greeze. "You're all right, too. Hurry, hurry! We must hide you and Rudger from the authorities."

"Mummers…Mummers!" Rudger said, trying to get Ridna's attention as she herded them inside and barred the door. "Please, Mum, you have to listen. Twelda and I aren't vandals. It was all a mistake."

"Well, of *course* it was a mistake. I didn't raise a son who would *intentionally* defile the True Hues! By the High Gnome's giblets, what a dreadful thought! The only thing worse would be your dabbling in this, this, this…What did you call it, dear?" She looked expectantly at Twelda.

"Science," the younger gnomette answered.

"Oh, yes. *Science*. Just a euphemism for magic, if you ask me. I do hope you've given that nonsense up."

Twelda and Rudger looked at each other.

"Ridna, dear," Rondo interjected. "I think maybe you'd better sit down. Rudger has something important to tell you."

Ridna Riggle Rump frowned but allowed her husband to lead her to a fireside chair. The other gnomes arranged themselves similarly. All eyes turned to Rudger.

The young gnome stared back at them, trying to figure out how to break the news to his opinionated mother. It seemed a greater challenge than facing the Logoleech itself. He opened his mouth thrice and faltered all three times. Finally, he slapped his thighs decisively and got to his feet.

"Come on, Twelda," he said as he strode toward his grandparents' bedroom. "We'll just show her."

Ridna emitted a tiny squeal of dismay as she witnessed the science-gnomette administering four drops of jawjackle juice to her husband's mother. Rondo stood close to his wife, arm wrapped around her as Rudger stepped up. Accessing the Source was becoming a matter of finesse now that hundreds of his resident eloquys had been returned to their proper owners. He was glad to release one more with the casting of the appropriate Wyrd.

Grammers' eyes opened, and the milky film over her pupils dissipated to reveal shining burnt umber irises. Ridna cried out in a combination of relief and confusion as her mother-in-law moaned softly. The old gnomette's wrinkled mouth turned up at the corners.

"Rudger," she croaked. "How nice to see you. Has it been so long? You've such a handsome beard now."

"Thank you," Vermis said, breaking his promise to Rudger to remain silent during the reunion. "I find the color invigorating."

The twitching, talking whiskers on her son's face were simply too much for poor Ridna. She fainted dead away into her husband's arms.

Similar scenes of disbelief and joy met Rudger and Twelda in each besieged burrow they visited over the next few days. So many successful un-Mutings were performed that Twelda was forced to distill bulk quantities of her jawjackle juice from the blossoms they'd collected across the river. Even the bush outside her own burrow was picked clean of the magical flowers before the flood of requests was stemmed.

"You're not wearing *that* to the ceremony, are you?" asked Rudger's mother on the morning of the fifth day after his return to Old Drungle Town.

Rudger looked at the colorful weave of the shoulder-hood the human King had awarded him before he'd left Castle Happenstance. At his current reduced size, it fell from his neck to his ankles like a brilliant stole.

"I certainly am, Mummers," he informed her.

"But this occasion calls for the utmost dignity," she argued. "You mustn't insult the Gnomister and his Gaffers with those horrible colors."

"The Gnomister has me to thank for magicking away the Mute-ation. Yes, Mum. *Magic*. You needn't flinch at its every mention. I'm sure the Gnomister will tolerate this little eccentricity. Oh, and that's with three *C*'s, no *K*, just like you taught me, remember? Anyway, I have a feeling I won't be the only person there sporting garish colors. Aunt Ragna's still on her way, right?"

"Wrong!" Rudger's former gnomeling-sitter announced from the door. "I am here!"

"Oh, Ragna, *no*," her younger sister moaned.

Aunt Ragna had outdone her nephew, combining every

brightly colored piece of clothing from her closet into one eye-scouring outfit.

"Aw, loosen up, Sis," she laughed, slapping Ridna on the back. "Life's too short not to *shine* a little."

The honor ceremony was a full showing of the pomp and circumstance done up best by the Humdrungle gnomes. The entire city was crowded around the Gnomatorium, watching the solemn procession of the Gnomister and the Council of Gaffers. Rondo Rump, fairly bursting with pride, could barely keep to his knees as he processed behind the sour-faced Sergeant Sartorio. Rudger grinned as the indignant official passed him on the platform. Clearly, the Sartorio did not share the popular opinion of Rudger's deeds.

"It has come to pass that one of the Humdrungles' own has distinguished himself in our greatest hour of need," the Gnomister began. "Today, we gather to honor this hero who has battled the odds and our preconceptions to master a magic that has delivered our salvation. Indeed, it is time to reconsider our long-standing bigotry against the practitioners of benign forms of wizardry and to embrace our brethren who manifest a talent in this heretofore repressed art. Rudger Rump is such an individual who deserves our praise and tolerance as he leads us into a new era—an era of increased safety and prosperity for all Humdrungkind. I give you, Rudger Rump, our first Magister!"

The cheers of two thousand gnomes made the amnesioaks around them tremble.

Rudger swallowed hard as he stepped up to the podium at the behest of the Gnomister. He looked out over the brown-clad crowd and nearly lost his nerve. But then his gaze fell on his loved ones—his mother wrangling the exuberant Terror Trio, Twelda beaming ear-to-ear in her new Healer's Guild shoulder-hood, Aunt Ragna in her multi-colored scandal of an outfit, and, of course, his beloved grandparents. That was when he made up his mind.

"Honored gnomes and gnomettes, I am deeply touched by your show of support. I may be a wizard of Wyrds, but I am not a speechmaker, so I beg you to forgive my fumblings.

"I have traveled the length and breadth of the Land of Lex in search of my father, the Supplico, who was gnome-napped by an evil human wizard from this very knoll."

The crowd gasped dramatically at the mention of a human in their midst. Rudger was emboldened by their reaction to his words.

"Yes, an evil wizard, but not the epitome of his species. Not all humans are the monsters we believe them to be, and as your Magister, I intend to build a bridge between Humdrungles and humans to our mutual advantage."

Concerned murmurings filled the pause in Rudger's speech.

"Not only this, but I shall continue to set right the wrongs of the aforementioned wizard by traveling far and wide with my great friend, Twelda Greeze, your newest Healer. Together, we shall finish the work we have begun, reuniting every being with his or her stolen speech, be they gnome, human, quadricorn, dragon, or leprechaun."

The Humdrungles looked at each other for approval to

approve. A smattering of claps grew into a healthy round of applause.

"But now," Rudger continued, "I make my first act as your Magister. In my travels, I have seen many things, and it is with great fondness that I recall the color and pageantry of the human ball I was privileged to attend. While I bear no ill will against our traditions, the Gnomister is correct; it is time to embrace the new. And in that spirit, I give you a gift. A gift of freedom from the humdrum tones to which our very apparel is dismally bound."

Vestivivido!

A tide of color washed over the crowd, turning the sea of tan, brown, ochre, and umber into a living, breathing rainbow.

The Humdrungles examined their clothes in shock. For a horrible moment, Rudger feared they might revolt.

Then they cheered.

The cheer was so loud it shook leaves from the amnesioaks. Suddenly, a giant yellow Fyreball appeared in the air above the trees' highest boughs. The Humdrungles accepted it as a celebratory gesture from their new Magister. But Rudger hadn't conjured it.

And he knew who had.

VESTIVIVIDO
©2022 Simerlein

Rudger stepped away from the podium and moved toward the Gnomatorium's entrance. Well-wishers flooded the stage, impeding his progress. His father negotiated the crowd to approach him. He was wearing a purple suit coat with red-and-green plaid trousers.

"Way to go, Son!" Rondo Rump said. "I have amazing news! Turns out you and Twelda may not be the only ones with new appointments. The Sartorio isn't on board with this colorful clothes business, so he's resigned. Looks like I may be the new Sergeant Sartorio. What do you think of that?"

Rudger congratulated his father as he continued to work his way toward the building's double doors. Bumping elbows with every other colorfully clothed Humdrungle along the way, he finally made it into the hall. He hesitated as he appraised the Gnomister's private entrance to the tunnels. The narrow earthen staircase made his stomach squirm.

"Hey, Mr. Magister," said a familiar voice. "Leaving before you admire my new dress?"

He turned to see Twelda Greeze in a blue-and-white checkered sundress. Two flaxen braids tumbled down from a bright red pointed cap to lay over each of her shoulders.

"Wow," he said. "You're positively glowing."

"Thanks," she replied with a wink. "I'll be sure to give you the name of my stylist."

Rudger chuckled but then grew serious. "I'm glad you're here," he told her. "That Fyreball out there wasn't me. I think Kallendar's lurking outside the Amnesioak blind. We've got to go and check it out."

They hurried down the private staircase into the restricted part of the tunnels. Rudger let Twelda lead him to a public flaphatch outside Gnomister's Knoll. They began a frenzied search for the rogue wizard.

And found a little boy instead.

Rudger had cooked up a half-dozen Wyrds to lob at Kallendar, but something in the way Kal was twisting his hands together stayed Rudger's lips.

"I…I know you're probably mad at me," the boy-wizard said, looking down at them shyly. "I don't blame you. I know what Lendar—I mean, I know what *I* did to you, and I came to say I'm sorry."

Twelda pounced. "How do you know any of that?" she asked harshly. "Are you saying you can remember what Lendar did?"

"No, but I finally figured out how to work this," he said, bending down to show them the Chronologue. "I really can't believe I'm going to do such terrible things. It…it hurts to think about it."

"Rudger, I must intercede," Vermis suddenly said. "This may be a trick. You've told me of this boy's treachery. He Muted me, for the love of tomes! Make him pay."

Until this point, Rudger had remained on guard, ready to counter any aggressive spells with magic of his own. But now, with Kallendar looking exactly as he had on the day they first met, Rudger knew he didn't have it in his heart to destroy the contrite boy.

"I can't, Vermis," he said. "Kal isn't to blame for his older self's crimes."

"Vermis?" the boy piped up. "He's in your beard? He's all right now? The Chronologue told me he got Muted."

"He's in Rudger's beard all right," Twelda growled. "But

not the way you think. Vermis lost his body because of you. Now his spirit is embedded in Rudger's whiskers."

"Oh," the boy said sadly. "I did that, too? I… really hate myself."

Kal began to cry. Even Twelda seemed to be moved by his youthful tears.

"Look, why don't you just go to the castle and turn yourself in?" Rudger suggested. "If you explain your Chronocurse to the Archmage, maybe he could help."

"The Archmage?" repeated Kal. "Oh, no. I could never go to him. He's a bad man."

Twelda spoke over the boy. "Rudger, Kal can't go there. They'd lock him up the minute they figured out he's Lendar."

Rudger nodded slowly. He was remembering something Lendar the elder had said through the spy-eye. *We are two incarnations of a convoluted timeline, Kal and I. What he learns, I remember. What he experiences enriches me.*

"Kal," he said kindly. "Do you remember all the fun we had at your cabin?"

"Oh, yes. Well, some of it, anyway."

"And you remember the nice Princess who saved you from that nasty arachna bush, right?"

"Uh-huh. Her name was Hildegarde. She was pretty."

"And you're going to try really, really hard to remember that Twelda and I are your very good friends, right?"

"Sure. I like you guys."

"Will you try so hard to remember you'll remember it a hundred, hundred years from now?"

"Oh, yes. I'll never forget."

"Okay, then I'm going to need you to trust me right now.

I'm going to do something so that bad Lendar can't hurt anyone anymore."

"Oh, that's good," the boy said cooperatively. "I was hoping you could. Can you…can you maybe take my magic away so Lendar won't have it anymore?"

Rudger was impressed. "Clever boy. That's exactly what I'm going to try to do. Can you sit down and relax for me?"

The boy settled himself on the ground. Rudger gathered his wits, hoping the few borrowed eloquys still left inside him would be enough to cast the great Wyrd. Then doubt crept in. Was there any other way to protect the realm without depriving the boy of his magic?

There wasn't.

Sequestrimagum!

A powerful force resisted the Wyrd, straining Rudger's diminished eloquary as he fought to impose his will on the boy's burgeoning magic.

And then the struggle was over. Rudger dropped to his knees, momentarily losing his bearings. Twelda hurried to his side as Kal frowned in confusion.

The boy-wizard tried to conjure something with his hands and failed. "I-I think it worked," Kal told them as Rudger recovered. "I can't make a Fyreball. Thanks."

"You're welcome," Rudger said unsteadily. "But you'd better get back to the cabin before dark. You can't protect yourself with magic anymore."

"But Lendar won't be able to hurt people with my magic

either," the boy said as he rose to his human-huge height. "Don't worry about me. I ditched Hieronymus half a league upstream. He's probably flying around trying to find me. He'll get me home safe."

When the boy was gone, Twelda let out a whistle. "That was something," she marveled. She helped Rudger back to his feet. "Just what did you do?" she asked.

Rudger staggered a bit. "I used every bit of Logomantic magic at my disposal to lock Kal's Elemental magic inside him. If I did it right, the stronger Logomantic binding should prevent him and Lendar from casting spells until it's removed, assuming the binding is durable across his Chronocurse. But even if it isn't, the message of friendship I've tried to drill into Kal will hopefully keep us all safe until I can figure out a more permanent solution."

Twelda shook her head ruefully. "What a mess. Don't you wish you could just go back to me being the know-it-all scientist and you the hapless country gnome?"

"Maybe, but then we might never have met."

Twelda stepped in front of Rudger, fixing him with her sea-green eyes. "And would that be such a bad thing?"

Rudger felt himself flush. "Uh, yeah."

"Tell me why."

"Because, uh, I never would have learned about science and logic."

She twined a finger playfully in his hair. "You know, logic's not always what it's cracked up to be. Sometimes, I find the irrational rather…intriguing."

She leaned in close.

Rudger felt her breath on his lips.

"Great gobs of osculation!" exploded Vermis the beard. "Sorry, lovebirds, but I'm coming between you. *Y-U-C-K*. Yuck!" Rudger's whiskers twisted to form each letter.

Twelda pulled away and rolled her eyes. "Ugh. Vermis, you're such a nuisance."

"It's what I do best," the beard said. "Besides training Logomancers, of course."

The gnomes grinned at each other, and Rudger reached out to take Twelda's hand. It fit perfectly into his.

"Shall we return to the party?" he asked.

Twelda quirked an eyebrow. "I don't know, Mr. Magister," she said slowly. "You have something urgent to attend to."

Rudger frowned. "What's that?"

"My lab. You still owe me a burrow-cleaning."

"I do," he laughed. "And a whole lot more than that."

Logofile

Property of Rudger Rump

with unsolicited! notations
by Twelda Greeze

Don't be mean,
Rudger.

Wyrds That Wyrk — Cute.

dwindiminish -- a mean Princess told me this made her dragon disappear. I blacked out. Shrinks things.

Take that, Logoleech!

corporsapiensi -- scared the Terror Trio with this one. Don't know why. Got woozy.

Oh, the humanity!!

hydroscleros -- Wingnut and Vermis said this saved my life, but I can't remember how. I was out of it.

Hydro = water
Scleros = stiffen

You seem to have trouble staying conscious, Rudger. Have you had your blood checked?

deft weft (?) -- pulse of energy in Standards Chamber

Can a Weird Wyrd be two words???

projectimentum -- beard attack! Compliments of Kal.

zephury -- This one was a breeze!
(zephyr + fury)

barbanimus -- Sorry, Vermis.

de-eloquarantine -- removes an eloquy

de-dwindiminish -- Herald's favorite Wyrd!
Unshrinks things.

dehumanifest -- Gnome, sweet gnome.
Transforms human back to gnome.

vestivivido -- bye-bye, True Hues.

sequestrimagum -- supposed to bind magic

Sure hope it wyrks!

Wyrds That Don't Wyrk

This is stupid!
Who cares about wyrds
that didn't work?

Good scientists are
as interested in their
failures as their
successes, Rudger.

Still not a scientist, Twelda.

barbibanish, whiskaway, beardectomi, elimafur, eradihair, rejectimentum, stubbelost, bristlioust, etc.

paternilocus -- to find Dadders. (pater = father, locus = location)

scleros-air/air-scleros -- worked on water, why not air?

ala generatum -- who wouldn't want wings?

Wyverns
do it best!

Ugh! Not you, too, Herald.

gravitinverto -- reverse gravity

Non-Magical Words

eccentric
~~ecentric~~
~~ecsentrick~~ = weird like Aunt Ragna

arachna shrubs = nasty, meat-eating bushes

carnivorous = meat-eating

hackerpede = black, eloquy-stealing centipede

Bibliorinctum = book convention

logofile = my file of words

logophile = word lover like me!

palaver = a chat

terminus = end

tragus = goat's beard ear flap

vibrissae = nose or ear hairs! Blech!

logomancy = word magic

etymology = study of word origins

quotidian = everyday

Rudger, this is disgraceful! How do you find anything in this mess? Couldn't you at least alphabetize your Logofile?

Hey! No scientist allowed! Wizards only!

logorrhea = diarrhea of the mouth

Like Vermis von Higglesbreath the Fourth!

I object!

Don't even think about consuming my Logofile, Vermis.

loquacious = talkative

xenophobia = fear of strangers

chignon = Grammers' hairstyle, a knot of hair worn at the nape of the neck

gnomelescent = an adolescent gnome

vermitome = the best-read, most erudite species in the Land of Lex

vermis = worm
tome = book

I did not write this! Stay out of my Logofile, Vermis!

superterrarean = above ground

Just ensuring your scholarly text is complete, Master Rump.

haberdasher = hat merchant

raiments = fancy clothes

retinue = procession

troika = group of three

vesture = another word for fancy clothes

discalced = shoeless, barefoot Four Toes and Go, anyone?

sartorial = related to Dadder's profession, tailoring

conduit = tool of focus

capisce = understand

quarantine = shut-in for health reasons

chilopod = centipede

chitin = hard material making up a chilopod's shell

burbled = a frothy method of preparing eggs

bioluminescence = glow-in-the-dark Mishamash mushrooms! Yum!

tatterdemalion = unkempt

auricle = ear

oracle = future-telling prophet

homophony = words spelled differently but that sound alike

prolixity = undue lengthiness in speaking or writing, like Vermis Indubitably!

narcolepsy = disorder of suddenly falling asleep

lexicologist = one who studies words

Glynt = aura around wizards or their works

alacrity = briskness

winsome = attractive, beautiful

plumage = feathers

sesquipedalian = a long word

I've got a longer one:

hippopotomonstrosesquipedaliophobia

The fear of long words!

Or of uppity vermitomes.

hypothesis = idea behind an experiment, for nerdy scientist types

Hey, I resemble that!

acerbity = bitterness

schnecken = cinnamon buns

frakus?

debacle = a violent commotion or upheaval

fraicus?

frakis?

<u>fracas</u>

cockamamie = crazy, ill-advised

incorrigible = uncorrectable

svelte = thin, slender

curate = to care for artifacts, as in a museum

Or my collection!

alias, pseudonym, nom de plume = false name

Wingnut, Hieronymus, Yeshirumon

provisions = food

victuals = food, pronounced "vittles"

tew = a state of agitation

metallurgy = the methods of refining metals

ferrum = iron

Ferrie = metal-urger, like Herald

eloquy = a person's word-intelligence

eloquary = a collection vessel for eloquys

ebullience = enthusiasm

mollycoddle = pamper, spoil

incongruous = mismatched for the situation

inveigle = confound

pulchritude = beauty

conundrum = puzzling problem

faux pas = social blunder

interlocutor = one engaging in a conversation

synecdoche = using a part of an object to represent the whole thing

Oh, like saying "brain" to mean "vermitome"?

No, like saying "beard" to mean "hairy annoyance."

Ouch.

multitudinous = many

elucidate = clarify

heliotrope = bluish purple

euphemism = polite substitute word or phrase

epitome = prime example

osculation = kissing

XXXXX !

Blech!

Twelda's ~~Contraptions~~ Inventions!!!

Auriculator – enhances hearing

Fire-flinger – instant igniter or your money back!

For klutzes like Rudger! → *Noggin-guard – head protector*

Eleminator – researches Elemental magic

Gnomellaneous Humdrunglisms

The Humdrungle
Entry Entreaty

"Gnome a'home?"
"Gnome a'home."
"Home to loan?"
"Welcome, gnome."
or "Go and roam."

The True Hues

Tempered Tan = rusty brown
Mudpud Brown = rich brown
Drear Ochre = dark orange-brown
Burnt Umber = greenish brown

Gnomish Words and Idioms (for non-gnomes' reference)

Pinch 'em = shut up, close your lips
Bump a rump = sit down
Lipflap = backtalk
Swale = dungeon or jail
Domar = idiot, moron
Bowbump = touch elbows in greeting
Pandypuss = scaredy-cat
Barmy as a boughbrat = crazy
By the High Gnome's giblets = mild oath of unknown origin

Flora and Fauna of the Land of Lex

Flora (Plants)

puxa pod bush
grizzlegrass
arachna shrubs
buffa beets
somna root (tea)
suzzleleaf (tea)
grummermelon
jawjackle bush
bricklebark tree
brickkernels (seeds)
canfa tree
gnarlic tree
collybloom
munxmoss
bugnought root
bippup vine
duchess-bloomers
fairy's-breath fern
bilgreed root
dringleberry
sunspray blossom
sniggleswort
skunkin sprout
pungleroots

Fauna (Animals)

dayna birds
blunderelk
boughbrat
wurblebird
flufferbunny
dillyhog
subterranean hackerpedes
vermitome
fiddlerfish
gabbler
zingbat
lummox
swampkunk
polydactopus
wyvern
dragon
quadricorn
chitterbug
manticore
marsh-shrew

The Magical Elements

First Element - Earth
Second Element - Water
Third Element - Air
Fourth Element - Fire
Fifth Element - Unknown

Assistant Lexicologist's Notes

Now that you've studied Rudger's Logofile, are there any words or phrases you think he missed? Help him complete his research by writing them in below!

____

____

____

ABOUT THE AUTHOR

Dr. Scott Simerlein is a graduate of Palmer College of Chiropractic, where he drew a comic strip for the campus newspaper. When he's not chronicling the life histories of gnomes and dragons in the Land of Lex, he passes his time in this world teaching anatomy and physiology to college students. Dr. Simerlein is the author of two more humorous gnomespun tales, each included in separate anthologies from Hydra Publications. *Rudger Rump and the Mage of Ages* is his first novel.